R.A.Y. A STEP TOO FAR

R.A.Y. A STEP TOO FAR

J.L. HUGHES

ROUGH
EDGES
PRESS

R.A.Y. A Step Too Far
Paperback Edition
Copyright © 2024 J.L. Hughes

Rough Edges Press
An Imprint of Wolfpack Publishing
1707 E. Diana Street
Tampa, FL 33610

roughedgespress.com

Cover design by Rough Edges Press
Editing by My Brother's Editor

Paperback ISBN 978-1-68549-431-5
eBook ISBN 978-1-68549-430-8
LCCN 2024947850

*For my greatest blessing
and all those who take pause.*

R.A.Y. A STEP TOO FAR

SURVIVING A BRUTAL CHILDHOOD OF CAPTIVITY, Nick understood no matter how the winds howled, windows shook, or ground trembled, no storm matched the wrath his sister would unleash if freed, and she was.

Nick knew storms. The natural and unnatural kind. Neither frightened him. He wasn't what you'd call easily moved or emotional. He'd almost died in battle. He'd seen many others die in the field and on operating gurneys. Men who died because he could not save them. Men who died because he chose not to save them. He lived a life on the fringe, watching those without conscience forge new paths of possibility on a map of depravity with no moral compass. He mastered control over emotion. That tool had kept him alive and of use and isolated. After twenty years of active service, he wasn't capable of panic. Nothing mattered enough to illicit that depth of emotion from him. There was only one living he cared for, one he feared, and she'd vanished from his screen.

He had watched Ray recover from captivity, find her place, always hoping the scars hadn't cut into the heart of her. He knew better.

Storm winds prowled over the water. They growled in the darkness surrounding the island. Their tremors shuddered up through the marble tile, into the soles of his bare feet and the marrow of his bones. Once peaceful palms slapped outer walls and windows, bending to near fracture as Ray came back into view on the security feed. A boat crossed into their waters, desperate to make land, and Ray was headed its direction.

Nick flew to the nearest exit, snatched a med kit on the way, and never closed the outer door. No time.

He ran following the pathway to the gardens before the dock, cobblestone driving the dull ache of the cold through his feet. At the beachfront deck tiering down to the splashing shoreline, he paused, squinting through the rain and dark, surveying the distance until he locked on her advancing toward the boat.

Tossed in and out of view, the beacon of a desperate sailor navigating a dying ship to the refuge of the island. That was how she'd found it.

The fight appeared futile. The vessel sagged into the drift; she'd taken on water.

Against the odds, the small vessel's captain made for their harbor, perfect trajectory to crash into the rock bed. Nick spotted Ray sliding down mud and stone for the impact zone. It'd be a vicious end to an ugly battle.

Seconds later, she halted as metal met boulder, and shards of the craft exploded in the crashing waves. It slammed hard twice before the wreckage locked in the jaws of the sea.

Storm winds made it impossible to maintain line of sight. Nick swept rain from his eyes as he ran. He screamed her name; its echo pushed back to him having stalled in the gust. His lips tasted of salty desperation, but he kept calling.

Thunder roared, and lightning split the sky in an explosion of light as he neared the cliff's edge. It lit the sea below, shining a spotlight on the boat's tragic state. What remained above waterline was being swallowed fast. Its captain clung to a side rail, struggling upward away from the point of descent. Every wave drove the vessel further behind the teeth and into the gullet of the beast.

Twenty feet below Nick, Ray leaped and dodged, closing the distance to the rock bed and the only safe place for the captain to abandon ship. Over the lip, on a downward slide, Nick watched her throw a rope. She scaled the embankment, gripping rock with her bare feet and fighting, like him, to see beyond the saltwater burning his eyes. One strong wave and she'd be cast to a watery grave between the ship and the rocks. There was nothing to tie the rope to. The sound of crunching metal overshadowed the fury of the storm. Ray lassoed a boulder as Nick lost footing and was forced to pivot into the wall of broken rock, grabbing hold with both hands and feet. Back turned, he couldn't keep eyes on her but knew the ship's dive was closing the window between her and its captain.

"Dutch." The captain's yell filtered up from below.

Nick found control, turning in time to see the captain bled from the head, an injury sustained in the collision, no doubt.

"Anyone else aboard?" He heard Ray shout back as waves broke over the rocks, forcing her to grip tighter on the rope.

Two colliding waves hit. The boat list throwing the captain down hard. He cried out, but Nick's eyes stayed trained on Ray. As he descended, she lost her footing and slammed onto the rock, sliding with the receding water to its edge. His heartbeat raced in his chest. Scurrying back on all fours, she disappeared, overshadowed by the ship's underbelly with its last lurch. She emerged tugging her way back to center.

She gained ground under her feet and threw the rope. The captain caught hold. The boat pitched. His feet took flight. Ray glanced back in time to see Nick traverse the embankment. He screamed, "No!" His voice sounding oddly unfamiliar to him, laced in anguish. The storm swallowed it, overshadowing with its own rage.

She couldn't hear him clearly, but the glint in her onyx eyes said she read the intensity on his face. He landed beside her, hands outstretched for the rope, a fraction of a second too late. She cut the rope and watched the captain fall between the wreckage and the rocks.

"Goodbye, Dutch." She spoke like the storm, without remorse.

The captain's legs and torso slammed into debris. When his head, astonished expression and all, smashed open on the rock below her feet, she turned back to Nick.

"You killed him." Nick swept water and shock from his brow.

"Uninvited," she said, stepping back, sure-footed, to view the mess.

"It's murder."

"Mother Nature, actually."

"For the love of God, Ray."

"Why does everyone insist on using Him as moral punctuation?"

She pushed her wet hair aside, giving Nick a clear view of her black eyes. After all their years together, the void of color still unnerved him. He preferred them hidden behind contacts, ones she refused to wear. "It's an idle threat," she said.

Peering over the lip of the outcrop beside him, she watched the broken remnants of the ship and its captain quake in the swell.

"Ask him how loving his creator is." She climbed past Nick. "As compassionate as mine," she said. "Don't take long. We have a surgery waiting."

She disappeared up the rocks and into the night, leaving only the sick sound of metal, wood, and flesh breaking the waves. Nick felt them break inside him. He knew the nature of violent storms couldn't be denied, controlled, or contained, but eventually, they died. And the panic he never felt before had come to life.

———

"Don't make me regret this." Behind a cold metal table, Ray operated as if infallible. She fought dying tissue, death scratching at its surface.

Out of the windswept night, palm leaves twisted and slapped the sleeping estate windows. Revolting against the atrocity inside. Ray didn't believe in the Almighty. Mother Nature, however, earned her respect.

"Most think when the body dies the brain's fate is sealed." Ray whispered. She knew life was about the pieces; she'd been made of them. Many superior, painstakingly selected pieces.

Defeat beaconed her by way of plummeting vital signs and a hesitant blip across a heart monitor. Surgical prowess was her way out. The metallic scent of blood tainted the air. Sterilized tools, precise in their cruel function, glistened back from silver trays. Ray's scarred bare feet clenched the tile floor. Her hands, sheathed in powdered rubber, operated with precision. Beneath them lay the brain of Micael Valeric. Savior. Mentor. Hero.

A dead man by anyone else's standards. Not hers.

On a landmass amid the dark Pacific's silken surface, his blood dripped from her surgical gloves, slid down her gown, and added to the puddle at her feet.

"It's coloring outside the line." She stared at the repaired frontal lobe; healthy eicosapentaenoic and docosahexaenoic acid, main components of the brain's synapses and blood flow, then glanced at her brother.

"What line is that?" Nick asked.

"The one between life and death." She drew in a filtered breath. "What's the count?"

He exhaled, distending his hygienic mask. "You don't want to know."

"Nick, give me the count." Ray's eyes were cemented on the patient. Distractions meant failure.

"Twenty-three, twenty-four...the clock to your left." Nick's sharp tone muted beneath the mask. "Most people accept death as a certainty."

"Most people aren't raised in glass cages and brain trauma wards. They don't read PDRs for fun at age twelve."

An alarm sounded. Nick silenced it then said, "Can't say I didn't warn you."

"We've been in here for seven hours." Her voice held an icy resolve, but her black eyes burned as they met his. "I'm not losing him."

"Who do you think you're saving?" Nick's words were met with a silence that held the length of the procedure.

The cerebral cortex transplant lasted fourteen hours. Prying expended gloves from her skin, her hands trembled. The statue of solidity she'd been now crumbled. She fought to focus on the washtub, the soap, anything. Her vision blurred.

Carnage, sweat, and fury emanated from her. She wasn't waiting on a miracle. She was one. She pushed back hard at self-doubt, seeing it as a product of exhaustion.

The swish and plunge of life-sustaining machines offered cold comfort.

Leaning on the sink for support, she stared through the hazed glass. An overgrown human-spider hybrid rested on a metal slab; not the man she sacrificed all to save. Tubes and wires extended out from his upper torso. His head was webbed in surgical gauze.

She weighed the cost of what she'd lost between the scalpel and sutures.

Life with him had been a symphony. Without him, her mind lost tempo and spun between broken notes. When Nick found her passed out on the hard tile floor of the scrub room, she blamed it on the blood transfusion she'd donated for their patient.

She lied, a hereditary talent she assumed.

She would've thanked her parents, all eighteen of them if she'd known who they were.

———

Nick carried Ray down the corridor to her bedroom, moving from the cool isolation of the operating wing to the elegance of their living quarters. His eyes followed the walls. Ceramic tile ended. Italian marble began. Cathedral ceilings, fifteenth-century mirrors, and antiques fit for the castle they'd once adorned mitigated dark memories.

He laid her on the bed inside her suite. She stirred when he picked her off the scrub room floor but was out again. Tantalizing decor should've lured the starving eye like a mirage. Numb, he saw the room in muted color.

He pulled a throw from a chair and placed it over her. He stood back, staring at a creature he should despise. He didn't. He despised her actions, not her. She'd come by darkness, honestly. Born into it. His eyes followed her sleeping frame from head to toe. One foot protruded from the blanket. Soft, perfect and dainty on top, scarred to hard, unfeeling leather on the bottom. This was Ray.

He stepped forward and slid the blanket over her foot. Instinctively, she pulled it further up, curling into the warm cover. His eyes burned with raw exhaustion as he turned and walked out.

Ray would be spared the potency of surgical aftermath. Even with the mess cleaned, the smell would linger for hours. Dread weighed on him walking back through the metal doors.

Everything assembled easily for the patient's transfer into recovery. For the majority of its existence, the estate had one owner, and Micael alone used its medical facility. Nick clamped, fastened, and double-checked each machine before journeying down the hall with the static form on the rolling bed.

He repeated the procedure in reverse once in the recovery room. Noting the white sheers shimmering in sunlight, soft fabrics, and smooth lines camouflaging the medical residence in serenity were a lie masking the birthplace of a modern-day Frankenstein.

With the patient secured, Nick headed to the janitor's pantry outside the operating room. Recovering a bucket full of disinfectants, he stretched on new rubber gloves and dove in.

He opted not to wear a surgical mask, feeling he'd lived in one for the last week. A mistake. The stench of blood, medical supplies, and related odors hit harder than they had an hour earlier. He powered up the air exchange.

He dragged a disposal can close to him and pitched steel and cotton. A waft of sour air floated up with every toss and every toss hit harder than the last. Expensive utensils that could've been sanitized and reused soon found themselves in a twisted melody of bloody metal glistening up from the dark cylinder. He didn't care to distinguish the salvageable from those compromised during surgery, only that their destruction served as a sliver of release for his rage.

His phone vibrated in his chest pocket. He shook his hand loose of a saturated rag, cursing its resistance. He checked the screen, smearing it in the process, a fitting misfortune. "Cage." A most unwanted caller. Government bloodhound. Keeper of secrets. Pain in the...

Nick surveyed the room. It mirrored a backdrop for a medieval massacre-everything awash in crimson. Saliva flooded his mouth.

"Bloody mess." He spoke to foul air, tossed the soiled phone back in his pocket, grabbed a new cloth, and kept wiping.

Clean-up lasted hours, the first three of which nullified Nick's appetite and earned him a deep appreciation for sanitation crews.

A military doctor for fifteen years, he was no stranger to the sight of blood, operating room graphics, or wounded, dying men. What struck him was applying those conditions to someone he gave a damn about. Detachment came easier under the pressure of surgery.

"The frailty of our existence just got frailer," he whispered, defeated. He scanned the transformed room one last time before fine-tuning the air purification and leaving to take a shower.

The stainless-steel doors slammed shut with a pronounced thud. Nick stood silent for a moment with his back to them. No sense turning around. What was missing couldn't be found there.

His loss weighed heavier with each footfall on the way to his room.

Inside, his handsome face distorted into monstrous defects across the brass spittoon on his desk. He would've spat but refused to soil his speeding ticket collection stored inside the vessel.

His hair, a mass of waves, bore the stress of him raking his hands through it. His clothes wore blood splatter in a violent abstract. He threw them in a garbage chute that led to an outdoor burning barrel. In the shower, he rotated the faucet to hot and let the water run. From the linen closet, he chose Patchouli mint soap. White beneath his dark tan, Nick stood before a mirror, wondering who appeared more alive, him or the guy who flatlined on the gurney down the hall.

"Savior or slayer?" His words drifted in steam. He wrote "neither" backward across the glass.

He walked naked past a bank of windows back to the shower. There wouldn't be any onlookers outside.

This was, after all, his island. No trespassers allowed. The captain's death was testimony.

He leaned under the spray. Blood swirled down the drain, but it wasn't his this time. The pulsating showerheads drowned out the guilt that would've plagued other men and subdued the rattle of his soiled phone vibrating across the vanity.

2

"HE HAD CHILDREN?"

Brook Cromwell read the Half Moon Bay headline in the crumpled remnants of the morning paper voicing her questions to no one save the cat.

"Son Bids Farewell To CRISPR Pioneer And Brain Surgeon"

Her husband Curt snatched the business section before leaving for work. Her son and daughter nabbed anything else of interest for the trip to university. She didn't expect to find the foreign news engaging, but one article gripped her. There, amid stories of an oil tanker, adrift, and seeping black death, and devastating war statistics, sat a tribute to Doctor Micael Valeric—the last reminder of Christian, her firstborn son.

The article spoke about his groundbreaking work using the CRISPR technology for gene editing and gave details of a memorial fund set up in Dr. Valeric's name for brain injury research. Vibrant, talented, and, like Christian, gone. She made a mental note to make a donation. The funeral was scheduled a week from Sunday, attended by immediate family and a select few well-respected medical associates on the island he'd owned and lived on.

The toaster buzzed out a warning it was jammed again. Yanking the cord free, she pried her burned toast out, threw it, a fried egg, and a handful of bacon on a plate, and headed for the kitchen nook. On route to the table, she balanced the plate in one hand and the paper in the other, reading the last sentence in the article. It referred readers to a tribute by Dr. Valeric's son on the back page.

She stopped short of the table and fumbled with one hand to flip the paper over. The plate crashed, shattering on impact across the floor. Food and ceramic shards splattered in a four-foot radius around her feet.

A face too familiar, trimmed in black outline.

If the color photo had been three sizes smaller, it would've impacted the same. His arrival in her life profoundly changed her world before and today it did again.

"Christian."

A wave of shock washed over Brook, throwing her back on quaky footing. She reached for the phone. Although his hair was darker and his skin flawless and fair, his looks resembled his younger brother Zavier's so completely that one could easily mistake them for twins. One difference set them apart. Their eyes were identical in shape, yet lineage couldn't account for his kaleidoscope of color. As vibrant as they were, Christian's eyes emitted an odd lifelessness.

According to the article, Brook's son existed under the Valeric name and was very much *alive*. And that was exactly what she'd tell her brother Mason, when he answered the phone.

————

"Face facts, you live for blood and sweat. You're creepin' over the hill and flatly refuse to take up residence anywhere close to suburbia."

Mason Stone stood in his cabin's doorway, laughing at his friend Jack's assessment. It made him sound like Rambo's grandpa. "What'cha expect from the only son of a military man? I was raised on testosterone. I'm too old to change."

"Your father was an ass, Stone, but he still had a wife."

"Yeah, she paid a price. Quit setting me up, Jack. It's a waste of time."

"I owe you. Family life can be a blessing."

"Remind me, aren't you divorced?"

"Ouch. Victorious crime fighter turned international hostage retrieval expert, and a coward nonetheless."

"Careful, buddy."

"Kidding. I still think..."

"I know what you think—I'm wealthy, accomplished, and better looking. You'd prefer if I were off the market 'cause you can't compete."

"Okay, High-test. It's the ego I can't compete with."

Laughter filled the air before Mason kicked Jack out and closed the door.

Mason's sister nicknamed him High-test in college because her friends described him like coffee. Smooth, strong, bold, and addictive.

The laughter hadn't left him when her call came in.

"I was thinking about you," he said.

"I'm glad you're home." Her response held no sense of humor.

"There's a world out there I'm avoiding."

Pleased to hear from his kid sister, seconds passed before he recognized the urgency in her tone.

"It's a cruel world," she said. He waited for her to say something anecdotal. She didn't.

"What's up, kid?" He heard the stutter before the tears. "Talk to me."

————

Brook couldn't form the words. Once spoken, they'd taint every facet of life with their blackness. When they did escape, they came out broken and frantic.

"I need help. I've made choices that have come back to haunt me and I'm talking a full-fledged resurrection." She set the newspaper down to break its spell.

Any other day, her description might've made him laugh out loud, but the tremors in her voice killed any chance of humor.

"I have a few days of hibernation coming to me. Hiding out at your place works." His ease was deliberate, but his quick assurance to come said he heard her.

"The kids would love to see you and...they're going to need your support." Her voice became shallow.

"Does Curt know about this...resurrection?" he asked.

"No, but he will before you get here." She promised herself as much as him. "Please, hurry."

"I'm out the door."

With the dial tone resonating in her ear, Brook fixated again on the newspaper. She dropped the receiver haphazardly into its cradle and walked through her smashed breakfast unaware. The outside world dimmed in the shadows of the haunting storm swelling inside her. She never got to say goodbye to her son. Now she knew why.

3

"ASTOUNDING, YOU CAN'T TAKE A HINT." Nick aimed for a clean shot at the hoop above his bookcase and missed as Doctor Locke's wimpy voice resonated over the speakerphone. Unbelievably worse amplified.

"I'm only suggesting—" he squealed.

"I'm well aware where your suggestions lead. No thanks. In fact, you sick, pathetic piece of garbage, if you ever call here again, I'll make sure Ray gets revenge for your years of torment."

He sunk the next one effortlessly.

"Hey, I worked on the project the same as—"

"Not the same. You took pleasure in the worst of it. Let me be perfectly clear. You've been delusional far too long."

He snatched up the rebound and spun the basketball on one finger.

"You figured Micael would tame Ray. That's why the team didn't end his involvement. You weaponized her. It wasn't strategic genetic manipulation, you idiot. It was her sheer hatred of you."

Nick sauntered to the furthest side of his suite.

"You're not seeing the whole picture," Locke squeaked.

"Now she can't be tamed or managed. She's spent years absorbing knowledge. Knowledge is lethal in her hands. She's going to make sure you die afraid. Exactly how you made her live."

With his back to the hoop, he tossed the ball overhead.

"And I'm going to watch."

Locke stammered and stuttered, then managed a half word of protest as Nick turned to see the ball hit, circle the inner ring, and fall through.

Flawless.

He marched to his desk and hung up, denying Locke further rebuttal. He had the upper hand, for now.

Cage, the man heading their sordid situation on the government side, forbid Locke direct contact with Ray. Locke broke all the rules while Ray was in their captivity, using his father's medical brilliance as a shield. His father long dead, he lost the benefit of prior protection. Cage acted as the conductor, ushering in a superior existence in silence with his hand over all the moving parts. Nick didn't believe duty was the only fuel for Cage's lethal dedication to the project or his particular disdain for Locke. Cage's reputation for exacting consequences stirred fear in everyone. Everyone except those just like him.

———

Nick found Ray in the operating wing hallway, fast asleep on a lounger. She never lasted a full night in her room. Her head rested on a white linen back cushion. Beautiful monster at rest. Micael, their mentor, ushered her into a different life, one dedicated to healing, or so he thought. In truth, he'd been the poison fueling an already lethal composition. Her dwarfed subgenual cortex, the ten percent reduction in brain density in the paralimbic system, the state of her orbitofrontal cortex, and caudate were a recipe for a cold, calculating psychopath. She still didn't look the part. CRISPR's technology for editing genes carried only superior aesthetics into her DNA chain along with those most dangerous.

Ray's perfected genetic make-up guaranteed she'd never develop cancer, MS, or Parkinson's. Her mind would never suffer the ravages of Alzheimer's, but it'd also never reveal more than cognitive empathy. No emotional empathy, or so the research promised. Nick figured they'd promised more than they could guarantee.

Careful not to wake her, Nick crept past and through the recovery room door. Inside, he reviewed Ray's instructions, monitored the patient's vitals, re-calculated the medicated drip, checked bandages, and administered appropriate morning doses into the IV. Easily mistaken for routine procedure. But nothing about their existence was routine.

He drifted back from his thoughts and found himself staring down on a face permanently etched into memory. Something had changed. Shifted. The morning light streaming into the room after so many dark days in the medical wing made it appear brighter, more alive. Or was his mind playing tricks on him?

If the operation failed, Ray might spiral into an inescapable hell. If it succeeded, it could ignite a fate far worse. "No upside here," he spoke to the air.

For the first time in a while, Micael's voice echoed in his head. "When you're fighting yourself, son, you never win." His sound bites of wisdom were growing louder.

"This is insanity," he whispered, assessing the unconscious man on the gurney. "You've all made her deaf to salvation."

He was on his way out when Ray screamed.

He ran to her, the weighted door sealed shut behind him. He shook her shoulders. "Wake up. Come on, girl." She lashed out with her left arm, a lethal reflex. Nick slid clear of impact, clutched the full water glass beside her, and doused her. Ray's black eyes sprang open. Their intensity made him retreat.

"Jesus, Ray."

"Not in the same sentence," she warned.

"How bad?" he asked.

"What do you think? They're night terrors. All bad."

"Do you want your journal?"

"I'll write it down later." Irritated, she tossed off the blanket and sprang upright.

The side effect of her otherwise perfect design, black eyes and scary dreams.

"What time is it?" she asked, wiping water from her face.

"Just after eight," he said. "You slept quite a while."

"When did you get up?" She spun on her heels to face him.

"Around four thirty. After an hour of vibrating windows, I gave up.

You, however, slept like a baby through the worst of the storm. How is that?"

"Storms never bother me."

"Nor guilt."

"Not the captain again." Typical Ray, incapable of remorse, lulled by thunder, haunted by silence.

When they reached the kitchen, she grabbed champagne instead of coffee.

"It was violent." He handed her a champagne flute from the cupboard.

"It was over in seconds. He didn't feel a thing," she said.

"No. I meant the storm...forget it."

Half full of fermented bubbles, she carried the glass to the refrigerator, filled the remaining space with freshly squeezed orange juice, and passed the container to Nick.

"How's he fairing?" She motioned with her glass to the recovery room.

"Fine. Vitals stable, nothing significant to report."

The phone rang. Nick grabbed the receiver before the second ring. Ray never answered the phone—ever. The change in Nick's tone substantiated why.

"Why are you calling here?" His voice was solid, unforgiving. "That doesn't grant you any leeway in the agreement! If you think he was risky to deal with, just ponder for a moment what we'll be like in comparison, with no one persuading our tolerance."

Ray didn't need to be told who it was or what they wanted. They'd both expected the call but had put it out of mind in the chaos of the previous days. Time had ticked by. But patience wasn't a virtue of their enemies.

"You'll deal with me until he has had time to recover from his loss, you heartless son-of-a-bitch!" Nick slammed the phone into the cradle hard enough to crack the casing.

"Well, why don't you tell them how you really feel?" Ray laughed.

"I'm shocked they waited 'til now," he said, theatrics over.

"We won't be able to hold them off indefinitely. I don't want Cage docking in our front yard. Our patient has to recover fast. I give us two weeks." She refilled her morning cocktail with straight champagne and raised her glass. "A toast before dying." She swallowed down half the flute.

Unimpressed, Nick set his glass on the counter untouched and walked out.

4

"I'M GOING, Dad. This story's worth the risk." Kyly Zuriel fed the friction with her father in leisurely tones from a lounge chair on their sun deck.

"I fought so hard to find us this peace." Cero may have understood her independence, but what underlied it he carefully avoided. "You're not using sound judgment."

Their home furnished the back of an outcrop perched on the edge of a high cliff, with a sharp break between land and sea. The barren sugarcane plantation on Maui's west side brought salvation from a painful past. A healing place for a minister, his wife, and a budding journalist. And she was abandoning it.

He continued, "You could get there and find no one will talk to you."

"I know what I'm doing. I'm surprised you're questioning it." Kyly spoke without glancing up from her laptop.

"I worry for good reason. I'm your father; it's my job. You hook into the Internet like it's an IV, but it's worthless to this cause? I'll never understand..."

His voice trailed as he headed back inside to his crystals, incense, and the latest religious reads he'd finish before resuming his ministerial classes in a couple weeks. Kyly heard him. She always heard him.

"No, you won't ever understand," she promised under her breath.

After two years in college, four in university, and three struggling to make a name in her field, she hit pay dirt on a worthy story and stuck her neck out to investigate.

Cero didn't agree. He liked her neck right where it was, not on a chopping block of controversy. It wasn't his decision anymore.

A documentary on rare birth defects had piqued Kyly's interest, prompting her current research. Months of canvassing unusually disturbing cases narrowed to one specific incident. It wasn't the rarity of the peculiar defect or the possible cause that intrigued her, but the lack of information, the initial handling of documentation. Missing pieces and a familiar failure became alluring bait.

For the last few months, she'd been engulfed in research. She'd numbed to her surroundings. Even the radical new age practices Cero and his born-again wife occasionally participated in didn't faze her. Kyly typed on her laptop, blind to the incense -laden fog.

A deep seeded injustice driving her focus.

Her mother died twenty years earlier, giving birth to her baby sister. Both infant and mother were lost. Cero, a doctor then, specialized in obstetrics. He swore off the medical profession after watching his young wife and new child perish beneath the hands of another's incompetence. After years of guilty mourning and a hidden existence in the novels he wrote on metaphysical healing, he found peace and assurance with someone not bound by this world.

Kyly adored her stepmother, even if she couldn't understand her kinship with the 'other side.' As sweet and kind as they came, Paris swept her dad off his righteous high horse while infecting them both with soulful temperance. Kyly was grateful. What she wasn't was at peace.

"He's giving you grief again over this trip, I assume?" Paris tended to a herb plant behind Kyly's lounger.

"When isn't he giving me grief?" Kyly said.

"When he's giving me grief, of course." Paris smiled.

As beautiful as the city she was conceived in, Paris bore its name as a reminder. Kyly prospered under her reserved loving nature. The two were as opposite in character as mother and daughter could be, one all faith, the other all fact. Yet, an underlying kinship bonded them, sacrifice for justice. Paris was a medium who worked with police in child abduction cases. The pain she silently carried resonated with Kyly.

Paris drifted onward with her watering can. A house full of herbs, fresh flowers, and an irritated husband awaited attention.

Watching her stepmother walk away, Kyly wondered what fate was worse, never experiencing conception, dying during childbirth like her biological mother, or giving birth to a fatally damaged baby like her research subject.

She located birth records, background on the doctor who delivered the flawed infant, and a listing of his very public accomplishments, then enlisted outside help. Her cousin worked for the FBI and, although straight-laced, he confirmed the parents' previous address. The rest of the digging was hers.

Kyly believed many women were ill-advised when receiving gender-specific medical care, particularly during pregnancy, often falling victim to ineptitude. A belief solidified by her loss.

"This has something to do with your mother's death, doesn't it?"

Kyly jerked up, sending her laptop in a slide for the stone tile. She snatched it before its corner made impact. "Dad, warn me next time."

"I'm right, aren't I?"

"Let it go. I'm not discussing it." She settled back into position, raising her eyes only after his footsteps faded.

She derived no pleasure from his frustration or the increasing tension it caused her parents. Their voices drifted to her from inside the house.

"Cero, you must trust her decision. You're always bragging to friends about her intellect," Paris reminded him.

"There's reason to worry!" he said. "Lee is never this quiet about anything, her secrecy is...it's personal."

"Honey, you can't control her. All you can do now is be there if she runs into trouble."

"Trouble is exactly what she's running to," he said. "I know it, and so should you."

Kyly would prove him wrong. She trusted her own judgment, not his. Not for a long time. Maybe not ever again. Proof waited on the other side of the ocean, a plane ticket away.

Paris drifted soundlessly onto the patio. Kyly was accustomed to sensing her presence rather than hearing her. She came into reflective view on Kyly's laptop screen. Her expression stalled Kyly's typing.

The distant stare of a psychic seeing a dark future she didn't want to reveal. The same intensity she wore during the last abduction case she'd worked on.

It ended badly.

How do you tell a family their seven-year-old son is never coming home?

You don't. Paris had given the news to the authorities. They did the rest. The burden of her mother's inner knowledge streaked silver shards into her hair and carved wise worry lines into her face.

Those wrinkles deepened, but now they were for her.

Kyly couldn't deny the dread her stepmother wore. Rising as surely as the tide, it wasn't enough to stop her. Why try? She'd learned the hard way; good or bad, destiny couldn't be avoided.

5

MASON STONE HAD reason to carry a gun and walk a righteous path. His father did neither and possessed a disdain for both. A fact feeding his commitment.

Despite a rescue rate for kidnap victims that said he deserved an Aston Martin DB9 and a bank account that agreed, Mason exuded a modest but hard edge class. His Cadillac Denali SUV sported custom brushed-nickel equipment to hold his gear in perfect order while concealing an unbreachable alarm system. His home reflected the same subdued style. Smart. Safe.

The lower level of his mountain estate was reserved for entertainment, sports, and weapons. Selecting his handgun, he glanced over the collection of arms. His life had evolved from one form of combat to another, surviving his father, the military, the police force, and then his kidnap and ransom assignments. Every departure came with the knowledge it might be his last.

He skirted the dark maple pool table, dartboard lane, and card table. None of them had logged sufficient playtime. Grabbing a remote off a sideboard, he hit a couple buttons and watched a 106" screen retract into the ceiling as the roof-mounted projector extinguished its image, no movie, instead a crime scene he'd been analyzing. Another touch silenced the stereo system pumping soulful blues of an unappreciated artist into the house through wall speakers.

Tossing the remote onto a sofa, he picked up the phone.

Jack, his only neighbor for miles and a brother-in-arms, was a loyal friend. Both bachelors, one by choice, the other by consequence, relied on their alliance.

"Hey, Jack. Could I saddle you with Riggs?" Mason said. He named the Irish setter pup after the character in the movie *Lethal Weapon* because he'd busted into a liquor cabinet and suffered the consequences.

"Sure. Dallas is back at his mom's. I could use the company. What's up? I thought you were lying low?" Jack said.

"It's personal. My sister called...I'm heading out of town for a while. Not sure how long. It's complicated."

"Family stuff usually is."

"That's why I avoid it as much as possible."

"How's that working for you?" Jack laughed.

"Funny, smartass."

"I'll pick him up in a couple hours for a run."

"You remember the code?"

"Yep. No Alzheimer's yet."

"I'll call when I get a handle on things."

"Okay. And, Stone, if you need anything—"

"Thanks, Jack."

He placed the phone back in its cradle and climbed the curved staircase to the second storey master loft with his four-legged companion in tow.

"Sorry, buddy. You'll have to stay here." The pup's head hung lower to the ground. "Jack's coming. You'll still get your run in."

Recognizing the name, the dog's mood reversed.

Everything in the house was oversized and masculine, an experience in gallantry etched out of a time of knights and kings. Surely a descendant of one or the other, it provided the perfect backdrop for Mason Stone.

A backdrop more abandoned than experienced.

In less than a half hour, he slammed his truck's back hatch, set the house alarm, and jumped in. He was nothing if not efficiently prepared for crisis.

When he pulled out of the driveway onto the tree-lined inroad, ominous clouds building in the distance shadowed his windshield.

Perhaps an indication of what lay ahead, something ulterior plagued him.

The fear in her voice? The fact she'd left Curt in the dark about whatever had her so scared? He assessed his thoughts while driving down the lane. Then it hit him.

"*Resurrection.*" Remembering her saying the word sent a cold sweat across his palms. He tightened his grip on the steering wheel. Brook was spiritual, had been her entire life. His sister refused to be caught speaking the Lord's name in vain no matter how mad you made her. She honored faith and wouldn't have made the reference lightly.

"Resurrection." He spoke it aloud, fumbling it over in his mind as he scanned the now-dampened pavement ahead. Contemplation cracked and snapped explanations together like links on a heavy chain. It lengthened with each exploding droplet that scattered across the blacktop's surface. The first rule of resurrection was death. He only knew of one ghost that haunted his kid sister, and, as irrational as it was, it fit.

"Christian?"

He remembered the hardest day of her life. The tears, the pain on her face when he came to see her in the hospital, the devastation, a birth but no baby to bring home. The experience cemented his already brewing choice never to have children.

If he was right about what tormented his kid sister, she needed a priest, not a retired cop.

Resurrected how he wondered.

That was the disturbing factor. Needing to confirm his suspicions, he spoke to the truck's satellite phone activating her number. Digits clicked across the illuminated faceplate. Her line rang out on speaker mode.

"Hello." She sounded exhausted and more heartbroken than she had a half hour earlier.

"Sis, I have to know. I've been throwing this around in my head and...does this have anything to do with Christian?" Guilt ate at him for bringing it up. He had to be sure.

"How'd you...yes," she said. "I'm not certain. I'm sorry I—"

Exactly what he didn't want to hear. "It doesn't matter. I'll be there tomorrow afternoon. We'll talk then. Take care, kid." His foot dropped heavier on the accelerator.

He hung up and spoke with the man upstairs.

"Watch over her until I can." It'd be a long night on a highway that now appeared to stretch further the distance between them.

VOICES ECHOED from the outer corridor to the patient wing, drifting down the hallway into his ears. Ray's airy tone laced with concern and determination.

Bleach in the bed linens and customary hospital disinfectant rose from the tile floor, coating the air. Underlying the medicated surface, the aroma of lilacs and lilies lingered. Someone brought flowers, or air flowed in from an outer garden. Before he opened his eyes, he pictured the room in sanitary splendor.

His lips were dry. Instinctively, his tongue drifted across them. The physical action triggered an onslaught of questions, the first wave in a hurricane of confusion.

Terror sheared through his body. His skin iced over. His heart clambered, its jagged rhythm pounded in his head. His mind, alert, remembered. Alive.

He couldn't move. Physically possible, the idea itself was implausible. He wanted to scream, the dark haunting bellow of a tortured spirit. He dared not utter a sound to the outside world, unsure his voice would be familiar.

Inside, an outcry reverberated across the caverns of his soul.

He needed answers.

His eyelids fluttered, fighting light.

Before his sight cleared, he heard footsteps down the hall. He was cognizant, post-op. A fact he intended to keep to himself.

Then, a flinch, swords of pain, and an eruption he couldn't contain behind new lips.

————

The patient's scream drove Ray's champagne flute from her hand with such force it cleared four feet before smashing against the high gloss cabinets, sending tiny shards across the floor.

She sprang from her chair, landing in a sprint. For precious days, she proved her mettle, retaining a calm endurance and unwavering confidence without a shred of evidence. She considered the possibility of an awakening, consciousness, and, yes, full recovery, but had it arrived?

She stalled outside the patient's room.

Nick arrived behind her carrying a towel, hair dripping from the shower. The scream had resonated through the intercom monitoring system. He read optimism in her eyes.

"Careful." He clenched her arm with a solid grip. "We don't know what we're walking into."

She pulled her arm from his grasp. "Not what, who."

Inside, light from the window cast a pale glow, bathing the room in the soft warmth of afternoon sun. For Ray, the darkness of the days and months before was, in this moment, washed away. She approached her shaken patient, and her worries, even the hidden ones, melted into the cracks between the cool floor tiles under her bare feet.

"Well, that's quite a greeting. You got my attention." She neared his bedside. "How are you feeling or should I assume from the thunderous holler you're less than comfortable?"

Nick appeared taken aback by her composure.

Her patient's eyelids quivered, caught in a state of semi-consciousness.

"Take your time." She brushed his cheek.

His face rejected the contact, and he let out a broken breath as if insulted. Unaffected, Ray guided his bandaged head and checked his pupils. She pulled back his right eyelid. He blinked and, for a fleeting second, focused on her.

"So you're in there after all." She checked his racing pulse with her left hand.

Less than amused by her comment, Nick rolled his eyes, then stood behind her, peering over her left shoulder to watch the patient's responses.

Shifting in the sheets, limbs jerking, quaking, and flinching, the ailing man struggled, uncomfortable in his own skin. He seemed unaware and out of control.

"I...can...can't focus."

His voice was raw, fractured, deeper than she imagined, and nice.

"It's normal. It'll take time. And time is something you now have." She leaned in to kiss his forehead, but before her lips touched his skin, the mysterious world of dreams and shadows claimed him.

His skin was warm. Warm and so very soft. She could've remained there with her lips pressed against him forever if her brother's piercing eyes weren't burning a hole through the back of her skull.

His stare was worse than anticipated when she turned to meet it. Unforgiving. Repulsed even.

"What the hell are you doing?" He didn't waste time concealing his protest. "I've put up with more than my share of free falling into hell with you. I've held the line, but there is *no* chance I'm going to sit back and watch you swoon over this man like an overzealous school girl."

Nick hardly managed a breath between sentences.

"Sleeping beauty over there isn't even conscious, and when he is, chances are he'll have zero memory of you, us, or anything else, and you damn well know it!"

With every word, he distanced himself further from the bedside. His voice maintained a solid military strength few would risk interrupting.

"Until he is ready, willing, and able, any physical interaction will be professional, or you'll have way more than medical malpractice to contend with.

"You may be superior to the average person, little girl, but you cannot do this alone. So snap out of it or this soap opera episode is going to turn into a horror movie overnight. Maybe you didn't notice, but you're standing in quicksand. You don't have the leverage to push me."

The door flew open with one jarring thud from his open hand. He didn't wait for a response. And she had no intention of delivering one.

Ray took orders from no one, but Nick was her sole confidant.

She'd been so relieved, euphoric, she'd forfeited logic for contact—not a mistake she had the luxury of making twice. Nick was right, any deviation from the plan could cost her everything.

If their patient woke confused and terrified, an overt display of affection could create stress, slow recovery, and result in an immediate lack of trust, taking precious time to rebuild. Time they didn't have.

Nick sat outside on the edge of the wicker lounger with his head in his hands. The sting of his reprimand faded.

"I'm sorry—" she said.

"It's been a hell of a ride, Ray. You can't afford to lose focus." He looked up, tired and resolved. "Too many years of programming," he gestured to the doorway. "Is he still asleep?"

"Yes. Sleeping beauty," she said. "You want to help me with the preliminary tests? I believe he's stable enough to run a few basic readings."

"Sure, if you promise we'll eat lunch like regular human beings when we're finished. I can't take another week of random snacking. It's making me cranky."

"You've never eaten like a regular human, and I've never been one, but yes. Lunch, I promise. Anything to put you in better spirits." Ray flashed a calculated smile.

When they walked back into the recovery room, Nick collided with her as she stopped dead two paces in.

"What now?" he whispered, holding onto her shoulders, almost having mowed her over.

"Look." She directed his attention to their patient's position.

He lay in the bed, arms folded over his chest despite the encumbrance of the IV and other paraphernalia. And, as much as it pained him to admit, Nick instantly recognized the familiar pose too.

"It may be coincidental." His transfixed eyes belied his calm tone.

"It's not."

Walking closer, she removed items from a cabinet hidden behind wall panels. "Are you going to help me with this?" She recited into a tape recorder mounted with other handsfree equipment in the wall. "Movement in upper limbs functioning normally."

She issued a subtle but victorious grin. Ray didn't fit the world she was born to. She forced new boundaries. So far, they were holding.

7

A FLASH OF GREEN, not a fair warning, lit the far corner of Brook's eye before the crash. It came at an angle on the driver's side. Tires screeched a wicked, foreboding regret. And, for a fraction of a second, their eyes met through the glare off the windshields.

She hadn't seen or heard him coming. She passed through the quiet intersection with reckless abandon, never stopping to check for oncoming traffic. Her mind hadn't registered the five-ton truck or the tightly twined load of spruce trees bursting beyond its box. The war waging internally had taken precedence.

It did not cease, even during impact.

Her hands clutched the wheel, forcing the SUV into the park. The other driver veered left too late. His front corner connected and tore metal on the driver's side. Shrieking far worse than any high-pitched sound she made. Pain jolted her body left. No time to locate its source. Brook's tires hit the squared curb, launching over the sidewalk. Her head slammed forward, striking with blunt force, to ricochet back before a hazy vision of red monkey bars threatening to cut through at neck level.

"No." Thoughts of Curt never knowing their son was alive pumped a fresh wave of adrenaline through her.

Her hands yanked hard on the wheel. She stood on the brake with her left foot slamming hard into her right as if sheer determination would halt momentum. Swing set chairs crashed into the side door. She turned her face away, shielding it from exploding glass. The tires dug into playground gravel and stopped spinning. A wave of brown hair flew forward as she twisted to see over her shoulder, fearing the tree truck bearing down on her. She focused in time to see it waver on three wheels and slam to a stop, jackknifed in the middle of the street, surrounded by broken branches.

Eerie silence, then pain.

Freeing her death grip on the steering wheel, Brook padded herself down. When she touched her head, her hands came back bloody. Her left side throbbed, making her wince, ribs bruised, not broken she hoped. She caught a glimpse of herself in the rearview mirror—a disheveled wreck, a nasty gash on the forehead. Marred but alive.

"Are you okay?" A voice spoke through chastened breath. The other driver had fled his vehicle and ran to meet her. "Jesus, are you okay?"

The young man wrenched on the concave driver's door until he forced it open and stood breathless at her side. "Are you in any pain? Are you hurt?"

"I'm...I'm so sorry. I think I'm okay. I didn't...are you okay?"

"I'm a little shaken but unharmed. Let me help you, make sure you're not injured. I'm an EMT. Liam. I drive for my brother-in-law's landscaping business on the side. How's your head? You have a pretty bad laceration."

Noticing protruding plastic on the interior door panel, he reached for her left side. "Can you pull up your shirt? I better have a look at your ribs."

Brook read the concern in his eyes and lifted her shirt above the injured area. With trained hands, he traced her ribs. "Any pain here?"

She winced, then climbed out gingerly with Liam's help and walked a few steps to a park bench that was unscathed by the accident. "It doesn't hurt too bad."

"It will. Shock staves off the pain for a while, not forever. I have a kit in the truck. I'll move it out of the way and grab the kit. You sit. We were lucky."

"Lucky?"

"The playground was empty."

"Oh god." Brook scanned the park, guilt overriding any pain.

"My truck's in one piece, big bumper. You've got some body

damage. The park's untouched, may need to smooth tire tracks out of the gravel. Could've been far worse." Liam smiled then jogged back to his truck.

"Thank you," Brook called after him, nursing her injuries. "I'm sorry...I'm so sorry."

He waved a hand and kept moving. He was about the same age as Christian, and she could've killed him.

———

"Brook? Are you okay? What happened?" Curt's voice echoed from the kitchen to the outer deck. "Who wiped our car out? Where are you?"

She heard him but couldn't respond.

Sun brushed the lush grass in their backyard like a gentle painter, glazing every strand with a thin gold veil. Even the cat, lulled by nature's tranquility, slept beside Brook's chair, sprawled on the deck's cedar planks.

Peace failed to penetrate.

The French doors flew open and Curt rushed out sporting a thick film of construction debris dust, sticky with the sweat of cold panic.

"What the hell happened?" He crouched to examine her.

"I was broadsided by a landscape truck." Brook shifted in her seat awkwardly. "The intersection of—"

"Are you hurt? Was the driver drunk, asleep at the wheel? Let me guess, texting?"

"It was my fault," she said. "It doesn't matter—"

"It doesn't matter? Of course it matters. I come home to find the SUV smashed up in our driveway, you tell me you're responsible, and it doesn't matter? Was anyone else hurt? Are we going to be sued?"

"No, his truck's fine. He's an EMT, very kind, and, minus tire tracks, the park is too."

"Let me see your forehead." Curt leaned in to inspect the bandage over her brow, only to have his hand knocked away.

"Have you seen today's paper?"

"The paper? Brook, the accident! What happened?"

"The accident is the least of our problems," she said. "Have you seen it?"

His face contorted with confusion, then he said, "You know I have. I always read the business section when—"

"The rest of the paper."

"What does that have to do with the accident?"

"Have you?"

"No."

"Well, I did. Then I watched reality crumble. It's why I had the accident." She passed him the copy she'd carried with her all day. "Curt... we've been lied to."

"Have you taken anything for the pain?" He reached again at her brow. "Looks bad."

"I don't feel it. Please read."

Staring at the photo on the front page of foreign affairs, he peered at it, then at her like the bump on her head had done significant damage. She read his expression and shook her head.

"Turn it over to the page I marked." She pointed to a bent corner.

The paper flipped in his hands like a thousand times before. She studied his face as he read the article with intent. Before he got very far, he became impatient. When dry throat impeded his interrogation, he grabbed the glass of iced tea beside her and swallowed half of it down.

"So the doctor that delivered him passed away. How does this evolve to us being lied to?"

"Flip to the back page where the tribute by his son is written."

"I didn't know he had a kid the same age as...you'd think we would've heard of him with all the doc's publicity." He refolded the paper to the back page.

"Oh, Christ!" His reaction was as forceful as hers had been that morning. Shock had weakened her into losing her grip on her breakfast plate; it strengthened his hold on the iced tea glass. Sheer rage snapped the hard plastic, sending the cat running for shelter.

"It's...he's our son. Has to be. It's Christian." His words were choppy, strained.

"I know. Mason's on his way."

8

NEVER TRUST STRANGERS. When one killed your mother and sister, these words hold a profound truth.

Kyly Zuriel focused on approaching headlights, ignoring the man who followed her outside from the baggage claim area.

Scanning the curb, she stepped into the rain from the sheltered airport exit. A cab pulled in behind two others awaiting weary travelers to Half Moon Bay. Its driver sprang from his seat to assist her before she crossed the distance.

Cleaner than the cabs in New York and minus the Bulletproof Plexiglas, the vehicle put Kyly at ease. She was as comforted by the older gentleman at the wheel who struggled to lift her luggage into the trunk as she was leery of the one in the trench coat ogling her in the rain. The cab pulled away, and she exhaled with relief.

Humidity poured through the cabby's open window, noticeably void of the lush tropical flower fragrance her island air basked in.

Leaning forward, she committed her attention to the veteran tour guide.

Taking advantage of his knowledge of the area, Kyly asked where the library, university, and other places of interest were. They discussed direct routes from her hotel. Pops, as he introduced himself, gave her the run-down of quick avenues to each. He even threw in histories of a few great diners along their trail, making the time pass.

"This is it," Pops announced, reaching to unbuckle his seat belt at the hotel.

"Don't trouble yourself." Kyly gathered her belongings. "They have bellhops for that."

A young man wearing hotel attire came to meet the car. Pops hit a button to open the trunk. "I'll keep an ear open for dispatches," he promised.

"I'll be around for the next ten days."

"You never said why you were in town." He kept a keen eye on the bellhop's treatment of his car and Kyly's luggage through the mirrors.

"Research," she said, getting out.

"If you need a ride, call the company and ask for Pops." He leaned out the window to hand her his card in the shape of a cab.

"I'll do that. Thank you again." She smiled as she exchanged the yellow card for the fare she owed. "Good night."

The cab departed with a slushy swoosh, leaving puddles of water waking in waves on the pavement. The bellhop ushered the luggage in on a trolley.

"Reservation, miss?" he asked.

"Zuriel, Kyly. Would you mind taking the bags up for me and having them leave my key at the front desk? I want to get a feel for the place." She handed him a tip and drank in her surroundings. The rain diminished into a light drizzle.

"Yes, miss, but don't go too far. People get lost in the fog, and it's pretty dark out here when you get past the streetlights." He pointed to the end of the block where only the headlights of a parked car lit the street. Then, blackness when its driver extinguished them. The bellhop disappeared inside.

Leather backpack slung over her shoulder, Kyly set off in the direction of an all-night diner Pops raved about during the cab ride. She checked her watch. After eleven local time and she was starving. Her small frame belied her appetite.

The rain dissipated. A moist breeze remained in the air. It rustled the leaves on large trees lining the street and sent down glittering droplets tapping out a random rhythm as they met pavement.

Even in the shadow of night, it was pretty here. Fog softened the edges. Across the way, she discerned a government building. She'd check it out in the morning. Faded in the distance, a lighthouse beacon sent a thick ray of white across the sky over the Pacific Ocean. Half Moon Bay was nothing more geographically than a ten-mile stretch of sand and rock clinging to the sea. But its founders made it a visual masterpiece from this vantage point. Dim light revealed a quaint village etched in Victorian charm and unique unto itself. As were all the small towns that made up the sea bound area.

Kyly's summer shoes were just high enough for her feet to escape the damp spray created with each step. A car door slammed, echoing from behind her. She turned but couldn't see it through the haze.

Crossing the street, led by a pale green diner sign with the word 'ALWAYS' written in Old English, she listened for footsteps. Nothing. She made her way inside through heavy ship galley doors.

After a quick gab with the hostess, Kyly learned the name was a tribute to the owner's favorite movie starring Richard Dreyfus. A plaque on the counter said, 'We're ALWAYS open, and you're ALWAYS welcome.'

"The restaurant was built in the late 1890s." The hostess sensed Kyly's curiosity. "A hideaway for sin seekers creeping under the legal blanket of prohibition, a Rum Runner's drop point from Canada. I hear it drew a thirsty crowd. Hasn't changed much. Chardonnay instead of moonshine. That's about it."

Surrounded by towering cypress trees, it lay nestled between coastal rock-bed and inland charm. Kyly drank in the nostalgia.

Taking her waitress's advice, she ordered the house clam chowder and home-baked bun. While she ate, she watched the crowd.

The amount of traffic suggested it was midday, not midnight. Savoring the juice from her bowl, she knew why. Enticing as ever. The place gave the expression 'midnight snack' new meaning.

Stomach content, fatigue set in. The diner sat a few blocks from clean linens. Despite the people scattered throughout the restaurant when she entered the street, it was abandoned. The only footsteps resonating down the block against the asphalt were hers.

Back at the hotel, a lone night attendant at the front desk handed her a room key and directed her to the bank of elevators on the left. She got off at the third floor and walked down a long, narrow, but stately deco-rated hallway to the corner suite. The silence in the corridor gave the illusion she was the sole guest in a ghost town. She paused midpoint in the hall. No one in either direction.

She appreciated the quiet. When her head hit the pillow, she was out, sleeping hard until the sun woke her. She'd forgotten to close the outer drapes. She stretched, checked out the view, then drew them shut, heading for the shower.

She was shutting off the tap when the washroom phone's old-fashioned ring echoed into the shower stall and bounced off its walls. The intrusive noise sounded in stereo with its partner in the adjacent bedroom. Well-orchestrated, the rings overlapped, creating a reverberation you'd have to be half-dead to sleep through. A thick towel around her, Kyly wrapped another over her hair while walking to the phone.

"Hi, Dad."

"How do you do that?" he asked.

"The relentless ring gives you away." She regretted the cold tone in her voice.

"Wanted to check in. Make sure you got there okay."

"I'm fine. It's late and I have a busy day. I should go."

"Your mother wanted to make sure you received the etransfer."

"I saw it, haven't accepted, it isn't necessary." She knew full well who sent the funds. "I don't plan on shopping while I'm here. It's strictly business."

"I thought maybe you could bring a keepsake back for your mother," he reasoned.

"I'll pick out something nice."

A silence passed, then Cero said, "Good luck...with your story."

She knew it was difficult for him to say. "Thanks." It wasn't much, but it was something.

"Keep us posted. I don't like the idea of you venturing—"

"Yeah, I got that," she said. "I've got to go."

Dropping the receiver back in its antique holster, she directed her attention to the suitcase on the holding rack, ignoring the pang of guilt for the distance between them—none of it measurable in miles.

———

Summer had been in the air for some time in Half Moon Bay. Still, Zavier Cromwell knew the woman was a tourist at first glance.

Her rich raven hair was sun-kissed with a golden sheen and streams of scattered highlights. Her skin tanned a warm brown. She would've made a fabulous travel agent. A glance in her direction inspired dreams of tropical holidays.

He was dreaming.

Here, the sun shone in spring and muted during summer months beneath the film of fog rolling in off the shore—insufficient conditions to have created her.

She exuded maturity beyond the average student on campus, flawless. Crossing the expanse of manicured lawn outside the library, he'd watched her capture the attention of every male breathing, oblivious to all of it. Then he followed her in.

"It's been sheets 'n' smir out there for a month. Where'd you get the tan?" He overheard the bubbly blonde working the information desk.

"I'm here doing research," the woman replied, smiling politely.

"If you don't have to be indoors, why come here *today*?" the girl questioned. "There's sun out there! Then again, you're already baked."

He wouldn't have put it that way.

Not responding, the woman departed after getting directions to public records.

Choosing a desk close to an aisle of interest, she set up for the day. Hours passed, and information mounted. With studies of his own, Zavier glanced occasionally in her direction, searching for the signs of overload.

Patience. One of his virtues.

———

Dangerously close to admitting her father had a point about the trip being a waste, Kyly picked up her first solid lead. The mark roster confirmed she was in the right wing of the campus to find him. It also said she wasn't going to be dealing with an idiot. Zavier Cromwell held the second highest grade in his class, according to those recently posted. She hadn't found a picture yet to track him down by face, but she didn't need one.

"There's a coffee house down the left wing. By now, you must be feeling withdrawal."

The voice, so close, startled her. She knocked over a stack of books, sending them sliding across her desk.

His tone was too deep and sensual for his age, she thought as she faced him. Midtwenties. Kind. She read him in an instant. Handsome and fit, with a medium build and obvious confidence, he wasn't quick enough to catch a peek at the newspaper in her hand before she discreetly flipped it over.

"I'm Zavier Cromwell, med student. And you are?" He extended his hand across the scattered heap on the table.

Nervous, she knocked the pile a second time. He chuckled.

"Kyly Zuriel, how did you know I'd been—"

"I've been studying across from you for the last three hours." He pointed to his table a short distance from hers. "You're not much for scenery, hey."

"I avoid it," she said, laughing off the fact she hadn't noticed her polite admirer.

"What faculty are you in?"

"I'm a journalist."

"Communications program?"

"No. I graduated a while ago. I'm borrowing your library." She escaped his gaze to shuffle papers.

"How about that coffee?"

Whether truly in need of a break from scanning over fine print or not, his offer was the gift of preparation meeting opportunity. She would've found him sooner or later. Sooner and instigated by him was better. Besides, she reasoned, it was difficult to turn down his aqua eyes.

"Is it okay to leave everything here?" she asked.

"Unless you have hidden exam answer keys in there, I think it's safe enough." He grinned.

No chance to study him without being noticed. He was one of the Cromwells she came for. She'd chosen this library for more than one reason. Today the research paid off. Where would it lead? She hoped in a direction opposite to what her father predicted.

Making small talk through the library's columns of texts, she was relieved to find him focusing more on her face than her hands. He failed to notice the newspaper page she folded into her purse while they were talking. The headline stated in bold black print the achievements of the doctor who potentially delivered his older brother. For now, she preferred to remain friend not foe.

"I take it you're not from around here?" he said, eyes grazing her tanned limbs.

"Maui," she answered, watching as his face lit up.

"An island girl. It must be a beautiful place. I've never been."

"I miss it already," she admitted.

"The fog here takes some getting used to." He redirected her around a corner to the coffee house. "How long have you been away?"

"Not long," she said, deliberately vague.

"More importantly, how long are you in town for?" He caught her gaze as he stopped at the end of the lineup.

"Ten days." She diverted her attention to the menu board, dampened by the realization it'd be long enough to unearth skeletons, open old wounds, and flee the wreckage.

9

THE RHYTHM of blood never sounded so good.

Ray's stethoscope confirmed a strong heartbeat. The patient's initial physical results were solid. Blood pressure, pulse, and temperature were optimal. An ophthalmoscopic examination of his kaleidoscope eyes brought relief. Even Nick couldn't dismiss the signs of success.

He'd become a reluctant but integral ally. Ray stroked his ego like the back of an aggravated cobra. Warily.

"What a team," she whispered.

"Yeah," Nick said dryly. "Like a sword and its sheath. Guess which part I am."

His negativity never penetrated.

The heart rate monitor reflected exertion caused by fleeting moments of sporadic consciousness. Generally, their patient remained trapped beneath a shroud of exhaustion, oblivious to poking and prodding. It didn't mean their intrusion wouldn't register. She knew firsthand every harm registered.

Content as she was with the recorded progress, Ray heard the clock ticking. She retreated to the privacy of her office, knowing the edge against her enemies hinged on a miraculous recovery.

Micael's surviving son, a stunning and threatening revelation to them, held the government hounds at bay by presence alone. Still, he'd have to be in attendance at the funeral.

She expected nothing less.

Ray wasn't designed to lose.

The patient down the hall was a living testament to this fact.

Equations flashed across her computer screen as she keyed in new data. Results. How she lived for them.

While the computer tallied, she scoped out her den.

She focused in on the corner bar behind the dirt-brown leather sofas. An ornate, crystal vase perilously perched there. Fresh white roses overflowed its rim, making it top heavy. Ill-fated, it hugged the edge, dreading a draft.

Ray stared at the vase. Its precarious placement curled the corners of her mouth into a cagey grin.

Her gaze drifted upward as she stretched out. The office roof reached sixteen feet high, surrounded on all sides by inset bookcases accented by hidden shelf display lights.

A coarse metal lamp sat on her desk. An obvious weapon of choice if a threat was ever posed within the dusk chamber. She ran a finger over it, admiring its severe edges.

The room was signature Ray—exquisite, ingenious, purposeful, and cold...so cold.

Its mahogany shelves housed the latest texts and novels written by experts in one field or another. She'd read them all—twice. Knowledge provided the power to master your enemy's tactics and manifest their defeat. And, since she despised humanity as a whole, she'd absorbed countless volumes. The books sat, meticulously placed, titles reflecting the dim lights pouring down from above.

She'd published two of her own under an alias. The first, a definitive study of CRISPR gene editing and cellular memory. The second was a psychological non-fiction on the unforeseen capabilities of the human mind accessing more than the standard five percent and the inevitable possibilities. Together, they told her story.

The expensive volumes were added to the curriculum of many leading universities, but few in the general public knew of their existence. She attributed their success more to her famous co-author than her own genius, but Dr. V knew better.

So did she.

A framed photograph faced Ray's workstation.

In it, she was seventeen, attending her first opera during a medical conference in New York. Though not in years, she was all woman.

The hotel manager snapped the photo on their way out and sent it to their room as a gift for what he presumed was "a lovely father and daughter" pair.

Fool.

She kept the photo as a reminder of the trip that initiated the drastic change in her life—Dr. V departed three weeks later for a two-year research trip halfway around the world, leaving her in the care of her brother, Nick. When he returned, she was no longer the girl he rescued, but the woman he'd abandoned. Guilt drove him places he swore he'd never go. Places she led him. Places of sin and redemption.

The island fortified and imprisoned. He gave himself. All she wanted. They were happy for a time. Then her happiness became his disease, he fell ill, and their lives were transformed.

A remote panel beside her desk hid a small television. She revealed it with the press of a button, and her patient appeared in crystal clarity on the screen. With another touch, the volume rose. She worked to the soothing cadence of his breathing.

It wasn't long before a rap on the door alerted her to pending intrusion. One touch and the panel slid shut.

"Come in." She knew who waited on the other side.

"Why work with the door shut? It's not like you're at the General with visitors mulling about." Nick rolled his eyes at her need for secrecy.

"Habit. What's up?" Ray rested her bare feet on the desk's edge. Nick's eyes drifted to her scars.

"Phone call."

Without questioning, she sat upright and spun her chair to face a second computer screen programmed solely to monitor the island. In the top right corner, a digital telephone symbol flashed. Ray moved the cursor, clicked twice, and waited briefly for a box to surface with pertinent information. Date, time, location, scrambling method, everything scrolled across the screen.

"They're close. Inside our waters." She invited Nick for a closer look. "See this?" She pointed to a line of description. "That's a wireless up-link signature. It could be coming from anywhere within a thirty-mile radius." She clicked the keys to request further data.

"A boat?" Nick searched out the window behind him. Ray engaged a security program on a second screen while the monitoring system sought to fulfill her latest request. An invisible inner pane darkened. Although Nick could still see out, no one could see in anymore.

"What did they say?" she paused for emphasis. "Exactly."

"Grief or not, they intend to restructure immediately. If he wants to be in the game, he has to play his hand now, or they'll play it for him. Locke's words." Nick looked back out the window. "I told them to go to hell, that they were forgetting who was holding the cards and hung up."

"Good. It might irritate them enough to call back. If they do, I'll trace them, and we'll know where to strike."

A majestic bluff with a spectacular view of the ocean marked the halfway point on Ray's run. Located on the south side of the island, cleared of trees, and lush with wildflowers, it was beautiful, open, and potentially very public—an obvious choice for the funeral site.

Normally, she stopped for nothing. Today was an exception. Cage and the boys back home hadn't called yet, a sign of a disorganized approach or a focused and deliberate choice. Chances were, the latter.

Scanning the open waters, she re-configured the layout of the upcoming service in her mind. This side of the island was unapproachable by boat. It provided a single outcrop without constant surveillance. If her opponents planned to penetrate, divers were the safest option. Ray had measures in place for that. Their tanks only lasted so long. A boat would be detectable from any dockable point. And a helicopter would be a mistake at any time. Ray, a born marksman, had impeccable aim and lethal deterrents.

Going over possible infiltration patterns in her head, her feet pounded the pavement again. Despite the heat, she never broke a sweat.

Humidity saturated her Body Armor. It clung uncomfortably to her athletic frame and tainted the air with the scent of antiperspirant.

Her routine forfeited vanity for stamina, the key to survival.

Outlast, outsmart, outrun.

Reaching the house, she slowed to a walk, drawing in deep breaths. She didn't collapse into a chair, slump her shoulders, or hang her head.

Standing straight, shoulders back, chin level with the ground, she surveyed the pool area.

Never exhibiting weakness. Never letting her guard down. Never forgetting who was watching.

Nick motioned to the table. "I won't be able to relax and enjoy my meal if you're making my lazy ass feel guilty."

"It's nice to get back into routine," she said. "What's been happening while I was out?"

"If you're asking about our admirers, no response. On the other topic, I think your friend is beginning to stir. His vitals are up, and his sleep activity was intriguing a half hour ago. He's resting comfortably again."

"What do you mean, intriguing?" She blotted her face with a beach towel.

"More motion than before. REM sleep. He's dreaming, but don't get any illusions about what."

His perimeter fence went up. Ray backed off. She'd investigate for herself later.

"What are we eating?" She dropped the towel and found her seat.

"Monkfish. Seemed appropriate. Brain food without the calories." Nick slid his chair closer to the table and leaned in. "We have to talk."

"After we eat." Ray shoveled a forkful into her mouth. "Umm. Delicious."

Nick lifted a file out from beside him and opened it on the table by her plate. Medical data and funeral plans. The morbid papers were intended to interrupt her appetite. Ray slid the pile closer to review its contents and kept eating.

———

The casket was flown in over a month earlier through a maze of precautions. Ray ran her hand down the side of its embossed edge. The warmth of the wood fed into her flesh. Micael's family name was etched into the front, while the rosary, written in Italian, lay below it. It was honorable.

And it was empty.

She admired the workmanship—the perfection of the design that was hers. Everyone would be touched by this graceful burial gift, and everyone would be saddened, even her, if for appearances only.

She understood the risk the funeral posed. There was no way to be confident a caterer or florist wasn't planted as surveillance. And a few would be. However, by leaving themselves wide open, they'd avert suspicion. Watchful eyes would detect nothing out of the ordinary. The casket would remain sealed. No one would question this choice. If they ever did, it'd be far too late. Ashes to ashes.

Put on a good show and buy more time for unimpeded patient recovery.

The casket was on a holding table in the six-car garage beside Nick's sports car. She glanced between the two and deliberated over which was more exquisite or more useless—a casket without a body or a racecar without a road.

Nick had the sleek silver Saleen S7 ultra-elite supercar flown in. The car, one of a limited few built, was worth over half a million dollars. Its design, Nick said, was sacred. "Rare. Scary sexy. Pure to its purpose."

Ray liked the car. It begged to be driven.

No roads.

She turned her attention back to the coffin. Invitations were hand delivered by a motivated courier. Each elegantly composed with sincerity and intention, as well as an itinerary outlining pick-up, flight times, and the particulars of the funeral service.

Patient recovery over the last nine days was nothing short of amazing. The medical attention exceeded levels other leading medical professionals could scarcely begin to imagine. Ray's formula for recovery mocked decades of conventional wisdom. Yet it held the modest rewards of scattered words making little sense and intermittent consciousness.

They needed more.

She'd have to do better. The garage mandoor adjacent to the medical wing flew open, and with it, the blinding light of day. A dying sun scorched her black eyes. Until then, she hadn't noticed she'd been engulfed in a shroud of darkness.

"He's awake!" Despite his strong faith in their science, Nick's voice pitched with utter astonishment.

"Awake?" She slinked out from behind the casket.

"Speaking, but I don't know for how long." Nick held the door as she passed under his arm. "He's asking questions. I told him I'd get the doctor."

Ray opened the outer door accessing the medical wing. He caught up and grabbed her. "Ray, he doesn't have a clue who I am."

She stopped.

A shiver made her flinch. The hall wasn't cold. "Are you certain?"

"He doesn't know who *he* is. You have to be careful here."

A moment of silence fell between them. Ray resolved to accept this temporary delay in her plans, deciding it might prove useful in the short term.

"Getting him to attend the funeral, no questions asked will be far less complicated," she said.

Nick's forehead tensed as he squinted and rubbed a hand across his brow.

"The long-term effects will cause nothing but havoc," he said. "Jesus."

"He..." Ray said, referring to the Son of God. "...isn't invited." Ray motioned at the recovery room door. "Shall we?"

Nick moved slowly, hesitant.

"Everything is going to work out perfectly." She grabbed her coat from the chair in the hall and settled into her doctor's role. "I could handle this in my sleep."

"Yeah, your dreams turn into nightmares," he reminded.

10

BROOK WELTERED on sorrow's stormy seas, and Curt felt himself a fallible life preserver.

Up most of the night, she'd agonized over her abducted son in tears of guilt and rage. Eventually, Valium created a crevice in her torment wide enough for the sandman to slip through. The drug didn't silence the demons, merely muted their voices to a wicked whisper.

Watching her deteriorate, Curt knew she couldn't maintain a casual illusion through another long day. He sent Sandy a message at first light explaining her absence at the office.

Brook's emotional decline fanned the flames of resentment building inside him.

Still, he refused to allow his own anger and remorse to overpower his empathy for her.

It shadowed her, an ominous storm cloud anxious to purge.

This Thursday work was manageable for him. His crews were working three jobs, all familiar blueprints. Yet, Brook needed time alone with her thoughts. They weren't sure when Mason would arrive. But, knowing his brother-in-law, he'd be at their door before noon. One person explaining this ordeal would be difficult enough.

After his shower, Curt decided to tour the sites and give the siblings privacy.

The kids were home late the previous night and still sleeping; neither had early morning commitments.

Before exhausting the conversation the evening before, Curt and Brook wrestled over how to tell their children without completely disrupting their lives. Regardless of their fears, they couldn't risk having Zavier and Farrah discover the truth on their own.

Tired and worn, Brook stared at him through her reflection in the dressing mirror. Her eyes said what she couldn't. Curt placed a supportive hand on her shoulder before heading downstairs.

A few minutes later, he was outside Zavier's bedroom.

Without breaking stride, he spoke through the door, "Son, join us for breakfast. Your mother and I need to talk to you."

The kids claimed the right wing of the house. Farrah's room sat at the far end. Glass French doors enclosed the area, and the ten-foot ceilings in the hallway echoed Curt's voice, reverberating it back at him.

"Hey, doll, rise and shine. Mom and I require your presence at the table."

Turning back to the kitchen, Curt knew nothing would be the same for his children, not even their identities. No longer only brother and sister, they'd become two missing one. For a fleeting moment, a wave of nausea washed over him. His legs weakened, his head spun.

Shake it off.

"What's up?" Zavier stuck his head out his bedroom doorway in time to see Curt pass through the French doors at the end of the hallway.

"Breakfast! You've got ten minutes, Doc." Curt spoke with his back to him. "I'll meet you at the coffee pot."

The hall door closed. Zavier flew over his bed to his dresser on the far side of the room, grabbed his shirt, then headed out. Half asleep, he still functioned with the precision expected of a future surgeon.

Farrah was shuffling like her linen PJ's were infused with lead. He dove out of his room into her with a minor thud, jarring her to the left.

"Good morning." His intrusion of her personal space was his version of affection.

"Can't you even enter the hall without causing a commotion," she said, mildly annoyed.

"Nice do." He smiled at her primitive wavy locks and stretched on his shirt.

"Runs in the family, rockstar." She laughed and flicked a chaotic chunk of blond hair standing on end.

"What's going on?" If anyone had the inside info, she did.

"Don't look at me, I just sleep here."

"Okay." He smiled and flipped a curl of her hair with his finger. Then, as expected, cut her off to beat her to the kitchen.

Curt poured pancake batter onto the grill's surface as Zavier rounded the corner.

"What a day. Smells good. I'm starved, how 'bout you?"

Curt flashed an inquisitive stare.

"What? I'm always this wonderful, don't you remember?" Zavier teased. "Maybe you don't. Early onset of Alzheimer's?"

Curt stopped pouring and stared deliberately, searching for something, then said, "Maybe it's a someone and not a something."

His father wore the all-knowing gaze of a man who lived to remember the inspirational passion of young love.

Zavier curled one side of his mouth into an evasive pirate's grin. "You can make me a stack. I've got to keep up my energy level." He flexed his pectoral muscles and beelined for the coffee pot.

"Morning, Dad," Farrah said from behind him. He turned to see her squeeze Curt's side in a half hug so not to disturb his cooking.

"How'd you sleep?"

"Not long enough," she said and then, taking after her father got right to the heart of the matter. "What's up? Why the family chat?"

Zavier's ears perked, but any chance of clarity was squashed when his mother entered the kitchen.

Sunlight warmed the tile underfoot. The cat, capitalizing on the heat, plopped down without warning, causing Brook to reshuffle to avoid launching her like a football.

"Hi sleepyhead." Farrah plucked the bag of limp fur from the floor. "Tripping up Mom again, are we?" With cat in hand and kettle brewing for tea, she skirted Zavier and headed outside to the deck.

"You're lucky we have camouflage foliage," Zavier teased, followed her out, and nabbed the nearest chair. "You could really scare someone with that mane." He finished the sentence with a grunt as she dropped the cat on his stomach.

"Watch it, or I'll command her to attack," she warned, flopping down in the chair next to him.

"You're sure you don't know what's going on?" he said, scratching the cat under its chin.

"Haven't a clue, but I have a feeling it isn't good."

"Any ideas?"

"Not a one, you?"

"Nope, I never know what's going on."

"Well, in this case, we're equal." Farrah's eyes squinted in the morning sunlight. Her brow tensed, and she stared through the glare at him, waiting for reassurance.

"We'll know soon enough." He handed the cat back and reached for the mass of paper tucked beside the chair.

The paper was crumpled, requiring wrestling to flatten. Zavier unfolded and unfolded until it was completely open. His eyes skimmed its surface for mere seconds before locking on a target.

Slowly, advancing into a prone position, his disbelief found a voice. "...Like now."

Preoccupied, Farrah had been interrogating the cat. Her teasing stopped.

Turning away from the paper, he revealed the photo in slow motion, unintentionally building the suspense around his discovery he'd aligned it beside his face.

"My god!" Her eyes caught the photo and darted from it to her brother and back again. "He's you."

The confirmation he needed. "We could be—"

"Brothers." They said it in unison while turning to face the kitchen and rising together, no longer content to wait for answers.

———

Chairs slid out and places were taken. Brook chose the seat closest to Curt. Zavier and Farrah sat across the table.

"Is he..." Zavier struggled for words, holding the photo up for Curt's viewing. "Family?"

"We believe he's your brother," Curt said.

"How?" Farrah turned to her mother for answers.

"Remember your older brother?" Brook said.

"He died," Zavier clarified.

Treacherous ground, Curt jumped in.

"It wasn't as simple as that, son. He didn't pass...immediately."

Unnerved, Farrah cut in. "But you always said—"

"I said this would be hard," Curt warned. "We were told he wouldn't last more than a couple days. He didn't have any awareness of us. The doctor convinced us there were precautions to be taken before we could see him. The idea of sitting idly by while he wasted away was...unbearable."

Farrah reached across the table and placed her hand over her mother's as Curt continued.

"The doctor transferred him to a special care facility. He guaranteed us he wouldn't suffer and promised to study his brain abnormalities to prevent other couples from going through our pain. He came in that same night. Before we were cleared to see Christian, he told us our son passed."

"We were lied to," Brook blurted it out, unable to contain it.

"But how could this happen?" Zavier's temper flared. "You're telling me I've had, we've had, a brother all this time and—"

Brook's shoulders slumped under Curt's supportive hand. Tears streamed down her face. Guilt, overflowing.

"Mom, it's not your fault." Farrah sprung from her chair to comfort her mother.

"Who did this?" Zavier demanded, kicking his chair back when he rose to pace the room. "Someone has to be held accountable."

"We're going to find our son," Curt said. "And whoever kidnapped him is going to pay for this. Your uncle is on his way."

"Jesus." Zavier stopped pacing and pressed his hands against the table for balance. His head hung in disbelief as he spoke for all of them. "What do we do until then?"

11

A LIE by omission is still a lie.

These words echoed in the recesses of Kyly's mind as she thought about Zavier Cromwell in the morning sun streaming into her hotel room. She hadn't mentioned the particulars of her story. If she had, he wouldn't have been so eager to spend time with her. But he'd fallen in her lap—strange twist of fate.

Her mother would say destiny. Her father? God's work. She existed in the shadow in-between. She set out to put herself in his path, and it worked.

Eventually, she'd come clean about why she was in town. Until then, her new friend would remain in the dark. As consolation, she vowed to protect him from anything disparaging. The family wasn't to blame. They were the victims. This, she understood too well.

Zavier gave her the opportunity to observe and assess the situation before approaching the Cromwells to seek cooperation. She hoped when she explained her own history and the motivation for going after the medical malpractice publicly it'd ignite a common goal.

If it didn't, she'd add them to her list of nonsupporters, right below her father.

Mindlessly, she thumbed through a hotel brochure on the desk, stopping at a page promoting local shops. It reminded her of her father's suggestion.

For all her unwavering support and acceptance, her mother deserved some memento from the trip. If not for Paris' voice of reason, Kyly's relationship with her father would be ripe with conflict daily. Paris was the buffer between Cero's overprotective nature and Kyly's free spirit. No, between Cero's failure and her anger.

God bless her bravery.

She glanced at the clock and sauntered to the closet to trade in her bathrobe for more appropriate attire. Research kept her busy from first light. Intrigued, she headed out.

In the hotel lobby, she paused to scan for signs of a gift shop. The corridor was flanked by glass cases filled with souvenirs, everything from wineglasses and tumblers with area etchings to teddy bears and embossed clothing. One display caught her attention.

Behind polished glass lay an antique brooch reminiscent of the days when pirates ruled the seas. Aged silver twisted around a carved bust of mother and child in opal. Kyly knew it'd set her back more than the typical gift shop trinket, yet she couldn't take her eyes from it.

Not even to notice she was being watched.

"It's my favorite piece," said the frail clerk.

Startled, Kyly glanced to her right to see a tiny woman stretching to gain a vantage view.

"Isn't it magical?" she said, a twinkle in her eye.

"It reminds me of stolen treasure," said Kyly. "Is it for sale?"

"It is for you."

While the elderly woman rummaged through her sweater pocket for keys to unlock the case, dollar signs flashed in front of Kyly. "How much would something like that cost? If it's authentic, well...it may be out of my price range."

"Oh, it's authentic, but I think you'll find it quite reasonable," the woman said. "Besides, some things are worth having at any cost."

Kyly wasn't sure if that was a sales pitch or a warning. Either way, her mother was about to become the proud owner of a piece of history.

"Would you mind, dear?" The slight woman handed Kyly the keys to open the front of the case. "I'm not as tall as I once was or as nimble."

"Oh, certainly." Taking the gold key from the gnarled hand, Kyly smiled, momentarily mesmerized by the woman's faded blue eyes. She popped the lock open. Careful not to disturb the other ornaments, she lifted the pin from its resting place on a mound of silver velvet and secured the case.

"You see, when you look closely, mother and babe are staring into each other's eyes." The old lady pointed out.

The eyes were tiny jewel chips. Mounted on a black backing, the silver image of the opposing face cast a reflective shadow. It would've been eerie if not for the perfection of the carvings.

"It's called 'Reflection,'" she said, smiling at Kyly's obvious appreciation for the piece as she retrieved her keys. "A hundred dollars if you take it right now."

"It must be worth far more," Kyly argued against her own good fortune. The woman didn't respond immediately, her attention taken by a man Kyly only caught a glimpse of. The old woman's expression said he was someone she recognized and didn't care for.

"Are you sure?" Kyly prompted.

"Oh yes. I've waited for a long time to make sure it had the right owner." The woman's slow smile exposed her secret.

"This is yours, isn't it?" Kyly fumbled for money.

"No, dear," the clerk said, folding the funds in her hand. "It's yours."

Kyly struggled with her book bag and purse to close her wallet. When she glanced up from the gift, she was alone. The elderly woman, who seemed so frail, had left the room in complete silence. Quietly as she'd materialized, she'd disintegrated like morning mist without so much as the whisper of a footstep.

The brooch weighed heavy and warm in her hand. Wrapping it in tissue before sliding it into her purse, she realized she never asked for a receipt. In fact, there was no box, no bag, or proof of purchase whatsoever.

She'd request a bill from the front desk when she returned. It was getting late. Walking through the hotel's swinging doors, she found comfort in the lump the pin created in her purse's zippered pouch.

———

"Pretty day," said the perky strawberry-blonde library clerk as Kyly returned some of the material she borrowed the previous night.

"Storms coming in, it's a shame." Kyly removed the last book from her leather satchel.

"Is that what they're saying? I never watch weather reports."

"It wasn't mentioned on the news. I can feel it in the air. I hope it hits late." Kyly fastened the latch on her case.

"Humm, a mystic," the girl surmised.

"Pardon?"

"My grandfather was native. He used to say storm trackers were mystics, spiritual teachers. Led by sunlight, haunted by shadows."

Kyly's expression showed something. Fear. Confusion. Disbelief. It led the girl to retract her assessment.

"Or maybe there's just a chill in the air. He also ate orange peels instead of the fruit. Never could figure that out."

Kyly shrugged the comments off, leaving the counter.

Anxious to get to work, she headed for the desk she chose the evening before, which sat unoccupied. A sure shot for Zavier to locate her after lunch. Although, she had a sneaking suspicion he'd be able to find her during halftime at a Super Bowl game amid a hundred thousand screaming fans.

Barely eleven o'clock. She had time to spread out her materials and work without fear of his inquiries for a while. He'd mentioned he had class until noon. She wouldn't have to conceal her papers until at least then.

From her previous findings, she knew Doctor Valeric traveled heavily a year or so after the birth of the infant with the functioning body and fractured mind. There was little information about him during that time. He left the hospital for a private hospital in Italy and transferred some patients with severe cases of brain abnormalities. No names. Her grip on her pen tightened. Damn.

She'd called the Italian medical board several times from the hotel before finally latching onto someone willing to offer assistance. Even then, the former nurse's memory was sketchy at best.

A local magazine clipping she located in the library was sprinkled with valuable facts. It featured an article on the good doctor with a page of background information. It listed organizations around the world he'd been affiliated with. Among the names was a restored, Italian, private hospital. It opened the summer after Valeric fell off the grid and noted him as a board member and generous contributor.

She jotted down the name and ran to the aisle designated for European historical buildings.

A collage of photos of key sites in the area, including the one of interest, wrapped a hardcover book she discovered. She almost walked into a wall on the way back to her desk fumbling through its pages.

Consumed, she flopped the book down in the center of all her material loud enough to draw unwanted attention from surrounding students.

"Sorry," she whispered. A girl two desks away glared back. The merciless annoyance of a straight 'A' scholar hard at work.

There it was. In Kodak color, the outstanding architecture of a perfect historic hospital gleamed back at her. Cleaner and brighter than its centuries of wear thanks to restoration, bordered by a row of its new founding fathers, including Dr. Valeric.

The hospital's history was traceable. And, with a little luck, patient records as well.

"Nice place, thinking of taking a trip?" Zavier asked, sending her book across the table in a startled launch.

"I didn't mean to catch you off guard. Our class was cut short. Professor Wilks likes to sneak away early on weekends."

Catching her breath, she glanced across the surface of the desk to ensure she hadn't exposed sensitive information. Content her secret was safe, she regained her composure.

"A morning of surprises. I wasn't expecting company so soon."

"I'd suggest a coffee break, but it appears you've had enough caffeine for the both of us." His comment was laughable, his tone somber.

"Coffee sounds perfect." She gathered her documents into an inconspicuous pile, though he wasn't watching close enough to notice anything incriminating. No eyes on her, his mind elsewhere. They walked to the coffee house. He wasn't paying attention. "A shot of espresso, and I'll cartwheel back to the desk," she tested.

"Could prove interesting." His response was dry and off base. She was staring at him when he veered too far left, narrowly missing a bookshelf.

She yanked him over before impact. "Those don't move, you know. You okay?" His demeanor said no.

"I'll be fine." He wasn't making eye contact, nothing like the previous day.

"I'm a terrific listener if you want to talk," she offered.

"Something I'd prefer to forget. Let's get that coffee." He picked up pace, leaving her trailing.

Now they were even, she thought. They were both hiding something. As disturbing as that was, every fiber in her said she *was* on the right track.

Unfortunately, even the right track can lead you headlong into a train wreck.

12

CLOSING the outer gate behind him, Mason fought his way along the narrow pathway to Curt and Brook's backyard, ducking below intrusive branches in desperate need of trimming. Then he saw her. Zombie-like, in a deck chair, staring into the past.

"How you holding up, kiddo?" He spoke softly. She didn't answer. He dropped his bag and crouched beside her.

"Time stood still," she said. "I'll never forget that moment when the pain slipped away...and I saw him for the first time."

Her gaze transfixed dead ahead on a ghost visible only to her. Then, in a haunting voice, she recited the events of Christian's birth.

"His tiny hands were perfect...I studied every digit. And the tuft of dark hair, barely recognizable beneath the film of blood yet to be wiped away. My firstborn, my greatest achievement. The doctor cut the cord between us. My body vibrated with exhaustion, then fear coursed through me. I asked if he was okay. They didn't answer."

Looking up for the first time, she continued.

"The fear of a future that may never be as pure and full of love as that moment. I thought of the struggle between *our* parents. I hoped Curt and I would carve a better path. The moment was swept away in the rush of doctors and nurses."

She bowed her head again and picked up dead flower heads that had fallen from a basket overhead. "Little did I know it was to be the first and last time I held my son."

He leaned closer. "You were consumed by incomprehensible pain. I couldn't ask you about it. I thought he was gone before he was born. I had no idea he was alive."

"Either did I!"

The flower heads bled, crushed beneath her fists. "We were told he wouldn't live. He wasn't complete. Nothing could be done. Oh, but it might not be in vain. Our loss might serve others if we agreed. It'd make it worthwhile. Bearable. His memory would live on." Her hands unclenched releasing fragments of smeared petals to the ground. Her body language said everything she wouldn't. "*Live on?*"

Mason interrupted her tirade.

"Agree to what? Brook, I don't understand."

"The experiment."

"Experiment? Are you telling me..."

Brook's hands folded over her eyes, her head dropped lower than before, and her shoulders slumped. A breath could've blown her over.

Grief and guilt leaped across decades to land squarely on her heart. "I failed him. I failed my son." He reached for her hands and removed them from her face. Moving closer to physically break her emotional fall.

"I know you," he said. "You're the best of us. The one all my friends would've sold their soul to marry. The one our parents cherished. I see the way the kids stare at you when you aren't looking. This doesn't define you. You did not fail him. This is a horrific deception you couldn't have imagined."

She raised her head. "I failed him." Her tone was unwavering. "You know our family history. I was young and in perfect health. So was Curt. Neither of us had inherited medical problems. No reason to think our children would."

She stood, walked inside, and paced across the living room floor. Mason followed, chose the nearest seat, and didn't flinch, fearing the slightest movement might break her courage and momentum.

Inner rage was the glue holding her together.

"We attended our scheduled appointments faithfully." An air of defense strengthened her. "We were excited, grateful to follow the recommendations. Lots of rest, moderate exercise, no drinking—not even a glass of wine. Curt wouldn't even allow the guys to smoke in my presence."

"I remember." He watched her lap the room. It made him dizzy. "You were strict to the letter when it came to the baby. You even refused my famous eggnog that Christmas."

She didn't hear him.

"The ultrasound didn't give any indication of a potential problem," she said. "We waited, he grew."

"You were early. I remember checking my calendar when I got Curt's call on the way to the hospital. That's why I showed up so soon. I was worried how it might affect the little guy."

"Three weeks early," she said. "But it wasn't a problem."

Her hands followed the momentum of the swirling sensations surely rising inside her, folding one over the other while she completed her final circuit of the room.

"He was a perfect baby," she said with a quivering voice. The energy of anger waning. She crumpled into a seat, forced by weakening legs. "I mean...he appeared perfect, but he never cried."

She did.

"I'm sorry," he said, though words were not enough. "I can't imagine how difficult it is for you to relive this. It's the last thing I want, but I have to understand. Was he alive?"

"Yes!" Fury flooded back into her voice. "Dr. Valeric described it as living, but not consciously alive."

Compassion and confusion brewed Mason an anger of his own.

"What the hell does that mean?" His demand was aimed at the doctor.

"He had a functioning body but wasn't conscious to life."

"Conscious to life? Over half the people on this planet aren't conscious to life!" Mason was on his feet. "I've filled jail cells and hospitals with them. This quack picked one hell of a time to get judgmental about my nephew's future prospects."

She moved from the sofa back to the chair closer to where *he* was now pacing.

"Mason, he was brain dead." Cold. Harsh. Reality. "The area that makes us individuals was missing. No frontal lobe activity, a beautiful baby devoid of humanity. His prospects for life weren't the issue, whether it could be called life was.

"They didn't think he'd survive long. It was a rare case, and they wanted to study him until the inevitable...happened."

She paused, shaking her head in defeat.

"Until he died, naturally." Tears spilled over her soft cheeks. "Dr. Valeric requested our permission to institutionalize Christian. After our loss, it seemed the only way to give his life meaning. We wanted to help prevent anyone else from feeling our pain—"

"You said, resurrected." The wheels in Mason's head hit pay dirt. "You're telling me Chris is alive?"

"Yes. He lied. Something was done. Our son became whole."

She rose from her seat. He watched the room spin. She returned with a newspaper in her hand. The room stopped. She thrust it at him. He grabbed hold, still absorbing the facts. Chilled, Mason's disbelief caught between his tongue and the roof of his mouth.

"Back page." She aided his fumbling and tapped the paper with her finger. "Alive...and wealthy."

His eyes locked onto the photo. He grasped the back of the chair for balance. Hairs at the nape of his neck stood at attention.

"That could be Zavier or his twin!" Fixated on the newsprint image, the theme song from Twilight Zone played in his head. He shook it out.

"His brother," she said.

"How?" Mason couldn't force his eyes from the picture. "Did he fix him somehow or lie from the start?"

"There was something wrong," Brook said. "A mother knows. What now?"

In any other circumstance, Brook and Curt would've turned to the proper authorities, but they gave that option no consideration. In truth, they'd willingly institutionalized their infant son. Not a choice celebrated or understood by society.

Desperate to be near him, they'd visited the neonatal unit. The baby was gone. Transferred to a special facility. They ached to spend what time he had left with him in their arms. Dr. V delivered the bad news before Brook could make the trip. He'd arranged for the baby's cremation.

Brook would never know whose ashes she scattered or buried.

They'd done both. She couldn't stomach the thought of worms...but they owned a family plot.

By all evidence, they handed their helpless newborn over to the care of Dr. V, a world-renowned physician, without a second thought.

What right would they have now to stand in judgment? Especially when the man they were accusing wasn't alive to defend himself. They were painfully aware of how bad things looked. They simply would find another avenue for justice.

Mason.

"I'll be damned." He fell back into the chair.

"No," she said. "He will, for telling me my son was dead. I failed him once. I won't let it happen again. I'm going to get to my son."

There was power behind her words. No threat, cold fact. The pain, raw, made her transparent and wrecked, a ragged diamond ready to cut through anything between her and her child.

13

DAY FLED, and something wicked scorched the night while Kyly and Zavier worked in the library. She intended to leave the campus before the weather turned, but couldn't neglect progress for the sake of a storm. Time ebbed between the intrigue of research and the rapport with Zavier.

Fog rolled into Half Moon Bay inconspicuous and silent. The tide, distant and muffled by campus buildings, failed to lash out any warning. Wind ceased to blow, extinguished under a chalky cloak.

Darkness clung close, veiled—waiting.

"Doesn't look pretty out there," Zavier said. "Can I walk you back to your hotel?"

Kyly smoothed her hands over her arms, sensing the chill. "It's only a few blocks, not worth the trouble. I should go before it gets worse."

She stood, gathered her things, and they both headed to the library's outer door. Zavier stopped her before the stairs. "Here, take my sweater. You're not dressed for this."

He was right. Stepping out, evening air grabbed hold of her exposed flesh with icy hands. She slipped the jersey over her head.

"Tomorrow?" he asked.

"Tomorrow," she echoed.

They left in opposite directions, Zavier heading for the east carport in gallant stride and Kyly crossing the west park. The edge of the outer buildings barely exceeded peripheral vision when the sound of shoes on pavement spun her on her heels.

Zavier?

The noise had the distinct tap of dress shoes on asphalt. Zavier was wearing Doc Martens, cushioned soles. When no one appeared trailing behind, curiosity gave way to suspicion.

She kept moving.

Without question, the eerie atmosphere was enough to send chills up her spine. The air was thick, weighted with impending rain. It commanded silence in its muggy grasp.

From all directions it suffocated, draining the brilliance of every hue in its wake, shedding a washed-out world in shades of gray.

Kyly's body temperature dipped.

It wasn't like her to be easily unnerved. She remembered this, scanning the park for a rational explanation for the footsteps.

Clink. A singular sound of keys colliding wafted into her ears.

Her pace quickened. Her hands held no keys.

Passing the familiar park statues, the towering figures loomed with incriminating judgment. Unlike the honorable guard, they held in the light of day. Her feet left the grass to the unclaimed pavement of the street with relief.

Murky air blocked out streetlights. Dim shadows outlined the roadside. Everything typical about the area became discomforting.

She strained to hear feet out of sync with her own. Nothing. The more she strained, the more she realized how much of nothing she heard. No birds overhead, no traffic, no ruffling leaves, no movement whatsoever.

It wasn't silence she feared. It was her primal instinct sounding internal alarms.

Visibility abated in the soupy mist. She recognized an intersection by its mix of lights alone. Making the turn onto Main Street, the reverberation of footsteps caught her mid-stride.

She froze, isolating the sound. Turning her back on her destination, she waited to see a predator materialize.

No one. Alone. Not alone.

She spun back around. Like a safety beacon, the bright lights inside the hotel lobby shone through its glass front a hundred yards away. No longer concerned if she was overreacting, she sprinted for refuge.

With a yank, the lightweight door flung open, colliding with a bang against the frosted adjacent window. Inside, she glimpsed back on her way to the elevator, expecting to see shards of broken glass.

No clerk stood at the desk.

Inside the elevator, she waited for the closing doors to be jarred open by an intrusive hand. She hadn't seen or heard anyone in pursuit since the block before the hotel. No sound beyond the noise of her running. The doors inched together. Her eyes darted back and forth between them. For all her aggravation of the button, they refused to seal faster.

She heard nothing over her own labored breathing and pounding heartbeat.

Finally, the panels closed. A modicum of relief calmed the swell of fear when the lift ascended from ground level.

Illuminated buttons flashed on the indicator board inset in the transom above, accompanied by a resounding ding confirming passage of the first floor.

Her room was on the third. She envisioned a dark stranger waiting in the hallway for her to exit the lift, despite doubts that a stalker would have her room number.

Ding. Two floors.

She leaned against the back wall, hands grasped to the rail and not for fear of vertigo. Her eyes focused on the crack between the doors. No point in searching the chamber for a weapon. An island. It offered only what she carried onto it.

The elevator lurched, and somewhere between the second and third floor it gained a passenger.

Like a demon materializing at the opportune moment, he came with full force out of thin air. Dropping from the grate above, he'd waited for a clear path of descent and attacked with enraged precision. He was in front of her, hands clenched around her throat before her brain initiated to fight back.

She scratched and yanked at the gloved hands around her throat without effect. Her vision was blurring even as she stared at the buttons behind her assailant, searching for an emergency alarm.

With no other ideas and consciousness fading fast, she pushed into him. He stepped back, adjusting for stability. Her fingers made contact. She pushed and slammed her palm into the panel.

"Hotel security. Is everything all right in there?" A voice came through the speakers.

God, how she wished she could scream no. She wheezed out a gurgled protest.

She kicked and pounded, avoiding eye contact with the masked man who was crushing the air out of her windpipe.

"Hello?...I'm not getting a response, Jack." The voice echoed around her. "You better get up there."

The elevator jumped into motion, but she was falling into darkness.

So this is how victims feel before the end. This sucks.

It wasn't an eloquent thought. She hoped it wasn't her last.

———

"I fainted," Kyly lied to the bulky security guard hovering over her. She'd pulled off Zavier's sweater, draped it over her back, crossing its arms around her neck seconds before he found her sitting on the elevator floor.

"Could you help me up?" Her mind raced. Police involvement wasn't a viable option. "Not suppose to use elevators."

"I don't know that you should be so quick to do that. We'll have someone check you out—"

"God, no. I've had this happen before. Nasal surgery. It hasn't fully healed yet." It was all she could come up with to explain her broken voice and place on the floor. "I should've known better. Please don't go to any more trouble. I'm embarrassed enough."

"You're sure—"

"I'm completely fine. Really. If you could just help me off this floor."

The guard, wider and inches shorter than her attacker, lifted her to her feet, keeping an arm behind her.

"Sounds like you're losing your voice. You sure you don't—"

"It's from the procedure. They have your mouth open for hours and...I'm sorry to be such a bother."

"No bother. I'll walk you to your room. What's your number?"

Kyly handed the man her key card and welcomed his assistance down the hall and into her room. He called for room service to bring her hot tea and anything else she needed "on the house" and made her promise to get some rest and use the stairs. When he left, she dead bolted the door behind him and cried.

Her eyes burned. Not as bad as her throat.

In the bathroom, washing her face, the results of the attack glared back in twisted shades of purple and black. She dried off and wrapped the towel around her neck before room service arrived.

She didn't want to open the door, but if she didn't, she feared never being able to again. A friendly woman attendant delivered her order. Kyly didn't want her to leave.

Alone, she poured and drank the tea. She checked the keyhole to the hallway twice during the first cup. By the third, she was staring out the window.

The owner of the hard sole shoes waited.

This wasn't her imagination.

The storm released its armor. Raindrops drummed at the window. They clicked and rattled against the hotel's stone outer wall and the balcony's metal railing. The wind, non-existent on the walk home, churned forth the cold off the ocean howling as it thrashed the landscape.

Fear turned her flesh to ice in a fluid stream down her back as she stood at the edge of the glass pane.

She didn't die tonight. She felt so very alone and lifeless despite the ragged breath drifting from her lungs.

And that posed questions. Why was she left alive? Either by necessity or intention, the assailant decided her fate. The void in his eyes that clung to her said it was the latter. The impressions he left said he was capable of completing his dirty deed. She'd wear the bruises for weeks if he'd let her.

The journalist in her wouldn't turn back or let go. She'd bit down hard and couldn't free her teeth, the taste of justice irresistibly bittersweet.

Fear's grasp loosened, and she left the window.

In the washroom, she avoided the mirror and changed into pants, a blazer, and a scarf. She'd fight back. She refused to be victimized. This time, she'd get to be the warrior, and she'd fight harder than her father had. It was the driving force behind her career, behind everything she did.

She left the lights on.

When she exited her room, her research went with her.

14

AMNESIA LEFT him a nameless patient plagued by a torment of demonic cable playing a hundred channels of horror in his head.

Either fleeting and blurred or cruel with clarity, none held any insight. When the final haunting flash of contoured faces startled him awake, he welcomed the room's blinding brightness and the ache on his retinas.

Squinting to filter the scorching sunlight, he scanned the upper adjacent wall for the watchful eyes of monitoring cameras. As suspected, one adorned each corner.

Realizing no part of him would escape the recorder, he wiggled his toes beneath the blankets, then his fingers, followed by a systematic flexing of each muscle.

A fraction of physical ability existed.

Relieved to feel the burning in his pupils diminish to bearable irritation, he moved to thoughts beyond his physical circumstance. Until halted by the imploding door.

Nick had returned to loom over him. Face awash with abject sympathy. This time, he brought a young doctor with him, her expression disquieting excitement.

"My assistant tells me you've rejoined the land of the living." She approached his bedside. Nick's displeasure with her particularly poor choice of words was obvious, even through blurred vision.

"Can you tell me how you're feeling? Are you experiencing any specific areas of discomfort?" She lowered the bed sheets, exposing his right arm to check his pulse manually.

His arm jolted closer to his body at her touch. The sudden reflex unnerved him. It had no effect on the doctor. Her hand held fast and she proceeded to count the blood flow within the artery.

"My...my eyes hurt." His voice was raspy.

Though bent over her wristwatch, he glimpsed a slow grin cross her face. It sent a chill deep within him. He wanted to yank his arm free from her grasp, but didn't. Choosing instead to stare at it, another perfect piece that didn't fit.

"It's to be expected under the circumstances. It'll subside in time." She returned the sheets to their original place.

"Circumstances?" He made a broken effort at clearing his throat.

"Your voice will improve in a matter of days," she assured him. "What do you remember?"

"Remember? About what?"

"Do you know what year it is?"

"Two thousand and twenty...something." He reached his hand over his eyes to block the incoming light.

"Nick, the drapes." Returning her attention, she said, "Close enough. Do you know where you are?"

"A hospital, I guess." He set his hand back down, relieved by the filtering of the heavy fabric now covering the window.

"Do you know what happened to you?"

"I see flashes...nothing makes sense."

"It will in time," she said. "Do you know your name?"

He opened his mouth expecting to respond only to be choked by silence when nothing escaped his lips.

"You were in a terrible accident. It left you in a coma. Physically, your prognosis is excellent. There's every reason to believe you'll make a complete recovery. However, you sustained considerable damage to the area of the brain that governs memory. Although you remember how to speak, other memories may be unreachable. We'll have to wait to see what returns naturally. In the meantime, we'll help you fill in the blanks. There's no need to worry. You're in very capable hands."

"What about my family?" he said. "I mean, if I have one. Have they been notified?"

A logical question in illogical times.

"We're your family, Micael. Name's Ray. You met my brother Nick earlier." Her voice rang with authentic sincerity and something hard he couldn't identify. "Don't feel bad. It will all come back to you in time."

Micael bowed his head, then raised it, meeting Nick's gaze. "I'm sorry."

"Nothing to be sorry about, MJ," Nick replied with a nonchalant smile. "Just get better. It's rather boring around here without you."

"You need sleep." The doctor inspected the IV drip bag and administered the contents of a syringe. "I've given you something for the pain. Rest is integral to your recovery. We'll be back to check on you in a couple hours. If your vitals are still improving, we'll take you off liquids and try real food."

She headed for the doorway, leaving no time for further questions. Nick followed close behind her, swiveling back as the door closed.

Strange, Micael thought. A sinister intensity betrayed Nick's jovial expression.

———

When Micael woke hours later, the dimly lit room comforted. Although he had an endless stream of unanswered questions, being alive was a gift.

Scattered and incoherent, the images bombarding his mind while asleep gave him reason to be grateful to be cognizant of the real world again.

The only fragment he retained was a distorted face in the reflection of a mirror. He couldn't place where he was, what type of room, or even if a floor existed below his feet. Nonetheless, the face of a man in his midfifties with black hair and dark skin stayed with him. Who was he?

More questions.

He wanted answers. Perhaps this desire was enough to motivate his body into action.

Anxious, he pushed slowly on his hands to sit upright in bed. The strained movement squashed any ideas he had about racing out of the room. Stiffness triggered every muscle to ache with the slightest shift. His body reacted like it had been compressed into a cardboard box while comatose for easy storage.

Time drifted by while the simple task of shifting positions stole all his effort. Once completed however, he had one knee pulled up as an armrest, sitting like a person and not a slab of meat when Ray and Nick returned.

"What are you doing?" Ray rushed to check the monitors. "You haven't been out of bed, have you? How long have you been awake?"

Her frantic state put him on edge almost as much as the panicked expression Nick wore.

"It's a crime to sit up?" He searched her eyes for clues—something off about them. "Don't you think I've been horizontal long enough?"

"That's debatable," Nick mumbled under his breath, escaping Ray's ears but not Micael's.

"Excuse me?" he said to Nick, whose shocked expression made it apparent he hadn't expected to be heard. "What's going on here? I'd think you'd be pleased."

With this, Ray spun on her heels from where she was crouched reading a monitor printout and stood to confront him.

"Your recovery is my only priority, Micael. In fact, the significance I place on your return to health cannot be adequately expressed in mere words. This level of mobility, so quickly, is unexpected. I refuse to place progress in peril by allowing an inordinate amount of physical strain on a body still suffering from injury."

Her explanation, intelligent and perhaps rehearsed, failed miserably to cover their irrational level of alarm.

"We're family, remember," she said. "We're a little more protective than the average medical team."

"If we're family, why does he keep staring at me like I'm Frankenstein come to life?"

Ray flashed Nick a murderous glare that swelled with intimidation.

"You're not Frankenstein, MJ," Nick said. "I can't believe you're up and moving around. You're really a medical marvel. One we prayed for. And now that you're doing well, I guess I'm shocked. We were worried."

Although exhausted, Micael recognized the opening.

"What happened to me?"

"Let's check you out before we delve into the past." Ray leaned in for his arm to check his quickened pulse.

"I'm fine." He yanked his arm back. "I want to know how I got here, and I want to know now!" His voice cracked under pressure.

For someone in his state, Micael's spirited insistence surprised even him.

Nick wheeled his chair closer to the bed then said, "You sure you're up for this buddy? It can wait another day 'til your stronger."

What the hell did that mean? Micael shook his head.

"Now." He focused on Ray.

Sitting at the far end of his bed, Ray warned. "This is going to be painful, so if you need me to stop, say so.

"Do you have any memories of your father?"

"I don't have memories of me, but I did have a nightmare. I can't remember all of it. I saw a middle-aged man with graying hair and dark skin. Is he my father?"

"Most likely. We'll confirm that with photos later."

He stared at an empty corner for a second or two, then asked Nick, "Why do you call me MJ when she says my name is Micael?"

"Micael Junior, kid." Nick patted his arm like it was something familiar. "You're named after your father."

"Are we brothers?"

"Not by birth," Nick said. "Your father was a father figure to me for most of my life. I've lived on the island with you for the last five. And yes, I've always considered you a brother."

"Island?" He stared out the window.

"Yes, we've all lived on the island together for years," Ray said. "Privately owned by your father."

"Was a father figure?" he questioned.

"Yes," Nick said. "He's gone, MJ, that's how all this happened."

"Gone? He left the island?" Confusion swarmed nearer and clear thoughts were difficult to cling to. His head hurt.

"Your father suffered from a severe illness for months. He lost the battle weeks ago. We kept him on life support, hoping you'd wake up to say goodbye, but...his heart stopped beating days ago. His funeral's this weekend."

"He's dead?"

"Yes," Nick answered. "I'm sorry, MJ. Are you okay?"

"I don't remember him." His eyes searched the room for something grounding and came up empty.

"It could be psychosomatic," Ray said. "You were devastated at the prospect of losing your father. Being a medically skilled family and not being able to save one of our own was more irony than we could stand." She placed her hand on his leg. "You got mad and drunk and then took a nosedive off the cliff on the other side of the island. When we found you, it was touch and go for a while."

"*You* saved my life?" He glanced first at Nick then Ray.

"Ray saved your life, little brother," Nick clarified as if it mattered. "In this hospital, I'm the assistant."

"I don't know...I should thank you. What you must have gone through. My father, then me." He said it through the fingers of his hand, rubbing his face in utter disbelief, tangling medical cords.

"You're worth saving," Ray said.

He avoided direct eye contact, but asked, "Are we brother and sister?"

"Not exactly," Nick spoke before Ray could answer. "Ray's my sister biologically. We had the same parents. Your father raised us from the time she was a kid."

"I'm sorry I don't remember you," Micael apologized.

"You will in time," Ray said. "In time."

How could she be so damn confident? Taking into account how close to death he'd come, it seemed unlikely.

She rose from the bed and excused herself, explaining she had to pull his readouts off the computer down the hall before switching his diet back to chewable food.

With Ray safely out of the room, Micael asked Nick to clarify the emotion emanating from his young doctor.

"Were we?" He wasn't certain how to proceed. "Were we a couple... before the accident? She keeps looking at me strangely and—"

Nick saved Micael from further awkward prying.

"You were about to be married. She understands how this has changed things, but tread lightly on her anyway, okay. Her blood's coursing through your veins. She not only saved you but risked herself with a blood transfusion to keep you alive."

Micael stared at the raised blue lines on his wrist, he said, "I'm sorry."

"I know." Nick patted Micael's shoulder before he left the room.

Ray hadn't been wearing a ring. Of this Micael, was certain. Her skin was tanned a deep bronze. No faithful band of white skin, previously sheltered by a ring of proud commitment. Her third finger was flawless-long, elegant, and sun-kissed from base to tip. Not that everyone subscribed to that anymore.

He glanced down at his own hands, constricted by a mass of wires and tubes. Confinement established by connections forced upon him. He resisted the urge to sever the ties...for now.

15

GHOSTS DON'T LEAVE TRAILS. Two hours on the phone confirmed this for Mason.

A fellow detective once swore if you were at all qualified, you could find anyone in the world in ten phone calls or less. Thirty-three contacts later, Mason decided the guy was full of shit.

Not a novice at the game, Mason held a humbling track record for locating missing persons, even when they sought anonymity. Of all his prior targets, this was his first time tracking a phantom. And, so far, not an ethereal wisp.

The newspaper article stated Christian was named after the father who deceived and kidnapped him from his real family. *Egotistical bastard that he was.* Yet, as the namesake of a highly educated man, Mason's search confirmed Micael Valeric II hadn't attended any college or university in the US, Canada, or the UK under that name. Other countries were being tracked.

The story highlighted the sizeable estate and legacy left to Dr. Valeric's only son. Attesting to the fact he was competent to control vast wealth, a network of organizations, and his own private island—clearly not a position for the brain dead.

There was no record of Chris, as Mason preferred to think of his nephew, being hospitalized anywhere for anything. He never acquired a driver's license, opened a bank account, obtained a passport, or traveled outside the US. Every link to his prior existence before the article was a dead end.

The question Mason couldn't put to bed was how he'd remained so perfectly off grid with such a public father. And why the hell would a man who defied all avenues of access to his son for decades leave him exposed after his death?

One piece of common knowledge in the charade was that Dr. V had been ill for eighteen months or more. Long enough to make necessary arrangements to prevent Chris' photo from being splashed across the newspapers of every city the doctor had ever worked in. Particularly the one Chris was born and kidnapped from.

Through his online search, pulling in favors with every influential contact he knew, Mason made quick progress unfolding the life story of Dr. Micael Valeric.

Chris' life remained in shadow.

Brook's feet darkened the bottom of the doorway repeatedly. They'd pause, then drift away without inquiry. Allowing him space to rip out the grassroots of the conspiracy involving her son. When he emerged from the room full of printouts to get a drink, her restraint failed.

"How's it going?" She pitched the question like it was the bottom of the ninth.

"Making headway on this doctor of yours, but I've got to be honest, I'm getting the distinct feeling there's more to this situation than kidnapping."

He bumped into the corner of the wall en route to the kitchen, a wall clock rattled; he silenced it with his hand.

Brook pulled out a chair for him and headed back to the counter talking with her back turned. "I'm grateful for everything you're doing. I don't want you falling apart. Let me fix you something to eat."

Mothering calmed her.

"This guy covered his tracks." Mason angled his chair in her direction. "He had the money to make it official. Legally, we wouldn't stand a chance of refuting his claim on Chris."

She turned to face him with eyes filled with sorrow enough to drown in.

"Chris is an adult now," he clarified. "He may not be pleased with Daddy Warbucks when he finds out how he became his son. He may have no clue *who* he really is. Either way, the man he knew as his father is dead. And from what I can tell so far, there isn't a mother in the picture. We're all he has left."

He lost her mid-sentence. Lured by regret, guilt, and shame, she fell victim to that facet of the human mind that works diligently against us.

"Will he hate me?" She held an empty water glass in one hand and a pitcher in the other.

Mason wouldn't allow her to go down hell's highway of contrition.

"He's a Cromwell. He'll love you and be damn glad to know the truth. There's another concern we need to discuss. The kids. They're old enough to become too involved in this whole mess and young enough to be targets if things get out of hand."

"You think they're in danger?" The pitcher smacked into the counter having never been poured.

"Like I said, I have a feeling there's more to this situation than Chris' kidnapping. Those involved have wealth and power behind them. It's not worth the risk."

"What do we do?" She set down the glass, retrieved the pitcher, and poured water splashing up to the rim.

"Remove the threat. Send them into hiding. We guarantee their safety."

"Where?" She stared at the glass, then dumped it into the sink, the water too warm to offer.

"They can stay at my place. I'll have Jack keep an eye on them. He's looking after Riggs. They'll be safe in Canada and we can focus on getting Chris back."

"Farrah won't go. She has a showing in San Francisco in less than a week. It's her first serious one in the city."

"We send her early, put her under another name at the hotel, and have her use cash. I'll make arrangements to ensure her safety while she's there."

"Are you sure—" She stopped short. This was his business, and he knew it better than anyone. "Okay."

His real concern centered on Zavier. The resemblance to his brother was uncanny. A case of mistaken identity in a situation this volatile was inherently dangerous.

Brook brought a fresh pitcher of iced tea from the refrigerator and two glasses to the table, but before she filled them Mason put his hand over hers.

"It'll be okay." He said the words but didn't fully subscribe to them. "We'll get this straightened out. Where's all that faith of yours?"

"I know." She mumbled the words on the way back to the counter.

Mason insisted Brook take a mild sedative to help her rest. He'd lie down after checking printouts and messages. Having driven around the clock he needed rest, but while the adrenaline was pumping, he needed to work.

With Brook fast sleep and the house silent, he was able to review things.

The first line of attack was the island funeral. Dr. V's son was certain to attend. Private or not, so was Mason.

In the past, he retrieved the daughter of a prominent doctor; the head of the medical review board one state over. He located the girl, a heroin addict, and tucked her away in rehab to protect the doctor's reputation. The man owed him one.

Through his connections, the doctor happily contacted a mutual friend and former college buddy of Valeric's.

When Mason called, the secretary said the doctor left to attend a friend's private funeral on a remote island. It didn't take much role-playing to extract the information he needed. Sympathetic, she faxed him a copy of the hand-delivered invite. Since, as he explained, "water damage smeared the instructions" on his copy.

Zavier and Farrah were usually home promptly after classes. Mason stared down at a picture of them laughing. Taken a month earlier, they appeared young and untainted. He wondered what a new snapshot would reveal.

He jotted down a list of essentials Zavier would need and confirmed plans with Jack over the phone. Jack had business the next day but committed to clearing his schedule before Zavier's arrival. They went over emergency strategies. Jack agreed to check in on Zavier regularly.

"Be watchful, but don't have the kid tripping over you," Mason instructed. "He's a man. Treating him like an invalid won't work, keep a safe distance."

He also contacted a former partner who relocated to San Francisco and called in a favor. Bobbie gave his word in an Italian Philadelphia drawl; Farrah'd be "guarded like one of the family."

Bobbie was a tough cop. Crafty as they came. And, a true Italian family man, he was fiercely protective of young women.

With the kids organized, Mason threw off his blue jeans and fell into bed. He'd driven some twenty-five hours and hadn't slept in over thirty.

Regardless of the clutter in his head, he needed rest, so he slept— another benefit of military training. He could sleep face down in mud behind enemy lines if necessary. He prayed it wouldn't come to that.

———

Mason woke to a heavy weight cramping his left leg and the undeniable hum of the house cat basking in his body heat. Not exactly a dream date for someone who wasn't particularly fond of felines.

Wiping imaginary cobwebs from his face, he pulled on his jeans, leaving them unbuttoned, and walked around to his laptop to check messages.

A glance confirmed a fact he dreaded. His legitimate contacts failed to secure a ticket to the island funeral to unite with his sister's son—the only way to be certain the young man was indeed a Cromwell and get close enough to extract him.

One ugly alternative hit paydirt.

Experience meant a history with some unsavory types. Mason washed most of them from memory, others he kept in a back pocket just in case. The one he knew could help was the least palatable of the bunch. And he'd want something in return. Mason retrieved the criminal's rap sheet, then tripped on route to a chair over the heat seeker who leaped from the bed and darted out from his feet.

"Okay, so you're stealth-like after all," he said, regaining his balance.

Sitting with phone in hand he dialed the number. The call connected, and he heard heavy breath but no voice on the other end.

"It's Mason Stone, Track."

"Waiting for this day, Stone. Demons catch ya sooner or later. Surprised it took this long. What ya need?" Track sounded sly as always.

"An invite to a funeral. Dead doctor. Transplant hero. And I can't go as me."

"Sounds...*i n t e r e s t i n g*." He lengthened the word for emphasis, then paused, mulling the proposition over. "Send me details."

Track gave him an email address and specific instructions on delivery of the information. While they spoke, Track issued orders to one of his many henchmen. Mason could hear fingers clicking madly on a keyboard in the background.

"Your request is granted. What you need...will be sent within the hour. You got lucky."

Yes, but no.

"You know what *I* need," Track said, his voice smooth and calculating.

"Evidence to vanish before the retrial or a back door for you to slip out." Mason knew the sacrifice he'd have to make literally and ethically to expunge the illegal pharmaceutical dealer's trail of evidence. His sins lay in the billions.

"Options. Wouldn't dream of making you responsible. You're no good to me compromised. Options, buddy. My crew will do the deed."

The phone went dead, and with it, a chunk of Mason's pride. He'd sold his soul, at least a piece. There was no way back and no time to dwell. Family. This is what you did.

When his computer announced incoming mail a half hour later, he acquired a new identity and a sealed fate.

A shady medical acquaintance of Valeric's was unable to attend. He'd acquired a debilitating virus that hadn't been made public knowledge. It remained under a shroud of secrecy, as its nature threatened his credibility and his income. He'd made friends with Track to keep his drugs in full supply without accessing public avenues.

The man was Mason's height, though lighter. Weathered by years of field research, few people knew his face well. A recent photo confirmed with the sacrifice of a razor for the next couple days, Mason would become a close match. As long as he didn't have to engage in advanced medical small talk, he'd be able to pull it off without being detected. Or so he hoped.

Turmoil abated any optimism. Even if he proved Chris was alive, Mason couldn't guarantee a happy ending. He knew the pain of losing him would be nothing compared to the knowledge he was alive and chose to alienate his own blood out of sheer disdain for choices made in the past. As much as he played down this possibility to his sister, it weighed heavy on his mind.

He headed back into the kitchen, his throat tightening around a reality he'd rather not swallow.

In the silence of the house, he downed a bottle of water, made necessary travel arrangements, and prepared to have Zavier drive to the cabin in his truck. The kid knew the way from past visits and could be relied on to follow instructions. Although not accompanying him posed some risks, chances were Zavier wasn't in immediate danger. After the funeral, he'd have to watch him like a hawk.

Vulnerable to an unfamiliar enemy, they were all potential targets.

Why would a doctor risk his career to steal a severely brain damaged baby? Was there ever really anything wrong with the child? Brook said he didn't cry. Didn't respond. If he was damaged, how did he end up alive and well in the newspaper article? And why unveil him now?

Another piece of the puzzle was truly disturbing. If the baby was brain damaged, and somehow this doctor had restored him, why hadn't he come forward?

He'd be the first doctor in history to refuse recognition for a medical miracle. Wasn't that what they lived for? Perhaps, in this case, it was what he died for.

16

HE WAITED IN SHADOW. A man Kyly didn't know. Keeping his distance. Emitting dark intention in waves that sent sinister shivers across her skin.

The temperature was in the eighties. Kyly crossed her arms and rubbed her hands to combat the chill of fear.

The hall leading away from the university cafeteria filled. Unfamiliar faces. The Doors were right. Life is 'strange when you're a stranger.' The song echoed in the caverns of her mind. Then, a ragged needle cut the music. A man's voice startled her from behind.

"It's a wonderful thing," he said.

"Excuse me?" The voice, thank God, belonged to Zavier. She waited for him to catch up.

"Running into you," he clarified. Shuffling to match her pace, he noticed the pile of documents under her arm. "More research for your story?"

She nodded, then said, "Do you ever actually *go* to class?"

"Not really. I just hang around, looking intelligent, hoping to run into a beautiful student." He gestured to his throat. "Your voice?"

"Too much dictation. There's a gorgeous blonde at the table across from me. I'm sure she'd welcome a study partner."

Zavier had a lot to offer, but not for Kyly. She knew her appearance said soft, but the heart of her was stone, impossible to break into so far.

His easy smile cast a shadow across it. Each time she saw him, it became increasingly difficult to conceal the truth. She was lying to him, and it was wrong.

Her expression turned serious, and Zavier noticed. His smile fell away. She'd expected him to jump all over her suggestive matchmaking. He didn't.

"Everything okay?" she asked. "Did I offend you?"

"No, no. I'm sure the blonde's cute," he said without conviction. "It's not you."

"Hey." She stopped him and locked eyes as they approached her table. Setting her documents down without a glance. "What's wrong? It's serious. Zavier?"

The happy-go-lucky med student who stood beyond reproach disintegrated. Stress furrowed his brow and a frown of worry added a mature tension to his face.

After a silence he said, "It's...my family." He sank into the extra chair at the end of the desk. "I've been broadsided. I'm processing it."

She wanted to support him, but the mention of his family sent pangs of guilt through her.

"Is someone ill?"

"No, no. We're all healthy...well. I think so. It's...hell, unexplainable. Let's drop it." He searched the room avoiding further eye contact.

"Anything you say, but if you need to talk...um, I've been through more than one family tragedy." At least these words were honest.

She didn't want to pry and, in truth, wasn't sure she wanted to know what was going on. For the first time since pursuing the story, his reality hit home. The trepidation Zavier wore reminded her she was delving into their tragedy.

"It's not that I don't trust you," he said.

Before she could speak, the moment passed, interrupted by a library clerk who'd helped Kyly prior to her coffee break. The clerk was a freshman, no doubt. Reserved, quirky, and incapable of focusing her attention past the handsome gent at the table.

Her stammering caused a simple answer to become a frustrating test of patience. Tactlessly, Kyly dismissed the awestruck girl.

"What was all that about?" He stared inquisitively at the stacks of research surrounding her workspace.

"You, quite obviously," she said.

"Not the bird, the topic she tripped over."

In the banter, the girl had divulged some tidbit of information, arousing his curiosity. Kyly was annoyed she hadn't paid closer attention to the subject matter. For she couldn't recall what the girl had managed to spit out.

"I'm not sure," she said. "I couldn't make sense of it with all her stops and starts."

"She mentioned three doctors who proclaimed the eventual possibility of successful transplant of brain tissue, one who worked on a monkey. The paper she gave you has their names." He clarified for her. "What are you writing about?"

Ambushed by his query, evasion became a delicate tightrope walk.

"The moralities of transplant advancements and possible fallout for the families involved. The aftermath of medical miracles." Her answer came so fluid and confidently from her lips it surprised even her.

"It hasn't been tried, has it?" Zavier's intrigue heightened, his medical background fueling the fire or something more?

"No, not to that extent, at least not on a human or on record. My topic matter hasn't narrowed in any specific direction yet." She deliberately appeared scattered and blasé—her efforts went unnoticed.

"Why this area?" Zavier pressed on.

"I saw a documentary about a family suffering through the emotional trauma of their child being treated like a guinea pig for the sake of research. It unnerved me." Truth rang in the air.

Zavier's complexion became deathly white. His expression lacked all traces of boyish charm. For a second, she wondered if he knew everything and had waited in anticipation for this very moment to confront her.

"Zavier?"

"I think we were destined to meet, you and I." He pulled her to seat level. "There's something I need to tell you. You better sit down for this."

Kyly grabbed a chair and leaned in. In whispered tones, inches from her ear, Zavier explained the recent plight of his family. Despite the formidable blow to her self-esteem, she maintained her exterior composure until his explanation came to a close.

Eye to eye, he waited for a reaction.

"I don't know what to say." They were the right words, spoken for the wrong reason.

"I know it's a lot to take in. My parents never would've let this happen—giving up my brother without a fight—if they hadn't been deceived." He paused and when he spoke again his next words hit deep inside her. "No one gives us a handbook, you know, guides us into perfect parenting. So it's love no matter what, and try, with what you know. They've done that. I won't see them pay for what they couldn't control."

"I..." She fought to focus. "I'm sure you're right. No offense to your profession, but some doctors take the playing God role too far."

Kyly's words revealed pain from a past he knew nothing about. His conviction and forgiveness opened a door for regret to seep in. She did see her father pay and secretly believed it hadn't been enough. Was it too late to see him with new perspective? With eyes like Zavier's.

"Will you help me?" He held her hand in his.

She couldn't refuse him but wondered if time would make him regret taking her into his confidence.

"Of course. What can I do?"

"Find out everything you can about this man." He spoke, head down, jotting a name she knew too well on a scrap of paper. "I have to go to class. Will you be here when I get out?"

"I have some things to finish at my hotel. I'll be back here tonight. I'll do whatever I can." She needed time to regroup. "Zavier, I'm so sorry."

Rising from the table, he smiled meekly. He mouthed the words 'thank you' before disappearing behind a bookshelf.

Kyly had stood with him. Now she collapsed in her chair, unable to move for several minutes, weighted by the sheer magnitude of Zavier's story and the scrap of paper that read Doctor Micael Valeric.

Last night, she'd narrowly escaped a killer. Here, confronted by the facts, she recognized it was but a taste of what was yet to come. The price of the little knowledge she gained had skyrocketed.

Her father was right, after all. And so was her instinct. This story ran deep.

Kyly was certain Zavier revealed the tip of an iceberg. Its arctic chill hovered in the air, then descended her spine.

With no regard for order, she shoved her material into her book bag and headed for the hotel. She thudded shoulders with a student on her way out and left him spinning behind her in the aisle.

She crossed the distance to her hotel, never registering the journey, and took the stairs.

Despite focusing all efforts on cohesion, the jigsaw of available information offered dangerous fragments of understanding. She'd known the story of a lifetime came with a price but pursued it anyway. She knew why. She just wasn't willing to face it yet.

Rushing to her room, she entered the keycard on autopilot.

If she was followed on her way back from the campus, her connection with Zavier was likely red flagged. Their time together wouldn't be seen as mere coincidence.

Kyly's legs shook when she slipped on jeans.

Zavier hadn't said anything about the family being suspicious of anyone watching their house.

If they were safe before and in danger now, the blame lay squarely on her shoulders. She led the enemy right to their door.

Her packed luggage wasn't the only thing weighing her down. Her injured throat not the only reason there were words she couldn't give voice to. She walked to the lobby and dialed Cero's emergency cellular. A noisy group of tourists were checking in. She welcomed the confusion. He answered on the second ring, his voice almostl as anxious as hers.

"Dad, it's me."

"What's wrong?" He responded as though he'd been privy to her every thought.

"You were right." Her head bowed while her free hand pushed her long dark locks from her face. "The story...it's a lot more than I bargained for."

"Are you in danger?"

"I'm being followed." It was all she'd reveal.

"I knew I shouldn't have let you get on that plane. I'll buy a ticket and come get you. Your hotel?"

"They're probably lurking outside, but you can't come. Not yet. I think panicking will make them close in faster. I'm not alone in this. The biological family is here. They're right in the middle of it and I may have put them there. I met the son, and if I'm careful, I think I can find out who's behind all this."

"I don't care who's behind it! I'm not letting you get dragged in further. I'm coming to get you now."

"It will make things more dangerous if you do. They're connected, in a position to monitor everything. If you book a flight, they'll know I'm on to them. If I play dumb, they may see me as incompetent. I might survive this."

He was speaking. All she heard were the words in her head.

'I might not, and you'll never know how sorry I am.'

17

NICK SAUNTERED to the wall of windows overlooking the ocean, opened the sliding glass door, and walked the length of the cedar deck to an out-cove considering jumping the whole way. Ray was in a teak lounger with a satellite phone pressed to her ear, her body rigid, and her expression merciless.

"Has she left the hotel?" she asked the caller. "Stay on her. If she's folded I want to know exactly where she goes and who she speaks with, understood?"

Nick shadowed her while she listened to the information being reported from the caller. His loose linen shirt blocked the sun and cast an outline of dark waves around her.

The satellite signal, filtered through a scrambler for their protection, Ray had initialized. Nick imagined who was on the other end. In silence, he waited for answers.

"A specific description, you imbecile." Ray didn't get louder. Instead, her tone became leaden. "I don't pay you to be general. Take the damn picture and send it."

Ray hung up. Heat waves in the atmosphere reflected off her black eyes, brewing murky intolerance.

"Who?" Nick stood a tower in front of her chair.

"A tracker who lacks the intelligence to operate a self-adjusting digital camera." She said, then murmured something inaudible. "I've had him watching the donor family from the day of the newspaper release."

"And." Nick shifted to the open chair, tossed its decorative cushion to the ground, and was about to sit down.

"And some novice reporter researching a medical story made inquiries through the FBI about them. I've had her tailed to ensure she doesn't become a problem."

Nick's desire to relax disintegrated. "The FBI? I'd say she's a problem already."

"She doesn't have anything tangible. A relative of hers is a new agent. She made a location inquiry. *She needed their address.* She could be writing about something completely unrelated. I'm being proactive here. Relax."

Ray swung her long legs over the side of her lounger and patted the seat, inviting him.

"The woman has relatives at the FBI and is in close enough proximity to the family to swap information. We have a definite problem."

Nick paced away from her. The wind caught his open shirt and transformed it into a cape. He was in no mood to play superhero. He stretched his arms back and let the breeze take it over the cliff's edge. He swiveled around in time to watch it disappear. Ray stood, moving to peer over the long drop.

"She's a kid, not a worthy adversary," she said. "If she becomes a complication, she'll be removed."

"Just like that?" Nick's temper rose as quickly as the draft that disrobed him. "Whoever *she* is, her motives may be innocent. You can't go around killing a kid for stumbling onto the wrong story any more than you should've a captain for crashing on our shores."

"Not that again. She's in no present danger. And she'll stay that way if she quits digging and keeps her nose clean. I've put some incentives in place to redirect her. We'll see how smart she is soon enough."

Everything was a game to Ray. She leaned into the wind, dangerously dependent on its resistance to prevent her fall. It shifted. Her foot slipped. She teetered then regained her balance.

Nick never reached out to catch her.

"Tell me where things stand."

"Take a load off," she said. "Quit worrying. You're killing off Hippocampus memory cells. This new wrinkle could serve as an asset."

He listened as she outlined their next moves then she left, seeking refuge in final funeral preparations.

Coming in the long way, Nick skirted the north end of the house and entered the garage through the side door.

Inside, the casket waited patiently for no one. He ignored it as he walked by, electing to find solace in the gleam of his Saleen S7.

Opening the driver's door, he slid behind the supercar's steering wheel, drinking in its power. Removing his left hand from the leather wrap, he arched his back, searching his pocket for the ignition remote. *Click, click.*

The engine roared, not of a car left sitting idle for months but of a beast waiting to escape its cage.

He hit a button in the roof panel. With smooth precision, the garage door lifted, exposing an advancing shield of sunlight. Its reflection bounced from the hood, blinding him. Unlocking the glovebox with a code, he reached inside and pulled out the letter. It hurt to read it. Still the attachment to its author compelled him.

I'm so sorry for what I've done to her, to you. I slipped down a slope there's no recovery from, no climbing back to solid ground. I knew what they did to her and now I'm no better. She trusted me, only me, and I took advantage. She was there and I leaned on her. You were right the day you told me if I loved her, I'd stay the hell away from her. My weakness will make the world pay. I'm so sorry, Nick. I failed you both. Forgive me.

Nick folded the paper and put it back in its box. For a moment, memories of life before the island sped like wildfire through his veins. His body temperature rose against the molded leather seat, saturating his back as he pushed hard into the upholstery. All his anger and general contempt for a world he found utterly disappointing poured like molten steel down his leg, anchoring the ball of his foot to the acceleration pedal.

This substantiated the collection of tickets housed in his brass spittoon; rage became octane transferred down his leg to the floorboard. He saw the past filtered through a customized rearview mirror until jolted back to reality by an ominous figure standing beyond the front fender. Torn from his trance, Nick killed the engine and his memories with the turn of a key.

Soothing purr gone, dead silence overtook the garage, drawing his gaze from his sister's menacing shadow to the casket a few feet to his left. It sat strangely close now, moments before it'd felt oceans away.

It didn't fit. Not any of it. Sitting in bed, cushioned by the finest down pillows, Micael became acutely aware he wasn't being treated like someone who stumbled aimlessly off a cliff in self-inflicted delirium.

Most relatives wouldn't be so accommodating. In fact, they'd likely be madder than hell.

Using the headboard for support, he leaned near the window behind his bed, peering over his shoulder. His attention drawn to the lush freedom of nature, the spray of color, the reassuring flow of flowers and leaves leading away from the house.

An intricate stone pathway wove beyond the pane. His eyes followed it. Smooth, intertwining rocks softened by years of wind and weather.

Beyond nature's masterpiece lay a creation it might not be equally eager to endorse, one who had lost her bedside manner.

Ray's expression, even from a distance, appeared tyrannical. She stood inches away from Nick, her small frame iron, her demeanor, staunch assertion.

Micael watched. No bowed heads in sadness, no physical embraces of support, no hopeful smiles of encouragement. He watched and waited.

One could imagine, at such a time, siblings drawing strength from each other. Their father figure was dead. There was none of this. Their body language screamed of strategic planning and information shared with urgent intensity. No question who was the boss.

Nick's head whipped around as if alerted to Micael's analysis.

Backing away from the window, he returned to the comfort of his pillows and reached for his nutrition shake.

Soon after, a car engine roared from the nearby garage. When the sound stopped, shadows of their voices lingered down the hall. Followed by the rhythmic beat of their footsteps closing the distance and the creak of his door.

"How was it?" Nick pointed to the empty mug sitting before Micael. "She makes a mean margarita too, but you can't have that for a while."

Micael smiled but said nothing as Ray came in a few strides behind Nick, her bedside manner having magically returned.

"How was your first meal?" she said.

"Fine," he replied without fervor.

"What? No rave reviews. You're a tough customer."

"Sorry. What's in it?"

"A multitude of vitamins, CoQ10, extra B, alpha-lipoic acid, D, fish oils, vinpocetine, and ginkgo to enhance blood flow to your brain. Huperzine A and acetyl-L-carnitine for neurotransmitter acetylcholine repair. And N-acetylcysteine and other super antioxidants," she said. "Regaining normal function and energy levels is crucial. It'll help."

He shook his head, not impressed by the ingredients, then asked, "I'd like to go outside."

"I don't advise an island stroll. The slightest change in temperature could be a shock to your system. You've been through a series of serious surgical procedures. Your health is delicate."

"You said vitamin D, right? If I can survive a dive off a cliff, I can survive a walk in the park." He didn't mean to snap, but the room had shrunk into a claustrophobic closet. "I'll take my chances. Nick, will you get me outta here before I lose my mind?"

Nick's face drained several shades. He nodded in agreement, silent, and left the room.

"I don't think this venture is in your best interest, but if you insist, I hope you'll give me your word you'll rest when you return. Feeling imprisoned isn't healthy either."

He agreed and allowed her to help him to the edge of the bed. Nick returned and lifted him the rest of the way into a wheelchair while Ray brought him a blanket.

"Don't be long," Ray insisted, vanishing into the hall.

Minutes later, rumbling down the stone pathway, he embarked upon his first line of questioning.

"What did he do here...my father?"

Nick hesitated, then said, "Changed the world."

"How?"

"He was a genius in his field, a top mind." Nick's tone was cynical and smart-ass.

"You sound angry."

"I am. I'm angry at the whole mess. How this turned out. Him dead, you in this condition. The state Ray's in."

"She's handling it well," Micael said, contrary to his suspicions.

"You don't know her like I do," Nick corrected. "You don't remember her."

"Sorry, I just—"

"No, I'm sorry. It's a difficult time. The stress is taxing. What do you want to know about him?"

"Everything," Micael said. "What kind of man was he? Was he kind...I mean, did he help a lot of people? Why a private island? What type of doctor was he?"

"Slow down, MJ, I'm running to keep up." Nick patted Micael's shoulder. "Very kind. In many ways, he elevated our existence. He was world-renowned in transplant and brain injury advancement in the medical community, and because much of it entailed saving children, he was sought after by desperate parents everywhere—hence, the private retreat. He saved many lives in his day and died wishing he could've saved one more."

Nick's voice drifted on the last sentence behind a depth of emotion. Instead of pressing the matter further, Micael left the subject, deciding to press in stages.

"I thought I heard a car engine before." He scanned the area. "Where are the roads?"

He turned his head slightly to meet Nick's gaze.

Nick laughed. "I keep asking myself that same question. It was my masterpiece you heard. Hope I didn't wake you."

"No, I was awake. Where *do* you drive it?" Micael saw no sign of pavement.

"Nowhere." Nick ran a hand through his hair. "We're building a road around the island later this year. Until then, it's in storage."

"Can I see it?" Micael asked.

"We're on our way."

"She has a lean fighting weight of 2,750 lbs with 575 horsepower at 5500 rpm, an astonishing ratio," Nick spoke while the garage door vanished overhead. "Her aerodynamics follow the stealthy footsteps of Formula One, making the wind an ally. They say, in theory, at 160 mph you could drive her upside-down, and she'd still hug the road."

The sun's reflection gleamed over every curve, introducing and emphasizing the impressive lines. Nick discussed performance advantage, unique features, and customization in exquisite detail, including "her record-breaking abilities in the 200-mph stratosphere," until Micael broke into his first laugh.

"I wish I could take her for a spin, but seeing as there are no roads and I don't have the full use of my legs, I'll be content to stare," Micael said.

"Don't feel bad, bro. I have everything but the roads and I get chastised for starting up the engine."

"Why is that?" Micael asked.

"She doesn't want me waking her patient." Nick nodded in the direction of the house.

Micael stared at the mansion for a moment, then at a waiting casket. The mood dampened.

"Where did you resurrect me?" he asked.

Nick didn't respond immediately. The ornate body box held his gaze until he physically shook it off. "Um, the infamous medical wing. Allow me."

Nick whisked Micael from room to room, briefly explaining the purpose of each along the way while sprinkling in comic relief at the expense of the décor. Micael liked the décor. They proceeded down the corridor swiftly until Micael stopped him at the operating room doors.

Fingers outstretched, his left hand shot up by the elbow like an involuntary reflex caused by some post-surgery twitch.

Halted in front of the heavy metal doors, Nick stood silent. "Bad memories," he said after a time. For reasons he wouldn't disclose, he made no attempt to enter.

"This is where you brought me," Micael stated matter-of-factly, "when you found me on the beach?"

"Beach," Nick echoed.

"Yes, after I dove off the cliff," Micael reminded him. "This is where you saved me, isn't it?"

"Yes," Nick said without volition.

"Is this where my father died?" He locked eyes despite Nick's evasion.

"We moved him to a room down the hall when nothing more could be done medically. I should get you back to rest before Ray has my head." The previous lightness in his voice was replaced by a weight of sobriety.

Through a side window, Micael saw a bank of machines. "I'd like to go in." A strange tube structure caught his attention. Before he focused, Nick shifted the chair.

"Not today, buddy. We've done enough."

The wheelchair spun away from the entrance and right into Ray's legs. She'd appeared with catlike stealth. The front wheel impacted her left leg with a bruising clang. One would've expected a howl of pain or at least a rambling of blue language cursing Nick's stupidity. Ray neither spoke or budged. The metal remained pressed hard against her shin, her expression undaunted.

"Sorry, we didn't hear you," Nick apologized.

"Obviously." She shifted her stance, her demeanor transformed as she redirected her attention to Micael. "You must be tired. Let's get you back to your room."

Nick relinquished control of the wheelchair and patted Micael on the arm. "I'll see you later. Listen to your doctor."

Little was said on the way back to the recovery room.

Micael lifted himself, almost without assistance, back into bed.

"You can't keep me here," he said, catching Ray off guard.

"Keep you?"

"Isolated in this room. I don't need protection. I'm healing."

This was the first time their eyes lingered. Strange eyes, he thought. She said nothing. Her expression birthed more questions. It dispelled no obvious emotion, an impenetrable mask.

———

Muffled voices wafted in through the crack in Micael's window. Nick and Ray's discussion floated down in broken adjectives and angry verbs while he struggled to piece them together.

He caught "misdirection" and "dispel doubt," "the objective," and "adversary," but no connecting words to clarify meaning. They mentioned a "problematic lock," but he missed the meat of the conversation. He knew enough to cast suspicion into the shadow of nightfall.

The camera directed at his bed was surely equipped with night vision. He wished he could throw a blanket over it. The invasion of patient privacy never occurred to him as a significant concern until now. He made a mental note to discuss the matter with Nick in the morning. In the meantime, he yawned and stretched for the camera, then pulled up his head and chest in line with the window behind his bed.

He gazed outside disinterested, then around the room with his eyes resting on a novel on his bedside table. For the camera, he picked it up, turned on the overhead lamp, and read propped up against his pillows in front of the window.

From the small surgical mirror he swiped earlier from a room during his tour, he watched outside activities on the deck. Much like a dentist's tool, its long handle and small surface offered a surgically clear reflection. He kept it hidden behind the book's pages.

Ray came into view carrying tan file folders with shimmering black labels and hovered over a burning barrel. She stood too close, not backing away after dropping the contents into the flames. With the descent of each new file, a burst of sparks and ashes escaped. She seemed mesmerized by the incineration of the documents tossed below the can's blackened rim. In dangerous proximity, she guarded their demise, transfixed despite the hot soot.

Micael wondered, if he watched long enough, would her eyes also turn ashen and drip into the pit below leaving black holes in their wake. A flash of them hovering above his face rattled him. A memory? A shiver caressed his spine.

For the camera, he flipped slowly to the next unread page.

Nick came back into frame several pages into the second chapter, grabbing Ray's arm to prevent another handful of documents from destruction. Harsh words were spoken, then a glance into the mirror. Perhaps the mirror's glittering reflection had given away his intrusion.

He was finished reading.

His thumb released the mirror, and it slid undetected beneath the sheets. He placed the novel back on the nightstand and crawled into a horizontal position, an innocent slave to the capture of dreams. Or to appear so.

In truth, he feared the dying of the light. When separated from the waking world, he was imprisoned in a far more dangerous place. A place where blurred faces swam, familiar laughter plagued, and black eyes beckoned.

18

"KYLY? HEY, CAN YOU HEAR ME?" Zavier weaved through hordes of students like a surfer cutting a wave, the surge of his panic amplified back at him through a bad cell tower connection.

"Yeah, it's me. Are you alone?" Her voice crackled back shakier than his.

"Are you okay?"

"I can't go back to the library...it's not safe. Can we meet somewhere close to the airport?" Airport? Had his situation drove her out of town already?

"There's a truck stop called *Grounded*. It's busy."

"Busy's good. I don't want to stay on the line." Her voice said she was in danger.

"I can be there in less than an hour. Wait for me, Kyly."

Zavier's car left the university parking lot scarred with rubber.

Normally a conscientious driver, he threw caution to the wind as his sports car flew, dangerously weaving in and out of traffic.

He barely remembered to put the car in park after it skidded onto his driveway. He tossed the door shut in mid-stride en route for the house. The front door imploded, bouncing against the adjacent wall and back at him with a thud, sending him stumbling into luggage piled in the foyer.

"Slow down, Doc, you're liable to end up on the wrong side of the operating table." Mason steadied him with a solid grip. "What's chasing you?"

"Nothing...no one. Is Mom okay?"

"As good as can be expected. She's outside on the deck."

"You plan on staying for a while?" Zavier dislodged himself from the heap of baggage. "Isn't this our luggage?"

"Yeah, it's yours," Mason said. "I'm not staying and neither are you or your sister. She's leaving early for the art showing in San Francisco and you're going to my cabin until we can make sense out of this."

"I'm not going anywhere until—"

"You are. It's not up for discussion. You're a grown man. Act like it. You can't help by staying here."

"When do I leave?" Zavier's attitude tempered beneath the gripping fear he may not reach Kyly in time.

"Now," Mason said with a quick glance in the direction of Zavier's room. "Grab anything you need while I load these in the truck. Your clothes are packed. Don't tell anyone where you're headed. No phone calls. We'll handle advising the school. And Zav, say goodbye to your mother with a smile on your face."

Halfway down the hall, Zavier nodded and hurried into his room to pack essentials. Doctors were trained to react without time for contemplation, a skill that thankfully had become automatic. Throwing a few items into his carry-on, he checked the clock and headed out.

"I know you're worried sick, Mom, it's understandable. I don't blame you for this. I blame the bastard responsible for taking Chris. Mason's on our side, and he doesn't know how to fail." Zavier's smile beamed through to his mother's darkening soul. A little light of hope shone back.

Mason gave him a new cell phone for emergencies and suggested he stay off the landline at the cabin. He walked him through instructions and precautions and said Jack would be there to greet him on arrival.

"If anyone else comes knocking, they're not there by invitation, son. If it gets dicey, you know what to do. Remember your survival training. I don't know who we're dealing with, but I know they've enough power behind them to make people disappear. They were willing to abduct one son, don't allow yourself to believe they wouldn't forfeit another. Don't take any risks." The next part he whispered. "I've locked an untraceable

.38 in the floor safe, driver's side, combo's one, nine, one, eight. It's loaded."

Zavier stood immobile absorbing the implication of his uncle's words. When he finished, he feared his legs had transformed into ice blocks, ready at first flinch to shatter into cubes across the floor.

Not the most courageous response to being given access to a loaded weapon.

"Get movin'," Mason commanded. "Call me when you're outside city limits."

"I th...think..." Zavier stuttered.

"Don't worry," Mason said. "You're smarter than you realize. Speaking of which, did your professor get a hold of you?"

"Who?"

"A teacher called here for you earlier. Something about a lecture? I gave her your cell number."

Zavier knew full well it was Kyly. "Yeah, I talked to her."

Mason hugged him, doling out a few reassuring slaps on the back before booting him out the door.

"Hey kid," Mason called after him, tossing the keys to his new truck. "You forgot these. Take care." Mason slapped under his chin, their signal for 'keep your head up.'

Zavier's steady voice was returning. "I'll be fine."

Brave front. In truth, none of them had a clue how things would turn out. Zavier prayed his instincts, honed by years of survival training, were enough to keep him and Kyly safe. They had to be.

Mason disappeared into the house. Zavier gripped the truck's leather wheel, grateful for something to clench. He pulled out of the driveway, focused on the road ahead—Kyly waited.

———

The house phone rang twice before Kyly's father answered. The line was clear and still so very distant.

"How are you holding up?" he asked.

"So far so...I'm okay. How are things there?"

"They'll be better when you get home."

His tone held no judgment. Hers did. In fact, she couldn't recall the time when she didn't judge him. The time before everything went wrong. A sigh escaped her. She drew in a long breath and began the dissemination of information.

"The baby was kidnapped at infancy to support Dr. Valeric's research, we think. And the family found out he survived because of a newspaper article. He's a grown man. Dad, they want him back. I've put myself smack in the middle—"

"Don't assume this isn't where you're meant to be," he said, surprising the hell out of her. "I wouldn't have chosen this for you, but God did. What can I do from here?"

He never doubted her intention. He'd simply seen further down the road than her and feared her path. Her only comfort now came from the very wisdom she once resented and railed against.

She gave him the computer code to access her research files. "Everything I know is on there, including what I've learned here. It'll give you more to go on if...if you need it. I lifted this phone off another tourist. It'll be safe to call for a while. Dad...I'm sorry."

"Did you find the envelope I gave you?"

"Envelope? No, I—"

"It's time you do," he said. "God's speed."

She rifled through her purse until she located the envelope. When she removed it, a prayer card fell out. She read it fighting the swell of tears. Her father was oceans away but closer than he'd been in years, and only because she was finally allowing him in.

Divine love overcomes all obstacles, defies all odds, and defeats all doubt. The question, in times of turmoil, is not whether there's a way out but if one has faith enough to recognize it when it appears.

She had to stay one step ahead until it did.

Downstairs, Kyly made an obvious exit chatting up the bellboy. If someone lurked in the shadows, she needed to avert suspicion.

"The Northern California coast is a nice place to visit, a bit dreary given the fog," she told him. "I'm homesick already."

"Why'd you come here to begin with?"

"Research for an article I was working on. Turned out to be more work than it's worth."

"Think you'll ever make it back?"

"Doubtful."

"Our loss."

One could only hope.

She excused herself, leaving him guarding the bags outside to return to the front desk.

"What can I do for you?" the clerk asked.

Kyly said. "I purchased a piece of jewelry from one of your display cases but neglected to ask for a receipt."

"Did the desk clerk forget to give it to you when they entered it into the computer?" the clerk questioned. "I can pull it up."

"Well, no. I never saw her enter it into the computer."

"Her?"

"Yes."

"I'm the only female clerk with keys," the employee explained. "Are you certain you were assisted by a female?"

"Yes, I'm certain," Kyly answered, annoyed. "An elderly lady had keys in her sweater pocket. She showed me the piece, and I gave her cash."

"That's impossible miss, you must be mistaken. Only Dylan, the night attendant in the photo behind me, and I have access to the display cases."

"I have the pin right here," Kyly insisted, pulling it from her purse. "She knew its history. Charged me $100."

Lifting the pin from Kyly's hand for closer inspection, the clerk said, "Then you received one heck of a bargain, but not from here. You must have bought it somewhere else in your travels. I'm sorry, I can't be of help," she said, returning the silver treasure.

"But..."

Kyly's attention drifted from the pin to the night clerk's picture mounted on the back wall, then to photos flanking it of past employees, top executives, and previous owners. She searched the employee lineup for the woman who helped her while the clerk told her politely she was out of her ever lovin' mind.

In a black wooden oval frame, behind thick glass in outdated monochrome, sat the woman who sold her the pin. Posed with quiet authority in a wingback chair that dwarfed her shrunken frame, she stared back. The photo caught Kyly's breath. The bronze plaque beneath it read, '**_Mrs. Carthwright, Original Owner 1909_**.' The fine print said she died years ago. Kyly's legs buckled as blood drained from her face.

"Are you all right, miss?" the leery clerk asked.

"Fine. I have to go, my cab is here. Sorry to have...troubled you."

Pops arrived curbside to retrieve her. Kyly rushed to the refuge of the cab's back seat, anxiously ducking in after he opened the door. Pulling away, she didn't look back. A part of her wanted to. The place had been so beautiful and peaceful when she arrived, full of promise. Now? Ghostly. There was an explanation, one she didn't have time to unearth. She hoped she'd fair better with the Cromwell's mystery.

"You okay?" Pops asked, slowing slightly.

"Fine."

"Everyone says that. It's seldom true." He adjusted his rearview and smiled at her.

Kyly fought to curl the corners of her mouth to smile back. Darkness was spreading into innocent lives. She prayed her stalker stayed focused on her and not those helping her. Regret consumed her as they drove in silence down back roads.

Nearing the truck stop, twilight crept in under the fog.

"Is someone meeting you?" Pops asked. "Do you want me to come inside?"

"No, I'll be fine," she said. "My friend will be here soon."

Paying before they hit the parking lot allowed for a quick exit into the diner. Pops agreed to wait until her ride arrived to claim her luggage. He found an inconspicuous parking space hidden by a Mack truck, turned his sign off, picked up a paper, and killed the engine.

"I'm really glad I met you." She slipped out the door. "I wish you could say the same."

She found a table overlooking the parking area and ordered tea.

Burning her mouth on the hot liquid, she watched through drizzle for Zavier. Unfamiliar with his ride, she scoured the windows of the vehicles pulling in. Minutes dragged. Between cars, her eyes followed the waning droplets of water succumbing to gravity, trickling down the smeared windowpane.

She laid out payment on the table and gulped down the remainder of her cup instead of sipping contently. Her inner chill remained.

"I'm out back. Where's your luggage?" Zavier covered her raw grip on her leather satchel with a calm hand. She hadn't seen him coming.

"In a cab around the side of the building," she said. "There's a second exit close by."

"I saw it. You okay?" He made eye contact as if more than words were needed to ensure an honest response.

"What do you think?"

She snatched her to-go bag and let Zavier lead the way. They had secrets between them but security in their alliance.

"I'll feel better when we're out of here," she admitted.

Truck stops were foreign territory, and although filled with mostly happy, harmless, hard-working people, the place made her skin crawl. The ominous atmosphere she attributed to the aging diner was unfairly misplaced, and she knew it.

Zavier held her hand, offering reassurance on the way to the cab.

"This is me," she said, nearing Pop's car. Eager to help, the old man leaped from the front seat, popped the trunk open, and lifted Kyly's bags to the pavement.

Zavier grabbed the heaviest luggage during pleasantries, and in no time he and Kyly strolled away, hands full, headed for the rear of the building.

"Take good care of her, son," Pops said from his car window before disappearing into the late-day schmear.

Dampened clothes and spirits, Kyly climbed into the SUV's passenger seat a bit taken back by the luxurious vehicle. Her eyes roamed over the high-tech interior and plush leather seats.

"It's not mine," Zavier said. "Uncle's, the K and R guy. And don't worry about the leather, it's waterproof."

"K and R?" Kyly asked, smoothing the dampened leather.

"Kidnap and ransom," Zavier said.

"Risky business."

Zavier's expression became serious. "Yeah. And it's about to get worse."

Regardless of her vulnerable state, Kyly's interest was no longer masked behind her eyes. Recognizing it, Zavier spoke first.

"You're shaking," he said. "What happened? I need to know before I tell you the extent of what I've got you into."

"I've got myself into this." She spoke half under her breath, wiping water off her arms.

Zavier paused at the parking exit and held her gaze in his. "This has nothing to do with you. I'm afraid I've put you in great danger—"

"You have not. I'm responsible for whatever happens to me, or you for that matter."

As the vehicle rolled onto the main road she scanned their surroundings for headlights.

"Lee, you wouldn't have any part in this if I hadn't been so stupid, confiding—"

"That's where you're right." She'd start at the beginning and be prepared to tuck and roll if he pushed an ejection button—which surely existed amid the unrecognizable controls on the panel in front of them. "Perhaps you shouldn't have confided in me and not because you were putting me at risk, but because I endangered you and your family and didn't deserve your trust."

"I don't understand." His posture became rigid.

"Zavier, the family I told you about, the story behind my research, it's *your* family's story. I came here to find all of you and the doctor responsible for abducting your brother. But I didn't know that part of the story until today."

She didn't leave room for protests. She needed to get everything on the table in one shot, certain she wouldn't be granted another opportunity.

"I lost my mother and baby sister to a contemptible idiot with an OBGYN license. When I became a writer, my first mission was to expose the issue of undeserved blind faith in physicians. I needed evidence strong enough to impact readers. After three years of informative articles and extensive digging, I found your mother's doctor. Issues surrounding him gave me the scent. I followed it. I never knew it would take me here. I never imagined the extent of his treachery or that my search would lead whoever is protecting his lies to you."

Sometimes silence healed. Other times it ate away. Rusting armor trapped Kyly.

Rain wept down the truck's windshield, eventually landing beneath its tires, adding to the sticky hum of their rotation.

She couldn't read Zavier's expression. He faced the windshield, leaving a handsome profile darkened by a lack of street lamps on the open highway. Focusing on the empty road ahead, she realized she had no idea where they were going. At the moment, it didn't matter.

Though he must've longed to shake her senseless, Zavier didn't waste time on retribution.

She waited. Eroding.

"You should've told me the truth." He reached across the seat between them for her hand. "I would've gladly helped you. After all, you didn't throw yourself into this maliciously, did you?"

Moments passed before Kyly answered. Moved by his integrity, her guilt intensified.

"I wasn't sure you even knew you had an older brother when we met. When you told me who you were," she explained. "I came here seeking records, something to go on to trace the doctor's history. Meeting you, well—"

"Not exactly a lucky break," Zavier noted. "Whoever is protecting the truth from reaching the surface knows you're involved. And since journalists aren't the first people one wants to hand their skeletons over to, you're a bit of a problem."

"Yeah, I got that the other night after being followed home from the university."

"You were followed?"

"Stalked is a more accurate description. He knew what he was doing." She turned down the collar of her turtleneck.

Zavier traded his focus from the highway to her bruised neck. "Damn."

"Yeah. I'll relive it for you some other time." She slid her hand over the discolored finger marks. "That's why I met you at the truck stop. I planted a cover story for why I was leaving and got carsick while the cab driver lost our tail to get to you. You understand why I feel responsible for this whole mess? I probably led them right to your doorstep with all my ignorant probing."

"Mason thinks they've had someone watching the house since the day of Dr. Valeric's funeral announcement. He sent my sister to an art show in San Francisco early, and I'm, well, we're on our way to his cabin across the border.

"You didn't bring them to our doorstep, Lee. They were already there, so quit beating up on yourself. If you want something to feel crappy about, lying to me works." His charismatic grin returned, lifting her spirits ever so slightly.

"We're going to Canada?" It was the first border that came to mind within driving distance and one she'd never been across.

"Go Canucks!" he said.

"Go who?"

"Doesn't matter." He laughed. "We'll be in the Canadian Rockies in about twenty-five hours."

"Okay. It's not like I have a bunch of alternatives."

After an hour or two of exchanging information in an effort to make sense of their situation, exhaustion took hold. At Zavier's urging, Kyly climbed into the back and lay across the bench seat. With a travel pillow under her head and his jacket over her, it wouldn't be long before the road's vibration lulled her to sleep.

"If the weather turns to crap across the border, and it usually does, the ground will be soft and slushy," he said. "It makes the drive in a roller coaster ride of fallen trees and ditches. Sleep won't be an option then. So rest. A little low music on the radio, SoBe Lizard Fuel in the cup holder, and I'm good to drive through the night."

Kyly's eyelids grew too heavy to lift. She wanted to stay awake. Images of the attacker's evil eyes loomed. In days her world had somersaulted, but this was the adventure she'd asked for. Now she had to do her best to survive it. Fading out, she saw Zavier in the mirror, searching the distance behind them. Waiting on unwanted company.

19

MICAEL STOOD, peering through the window when Ray walked in. Dawn left no trace of the turbulence of the previous night. He'd managed to get out of bed, leaning on the wall for support, and carry his weight unassisted. He was gaining strength.

"Have you been up long?" Ray had fruits and oatmeal on a bed tray.

"Not long, found solid footing." He stared into the field a moment longer, imprinting the scene on the back wall of his mind, then turned to greet her. "I'm weak, but I'd like to shower standing up instead of using the seat system in there."

"Maybe later, after you eat. I'll send Nick in to wait out here so you can call him if you need help."

"Sure."

She wasn't dressing like a doctor anymore. Her physique was outlined by denim clinging to all the right places and a white stretch-cotton tank that did the same. Athletic, perfect outside anyway. One less illusion, he thought. Soon they'll all slip away. There may be nothing pretty left.

She caught him staring. A devilish grin brought a surge of color to her lips.

"Tell me," she said. "Any memories, dreams, disturbing visions of any kind?"

"Nature." He swiveled away, facing the window. "I keep dreaming about the grounds, I think." It wasn't a lie. He dreamt of those too.

"Figures, you always appreciated nature." An odd lightness colored her voice. Relief?

"Is it necessary for me to be monitored twenty-four, seven?" He turned back, gesturing at the wall camera angled at his bed. "I realize it's mandatory for patients in the condition I was in, but I'm obviously improving. It's the lack of privacy, you know. I can't sneeze or...anything without it being caught on film."

Her strange eyes were transfixed on his. Not a time to flinch. He shrugged and gave a quick pirate's smile.

"Don't I have a room outside the medical area? A regular bedroom."

"Of course. It's serene and cerebral. Would you like to see it?"

He'd drawn her in. Evidently, this was a tour she endorsed.

"Yeah, if you don't mind. I mean...I want to get back to living normally. Maybe it'd help me remember."

"You eat. I'll come back after you've showered, and we'll see about moving you."

He suspected Ray assumed his request to return to his room indicated subconscious links to his prior existence—an existence that included her. And relocating would bolster their united, grieving family appearance for watchful eyes during the closely approaching day of mourning.

After she left, he wondered if it was such a great idea. Moving closer to the lion's den.

He devoured the soft food on his plate. His body ached for energy. He found solace in walking, unsteadily but unassisted, to the washroom.

He'd showered, towel dried his hair, and was mapping the camouflaged scars near his hairline when Nick entered the outer room.

"You okay in there?" Nick called.

"I'm tracing my past."

Nick appeared in the doorway in a rush.

Micael read the tension in Nick's expression. "You okay?"

"Thought you might have fallen." Nick stared at the exposed wounds in the mirror, seemingly avoiding eye contact.

"Why would you think that? I'm fine."

Heading back to the door, Nick said, "I'll make sure we're ready for you."

"Ready or not," Micael whispered. "Here I come."

———

Nick's smile held from Michael's temporary lodgings and the length of the hallway but collapsed into a frown upon entering Micael's bedroom.

Ray stood at the fireplace mantle, a box by her feet, collecting photographs she deemed detrimental. Many personal pictures had long since been removed. A couple of Nick racing, a distant one of Dr. V on his sailboat in the sun, and another of him, much younger, accepting an award were all that remained. Ray stole center stage in a pricey Jay Strongwater frame. Wearing a white knit bikini, stretched out in the sun, she smiled at the camera the way one does when a lover is behind the lens. Nick couldn't recall being around when it was taken, but he recognized the deck of Dr. V's boat in the background.

"What are you doing in here?" He startled her from behind.

"Making preparations," she said.

"Preparations for what?"

"For whom," she corrected. "Micael. I'm moving him out of the recovery room."

"Are you sure that's wise?" He was certain it wasn't. She appeared far too pleased with herself.

"It's all part of the plan, Nick. Guiding his memory. This will help things along nicely. Not to mention the benefits for show time."

"The funeral?" he said miserably.

"Yes. By the way, what are you doing in here?"

"He asked for jeans." Nick halted her in her tracks before she began selecting. "I think we should at least let the man dress himself."

Storming by her into the closet, he clanged hangers together, pushed, pulled, and tossed until reappearing with a black shirt, faded blue jeans, and clean underwear in a heap. He never spoke a word on the way to the door. Pausing in the threshold, he turned to face her.

"If he knows you agreed to moving him, you better hurry and finish in here. He's showered; he'll want to see it right away."

Nick walked, feet heavier than before, back to MJ.

Micael had combed his hair, avoiding stitches. And, although still clothed in nothing but a towel, he appeared healthier than ever.

The man before Nick was no worse for wear—definitely not the reflection of a long-term coma patient. Though thinner than his body type demanded, his muscles were long, lean, and defined. His skin was impossibly flawless for a man his age, and if you didn't know better, you'd swear he was an athlete in perfect health.

"You keep staring like that I'll begin to wonder if the muscle car and low voice are a front." Micael grinned.

"You keep talking like that and you'll be the first person I run over." Nick set the pile of clothes on the bed. "It's...you look unbelievably good considering..."

"I must've been dog meat when you found me. The way the two of you are so astonished by my meager existence." He stretched into his black shirt.

"You wouldn't have qualified for any triathlons, but enough about your looks. How do you feel?"

"Weak. And, frustrated at that."

"There's no rush. Life can wait. Don't try to be any more of a medical breakthrough than you already are. Believe me, it's enough."

If he only knew. Nick wondered if he ever would. It had a way of coming back to bite you in the ass. The truth was a dangerous opponent, perhaps the only one to have an edge over Ray.

Nick glanced around the room. Memories. "You woke screaming a number of times when you were coming out of the coma. Do you remember anything, any reason why?"

"Falling." Micael pulled on his briefs with minor difficulty under the towel. "All I remember is the sensation of falling."

"Huh."

Nick sauntered out, giving Micael a minute to compose himself before the big move down the hall.

The sensation of falling. Interesting. Micael hadn't fallen an inch.

———

With the closing door, Micael dropped the cumbersome towel to the floor and reached for his jeans. He shook them free from the ball they were in. A distinct *ting ting* sounded. Tossing the pants aside, he searched the floor. A single key lay at his feet.

Cautiously bending to avoid the dizzying onset that accompanied any such movement, he grasped the old metal piece and flipped it over in his fingers. It wasn't a house key. Not for this house anyway. The aged pewter finish had the markings of a time long before luxury estates were key-carded and protected by interlinking computerized alarm systems. Its round looping head and long neck were fitted to a well-aged barnyard padlock. Despite the lack of rust, intense weathering left black soot on his fingers as he turned it over in his hand.

The object intrigued him. He placed it back in the pocket from which it came. After putting on his jeans and sandals at the foot of the bed, he slicked his hair back with his hands and patted the black soot from his pocket.

With nothing else to take, he scooped the novel he'd pretended to read from the bedside table. The door swung open while his back was turned.

"Presentable?" Nick asked.

"As ever I could be." Micael headed for the door. "Are you sure these are my jeans and not yours?"

With each step, the well-worn denim shifted lower on his hips, forcing him to nudge them back up by the belt loops every few feet.

"They're yours, bro. My hips couldn't fit a size 36 if I were skeletal," Nick answered. "I'll help you find a belt when we get to your room."

"I think you may have to reintroduce me to everything. I won't remember where anything is."

"We'll let you get comfortable, then we can spend time riffling through your stuff." Nick's smirk suggested the investigation might lead to Micael's embarrassment and his subsequent entertainment.

"I'd prefer it was just you and me. What if I have something...you know, Ray shouldn't see," Micael said.

"Haven't been awake for more than a week and already you're coming to the conclusion you're some kind of pervert. Not a lot of self-confidence there, hey?" Nick laughed.

Micael shrugged, and they both chuckled rounding the corner to intersecting hallways.

Glancing over Micael, Nick shook his head with a smile.

"What? I won't ask if *you know something I don't*. That's a given, but what's with that look?" Micael asked.

"You're too normal, man. I'm having trouble adjusting," Nick admitted. "I've seen you horizontal for sooo long..."

"So you *do* prefer me flat on my back! I'm worried about you. You had any dates lately? You know, of the female variety?"

"Watch it little man, or you'll end up with a few more Frankenstein stitches in that pretty head of yours." Nick pounded his fist into his palm for effect.

"I'm getting the distinct feeling that 'you fell from a cliff' story's a cover-up."

"We saved your life, and now we're liars?" Ray appeared from the opposite corner, meeting them on the way to Micael's room. Homing in on the last sentence of their banter, her tone confirmed she'd taken it literally and was seriously offended.

"No, no. Wait. I...I didn't really—" Micael stammered.

"We were just breaking each others'... We were kidding around. Relax," Nick said, returning his attention to Micael. "Let's see your humble abode, shall we? We'll discuss my sex life later."

Nick led the way, giving Micael time to yank at his ever-falling drawers while he shuffled beside him. Ray remained ever watchful behind.

"You should be in the wheelchair," she cautioned.

"I figured I'd wear myself out so I could have a nap, wake up in what should be a familiar bed, and if we're lucky—"

"Your memory will return," she finished his sentence. "It doesn't normally happen in a sudden blinding flash. Don't expect miracles. It can take months, years even."

"We'll see," Nick said, ending the speculation. "Here we are. Your boudoir awaits, malady."

Taken from the remnants of an ancient Italian church, Nick explained, worn and damaged by both the merciless hands of time and thieves, the doors to his suite captivated him. Micael ran his fingers over the wooden bodies that made up their outer border. A few angel-like figures lay gouged and cracked at the edges. Others were missing limbs, amputated by blunt force. All, however incomplete, were hauntingly beautiful.

"You *can* go in," Nick urged. "In fact, I highly recommend it."

"*This* is mine?"

"Yeah, I know it's not much. Well, with the 16-foot ceilings, ancient artifacts, Roman statues, and centuries-old artwork, I'd be disappointed too, but you picked it, even if you can't remember. It's like getting outta hand and waking up with a tattoo. It's still yours in the morning."

"I don't remember buying, importing...I couldn't be responsible for all this."

"You had some help," Nick said. "Enough drooling, go."

Floor-to-ceiling built-in bookcases adorned the wall on his right, full from top to bottom with ancient texts, many in hand-bound leather. The rich dark maple still cast a warm musk into the air.

He breathed it in.

Above a grand antique desk, skylights filtered concentrated light to the work surface—natures equivalent to a reading lamp. Drinking in the room, his eyes found everything synchronized, orderly, and specific.

Micael chose a comfortable chair by the desk and transferred the weight off his exhausted legs with Nick's assistance.

He reached for a pillow lying along the left side of the chair on the floor and tucked it under his head. He didn't search for it. He knew it was there. This caught the attention of Ray and Nick, who were still staring at him when he finished adjusting it.

"What? I saw it before I sat down. Don't get your hopes up."

"It's not the pillow. It's your favorite chair. It's where you could always be found, thinking, napping," Nick explained.

"So maybe I *will* wake up and remember, after all." Micael's speech slowed a little more with each word.

Their cue to leave.

Nick shrugged then ushered Ray out with insistence.

Peering out floor-to-ceiling windows at the ocean lapping against the rocky shoreline far below, he listened to their footsteps fade. Propping his feet up on the footrest, he balanced his novel against his stomach and tucked the fingers of his left hand into his pocket. There, hidden from the light of day, a cold metal key to the past.

20

CERO WITNESSED the merciless shredding of peace through bloodshot eyes. By 5:15 in the morning, his home had transformed from island paradise to command post. Kyly's phone call changed everything.

There'd been no sleep. He'd barely eaten in the last twenty-four hours. Paris marched down a list of preparations for Kyly's return. For all intents and purposes, their daughter needed to vanish until life resumed to normal—if it ever would. To this end, the phones and computers were constantly ringing out responses to requests Cero placed to trusted friends and much-needed alliances.

Yet, the fingers of an enemy would dial the call he waited on in desperation. A man Cero regarded with animosity, contempt, and utter disgust. Fear for the life of his child forced him to unearth a toxin.

Immoral, elitist bastard, Cero seethed.

The island preacher had given a lifetime to God. For all his words of guidance to others in search of faith, for all his mutterings on the mountaintop, he couldn't justify why the Almighty let such creatures roam the planet until now.

He needed answers. His daughter's life depended on them. And, by god or the Other, he'd get them.

When the call came in, Paris, monitoring the caller ID, summoned Cero to pick up the mainline handset by their patio.

"Be silent," he warned. "I don't want him overhearing you in the background." She agreed, leaving him to deal with the killer from his past.

"You called." A voice taunted Cero from three thousand miles away. "I was, quite understandably, taken aback by your insistent summons. I found your query unanticipated, of course. The prospect of hearing from you again, for obvious reasons, was remote at best."

Disregarding the pompous dribble spilling from the phone line, Cero said, "I'm collecting on a debt."

The clergyman's voice hardened, with intent cold enough to freeze the line to ocean bedrock across the Pacific and seep a lethal chill out the other end.

"All this time, Cero, and you sound as you did when last we spoke. I explained then, with considerable effort I might add, that I really can't make amends, but if there's anything you need–"–"

"I want information.",", Cero demanded. "No questions, no excuses, or we both know what I'll do to you. I want everything you can get on a Dr. Micael Valeric. Who his children are, where and when they were born, mothers, wives, girlfriends, adoptions, charges, and military involvement. Who hated him? Who loved him? Everything. You have twelve hours. No holding back. No lies. I want details. You understand, you smug, murdering, son-of-a-bitch."

"Cursing. Time hasn't softened you, old friend." The voice was laced with mocking charm.

"I'm no friend of yours." Cero snapped back.

"Oh, but you *were* once, not so long ago."

"Until you killed my family!" Cero raged. "Get me what I asked for. Once I have it, lose this number. Permanently. Don't even consider toying with me."

He slammed the phone down with an intensity that forced out a distorted ring of protest. The sound ricocheted across the patio and down the waterfall shattering, into broken chimes among the rocks at the jagged edge of the ocean.

He stood and followed a pathway bordering the waterfall, ducking beneath branches, and stepping haphazardly between rocks, tree roots, and softened moss. Determined to walk off the phone call's effects, he combated the eerie images in his mind with every footfall—his wife dying on one table, his newborn dying on the other.

He shook his head as if the physical act would rattle away the visions like a pinball machine, bouncing them back into discarded depths.

"*Bastard.*" He arrived at the cliff's drop- off.

He searched the rocks, too close to its lip. Physically, like mentally, he teetered on the edge. If he continued down memory lane, he'd fall into a dark abyss—one that had almost cost him his life once before. One that had most certainly cost him his daughter.

The water below crashed hard against the stonewall, splashing up in explosive white spray then retreating to hit again, leaving frothy foam clinging to the coast.

Hundreds of years ago, not far from where he stood, Hawaiians dove from the top of an 8o-foot cliff called Pu'uKeka'a. Hill of Rolling Stones. Now, locals called it Black Rock. How appropriate.

Ancients believed only one possessing great spiritual strength could survive such a leap of faith into this holy place where the spirits of the dead dwelled before leaving for the world beyond. Every evening at sunset, natives repeated the ritual with a graceful dive into the sea. An offering of the soul, rewarded when they reached the shore, asserting their spiritual power and physical strength.

Cero knew with every ounce of his being if he leaped, *he* wouldn't survive. The spirits of the dead waited to claim him, and his daughter needed him alive. He wouldn't abandon her twice.

———

"I beat the clock. Though I'm not certain what real consequences existed had I not. Are you impressed?" The bastard called back. Cero was surprised, not impressed.

"Nothing you could do would elicit my admiration," Cero said.

"Ah, but you haven't heard all the juicy intelligence I've accumulated at your beseeching. I must admit there are startling revelations to behold, Reverend Cicero."

"Lay it out." He placed the microphone relay on the handset and pushed play on his recorder, then reached for a pen and paper.

"Still deemed unclean, am I? Afraid you'll be tainted through the phone line? Where's your faith, Father? And what about forgiveness—

the elusive brass ring you just can't grasp? No matter. My conscience is clear enough for the both of us."

Cero snapped the pen in half, spilling ink across his notepad. He grabbed another and tossed the damaged sheets in the trash while the wheels on the tape recorder spun.

"He had no wives, no marriage in any country, and no public relationship of recognition. He dated in college. Normal behavior, but to work obsessed to commit to the enslavement of marriage..."

Cero hated to listen but trusted the validity of the information. The corrupt soul delivering it made an art of gathering the worst on world "so-called" healers. It was his obsession, and no one did it better.

The voice broke in again. "Here's where it gets interesting. For the first decade or so of his achievement, he's the lonely professor. Then, as if she were dumped on his doorstep half grown, it appears he has a daughter. First photograph on record, she looks about twelve, caught at a fundraiser holding fast to dear old dad. Not your typical kid either. One of the nurses had a conversation with her while he managed the podium. Still remembers it. Said the child was scary, smart, and edgy. Unnerved our poor lady in white. Still creeps her out today. Second photo opportunity was taken in New York at a hotel lobby. VIP guest scrapbook. Only this time, she looks more like an underage girlfriend than a daughter. Who knows what dirty dealings Dr. V had up his sleeve in that department...single for so many years—"

"Get on with it. I don't want your opinion, facts." Cero made notes while he listened.

"He and his mistress hid away for four years. Next we meet Ray. He introduced her at a conference on degenerative diseases, and her older brother Nick, who didn't exist until then. He appears to be in his late twenties or early thirties and announced to several others he was a surgeon with military training. Dicey bedroom theatrics if you ask me."

"I didn't! What about a mother?"

"That's the interesting part...there isn't one."

"Test tube babies, there has to be something—"

"There isn't. Nothing recorded in any hospital from here to Nigeria. No backwoods birth. No medical records for any treatment since, nothing. It's as if they fell from the sky. And, if the military knows anything, they're not willing to divulge it. I've built dossiers on a couple high-ranking officers that guarantee compliance, yet I couldn't squeeze an ounce out of them. All I have now are frightened contacts and dead ends."

"If you're playing me—"

"I don't give a shit about this dead doctor. I'm telling you, these two don't exist on paper!"

"Your true colors are showing," Cero said.

"There are no adoption records. No marriage certificates, birth certificates, social security cards, insurance plans, bank accounts, criminal records, driver's licenses. Nothing. The guy had no enemies to speak of. Coworkers, patients, and the medical community revered him. And he doesn't have a single blemish with the law. Which, I might add, is a minor miracle for us doctors, as you yourself are quite aware."

The man paused for effect. Cero remained silent.

"The military conducted several reconnaissance missions of his island over the last fifteen years or so. That's the red herring tied to our dear doctor. There must've been something he was working on that evoked their interest, but they were concerned enough not to even log it in top-secret files. The missions are listed with info on his activities on the island as seen from the air or water, but there's nothing stating why they were there in the first place. Your guy is one shifty character. I'd even hazard to say he has me beat, and *you know* that's saying a lot."

Cero's fax machine warned of incoming data.

"I'm sending you the photos and information from a non-traceable line. I don't want any part of this mess."

"You won't be involved, just cover your tracks."

"Worried about me? I'm touched."

"Never. Worried about any link to you."

"There's someone nasty behind this, isn't there?"

His words slithered like drool. Cero's stomach turned.

"What about recently?" he asked.

"The good doctor was expanding the family. When news of his death hit the papers, so did a picture of his only son and successor."

"The military doctor?"

"No, whole new character, pretty young thing. Maybe still in his twenties. Doesn't resemble Daddy in the least. And his birth certificate was certified a month ago. It miraculously appeared on files in Italy with the mother listed as a Caucasian woman, died giving birth. Sorry, these things happen."

"Bastard...what else."

"The son gets it all. Everything, including the island is his. All the bank accounts have been transferred into his name. Before then, nothing."

"What the hell..." Cero was thinking out loud.

"There's a funeral planned tomorrow for your devilish doctor and, not coincidentally, a recon mission is scheduled the same night. Curious. Should prove to be a stimulating weekend. If I were you, I wouldn't touch this."

"Well you're not me, could never be me, and I don't need your damn advice."

"Oh, I think you do."

21

"WHERE ARE WE?" Kyly studied the strange dark forest flanking both sides of the highway from the rest area. "Zavier, why didn't you wake me sooner? You must be exhausted."

"I'm a med student. I'm accustomed to 36-hour days. Besides, you needed the rest. How's the neck?" He stretched his legs and took in the mountain scenery.

"I'm okay. Why don't I drive the rest of the way?" she offered, following him to the break between the parking lot pavement and the forest.

"Thanks, but my clock's off. If I fell asleep, you probably couldn't wake me until tomorrow. I'm working off my second wind. We're starting through British Columbia, great views."

"I've never seen anything quite like it." Her eyes followed the ocean of green.

Rock walls in the distance shot up from ground level without so much as a brief incline. No gracefully rising hillside here. Everything, including miles of dense trees, reached straight for the Heavens with no pretense. Beautiful, ominous, and amazing. "I'd prefer to have a clear mind to enjoy it," she admitted. "We crossed the border?"

"Yeah, luckily they were in a good mood. They asked to see our passports, glanced over them, and waved us through. I said we were vacationing in the Rockies."

"I was worried we'd run into problems there. How much further do we have to go?" Her stare drifted deep into the pine trees, wishing they could escape into them.

"You're not going to start that, *are we there yet*, stuff, are you?" He smiled at her, refolded the map, and headed back to the truck.

Focused back on him, she smiled and said, "You're very funny, you know that?"

"You wanted to drive. There's a town not too far from here where we can stop and eat, pick up supplies for the cabin. I'll take over from there."

"Sure." She skirted around him to the driver's door. "I'm sorry I flaked out for so long."

"It's seven a.m. Hawaii time. You're up early." They shut their doors and left the rest area. "We're headed for Kelowna, it's a beautiful place built around the Okanagan Lake. From there, it'll take us about six hours...if I drive."

"Five if I stay behind the wheel." Pulling away, she accelerated around the winding mountain highway, checking and rechecking the rearview mirror.

Their conversation was light into town and remained so while they ate, but as the food diminished, so did Kyly's resistance.

Fear was proving a stealthy adversary. She thought she'd shut it out, but it seeped into the back door, tainting the conversation.

"I'd really like to survive this." She spoke without volition.

Zavier leaned across their small table, his expression gaining a mature seriousness; he locked his stare and whispered. "Do you know how to handle a weapon?"

"I've never seen a gun up close," Kyly admitted. "I've taken self-defense training. I did an article on it. The instructor left me black and blue for a week. I don't think he liked reporters."

"Let's hope you don't have to use it." As he uttered the words, doubt shadowed his eyes.

"What about you?" she asked. "You said you were a hunter?"

"Since I was a kid. I was a marksman by the time I'd reached my teens. Compensating for a scrawny physique."

"You are not scrawny."

"Not now. This is the result of hard work." He laughed. "It was a good way to gain respect around the schoolyard. If a bully eyed me, I invited him to target practice. One trip, and we were best of friends."

"Oooh, you're good," she said, clinging to every ounce of normal.

"Let's hope you never have to see how good."

"Your lips to God's ears." They both knew how serious the situation was and shared the need to savor every safe second they had left.

He mumbled something while staring out over the parking lot.

"I gave my father access to all my research information," she said. "I'm sure he'll have something new to tell us when I call him. I pray whoever is after us doesn't target them."

"We should get moving." Something distracted him but he wasn't willing to share. "Don't want to be dodging rough terrain in the dark. In Alberta, the summer sun doesn't sleep until late evening. Mason's cabin is well removed from city lights, sheltered by a forest too thick to penetrate. We want to be there before sundown."

The more Zavier explained, the more anxious Kyly became. She left cash on the table and handed Zavier his coat.

After driving for a half hour, occupied by alpine scenery, Zavier asked, "How did you find us? It's not like my brother's birth was common knowledge. You must be a hell of a journalist."

"I'm good at pooling resources. I also have a cousin in the FBI," she admitted.

"The FBI knows?" Losing sight of the road momentarily, he turned to face her, astonished, then swerved back into the center of the lane.

"I asked him for an address. Never said why I needed it. Watch the road. The research on your brother's birth was scarce and difficult to piece together."

"Well, maybe your cousin could help. I'll let Mason know if he's willing to discuss it after I tell him about you. He's not going to be happy. You're an unexpected wrinkle."

"Gee, thanks. It appears there's a growing list of my well-wishers."

She picked up her go-mug of tea, spilled it over the rim, sipped the top clean, and set it down again. When she stared out the truck's window, the blurred scenery made her dizzy. Shifting her eyes back to Zavier helped, but fear was sapping her concentration. Each passing mile corroded her resolve. When darkness fell, and they left the RVfilled highway for the isolation of cut line roads, her plush seat lost its comfort. Propped on its edge, inches from the window, she gazed back into the night. She couldn't see much beyond the truck's headlights. Yet, every few minutes, she swore she glimpsed red eyes glowing back from the forest floor.

The closer they came to the cabin, the rougher the terrain. Kyly clenched the armrest to stop from smashing her head into the roof when they hit potholes.

"Well, this is relaxing," she hollered, being flung by impact like a rag doll.

"It's intended as a deterrent," Zavier kidded.

"I imagine it works well for preventing unexpected visitors, but what if the bad guys are already there? It's not exactly what I'd call an easy escape route."

Zavier didn't respond but muscled the steering wheel to maintain proper trajectory.

"We're almost there," he belted out a few minutes later, above the noise of snapping tree branches, spinning tires, and the high revving engine.

"How could you possibly know that?" she yelled back.

"I've done this once or twice before."

"That's comforting."

Kyly was glad she hadn't said more. When the words left her lips, the truck hit pavement, the roller coaster ended, and her voice would've bellowed in the sudden quiet.

Low lights brightened their path to a peeled log arch and wrought iron gate. Zavier hit a button on the dash, and the gate swung open. It closed again as the truck cleared.

Once inside, the silken shroud of nightfall overtook the reclusive property, leaving well-placed motion sensors flashing on in succession to lead their way. Main floor windows illuminated the cabin's elevated entrance. Beautiful, at least what she could see of it. For a few seconds, she forgot to be afraid.

"The lights?" she asked.

"It's okay. It's my uncle's buddy, Jack. He's meeting me here to go over a few things. You can relax."

"Not likely," she assured him. "Is he going to let me in, or should I duck?"

"Trust me. He won't be the one tackling you to the ground," he said slyly.

Zavier stopped the truck in front of a curved elevation of steps. They led to a front porch and double-door entry several feet above the truck's roofline.

He barely set foot to the pavement when an alarming battery of barks erupted from the side of the cabin. Kyly removed her hand from the door release and elected to lean out Zavier's side. A large pile of fur ran full throttle toward him.

"Whoa, boy," Zavier uttered the words before being slammed into the truck's side panel by an enormous red heap. The defensive barking transformed into joyous broken yelps between licks. Kyly figured it was safe to abandon the vehicle.

"Lee, meet Riggs." He moved aside so Kyly could introduce herself.

"Hi Riggs, hi ya fella." She ruffled his fur face with both hands. "Nice to meet you."

Riggs greeted her like an old friend, an unexpected warm welcome. While Zavier unloaded their bags, something in the forest caught the dog's attention. His ears perked, his tail straightened like a lightning rod, and his hackles rose.

"Umm, is that normal?" Kyly pointed to the dog's frozen stance.

"It's probably an animal in the brush." Zavier swung a bag over his shoulder. "Come on, boy. Don't make our guest more edgy than she already is."

"Funny," Kyly said. "Very funny."

She really didn't think so. Zavier climbed the stairs to the cabin, Kyly and Riggs stayed behind—both watching the woods braced for an intruder.

———

Zavier caught Jack peeking out the library window for a brief moment. He looked Kyly over perhaps a moment too long. His expression said he assumed she was his girlfriend.

"I see you brought a friend," Jack said, peering down from atop the staircase as Zavier entered the lower foyer.

"It was crucial Jack, or I wouldn't have brought her."

"Long legs, perfect smile, and hourglass figure don't have anything to do with it, right son?"

"Actually, no. They don't," Zavier refuted. "Not this time, Jack. She's in trouble and we helped put her there."

Jack said nothing more, descending the flight of stairs to help unload the truck. Before exiting, he handed Zavier a handgun and two fresh boxes of ammunition. "Throw em in your bag. Mason said it might come in handy."

Zavier read Jack's friendly, weathered face. Seriousness belied his jovial grin. Like all of them, he knew enough to be worried.

———

"Name's Jack," the mountain man said, offering a rugged handshake. "Pleased to meet you. Any friend of Zav's is a friend of mine. Make yourself at home."

"I'm Kyly. Thank you, Jack." She followed him inside the house.

Despite the constant references to this being Zavier's uncle's cabin, it was no cabin at all. Cabin suggested a shack out in the brush barely held together by rusty nails. This was anything but. It may have been one of the most formidable structures she'd ever stepped foot in.

The walls were solid logs locked together so tightly mites would be hard pressed to find an opening. Their thickness transformed window seats into daybeds. Safe seclusion reinforced by heavy-paned storm windows. And, inside walls maintained inner privacy separating rooms with superior insulation. Shutting her guest bedroom door muffled lingering sounds from other areas in the house to meditation waves.

Virtual silence.

Beyond the fortress-like impenetrability lay a warm, comforting atmosphere. Kyly felt safe for the first time since leaving Maui.

The billowy goose-down duvet on the guest bed tempted her. Nice thought, unrealistic, but nice.

Zavier was in the kitchen going over particulars with Jack when she found him. Jack was making his exit. "I bid you both a pleasant sleep," Jack said on his way out. "There's a hike ahead of me and not much twilight left." Riggs walked him to the door but stayed behind, of course, to guard his own.

Flopping down at Kyly's feet, the Irish setter stared up, comforting her with big brown eyes that said, 'Don't worry, I'll protect you.' Kyly patted the top of his head then shifted her chair to face Zavier.

"Who do we call first, my father or your uncle?" she asked, uneasy.

"If your father's connections might give us new information, him. Mason might be easier to deal with if he sees a benefit to your involvement."

"He doesn't sound very welcoming. Under the circumstances, I wouldn't be either." Kyly put her head in her hands; everything from her shoulders up throbbed demanding Motrin.

"Don't worry. Once he meets you, he'll think you're great. He's a nice guy, protective."

"I know someone a lot like him." She dialed her father's number. Cero picked up halfway through the first ring.

"Are you somewhere safe?" His words were calm, his breathing frenzied.

"I'm fine, and yes, I'm safe." It was comforting to hear the worry in his voice.

"Where are you, can you say?"

"I'm across the Canadian border in the Rockies with Zavier. This has been one heck of a journey. I'm glad I'm not in it alone." She needed him to know she saw him now, how he'd been there, dedicated to her life for more time than not. The time he had not been there, in hindsight, had been brief but had done so much damage. It was the avoided conversation plaguing their life together waiting for the right words and now the right timing.

After explaining everything she and Zavier had pieced together over the last twenty-four hours, she made introductions and put Zavier on the phone. Internally defeated by the things she couldn't say.

The night outside the window leaped through the glass and sent shivers up Kyly's spine as the men formulated strategies for survival. The cell phone beeped out a low battery warning as their conversation concluded. Kyly snatched it from Zavier's hand; words flew from her lips. "Tell Mom not to worry and know..." Then they stalled. As she searched for the right phrase, the phone lost power. Zavier waited for an explanation.

"Things weren't great between us before. This hasn't helped," she said, deflated.

Time ticked by. Zavier wanted to be the one to broach the subject of his unexpected houseguest with Mason. Jack wouldn't delay his check-in for long.

Kyly was drained from the swarm of information and ensuing implications. They hadn't eaten since noon, and fatigue gnawed away any remaining bits of energy.

She suggested tea, a weak but sincere way to fortify them.

The next call demanded fast and efficient delivery of information. She physically braced herself for an onslaught of Mason's criticism.

Waiting for the kettle to boil, she searched towering gray mahogany cabinets for tea bags. Expecting empty cupboards or junk food, she was surprised to find gourmet ingredients. Unfortunately, she also found an extensive assortment of teas, sugars, and honey. No further reason to rummage. Her investigation concluded the man knew how to eat.

Straining loose-leaf Bourbon Street Vanilla into two gray mugs, she added a few drops of Tubilo honey and set them on the table. The few minutes of peace the warm liquid instilled offered a measure of absolution.

"I should make the call alone." Zavier gulped from his cup, seemingly immune to the scolding liquid. "At least at first. Let me smooth things over. Explain how this happened in a way he can understand, then I'll call you in."

"What you're saying is you want to break the ice instead of having him break it over my head."

"Something like that. This isn't about you. It isn't your fault this happened, but right now, Mason's only concern is for *his* family. He'll see you as part of the problem if we're not careful and none of us have the luxury of time for a meltdown. Let me deal with him. Then we'll put our heads together and find a way out of this godforsaken disaster before we all end up with invitations to the Jerry Springer show."

"Are those reruns still playing?" Kyly didn't argue. Zavier was right. Their situation had all the makings of a bad talk show. She could see the headlines—Doctor Kidnaps Brain-dead Baby / Baby Found Alive & Well, Inherits Island / Doctor, Criminal or Genius / Journalist Goes Missing, Presumed Dead—they weren't comforting.

She nodded and carried her tea elsewhere.

Sleep being improbable, she wandered the cabin—all 7,000 square feet of it. Well, perhaps not all, but at least a fair portion—once a journalist, always a journalist.

She began in the large open living area, the first welcome to the house after climbing the thirteen steps from the lower foyer.

The ceiling stretched twenty feet into the treetops held by salvaged cross beams adorned with skylights. Shadows played across the wooden roof ignited by a black crystal chandelier at its center.

At the far back, facing the forest, a stone fireplace stole center stage, flanked on both sides by windows reaching a half-moon curve across the top.

She stood dead center in the room, absorbing the panoramic view. The placement of the windows was calculated.

A rich woven rug, soft to the touch, in a raw, natural, linen shade ground leather furniture, Scottish tapestry, and other accents, all united by a knight's motif carved into the fireplace mantle.

Zavier shared many of the photos adorning it; the man standing next to him caught Kyly off guard. She imagined Mason a rusty recluse. What she saw was a striking man far younger than his years.

Picking up the frame for closer inspection, her head tilted capturing muffled sounds escaping the kitchen. Zavier was still on the phone with the man staring back at her from the photo.

He didn't appear nearly as cold or coarse as she figured, especially in the photo to her right. Mason, drenched by a waterfall, fully clothed. Though water poured down in copious amounts, his warm smile was still visible, and his energy intoxicating.

———

Zavier consulted his notes as he spoke, knowing there was no room for errors with Mason. "So there has to be at least three of them. Who knows if he acquired the other two the same way, but they're apparently loyal to him despite not being mentioned as beneficiaries to his substantial will," Zavier said.

"Our boy is the only heir according to this doctor?" Mason asked.

"Yup, but he hasn't been made public until now, which makes you wonder."

"How did you get this information?"

"I'm not exactly up here alone," Zavier answered, wanting to come clean.

"I know Jack's a great tracker on land, but—"

"I'm here with someone I met a few days ago—"

"What!" Mason shot back. "Are they listening? Don't you realize who they could be working for and they're in our only safe house, my house! Getting to you to get to the rest of—"

"She's not one of them. They tried to kill her! I had to keep her safe and compare notes. Together we might have a fighting chance, but from what her father just finished telling us, it's going to be a long shot."

"Her father's there? How many people did you take with you?"

"Just her. Her father called from Hawaii. He's the doctor. That's how I accessed the information I gave you. He's fighting to keep his family alive like we are."

Mason drew in a deep breath, slowly exhaling into the line, madder than hell. Patiently, Zavier waited for him to compose himself before speaking again. "Cero, the doctor, lost his wife and newborn, Kyly's mother and sister, almost twenty years ago."

"Does he think they're alive? Were they taken?" Mason asked, his calm tone returning.

"No, he watched them die. He buried them. Let's just say the experience left him with unresolved contempt for the medical profession. It's why Kyly started researching our story—and—"

"She's a reporter? This keeps getting better and better." No optimism colored Mason's voice.

"She couldn't have known where it'd lead. By the time she did, it was too late. She was being stalked."

Zavier explained, Mason listened. After the conversation fell to a low growl Kyly came into the room with one of the mantle pictures in her hands. She pointed to a figure in the frame and mouthed the words, 'Is this him.' Zavier nodded with a smile.

"Well I suppose it's time for proper introductions. Shall I put you on speakerphone?" he asked his reluctant uncle.

"Now is as good a time as any. But before you do, tell me, do you trust this girl, or do I need to call Ash in for a background check?"

Ashton Anden was a child protégé turned goofy, eccentric forensic scientist out of the San Francisco crime lab. Decades earlier, he'd become integral to solving one of Mason's more challenging cases—the homicide of a boy barely thirteen. They unearthed justice together. The two had remained chummy ever since.

"She's a great lady," he said, drawing an appreciative smile from Kyly.

"Hello," a deep voice said from the speaker. "How are you enjoying the cabin?"

"Your place is amazing, but I wish we were meeting under better circumstances," Kyly said with soft confidence.

"Zav will go over things with you. Stay together and stay safe until I get there. Keep him out of trouble for me, will ya? I hear you're a few years older than him."

"More than a few," she replied with a grin. "I'm happy to oblige. I'm foolishly hoping there won't be any. Mason, thank you, and I'm sorry if I've created problems for your family."

"The one responsible is dead and buried. If he wasn't, I'd put him there myself. We need to find out who his disciples are. You leave that to me. How do you feel about me calling your father?"

"If it will help, sure. I'll reach out and explain so he expects your call."

They traded numbers and mapped out contact times. Mason gave instructions and reassurances. After all, he was the most equipped to handle the situation. They were relying on his expertise to see them all through it.

"Mason," Kyly said. "You have an honest smile."

Caught off guard, Mason said nothing for long enough that Zavier deemed it necessary to break the awkward silence. "We'll talk to you in the morning. Take care."

"I will. You too. Good night," Mason said, and the line fell silent.

Zavier looked into Kyly's eyes. A grin crossed his face.

"What?" She evaded eye contact, but it was useless to hide what she was thinking or feeling—Mason's picture still rested in her hands.

"I've never seen a woman render him speechless, certainly not on first meeting."

"Oh, you're making something out of nothing. He has a lot on his mind."

"Well if he didn't before, he does now."

22

HOLDING Edmund Spenser's book of poetry in his hand, Micael realized time had taken its title and author. The ink, worn away by the oily rub of human interest, was replaced by fragmented etchings resembling cave drawings. Carefully, he opened the cover. The paper crackled and scraped.

Sonnet 64 began at the top of page 172, it blurred before him, and his mind's eye overlaid a map of the residence. He'd been through the halls, at least in the wing their suites were located. One was missing, the master's. He scanned the room around him and then, staring back at an invisible page, drew silent conclusions.

"You're up early." Catlike, Nick had crossed the distance to the desk and was upon him before he detected intrusion. "How was the old cot?"

Startled, Micael slammed the book's cover shut. "I didn't hear you come in. I must be half asleep. It...it was marvelous."

"What are you reading?" Nick stared down at the book still partially hidden under his hand briefly before the disheveled room diverted his attention.

"Poetry, I guess."

"Better not let Ray catch you. She hates the stuff." Nick spoke while absorbing the mess. "Says it's nothing but the ramblings of dimwitted saps who manipulate linguistics into a contorted mess for their own pathetic amusement. And I'm quoting."

"Well, in that case." Micael shoved the book under a pile of others, propping another novel sideways to conceal even its illegible spine. "She'll never know."

"What the hell happened in here?" Nick waved a hand at the overturned room. "You have a break-in?"

"It's my attempt at jogging my memory."

"Did it work?"

"Not in the slightest. I'm no better off now than I was yesterday."

"You may be worse off when Ray sees this hurricane."

"Yeah," Micael agreed. Taking in, for the first time, the appearance of things. "I really went to town, didn't I?"

"Let's see if we can lessen the impact, shall we? If she comes in, we'll tell her a bookcase fell on you, and you can't remember anything after its crushing impact."

"Don't tell her that! She'll have me riding around in a wheelchair for the rest of my life."

―――――

Silver blades sliced the air, scattering inland tidal waves of ground debris that made it impossible to be heard without shouting. Nick stood back as Ray signaled the helicopter pilot to kill the engine so the setup crew could exit without risk to the funeral supplies. The steel bird's wings slowed.

Nick shielded his eyes but stayed on the tarmac. The crew had two hours before the first infusion of guests arrived. A barrage of commands flew from Ray's lips before the workers had time to regain their land legs. Typical.

He watched as they were corralled down a stone pathway to island transportation in the form of modified golf carts.

Hidden behind dark glasses, Ray barked instructions, tapping her watch for emphasis. She never let up.

"Load up and head to the funeral site," she ordered. "Follow the directions on your maps to the west side of the island. *Do not deviate.*"

They couldn't miss it if they tried, Nick thought.

A tent was erected at the back left of the funeral site. Elegant white arrangements led them strategically down the length of the walkway.

Consumed with duties of his own, he'd left the funeral planning to Ray. A task he now feared they should've shared.

At first glance, the decor appeared strangely inappropriate, creating an atmosphere more suited to an outdoor wedding than a funeral. At the very least, it didn't possess an ounce of funeral lament.

If given a choice, he would've elected for something darker and somber. In his opinion, Ray had gone overboard in an effort to purify the appalling circumstances of Dr. V's so-called laying to rest.

He sought solace in the black chairs, podium, and runners, but they only offered a modest reprieve.

Ray harbored none of the expected grief-ridden characteristics of the bereaved. He hoped she was saving up for the right moment. If the guests saw her like this, adrenalized by funeral arrangements, surely they'd find her attitude absurdly out of place.

Realizing his hands were tied, he headed back to the house to check on MJ. He'd slept through breakfast and lunch. Nick decided to let him wake on his own. He knew he'd need his strength to get through the service, which would be long and uncomfortable at best.

Hearing motion beyond MJ's bedroom door, Nick tapped twice, then entered slowly.

"You awake, buddy?" Nick leaned against the door casing.

"Yeah, come on in. How long did I sleep for?"

"Four hours. It's good. It's gonna be a tough day."

"How long until guests arrive?"

"A couple hours." Nick sunk into a chair by the door, shouting into the walk-in closet MJ riffled around in.

Joining him in the sitting area, showered and back in his blue jeans and a clean light sweater, Micael asked how long he had.

"Don't worry about getting ready for a while yet," Nick explained. "After they arrive, Ray has them touring parts of the island and sitting through a life history before we come on the scene. We'll have plenty of time for reflection after they leave."

"In that case, can I venture to the kitchen, or is it being commandeered by chefs?"

"No, no one's allowed in the house. They're all working out of tents at the site."

They walked together to the kitchen. Sunlight streamed in soft thick, beams from the back windows, casting a warm glow Nick hadn't noticed before. He was glad Ray wouldn't be around to disrupt the atmosphere with her intensity.

MJ's appetite couldn't be quenched. And, with a positive prognosis, Nick encouraged him to eat heartily.

Out in the sun moments later, Micael closed his eyes and rested in the lounger.

"How do you cope with the isolation?" he asked, eyes still shut.

"Pardon?"

"I asked how you cope with the isolation. A guy like you trapped on this island."

"I'm not trapped. I can leave anytime I want."

"Really?"

"Yeah. I mean, it doesn't have the action of Miami or LA but...what do you mean, a guy like me?"

"You love the pulse of life," Micael said matter-of-factly.

"How do you know what I love?"

"Come on, Nick, the car. Admit it, you have to miss the freedom. The anonymity of a crowded city."

Nick wasn't sure how MJ could read him so well, but he couldn't deny he was right. After a few weeks, Nick *did* feel trapped, even if he wasn't. The island didn't give him a sense of calm or tranquility. Just the opposite, it made him feel dead inside. Like his life was devoid of meaning. The thought ate at him.

"I fly out periodically, but right now, Ray needs me, so do you."

"What about your needs?"

"What about them? They're not exactly a priority."

"They should be." MJ's eyes remained closed. "If you could do anything, be anything, what would it be?"

"I stopped daydreaming when I was a kid." Nick shrugged the question off.

"Anything. Come on, it can't be that difficult to imagine," Micael persisted.

"Okay, a cop. I wouldn't mind being on the inside of the law." He answered honestly without thinking of the possible implications of his admission, and he didn't know why. Micael sat up, eyes wide open, facing him head on. Nick had never been so intensely aware of the unique kaleidoscope of color in those eyes.

"So what are you doing wasting your life here?"

"I told you. You and Ray need me. I couldn't become a cop now."

"Why not?" Micael persisted.

Nick paused, contemplating his phrasing, then said, "Too many infractions."

"What if God himself could guarantee you a second chance at life? Would you dedicate it to law enforcement?"

"Sure." Nick flashed a cagey grin.

"You're nonchalant because you see the prospect as improbable."

"Impossible, MJ, not improbable."

"What if you're wrong?" Micael leaned forward and placed his hand on Nick's arm for emphasis. "You choose in every moment who you are, and who you are is transformed in every moment by what you choose. Chose differently."

Micael climbed out of the lounger and walked the expanse of the deck to disappear inside the house before Nick moved.

Something happened.

He wasn't sure what. He couldn't escape the film footage reeling in his mind of all his past choices and where they led. He glimpsed where he would wind up if he remained on his current corrupt path.

Every detrimental situation played out in his head, filling him with a bottomless dread—though, strangely, not for the repercussions he'd face, but for the life he'd wasted.

Then Ray walked up. Damned again. He held his stare at ocean level, refusing to meet her raven eyes.

"You daydreaming?" Her tone was sarcastic.

"Interesting choice of words," he said under his breath.

"What?"

"Nothing. Everything going according to plan?"

"It's a competition for most incompetent. Aside from that, everything's lovely."

"Quite possibly too lovely." Nick didn't hold back his criticism. "Last I checked, it'd provide the perfect backdrop for a Hollywood wedding."

"It's going to be an elegant place of remembrance when I'm through with it. I don't need your opinion."

He baited her already morose mood. Falling silent, he let her have the last word in an effort to end the banter. She stormed away. His eyes followed a perfect silhouette, perfect but empty like the coffin she'd bury.

Willing to see the truth, the question remained. Was he shrewd enough to pull a sliver of clean conscience from the soiled trash heap that had become his life or was he destined to be buried by the grime? The funeral gained new meaning.

———

Ray became an absolute picture of grief at the podium.

Standing, hair tied back by a black satin ribbon, conservative suit revealing nothing but sorrow, and face devoid of make-up discretely shaded by a black veil.

Sacrilegious.

The transformation.

She glided from fierce to fragile with such ease, it was unnerving. Whether Nick's emotions were hidden or contained , Nick was always Nick.

Not Ray. She became something, someone else.

Weakened by sadness. So much so in fact, two men in attendance rushed to help her to the microphone and offered to stay with her. She declined appreciatively. A wave of acid edged up Nick's throat. He swallowed it down.

Even her voice, normally stricken with control and expectation, converted to a soft, shallow echo of sympathy and kindness. He'd never heard this version before. Then again, who had?

She began the eulogy. Those in attendance were quickly moved to tears. If he didn't know the truth, perhaps he too would weep. The icing on the cake, the hint of her, was revealed last. He shifted in his chair as MJ glanced at him with questioning electric eyes as she began.

"A Litany in Time of Plague
by

Thomas Nashe
1567 - 1601"

"Please refer to your program to follow along," she offered. "This was one of Micael's favorite pieces, appropriate that I read it, as he requested, on this day. It holds a truth he came to accept, such a brilliant mind." Her voice quieted. "Loved his mind."

> "Adieu, farewell, earth's bliss;
> This world uncertain is;
> Fond are life's lustful joys;
> Death proves them all but toys;
> None from his darts can fly;
> I am sick, I must die.
> **Lord, have mercy on us! . . .**
>
> . . . Haste, therefore, each degree,
> To welcome destiny;
> Heaven is our heritage,
> Earth's but a player's stage;
> Mount we unto the sky.
> I am sick, I must die.
> **Lord, have mercy on us."**

She brought the house down, electing sobs and standing ovations. From two rows behind, women whispered over the burden Ray handled with such grace.

"How awful to be forced to read something so morbid. Didn't he consider her feelings?" they chastised.

Nick was a ticking bomb, seconds from detonation. And, by the expression on MJ's face, his instability showed.

Ray thanked those in attendance for their support and dedication to such an admirable human being. She instructed them to make their way to the tent at their leisure and then left the stage.

MJ's eyes hadn't left him. He said nothing but rose with the other guests, leaving Nick, his inner fury, and the empty casket behind.

———

Avoiding prolonged conversations, Micael walked on the far edge of the path. Occasionally, Dr. V's friends offering condolences slowed him. Most were brief and professional in their delivery—most, but not all.

The crowd thinned when Micael hit the halfway mark to the dining tent. Still recovering, he plodded behind the others. Despite their sorrow, the mourners hadn't eaten. And even the sadness of death couldn't dampen the alluring aromas wafting from the dining area. A plump lady issued her regrets. After her, he was alone, save one aged man. He walked at a snail's pace. Curious, he turned to face the lagging stranger.

"Did you know my father?" Micael asked.

"Yes, very well," the stranger said in a deep, surprisingly strong voice.

"Did you work together?"

"No, not really."

"But you're in a related field?" Micael assumed.

"You could say that, yes."

The mysterious man flanked Micael and appeared in far better shape than his slow steps reflected.

"Should I know you?" Micael sensed it was a necessary question.

"No, but I know you." The man glanced around them to ensure they were alone on the path. "And you *need* to know me. Why didn't you speak at the service?"

"I couldn't have added anything."

"A lifetime of memories and nothing to say?"

His words were leading.

"How do you know me?" Micael whispered, veering onto a side pathway away from their original destination.

"I knew you...even before you were born."

"You're a doctor?"

"No. A relative," he stated.

"Micael Valeric had no living relatives aside from us," Micael said.

"That's correct, but you do. Son, I don't know what you've been told about your past. Whatever it is, it's a lie. We don't have much time before someone comes looking for you. And, if they find out who I *am*, I won't be given a second chance to explain. And you need to hear this. I've come on behalf of your birth family to bring you home. I'm your uncle. Name is Mason. The man in that coffin isn't your father. And if I don't get you off this island, you may never see your real parents."

Honesty and desperation brightened the man's face. Micael sympathized with his uncomfortable urgency. He knew Ray and Nick were withholding information. He'd known the truth the moment he woke. With no escape, he'd waited silently.

"If we try to leave now, we won't make it off the island," Micael said. "We have to wait until the fireworks display."

"Fireworks, what kind of a lunatic has fireworks at a funeral?" Mason asked. "Don't answer that."

"Cameras and monitoring equipment will be disabled. There'll be a ten-to-fifteen-minute window to get out. Find me. And you're right; my father isn't in the coffin. No one is."

Mason reeled in the realization Micael—damn that, his name was Christian—Chris knew the truth, at least part of it. He'd shouldered the news without the slightest hesitation. The kid had unearthed evidence of his own. No one in the coffin? He knew a lot more than expected. Whatever it was, he wanted off the island.

All Mason had to do now was hold out until the fireworks display, escape suspicion, slip away undetected with Chris, and make it back across a couple thousand miles of ocean alive. Should be easy enough.

"Damn near impossible," he said, regrettably out loud.

"What's that?" a woman asked from behind him.

"I'm sorry?" Mason forced bewildered into his voice.

"What's damned near impossible?"

Miraculous, she hadn't been seconds faster and seen them together.

"To make it to retirement alive," he lied. "I've buried three friends in this last year. I guess it's a bit disconcerting."

"Death always is." Ray took his arm. There was a truth in her tone.

Without her veil, she was breathtaking. Her eyes were an impossibly deep forest green, or was that a reflection? Upon closer inspection they appeared black, quite fascinating. She caught him staring into those dark pools and blinked.

The color shifted off, revealing a shard of solid black.

Colored contacts? Why?

"Walk with me," she insisted. "I've just the thing for you."

"And what's that?" Mason mustered his acting abilities to appear grief-stricken.

"Comfort food," she replied with an easy smile.

If she suspected anything, she hid it. Mason let her escort him to the dining tent, thanked her for her compassion, and grabbed a plate at the buffet. Three hours to go. He scanned the gourmet assortment, a fool's banquet. He was first in line.

23

FRACTURED, and frail in the wake of cruel truth, Brook Cromwell's resolve crumbled. The dark seed of regret became a wrecking ball, swinging with impunity at the heart of her world, demolishing hope with each direct hit. Helplessly, she watched her family disband.

Despite Mason's reassurances, Brook knew the odds were stacked against them. Danger accompanied every avenue back to her son. Who were they against the enemy? She didn't even know who their enemy was, exactly. Thirty years ago, they trusted someone because of his position, accomplishments, and history. That choice now threatened to decimate everything good they fought to build after surviving a tragedy. They did nothing to deserve this mountain of chaos bearing down on them, but it would crush, nonetheless.

This evil, she feared, couldn't be outrun, outsmarted, or outmaneuvered.

Mason left for the airport before dawn. His footsteps had echoed down the hall. She didn't see him off. What she'd asked of him was too great a burden. The task had taken on a life of its own—one that may cost him his.

He'd said he'd handle things. She didn't doubt he would, but alone?

Hours inched by. Night fell, and Brook lay in bed until the rhythmic cadence of her husband's breathing assured her he slept. Sliding out from under the covers, she drifted down the dark hallway, a soundless apparition.

She dressed without light, stealing clothes off the laundry pile. She pulled out of the driveway in Zavier's car, bringing nothing save keys and a pocketed cell phone.

The dashboard clock said quarter to three when she pulled up to a dark estate house. A dim light shone inside.

No rest for the wicked, she thought as she climbed to the front landing and pounded her fist against the heavy wooden door. Lights came on inside, and soon they stood face to face.

"Hello, Warrick." Brooke hadn't the capacity for contrived sincerity. "I need you to call in favors for Mason and I. You owe us that much."

Still a towering figure in his sixties, the man held the door aside and allowed Brooke entry to his lair. A stately home to newcomers, but as cold as an underground cavern to her.

"Haven't heard from you. You changed your number. You could've called first."

Brooke stood inches inside the door. "You still have your connections?"

"I know it can never be forgotten, but we all need to move on—"

"Connections?" Time hadn't changed the interior. It'd been impeccably maintained. He'd settle for nothing less. None of his commendations or metals could be seen from the entry.

"It's been over twenty years—" He backed up, welcoming her into the parlor.

She leaned against the staircase banister, announcing no wish to get cozy. "Yesterday for me. Are you going to help me or not?"

"You could ask me for anything. You know that." He came closer, giving up on any chance of meaningful conversation that required seats.

"Anything but what I needed from you."

"I wish you'd let it go." The tone of his plea was sincere, but the timing was too late.

"Let her go." Brooke's voice rang back, laced with a rage spared for only him.

"Pardon?" He watched her more than heard her.

Brooke leaned forward, anger drawing her to him. "Let *her* go...the way you did after you failed her and your son. After your tyranny drove her into an early grave."

"I did everything possible to save her. I quit the military, hired the best care, and was there—"

"Too late." Brooke reached for the door.

He blocked her exit. "What kind of trouble has Mason got himself into?"

"Wrong again. It's me who screwed up and him sacrificing. Bet you never saw that coming, did you?"

She pushed past him. He stood aside but slowed her with a hand on her shoulder.

"Whatever you need. I'll do it."

"Now you will." She hated that his physical contact evoked memories of childhood comfort.

"I would've then too. I just didn't—" He tried.

"No. You didn't." She wouldn't.

"I will."

Pausing beyond the threshold, she said, "Good."

He shadowed her, blocking out the light. Fitting metaphor. She resented the familiar scent of him, the way his soft musk suggested reliance and protection. She'd enjoyed none of it for so long. Worse still was the knowledge that others had, those that came after, that didn't know him like his children did.

"You remember my name?" he asked. His eyes locked on hers.

"Yeah. I remember."

"It'd be nice to hear it." He didn't shrink back or waver.

Brook stood silent, unwilling to grant his request. "I'd say not to expect forgiveness in this lifetime, but then I'd be like you."

"I wasn't always cold. Life made me this way. Tainted. Jaded. The aftermath of bearing witness to death and injustice." He paused. An incurable sorrow deepened the blue of his eyes. "Don't think it can happen to you? You hate who I was. I'm asking you to find out who I am. I'm your father."

She walked away a thousand times before without looking back. This time was different. If she lost Christian again, Mason, Curt, or one of the kids, who would she become? New perspective held the terrifying possibility that she could become him.

"I'll call you with the details," she said, a hesitation held her for a brief second.

"I'll be waiting." He would.

It wasn't reconciliation, a few strides across a smoldering crater of pain.

Not nearly far enough.

She descended the stairs with solid steps, entered the car gracefully, pulled away with precision, turned the corner down an unfamiliar block, pulled over in the dark space between streetlamps, and sobbed.

24

PICTURES LIE. These ones did.

Keepers of a thousand words, all staged, none accurate. Nick knew because he'd taken them. They offered nothing more or less than partial truths in monochrome color.

Strategically placed throughout the memorial, they surrounded funeral guests with the doctor's smiles and laughter. The decorations were white, but this personal touch overshadowed them, creating the perfect environment for reflection.

People lingered at the images—everyone except the doctor's son.

Collapsed in a chair at the front table reserved for immediate family, MJ ordered iced tea from a waiter with his back to the crowd. His behavior could've been viewed as antisocial. Under the circumstances, it was accepted with sympathy.

Nick watched his expression from across the room.

Worn from overturning his room last night in a reported effort to jog his memory, he didn't possess the energy to hover over snapshots of the past. He didn't glance from his seated position at the images closest to him.

Nick slid in from the sidelines commandeering the seat to MJ's right, nearest an exit. "Bringing back any memories?"

"Sorry?" MJ fidgeted with something between his fingers. Quick to shelter it, Nick couldn't catch what it was.

"Thought maybe the photos would jar some memories...but then, you aren't looking."

"I'm avoiding them. Averting a meltdown in front of all these strangers. I'll look when they're gone."

Nick shifted in his seat, directing his attention to a surgeon at the microphone spewing the late doctor's operating room heroics with a fervor that screamed he'd taken ownership of the achievements and was using this forum to advertise. Little did he know he'd missed the grand finale.

"It's a daunting effort," MJ said. "You're not impressed."

"I'm not. I hate this crap. He's not here to appreciate any of this. What's the point?"

"Then, why?"

"It's expected. For all of them." Nick leaned back and surveyed the crowd. All were focused on the podium. When he turned back, he realized MJ's eyes hadn't left him.

"I hope they appreciate your efforts," MJ said.

The screen collection spliced from a forty-year-old film reel. The computer-enhanced imagery, eventually ended, as did the tributes. A small orchestral melody announced the break for coffee and conversation, serving as a window to wait out ideal evening conditions to begin the final fireworks and send off.

"I'm sure he's smilin' down on us," MJ said.

"Don't be so certain."

"I don't know how anyone could ask for more."

"I do." Nick stood, having spotted Ray on approach. "He could still be breathing."

Summoning a waitress for something stronger than coffee, Nick watched Ray collapse into the chair he'd vacated. She rested her head in her hands.

Her emotion, for all the wrong reasons, was real.

MJ placed his hand across the back of her slender neck.

She was motionless beneath it. They remained frozen in space. Guests passed their table, dessert plates in hand, nodding quaintly, considerate not to interrupt a fragile family moment.

Fooled, all of them, Nick thought.

Now, he was impressed.

Nick could scarcely remember the truth. And, reading Ray's body language, she'd rejected it completely. Surrounded by mourners, on a stage of insincerity, he feared it irretrievable.

———

Mason watched catering staff summon the female conductor of the event away from Chris. She left reluctantly, smiling at his nephew with a glint in her eyes. Her counterpart, Nick, was preoccupied across the room, chatting up an attractive cardiac specialist.

Ray exited the tent. Chris wandered to the coffee station and signaled with a nod. Setting down his coffee cup, Mason collected his jacket and approached Nick, knowing the pretty woman made a perfect distraction.

"I'm sorry to interrupt," Mason said. "I wanted to thank you and your family for allowing me the opportunity to pay my respects and share in such a beautiful tribute to a man I deeply admired."

He lied. Oh, did he lie.

"I have responsibilities back home I must tend to. I informed your sister I'd have to leave early. So sorry I'll miss the fireworks. I'm certain they'll be memorable."

"Oh, you're the one with the eight o'clock pick-up on the helipad," Nick confirmed.

"Yes, that's correct."

"You'll need a ride back up. Tell the cart attendant your name. He'll give you a lift to the pad. Thanks for coming."

Nick shook Mason's hand. Mason was careful to weaken his grip, though he would've thoroughly enjoyed a crushing clench. Nick dismissed him, returning his attention to the young woman. Mason slipped out of the tent and down to the golf cart holding area.

Before the driver pulled away, Chris appeared, halting him with a wave.

"Mr. Valeric?"

"Can you give me a lift back to the house while you're at it?" Chris requested nonchalantly.

"Certainly, sir," the attendant obliged. "Hop on."

Sitting alone at the back of the cart instead of sharing the middle passenger bench with Mason, Chris settled in and instructed the driver to make haste.

"We don't want to delay the doctor here," he insisted.

Mason made small talk with the driver, averting suspicion of a conspiracy between him and Chris.

Ray would put the pieces together, but Mason intended to scramble them first.

Chris remained silent until they reached the landing pad. There, he instructed the driver he'd see their guest off then return the short distance to the house on foot.

"Fresh air will be good for me," he said. "Do me a favor, though, won't you? Find Ray when you return to the site. Tell her I'll be soaking in the Jacuzzi if she wants to join me after the guests have left."

A small diversion with a suggestive nature capable of throwing off her suspicious intuition long enough to buy them a head start.

She *would* come after them.

And she'd keep coming until someone ended up dead. Of this, Mason had no doubt. He'd read it in her artificial eyes.

Darkness stole daylight quickly on the island. Like a grand hand of nature, it slipped under the sun, blocking its rays in silent shadow. Chris could almost see it creeping off the ocean. In the center of the dying light, the nighthawk approached, on schedule.

Not your typical touring helicopter. Chris was grateful no one could monitor its approach from the funeral site.

Lowering quickly for retrieval and rising back into the cover of the night's sky, the bird of prey collected her escapees and flew off with her belly low against the ocean. The pilot nodded at Mason, then said, "Turbulence ahead."

Chris sat closest to the open doorway, deep in thought, eyes locked on the sea. Spray from colliding waves shot up like angry, pallid spirits driven from watery graves. Their hands reached for him.

Chopper blades sliced the air in relentless rotation. Despite the thunderous rhythm overhead, an uncanny silence rested between the men onboard. Like the weight of the ocean, it was dense enough to drown.

Mason, equipped with a headset, nodded to the pilot then removed the earpiece to speak off microphone.

"Chris, you see the thunderheads out there?" he shouted beneath the chopper noise. "We're in for a hell of a storm. So much for an easy exit."

Smiling, he added, "Get on your life jacket, just in case."

"That's reassuring," Chris shouted back, taking the vest from Mason.

"Trahern says we might arrive under the wire before the worst of it hits. It's good for us. Might slow them down if it doesn't stop them altogether until the storm clears."

"It won't stop her," Chris said, turning his attention to buckling his vest. "Nothing will."

The kid fell asleep two hours from the coast. Turbulence or not, he was still exhausted. Anticipating what lay ahead, Mason let him sleep, watching over him, tracing their heritage in the contours of his face.

Trahern was an experienced combat pilot and a good friend. Mason had collected on every favor and infringed on every connection he had. It was worth it. Chris was worth it. Mason didn't doubt he was blood. Confirmed in the way he spoke, looked, and moved, even in his level-headed approach to escape.

Having switched places with Chris earlier, Mason dangled a foot outside the door. The chopper's ground searchlights refracted off the glimmer of silvery waves, northern lights underfoot.

Beyond lowering cloud cover rolling in from far out at sea, the night was crystalline.

Trahern gave Mason a small measure of relief, confirming the air remained clear of predators. Their rendezvous point on the Northern California coastline possessed some of the strongest rip currents known to man, capable of tearing even a highly experienced swimmer off the shoreline. Its wave activity could wear down an athlete, but hypothermia would be the first to kill. Knowing this, the most Mason hoped for was a land battle.

He stared at his nephew stirring back to life wondering what he'd endured in the years he'd been away. In their brief encounter, he'd seemed a stable man. But how?

A half hour from their destination, Trahern picked up radio traffic. A military frequency—they were being hunted. Trahern called in using their planned cover story and offered assistance in the search. The military asked if he'd seen a Bell 222 helicopter in the area.

"Negative. I'm running the northern coastline two hours out, and it's been clear sailing boys. Hope you find your bird. Iron Cap out."

It wasn't much, but every misdirection counted.

Mason regretted putting his friend in danger, but Iron Cap—a handle he earned as the only survivor of a combat crash—didn't require a whole lot of protection. Standing six foot four, as smart as he was solid, and the poster boy for the expression *built like a brick shit house*, he didn't scare easily, and he'd been paid handsomely for the risk.

Drizzle became droplets, which soon band together into cascading sheets through the open door. Cool air spun off the ocean and whipped through the cargo hold. The machine rammed hard against the chop.

"Landing's gonna be a treat," Mason said.

Christian, more awake and aware than he cared to be, nodded and held on.

If violent crashing waves weren't enough, the closer they came to the coast, the more evident it became. This was a shore without sand. In its place, a thick band of jagged rocks stretched as far as the eye could see.

"You sure know how to pick 'em," Chris said.

Mason grinned but didn't return the banter. It was something he would've said.

Instead of heading inland to open pastures and well-lit flat terrain, the helicopter veered right and ran the coast until it met with a dark industrial storage area.

"This it?" the pilot asked.

"Yep, drop us down gently," Mason joked.

"Drop us down? Where?" Chris asked. "This is the middle of nowhere."

"Exactly."

Without finesse, the pilot sunk low above a rooftop, waited barely long enough for Chris and Mason to jump to the unforgiving steel sheathing, and disappeared into blackness.

Their haphazard descent marked a rude awakening to life on the run. On Chris' landing, his right knee sustained the bulk of the impact, making it difficult to regain his balance on the slick metal, let alone traverse the distance needed to locate the truck Mason had waiting for them.

Mason caught an ill-fitting corner section of a rough patch job, and protruding screw heads tore a one-inch gash in his left palm. The damage wasn't life threatening, but a blood trail would be. He scanned the area for shelter from the deluge where they could patch up.

Shouldering Chris down a short staircase to a lower roof level where a door appeared, Mason prayed the damn thing wasn't bolted shut. As night followed day, it was.

A standard lock, thank God, no dead bolt. It broke open without too much coaxing. Inside, a dry alloy cave. The strong metallic stench of iron shavings filled their nostrils. The blackness of the space made the dark night outside appear well-lit.

Mason searched for a wall and leaned Chris' back against it, freeing his good hand to wrestle off his gear and locate the flashlights. He was grateful they hadn't ventured another step beyond the entrance. The beam of light confirmed they were suspended on an entry platform to an overhead walkway a good thirty feet above the ground. Its once secure side rails were eroded by the hands of time.

In the flashlight's glare, a shadow and light game of snakes and ladders came to life. Criss-crossing walkways with parallel tracks for once-existent heavy machinery intertwined. Waves of massive gray tarps covered expensive, abandoned cranes. The scattered skeletons of an iron shop graveyard.

The exit stood opposite them and, before it, what appeared to be an office area. Mason hoped for a stash of medical kits. If they could safely make it across, he'd dip into the remaining inventory.

"You see the office at the other side?" Mason asked.

"You're not serious?" Chris wavered, unable to put pressure on his wounded leg.

"I am. Think of it this way, you're out of the storm."

It didn't take an expert in metallurgy to ascertain the cross section leading to the other side wasn't structurally sound. Overlapping cobwebs bridged the railings, making short pale café doors meant to remain closed. Flashlight beams were captured and expelled in a haunting glow in all directions by these ghostly barriers. Many constructors of the elaborate sticky lattice, black and dangerous, scattered back into dark corners.

"The ground moved," Chris stated dryly, staring at the shaky walkway before him.

"No, our welcoming committee," Mason said. "Let's get this over with."

"Poor choice of words."

The chemical and gasoline-stained concrete below filled the air with an incense of stale industrial mold. Grabbing the metal handrail with his uninjured hand, Mason wrapped his left arm around Chris to alleviate the weight on Chris' bad knee. Together, they began the slow rickety climb across the tarnished catwalk.

Chris' flashlight scanned for open fissures in the floorboards. Ailing beams, pressed to support the weight of one man, appeared incapable of sustaining the excess of both their heavy frames. One crack would plunge them to a cold death in this desolate building, leaving them undiscovered until all but skeletons and mystery remained.

Aged steel moaned and screeched beneath their weight, reminding them with every step how precarious their crossing was. Chris' flashlight beam, tossed out past the guardrails by their awkward momentum, revealed nothing but long cold drops on either side.

"How could anyone feel safe dangling up here?" Chris gaped at the abyss.

"It's a built-in incentive," Mason said, distracted by a spider claiming a free ride on the edge of his boot. "You slack off, you walk the plank."

Chris wore an expression of mortification.

"I'm kidding." He tossed the creature off.

Halfway across, the bridge let out a long slow creak, paralyzing both men as they waited for its fall out. After a few seconds, when the metal mesh did not give way, they started again past the waning center point to the last leg of their trek.

The boxed-in area drew nearer. Light confirmed it was a foreman's office with windows facing the main shop below, one doorway to the walkway, and another emergency exit leading outside.

A sharp crack resounded. Mason's footing became unstable. The board below his right foot, the one sustaining both his and Chris' weight, broke free. He would've grabbed Chris, thrown him the remaining distance, and gladly fought to cling to life alone. He never had the chance. Before the echo stalled, Chris pushed him away with a force that landed Mason at the threshold five feet out of rescue distance. Clenching the weak railing with both hands, Chris' chance of survival rested on his grip and a bad leg.

"Stay back," Chris ordered, his voice raw with determination.

Having lost his flashlight, Mason searched the dark for rope, cord, or any lifeline. He turned his back and heard the railing collapse. When he spun around, Chris slammed into him. He grabbed the kid with both hands and hurled him into the office.

"Jesus," Mason said, his body stretched across the floor. "I thought you—"

"Not yet," Chris said, clutching his injured knee.

Mason composed himself and tried the light switch. Nothing. Power had likely been cut off years earlier. He located a battery-operated lamp still in working condition. With its light, he searched the room until he found an emergency kit. Despite a heavy film of soot and dust on its exterior, its contents were clean and fully stocked.

He gave Chris ibuprofen for swelling, activated a cold pack, applied it to his knee, wrapped it, and then cleaned and dressed his own cut. After removing a few supplies, he returned the kit to a closet.

Peering out the emergency exit, he confirmed the long jaunt to the truck was fraught with obstacles. There was no let-up in the pouring rain, and visibility was minimal at best.

Chris pulled bottled water from his pack and handed one to Mason. He grabbed it with his left hand. Bloodstains on the bottle revealed his bandaging hadn't gone well.

"Let me have a look at that," Chris insisted. "Trust me, you can't get what I've got from casual contact."

Feeling foolish, Mason let Chris tend to the wound. He removed the bandage and cleaned it with water from his bottle. Once dry, he used sterile glue to secure the wound. When Mason saw the gash, it appeared strangely less atrocious than it previously had.

"Man, I must be getting old," he muttered. "My eyes are going."

Once wrapped, the pain subsided.

"You must know what you're doing, living with a bunch of doctors for so long," Mason said.

"Yeah, I know what I'm doing. We should get moving." Chris shifted his attention above. He listened for noise overhead.

"There's no way they'd battle hurricane winds and find us here that quickly," Mason exaggerated. "Besides, the storm is strong enough to blow us off the rooftop. We should wait until she loses her momentum."

"I'll take my chances with Mother Nature," Chris said. "She's a far safer bet."

"How's your leg?"

"I'm fine," Chris replied. "Really."

"Okay. You want to get out of here so bad...after you, Doc."

25

EXHALATIONS EXPELLED from Mason's lungs became fading shallow white mist in the already dense fog outside the attic entrance. Instead of appearing as refuge from the relentless icy thrashing of the wind swept night, the eerie shelter seemed only a darker cavern of hell.

Exhausted from dodging Ray's bullets and traversing rooftops, Mason spoke between gasping breaths in a drained whisper.

"She's bright...and damn determined to ruin my vacation," he said, more to the air than to Chris. Looking back, the rooftops were an endless tide of oily steel waves.

"She's beyond intelligent," Chris corrected, panting between words. "A genius." His long hair, drenched and matted back, revealed a roadmap of scars.

Breaching the threshold, Mason's pen light revealed a thick maze of crates and worn cardboard boxes. Cobwebs quivered in the faint beam as tremors from his footsteps sent eight-legged residents scattering to concealed corners beyond the wisp of wind he brought with him.

Awkwardly contorting his large frame beneath the steeply pitched metal roof, Mason chastised, "I thought you, of all people, wouldn't be a fan or did you miss the sound of bullets grazing your head!"

The stark reality of the situation made him irritable.

"I'm not a fan. I'm the enemy." Chris hunched over to maintain his level of gravity, coming through the attic window.

The space emitted a now familiar foul metallic scent.

"It's how she was designed," Chris said. "She's more than a raving lunatic who wants me dead. She has purpose."

"I really don't want to hear this, do I?" Mason spoke through a wet sleeve screening his mouth in an effort to avoid inhaling the musty plumes of dust escaping their tomb-like hideaway. He refused to give the kid's information validity by facing him. The sense Chris wasn't who his sister believed him to be, and the possibility he was more, left Mason torn.

Chris kept one hand on the rafters overhead, steadying his crawl and reminding him to crouch low enough not to cold cock himself on looming overhead beams. Every movement brought to life ghostly shadows from the heavy layer of dust spawned by years of desertion.

"You might as well lay it on me while I'm too damn tired to leave you stranded here," Mason said. "I'm fairly certain I'll be resentful if I live long enough to get my strength back."

Mason collapsed onto one of the sturdier boxes. He doubted Chris' secrets were any more alarming than the countless confessions he'd endured. "Explain designed."

Chris made his way to a space directly across from him. He was forced to arch forward to fit beneath the slanted rafters. Mason studied him while he was preoccupied with his footing.

"When Micael first came to this country from Italy, a friend of his had connections in Northern California and told him about a terrific university near here," Chris began. "It had gained international acclaim. Not for its medical program but for one doctor's independent advancement in human DNA mapping. Doctor Lawrence Locke was making history. He became renowned and sought after by many in the field. Micael *fell* into making his acquaintance."

Coughing, Chris shifted on the dirty crate.

"How did he fall into Locke?" Mason peered into the rain, focusing on the information and ignoring the reverberating thumping of his own driven heartbeat. It had yet to resume anything remotely close to a natural rhythm.

"Micael tripped in the hallway and landed on Locke," Chris continued, oxygen deprived, breathing labored.

"Couldn't have made a great impression." Mason disregarded the rooftops to face Chris. His image, half consumed by shadow, was eerily angelic.

"Actually, it did. Micael had seen Locke's picture. He recognized him instantly. He apologized. Locke had a great sense of humor. A genuine love of life and people. It made him an outstanding professor... anyway, he forgave Micael, helped him to his feet, and they became life-long friends right there in the hallway."

Chris smiled as if reclaiming the memory propelled back in time forty years. Mason ignored the expression.

"This sounds like a great story, but what does it have to do with Ray being designed?"

Before he finished the thought, it struck him.

"Did he make Ray? Are you telling me she was genetically engineered?"

"It's a long story...short version, yes," Chris said.

"How?" Mason examined the rain-swept night beyond the attic's opening. "I'll let you know if our visitor's back. *This*, I have to hear."

Mason sensed missing pieces of the puzzle dropping into place. His investigative instinct became a deep well waiting for secrets to quench its thirst—despite his digging, days passed produced only a steady trickle. Now, a deluge.

Shifting his weight, causing floorboards to creak and snap beneath him, Chris paused to ensure the sinister sounds of their predator didn't lay masked by his movements.

"Micael acquired an advanced education from more than one university, yet his greatest teacher was one he never had a class with. His parents died in a car crash. Locke became his mentor and father figure. When Locke died off the coast of the military complex he worked on, Micael never forgot the anniversary," Chris' tone depressed with a loss that couldn't be his.

"How did he die?"

"Capsized in a storm, they said, five miles off the dock. Pieces of the wreckage washed ashore. His body was never recovered. Locke left a prime piece of real estate not far from the secret base—the island we just fled—to Micael, but that wasn't all he left. Six months after his death, Micael received a package. Wallpapered in stamps, its route traced a succession of remote destinations around the world, finding him last. It had never been opened."

"Not a good sign. I was a cop long enough to know good things don't always come in small packages. What was inside?"

"Hard to say, he never opened it. On an outer envelope, Locke instructed Micael to stow it away and never expose the contents unless his life was threatened."

"I think we'd best be taking a peek." Mason's voice gained a back-woods accent. The light humor flailed in the wake of a hell of a reality.

Christian continued, "He said it held the genetic link to humanity and his death sentence. Still want to see it?"

"You go ahead, kid. You're full of good news, aren't you?"

Mason slid his crate further into the gloom and away from the hard rain driving in through broken seams in a roof hatch. Glancing around, he realized the attic provided the perfect backdrop for a ghost story. A chill ran down his spine at the irony of it.

"Micael knew Locke's death was no accident," Chris said as rolling thunder replaced an ominous studio sound mix. "He drove his yacht near the last known location, hoping to make sense of things, but couldn't do more than survey the island base from afar. Security patrols were ever watchful. It became nothing more than a memorial ritual until eleven years later."

"Okay, so the military base was this remote island geared for genetic research with security and no visitors allowed," Mason said.

"If you can map human DNA down to the last gene, you can control everything before birth," Chris said. "Design the world's best or worst simply by selectively altering the code. Theoretically create...a manufactured race."

Christian's reply had impact. The eerie tale escalated into one far worse than Mason first suspected. Perhaps there wouldn't be sleep again. He couldn't put his finger on it, but like the cold drizzle above him, something sinister slinked closer.

"Eleven years later?" Mason prompted, deciding it best to hear it all at once, without time to contemplate repercussions.

"Micael wallowed in Italy's finest red wine hovering around the dock area. By this point in his life, he enjoyed being a menace to the bastards responsible for killing his friend. Then, faint lights from above punctured the mist. Soon they came from everywhere, above on the high cliff wall of the island. Then lower, nearing the shoreline. They couldn't see him, masked by fog, but when the beams and sirens intensified, he figured they were getting serious, so he left. Slowly, quietly."

"Were they for Micael, the lights?" Mason asked.

"No, but they were for someone."

"Who?"

"An eleven-year-old girl Micael found battered and bleeding on the back of his yacht fifteen minutes later. She crawled on board without a sound," he paused. "Maybe the sirens drowned out the splash of her entering the water. Perhaps the wine...vice of fools." Chris' voice trailed.

"What girl?" Mason said.

"RAY, Reconnaissance Assassin Y. Three more failed attempts, perhaps they would've given up."

The evil Mason sensed gained new strength. He rubbed his brow, but couldn't lessen the mounting tension between his eyes.

"You're telling me they toyed with twenty-five prototypes...human babies...the alphabet before they were successful?" Mason asked, dreading the answer.

"Yes."

"What happened to the other babies?"

"Mason." Chris stopped, and a depth of unarguable wisdom crafted his next words. "There are things in this world one should not lend the energy of the spoken word to."

"Sweet Jesus."

Shocked and fervently focused on cohesion, Mason shook his head, sending information bites rattling through his brain like loose coins.

"He was as confused then as you are now," Chris said. "And he would be damned if he'd let those murderers get their hands on her again. He sailed back to his island, spent months helping her recover, got the story out of her three months later, and used it and the package to ensure their safety."

"He raised her? Protected her? And now she wants you, his son and the only link to him, dead?" Mason tried earnestly but failed to see the logic.

"It's why she wants me dead. They designed her as a masterpiece. A genius, a weapon and a caged one. Isolated like a lab rat."

An underlying anger in Chris' voice became more apparent with each word.

"Created, abandoned, and feared her. Micael used their failure against them, threatening exposure and her eventual wrath. They struck a deal. He worked for them. Did limited research, and they stayed away."

"Limited research like hell! If it were so limited, you wouldn't exist." Mason wore his disdain for the man who essentially kidnapped his sister's first born like a badge of honor.

"They didn't know about me," Chris said. "I'm a project constructed...much closer to home."

So he *was* a project, and he knew it.

This admission confirmed Mason's theory was accurate. Dr. Valeric needed a test subject. Baby Christian fit the mold, so he acquired him like a guinea pig. What Mason couldn't understand, among many things, was how Chris had found out and why he seemed undaunted by such disturbing knowledge.

"Did you know about this growing up?" Mason asked.

"Not...exactly."

"When did you find out?"

"Not long after, I woke up from my coma."

"Coma. You were in a coma?"

"Apparently, for quite a long time. They told me I walked off a cliff after drowning my sorrows in a magnum of red wine—family trait."

"How long is quite long?"

"Well, how old am I?" Chris' tone gained a lighthearted air.

"Years. Are you saying you've been comatose for years?"

"In a manner of speaking." Chris wiped away a cobweb hanging beside him from the underside of the rafters, mindfully transporting its designer to the next available beam.

"What *exactly* does that mean?" Mason relented.

"I haven't really been conscious for the last thirty years or so. Like most people on this planet, I've been alive without consciously living."

Mason's skeptical expression reflected back at him in the dark murk of the attic window.

The kid's insane. One bump on the head and the elevator's permanently stuck between floors. He didn't trust him. Though he realized more with every passing moment, the kid had turned against everything he knew to place his life in Mason's hands. Foolish to be second-guessing his honesty after all he risked, yet...

"Mason, there is a great deal more you'll have to understand before this is over. This isn't the best time to delve into my past. Let's focus on Ray, Micael, and Doctor Locke's research."

Mason rubbed his temples to ease the throbbing in his head.

"She compared you to Locke tonight. No offense, but I don't think it was a compliment." Mason could still see the rage in Ray's eyes on the rooftop and hear the sound of her bullets ricocheting by them.

"That's his estranged son, Locke Junior. He lacks everything sacred his father stood for. Consumed by money and power, he has no concern for humanity."

"I'm no genius, so help me out here. Why does she want you dead?"

"Three reasons: I know her weaknesses and all the secrets, I lied to her about my memory, waiting for an opportunity to escape, and she's a woman scorned. Capable of amazing things, she can't cope with rejection. You know, hell hath no greater fury."

"The first two we could've handled, but the last one is going to cause us a significant degree of trouble." Mason rose, with fresh memories of their predator, to check their path in.

"I've dealt with scorned women before, but this one...powerful and lethal."

The weight of truth and the crush of discouragement hit a lancing blow. Whatever he embodied, to his sister, Christian was a son. Mason knew the odds they faced. Chris threatened everyone: dark holds of government, a manufactured killer, and perhaps social stability in general. Society lacked the grace to see Chris as innocent standing at the center of such an unprecedented conspiracy. Even worse, Mason had vowed vindication, a promise that may prove empty in the wake of reality. Instead of one twisted doctor, he set against a secret army who fashioned their weapons from flesh.

"I have to get you out of here, kid. Let's move."

26

AN AVALANCHE of chaos buried the funeral morbidity alive.

Choppers scattered on the heliport vying for flight position, and Nick watched mourners, once handled with kid gloves of formality, discarded off the island like tourists from enemy countries amid a declaration of war.

He preferred a semblance of order to prevent frightening the guests. Ray didn't give a damn about their fragile sensibilities.

Her expression, when she came looking for him, cast a vehemence that couldn't be concealed. An indelible film coated her eyes. She skated beneath it, strangely detached.

She'd shed the colored contacts. Highlighted by the last blast of ill-timed fireworks, her black irises bled, a barren backdrop for the red flecks shimmering down from the sky. Dr. Valeric's final farewell ended with the windows to Ray's soul revealing the dying of one light and the dangerous gleam of another.

"He could've passed out on the grounds. Fatigue. The trauma of all this might have gotten to him." Nick rationalized, He didn't know why.

"Nick, bullshit is a pathetic waste of your potential!"

He gave up.

They returned to the house, leaving the remaining guests in the hands of hired help. Ray wanted them airborne before she geared up to find MJ. She used the impending storm as a cover for the urgency. Pilots were ordered to follow a flight plan detoured to avoid intercepting hers.

In the office, she brought the security system back online and linked into military satellite surveillance scouring for the mysterious doctor's helicopter. His pilot evaded tracking by flying beneath the radar. Evasive maneuvers.

There were more ways than one to find him, and Nick expected she'd use everything in her arsenal.

Moments later, Ray left through the back exit, dressed and loaded for combat, to board their Black Hawk. She signaled for take-off with Nick racing across the tarmac behind her and jumped aboard, never closing its door.

"They'll have monitored all the commotion! They'll know." His voice swept up in the rotor wash. "How do you suppose I explain this?"

"I'll call you from the air when I know something." Pulling a black balaclava over her face, she motioned to the pilot, and then they were airborne. "Hold them off," she yelled.

"Right," Nick breathed as Ray disappeared into the night.

She'd left them exposed and vulnerable. No, she'd created their vulnerability. She created all of this, risking everything for her ambitions.

Percolating for days, his resentment hit a boiling point. His mind wandered through the ruins of his life. Thoughts compounded into a swelling compulsion to scream. Swallowing hard against his anger, he returned to the house and the seemingly unavoidable business of deception.

———

Waves broke, colliding in shards of black and silver, shattering wet fragments at the underbelly of the chopper. The rhythmic swell hypnotized Ray in its cold darkness. A mirror. It reflected the determination inside her.

Her opaque eyes captured the scene through narrow slits in her mask. There was no need to remain concealed across these waters, black in black. Occasionally, she glanced at a handheld guidance system sweeping for the faintest signal, out of range. With each mile, anger mounted. Too much time to ponder how long MJ had known the truth and deceived her.

It never occurred to her that she'd lied to him from the moment he gained consciousness, that her deception, like the dark ocean below her, ran leagues deeper than his ever could.

She wanted him with her in every way. A dying dream she'd do anything to revive. And she was the master of revival.

The more scenarios she played out, the more MJ being taken against his will became improbable. She hated the doctor or whoever the hell he really was. He would pay for interfering.

When she brought MJ back to the island, even wounded, she could restore things. His memory would be forfeited for their future. They'd build new memories.

Contorted images of surgery whirled across the black screen of her mind.

She would find him. No place existed where he could stay hidden. They'd be together eventually, but time corroded. She'd waited through Micael Senior's illness, through the deterioration, pain, and inevitability. It aged her internally, throwing her into a perpetual state of inescapable stress. It gnawed at her. She resented the lost days. She'd find a way to take them back.

Her conscience was clear but cold.

The impostor at the funeral could come from one of two obvious sources—either sent by the government to gain control by ransoming MJ, or he knew his true origins. Either way, someone stood to gain from his capture. It wasn't practical to assume MJ would willingly cooperate with the government. He'd shown resistance to her. But wasn't ignorant enough to believe the government trustworthy.

This left an outsider.

Anyone close to the island projects wouldn't risk coming up against Nick or her. Even the military kept at bay, aware of the weapons held against them. The only rational explanation pointed to someone naive enough to think they could get away with this.

Emotional attachment made people stupid.

Blood was thicker than water; Ray was comfortable swimming in both.

Her spies tracked the birth family before the newspaper announcement hit the press. Phones were tapped, information compiled, and sources constantly fed her ongoing research. All their residences, even the cabin hideaway, were known to her long before the game began. This family of fools never stood a chance. Yet, here she was, traversing an ocean because of them.

Their abilities weren't underestimated, their fortitude perhaps.

The onboard computer printed out pictures of both the doctor on the island, his medical board photograph, and Mason Cromwell for comparison.

As she suspected, the former cop had crept in disguised, taken a trophy, and disappeared. She'd shown him compassion, revealed he'd see none. He didn't know the deadly nature of his opponent, but he would.

Bleep, bleep, bleep.

A faint signal grazed the shoreline.

"You see it?" Ray asked the pilot, who nodded confirmation. "There! Now!"

———

The phone rang when Nick's hand hit the doorknob. NASA satellites waited on standby, surveying the property and monitoring the helicopter activity the second the alarms disengaged.

Disabled once again by island security measures, they were reduced to threat tactics over the phone.

Given a choice, he wouldn't have answered. Avoidance would only serve to fuel growing suspicion. Nick knew their keen noses had picked up a familiar stench.

Desperation drew them.

Nick thrashed about, trapped in a hellish covert undercurrent. The only escape route, swim to the bottom and find an opening.

"Got another peek at the place, eh. Must've been gratifying considering all the wasted government time waiting for a breach."

"We want to see him. Funeral's over, Nick," the familiar voice demanded.

"Not tonight, Cage. He needs his beauty sleep." Nick's tone revealed none of the fear brewing inside him.

"Your stall tactics are becoming more pathetic than usual."

"Yes...or I could deem you unworthy of an explanation. Basically I don't give a shit what you think. Face it, Major, you've been reduced to nothing more than a schoolyard bully. My time is far too precious to waste another moment on this phone line with you. The Jacuzzi awaits."

Nick slammed the phone down before the caller had time to utter protest, but he didn't stride away the defiant man he'd portrayed. Instead, he stood shaken. Hunched over the counter, he pounded his fist hard against the granite.

"Damn you, Ray!"

He knew her response. He'd heard it before.

'Get in line.'

———

Sitting undaunted behind his desk, Major Romulus Cage offered nothing to Doctor Locke. His face revealed no emotion. His expression remained, as always, stone cold. He pulled one of Cuba's finest from his desk humidor, trimmed, and lit the cigar, slowly puffing it to life, as the young doctor fumed and shifted in his seat.

James Lawrence Locke II was an impatient, egotistical, chauvinistic heathen, but even he recognized Cage's authority if only to guarantee his own survival. Seconds before Locke opened his mouth to put his dwarfed size nine in it, Cage broke the intolerable silence.

"You're shakin' like a new recruit after introduction to hell week. Quit sweating in my presence. We'll have her back here soon enough."

The man was a living monument to ineptitude.

"What did he say, damn it?" Locke's demand had the strength of a whimper.

"Don't pull rank, little man, or you'll find yourself in a small, dark space."

The threat made Locke squirm. He chewed his lip rather than enticing further criticism. Surly, he wanted, so badly, to lash out but knew better than to push the boundaries of their alliance. One Cage found detestable.

"I'm not pulling rank. I'm asking to be kept in the loop," Locke sniveled.

"He's not giving up anything, but he's nervous. He senses a break in their defenses. He knows we're at his back door," Cage said. "I'll call you in when we engage the target. Until then, get the hell out of my office."

Locke stood to his full, gangly six-foot-three height, turned to exit, then said, "He didn't sound nervous." He sauntered out of the smoke-filled room, leaving his contempt lingering in the haze.

Cage dialed after Locke cleared the doorway. Walking as the call connected, he sealed the room behind him. Heavy and soundproof, the door had a formidable lock he'd never double-checked before. In the fifteen years Cage commanded the office, his reputation had proved deterrent enough. No one dared enter without permission.

Secured, he sat again, cigar hanging off his lower lip, waiting for an answer.

"Where're we at?" A calm dignitary asked across the line from Washington.

"Progressing as expected, sir," Cage reported. "Nothing we can't handle."

"Good to hear it, Major. The update on our timeline isn't what we were hoping for. We require the package wrapped, delivered, and primed to go within the month. Any longer than that, and we're dead in the water."

"I can guarantee you delivery, sir, but whether or not she'll work..."

"Don't concern yourself with that. Once it arrives, there won't be any choice. Any movement on the notepad?"

"They lifted security for the fireworks. We acquired surveillance photos. We're analyzing data now," Cage replied.

"You know where to find me."

The line went dead, and Cage paged his visual data team for an update.

Locke Senior stashed his arcane research on the island—this they'd always known. But things had changed, making its immediate retrieval imperative.

His cigar lost its appeal. He snubbed the end out on a file with Locke's face on it, leaving his image smeared in soot. Cage had proved a crucial weapon for the most powerful players for reasons they all assumed secured his own purposes. In a way, they were correct. In another, they couldn't be more off base. Even Locke believed Cage shared his twisted hatred and jealousy of Ray. His interest in her certainly appeared obsessive. And they were, but not for the reasons on the books. He was watching every move she made, apprised of every breath she'd take, and orchestrating every challenge she faced, but the outcome he had planned for her was nothing any of them expected.

27

CLUMPS OF SATURATED HAIR, like black tar, oozed down Ray's back, shoulders and into her eyes. She didn't brush them away, flinch at slithering trickles of moisture draining from them, or blink heavy droplets from her lashes. Water snaked down her back, crept down her arms, and blurred her vision.

Numb.

Her only focus was her target.

She remembered her quest for freedom from the days, months, and long years trapped behind glass.

This was a much different affliction.

She dare not dampen the fire raging inside her. The anger fortified. It permeated the air she breathed—without it, she'd drown in a river of mourning.

The .45 caliber Colt became an extension of her. Not a weapon she held, but a mutation necessary for both their survival. She wanted MJ alive.

Her aim, pure precision, compensated for wind, distance, velocity, and drop. She failed to hit her mark. She never failed. She couldn't account for their good fortune.

A falling beam took a bullet. Then an accidental slip passed one target an inch too high. A snap of a head—as if a warning was issued from a dark corner—saved the abductor from certain death.

There was no explaining it.

And then, police.

Risking apprehension or imprisonment wasn't acceptable, not now. Revenge such as this couldn't be served by the hand of another, only her own. She gave him life, her very blood, hers to reclaim.

Damn them. The brief distraction of the flashing lights caused her to lose sight of her prey. They couldn't have traversed any great expanse, for the perilous terrain wouldn't allow it—metal and water were not a stable mixture underfoot. Regardless, they slithered away, and without light, she couldn't easily locate them.

Using a flashlight in the wake of the circling patrol car would draw too much attention. Rain and rolling thunder manipulated sound, so even the keenest ears became unreliable. For the time being, her stronghold weakened.

Their luck *would* run out. When it did, she'd be waiting, a shadow, refusing to shake free, a dark cloud looming overhead, a dead end.

They'd meet their maker. She could hardly wait.

———

Stepping out into a void of darkness, Mason feared the ghost story had come to life, casting him among its doomed characters.

Blackness deepened beyond the reach of the compound's perimeter security lights. Even the distant lighthouse beam, once a beacon of hope, shedding a glowing path over the treacherous metal shingles, dimmed beneath the frigid stone sky. The moon, melted ice, cried clear, cold blue.

He inhaled salty sea air. It dried his throat forcing him to breathe through his nose, never satisfying the need of his restricted lungs, weighed by panic.

Fear of death was no match for fear of failure. He had no children to leave distraught. But to stand idly by while his sister's long-lost son fell victim to a murderer? This would decimate him.

The deluge saturated his hair. He brushed water from his brow to maintain, at best, a blurred line of sight across the maze.

The dead weight of his weapon should've emitted a measure of reassurance, but moisture crept under his grip and stole any fervor it normally held. That, unsure footing, limited vision, and sheer exhaustion, made him and Chris slow-moving targets. Forced into the open with a circling predator.

He could only hope Ray'd vacated the area, choosing her own safety as priority over a quick kill. Chris reached forward, placing a hand on his shoulder. The silent connection fused a fortifying link. This was why he was here.

Lightning created a split-second spotlight amid the steely cascade. Mason examined Chris like a dedicated bodyguard, only to be taken aback by his youth and uncanny resemblance to his younger brother—save those intense hazel eyes. This *was* his nephew, damn it! He wasn't losing him without one hell of a fight.

The surge of anger fueled his determination, clearing his mind and allowing it to map a safe line of exit.

Walking downslope from his nephew, Mason became the human barrier between Chris and the roof's edge. If he died tonight, he was fairly certain it wouldn't be from tumbling off the top of a building to cement and metal scraps below.

Or would it?

Out of the corner of his left eye, a flash. He jolted his body upslope into Chris, knocking his unstable footing. Chris grabbed Mason's shoulders in an effort to prevent himself from sliding, catapulting them both off the edge into a slippery, horrid heap.

Instinct triumphed before Mason assessed the source of the distant burst of light. He threw himself in the line of fire to protect Chris. His body tensed, awaiting a piercing bullet's entry.

Being shot twice on duty, memory wouldn't let him forget the searing heat of fiery metal.

No impact, no burn. Mason searched left of the complex. Reaching behind, he pushed Chris down, minimizing him as a target.

Again, a flash broke the darkness. Blue, not red. With both eyes fixed upon its origin, Mason ruled out gun flare. It hadn't come from a direct source. A reflection on metal from the flashing patrol car's lights as it circled the area.

Huddled, relieved, body aching from his gut reaction, he whispered, "The patrol car's still here. She fled the complex or is in hiding and probably won't risk being fired on to take us out."

Pointing to a lower roofline where the patrol car passed, he slicked his wet hair back smooth to his head, blinking rain from his eyes. "If we go down quickly, we'll have a better chance of following them out and back to the truck."

"Right behind you," Chris said. Both longed to feel solid ground beneath their feet.

The police offered them a few moments reprieve. Nothing more.

Increasingly difficult to traverse, the metal rooftop transformed into a wet rink worsened by the severity of its slope. The jeans they wore, soaked through, became binding plastic wrap tightening around the muscles in their legs, restricting any positioning save an uncomfortable hunch.

Still, they ran.

Not leaving his feet in any step long enough to slide, Chris crossed the distance like a sly cat in pursuit behind Mason until a hand signal of caution slowed him.

At the metal rungs of a side ladder, Mason dropped his thick frame to a horizontal position across the cold steel roof. Peering over its edge, he shook the pipes, testing for stability.

Chris fought to maintain a firm stance near the roof's drop off. Beneath them, some thirty feet, stood a numbered emergency exit door with an overhead light. Its glare pushed back the shadows between buildings enough for Mason to see a safe landing beyond the ladder.

The building connected to the next by a cement sidewall, preventing attack from behind. Ahead, the open street lay empty. Ray would be seen coming if not heard, rendering this avenue ineffective for a stealthy approach. The roof of the adjacent building sat lower and clear of predators. The concern waited behind the door at the ladder's end. What were the chances?

Deciding to send Chris down first, having an advantage from above, Mason gave the go-ahead and helped him over the side.

Suction of the material glued to Chris' flesh could be heard tearing loose while he swung his leg over the railing. Mason held his wrist until certain Chris had found his footing.

No movement other than their own.

Chris focused on the rungs with each step as the rainfall and cold breeze turned a simple climb into a game of chance. The slippery steel appeared sturdy enough when Mason wrenched on it, but as Chris fought for footing, it creaked and groaned of weather and age. Legs aching from both cold and restriction, Mason understood why he skipped the last few rungs to jump to solid pavement.

He just did it seconds too late.

Mason watched it happen as if in slow motion. Chris had moved far beyond his grasp and so near the ground. He assumed he was home free. He was wrong.

The lower half of the ladder broke away seconds before Chris let go. The metal, rusted at the joints, severed off below Chris' hands at wrist level. Sharp brackets protruded from the cement wall. His full body weight, resting on the fractured section, tore his hands from the slimy wrung above when the steps gave way. Without warning and no time to react, both wrists were speared clean through. Left dangling, silencing his own screams of anguish, his body hung, suspended against the wall by his own flesh.

Industrial crucifixion.

Mason scaled the upper section of the ladder like a fireman down a slide pole. Leaping past Chris, he slammed into the pavement with a crunching blow to his left shoulder. Piercing shards of pain shot through to his neck. He rose quickly beneath Chris, supporting his full weight so he could tear himself free from the iron spikes. Blood sprayed overhead. It burned Mason's eyes. He couldn't pull Chris loose. When the kid's body finally fell back, he readjusted to catch him and deliver him to the ground.

Bleeding out on the frigid, sodden pavement, Chris grasped, in vain, at both open wrist wounds with useless hands. Mason ripped off his jacket and tore his shirt in half—tourniquets to stop the blood loss. Chris thrashed his head in pain as Mason yanked tight the makeshift bandages. Both wounds tied off, Mason held Chris' face.

"Stay with me," Mason pleaded.

Mason glanced up. Beneath the tattered metal mess, two solid streams of Chris' blood stained the wall.

"Can you hear me? Come on, kid."

"I hear you," Chris clenched the pain behind his teeth. "We have to leave, she could've heard."

"Can you walk?" Chris needed immediate medical attention.

Carrying him would slow their exit, and the nearest doctor lived miles away.

"Help me up," Chris said.

Careful to support him without placing strain on his damaged arms, he helped the kid to his feet. Mason's expression steeled against the gore. Too much blood. Chris could bleed to death before they escaped.

Mason scoured their surroundings——if the boys in blue decided to backtrack, they were in clear sight with nowhere to hide.

Ravaged and raw, Chris followed him to the front of the building, away from the door light's glare.

"Keep the wounds elevated against your chest," Mason said. "I'm going to get you outta here."

Doused in blackness again, Mason used the reflective white warehouse numbers to lead them to the truck. Each number offered a small measure of relief.

Two more to go.

The patrol car's headlights neared them on the opposite side. Mason paused to meet Chris' eyes. Still standing. Scurrying like wounded dogs, they disappeared into the trees surrounding the complex. The truck sat twenty meters away, hidden effectively by surrounding brush.

Dizzy and weak from blood loss, Chris prompted Mason to bolt for the vehicle's safety before he lost the ability. Mason held him back.

The truck had an unbreachable security feature. Even a genius would've required a couple hours of pouring over manuals to learn enough to disengage any one facet of the system, and much longer to acquire the code for an override. If Ray had located the truck, she hadn't had the time to mess with it.

Mason pulled keys from an inside pocket and pressed a small orange button. It blinked then became solid red.

"Sweeping for bombs, bugs, anything giving out the slightest traceable signal," he offered.

"What line...of business ...are you in?" Chris whispered, his words broken by pain. Brave, but fading quickly.

Confident Ray hadn't found the truck, Mason grabbed Chris without warning and carried him to the passenger side. Unlocked by remote, he opened the door and transferred Chris onto the leather. Shutting it quietly, he dashed around the front of the vehicle and slid behind the wheel.

Lights off, engine silent, together they surveyed the complex for the patrol car's whereabouts. They needed to put enough distance between them to allow the pounding rain to muffle their engine noise.

Spotting the faint beam from headlights turning onto the entry road at the opposite end of the complex, Mason said, "Okay, let's get out of here."

"Shouldn't...weeee...waait?" Chris slurred, his strength slipping away, pain overriding the rush of adrenaline.

"While you bleed to death? Hell no."

"Not leaving...'til I...I'm ready." Chris barely said the words before slumping in his seat.

"Spoken like a true Cromwell," Mason said, praying the kid's will to live would sustain him. Turning onto the main road, a streetlight illuminated Chris' shabby bandages. Saturated in blood, they told a different story. Mason was watching his nephew die.

28

THE PRIMEVAL ROCKY Mountains majestically towering over Alberta's western foothills kept watch like a row of sentinels, and the canopy of dense green spruce huddled its residence safely beneath, sheltering them from whispering winds. Below the forest cathedral, night fell. Above it, white drifts of cloud hugged the mountain peaks. Between, a single bald eagle screeched across the sky.

Kyly couldn't rest; nightmares broke the solace of sleep and tainted waking hours.

The unfamiliar setting, which should've contributed to her uneasiness, strangely gave her comfort. Restless, she circled the cabin's upper level before pausing in front of a collection of photos.

"You admire him, don't you?" Zavier asked from behind.

"Who?"

"Oh, give it up, girl. I had your number when you walked around for an hour with his picture in your hand."

"I find your uncle interesting."

"Yeah, right, that's what they all say."

"All?" she said.

"Oh boy, he *is* in trouble."

"Trouble?"

Zavier laughed, stole an empty cup from her hand, and left to refill it.

"What?" she called after him.

"You know what," he said slyly from the other room.

He was right.

Mason did more than interest her. She hadn't met him in person yet she was certain few men of his caliber existed. Perhaps it was the safety and comfort of his home, how he valued family, privacy, and harmony as she did, or his strength and masculine good looks. It didn't matter why. The feelings were just another irrational facet of her distorted emotional state.

It'd pass.

Riggs had sat loyally at her feet for hours.

Off duty, the dog slept while they talked. Then, as if called on shift when Zavier left the room, he bolted upright by the sofa, staring out at the night.

Sitting beside him, Kyly patted his soft head, rustling his ears and scratching behind them. Occasionally, he responded with a sloppy lick of appreciation or a reminding nudge.

She read over notes compiled on their situation with neurotic zeal. As if burning the details into memory would somehow pull forth a solution.

Deep in contemplation, she remained oblivious to the change in the dog's behavior. Minutes passed with the absence of nudges, licks, or whined pleas for affection. Eventually, his perked ears and stiffened state caught her attention.

"What's up, boy? You getting sick of me already?" She leaned close.

This time, he didn't turn to nuzzle her. In fact, he didn't acknowledge her at all.

"What's the matter?" She relinquished her papers, curious about what demanded the dog's concern.

Riggs made eye contact, then returned his focus dead ahead. On all fours, he stood in front of Kyly. The wind lashed at the window wall. She suspected it was responsible for the canine's discontent.

Not yet alarmed, Kyly said, "Don't like the wind, hey? Me neither."

Riggs padded a few steps nearer the glass panes, glancing back with a pleading stare.

She rose and the dog advanced with her trailing behind.

"What's bugging you? Are you trying to scare me?" She walked with her head down, attention on the dog.

Approaching the window, she saw little beyond it. Night swallowed every detail, leaving nothing but drifting shadows in the wind. Shades of darkness, dancing tones.

She leaned into the window, straddling the dog. A black hole amid the night lay dead ahead. It lacked a recognizable shape. She pulled back, crouched, following its outline. The sides were defined, two feet across at the base. It blended into the ground stretching upward.

Gradually, her eyes traced up the shadow.

A breath away from the glass, straightening, she strained to decipher its origin, a nearby tree, lawn furniture, the roof's overhang...

At full height, she found an unwelcome answer.

Something stared back. Two black onyx hidden in the bleakness of a coal mine wall. Towering her, its eyes stared into her own.

It didn't blink.

Fear gripped her like a steel vise. She froze solid where she stood. It failed to silence her. The scream should've disintegrated the glass pane into tiny fragments. Riggs attacked, jumping against the glass, teeth bared, anxious to fight.

Zavier flew from the kitchen, weapon in hand and slid across the hardwood floor. Slamming on the exterior house light, he came face to face with their adversary.

A formidable trophy buck stood illuminated. Then, without the slightest flinch of nerves, the animal turned his back, receding from the window to pause at the deck's edge while the last of his herd crossed the rear yard.

He stood guard protecting, the females.

This time, *they* were the enemy.

Kyly fell still, tranquilized by the sheer beauty and size of the animal. Graceful and majestic, he held his head with such honor and dignity it humbled her.

Zavier killed the lights but remained staring out, though neither of them could make out more than its outline in the distant darkness. Night transformed the window to a mirror surface clouded by their reflections.

"Safe trails, old man," he said, giving Kyly's shoulder a squeeze before leaving her alone with her reflection.

Riggs, who remained by her side, emitted a low growl.

———

Thunderheads brought heavy rain, blurring the lines between night and day. From peak to peak spread an infinity of overlapping clouds heavily weighted with an endless supply of gloom.

Staring into the morbid drizzle, Kyly dreamed of home.

Zavier sauntered in as the kettle clicked off. In sweatpants and a housecoat, his appearance mirrored hers. He crossed the kitchen to where she sat, wrestled her hair, then pulled her from her seat and hugged her.

"We're going to get through this," he said. "Stay positive, doctor's orders. Now let me have a look at that."

Together they retreated to the living room, and with gentle hands, he inspected, for the first time, the full extent of damage to her neck. "This guy knew what he was doing."

"Yeah," she said. "I got that."

Thousands of miles away, sometime during their dreams, Mason had risked his life to retrieve Christian. Despite repeated efforts, Zavier couldn't reach him. A dangerous reality crept in—an inescapable, savage possibility.

An inner storm moved in tandem with the one shrouding the forest. Kyly felt their safety receding. She couldn't predict how danger would come, or in what form. She just knew they were in its path. Waiting.

Waiting was all they had now. It drove them both into a quiet state of panic.

Huddled in front of the fireplace, finding strange solace in the memory of the buck standing guard, she called home. Somehow, the dark day seemed unbearably colder than its temperature reflected.

Her father answered, sounding optimistic. A tone she suspected tailored for her.

"Hello, dear. How are you?"

"I'm fine, Dad. Have you heard anything from Mason? We're starting to get concerned."

She lied. They'd been worried as hell for longer than she cared to admit.

"No, not since yesterday."

Her heart sank along with Zavier's, who read her father's response in her eyes.

"But I did hear from a reliable source, a military unit deployed last night to track a rogue helicopter, searching a certain area of concern. Sounds like someone has lost something rather valuable and is desperate to relocate it."

Her face accepted a smile. Hope.

"Truth is, they'll need to lay low. Mason needs time to explain things to Zavier's brother. This situation is so complex. How are you fairing, be honest?"

Terrified. Devastated. Forsaken. All feelings she refused to verbalize or embrace.

"We're safe for the moment. Zavier contacted his parents. Everything is okay there. We'll manage, one minute at a time. I can't stay on the line long," she said.

"I understand, but please keep in touch. Things are going to get dicey. They know, we know. We don't know what to expect."

"Speaking of unexpected, I saw an eleven-point buck yesterday."

She wanted to lighten their reality, if only for a few seconds. She wanted to share with him.

"Wow, that's not something one sees every day."

"Have to go. Give my love to Mom."

"I will, and you have ours."

Hanging up, Kyly couldn't get the words out of her mouth fast enough.

"Mason got him, Zavier. They fled the island. My father heard from a source they were followed." Her voice dipped. "We have to pray they don't find them."

"They won't find Mason," Zavier boasted. "He has extracted people right out from under the nose of the Secret Service. If anyone is discrete enough to go undetected, it's him. As much as I'd love to tell my parents the news, we better stay off the phone. Mason will reach all of us as soon as it's safe to."

"I hope so."

They spoke over each other, hypothesizing possible escape scenarios, what Mason's next move would be, and how to prepare.

Riggs stood in pointer position halfway across the room, facing the wall of windows once again. Turning, he stared at them as if to say, "Fools, you let down your guard too soon." His low growl gained intensity.

In mid-conversation, it registered somewhere at the back of Kyly's mind. The quiet warning grew in strength and volume, shifting her attention away from Zavier, the rush of blood drained from her face.

What were the chances of the buck returning?

Zero.

————

Light exploded in their line of sight, blinding them. Zavier rolled from the sofa across the floor to Kyly, pulling her down with him in one fluid motion.

A second flash.

He waited for the bulletproof glass to take the impact, but there was no sound. With Kyly covering her head crouched beside him, he peered over the furniture.

A third flash, and with it, an illuminated glimpse of a cameraman in the rain. Their eyes locked. The man startled, then ran.

"Stay here," Zavier bellowed above the barking, calling Riggs back from his position between them and the figure beyond the glass.

In sync, Kyly grabbed the dog's collar with one hand to pull him close.

Leaping from the floor into a full-out run, Zavier flew to the kitchen for the gun he abandoned earlier on the café bar.

Weapon in hand, he sprinted to the right side of the house, watching through windows as motion sensor lights broke the darkness tracking their predator's trail. Heading him off at the front of the house, Zavier flung open the door to see him flee deep into the woods at the west end of the property.

He wasn't sent there to kill them. Why risk exposing himself for mere photographs? Low tech and afraid, armed with only a camera, he was a messenger. Sent to survey, a watcher in the woods? The flash could've been mistaken for lightning if he'd kept his distance. He wasn't very good.

Zavier slammed the door, reset the alarm system's motion detectors, and engaged a perimeter breach warning.

He half-expected Kyly to still be crunched at the floor between the sofas when he returned. Instead, she paced the room filled with fury.

"Camouflage gear!" she barked.

"I saw."

"He wasn't more than five foot ten with thinning hair, and he's a smoker."

"How do you know that?" Zavier questioned, his brow furrowed in disbelief.

"Because I'm sure he's the same son-of-a-bitch I saw skulking around my hotel. We've been followed."

"No way, I watched the highway like a hawk," Zavier defended.

"It wasn't your driving. Someone knows about this place. They found us. I don't know how, but they know where we are. We can't stay here."

Their situation was dire, even if they weren't ready to face it. Anonymity had been obliterated, leaving them isolated and mercilessly exposed.

"If we leave, we'll be at a greater risk on the highway than here," he reasoned. "I think we should wait to hear from Mason. Maybe we're blowing this out of proportion."

"We were lucky those shots came from a camera. The next ones will be far more lethal. We have to leave," Kyly insisted. "We have to leave tonight."

29

TEN PERCENT DREAD is enough to kill you.

Ninety percent of what you worry about is never realized. Paris contended it *was* an adequately tested theory. And, if you include every apprehensive thought that crosses your mind, the premise gains merit. If ten percent is bound to come true. And it's the ten percent telling you your daughter's life is in jeopardy?

Then, ten percent dread *is* enough to kill you.

There are times when panic exists, like a cosmic warning system proclaiming something wicked is coming. And no matter how you deny it, *some* things you cannot lie to yourself about—even when you desperately want to.

Paris lived and breathed this truth.

Second sight drifted in with the torment of a demon or glowed with the hope of an angel. This, she accepted, praying against the odds. Against a day like today when dark insights targeted someone dear to her.

"What? What is it?" Fear shadowed Cero's eyes.

"Trouble...it's headed her way."

"I spoke to Kyly. She was worn but safe."

"She's not safe. We can't afford to trust in a false sense of security."

Veiled light cast dim shadows in their living room. She lit scented candles at alcoves along the sidewall. An aroma of peaches filled the air.

Paris waited on its promise to bring luck and happiness. Beneath the fruitful fermentation, dread lingered, refusing to be obliterated by anything as simple as summer fruit.

Cero rose from his chair. She placed a somber hand on his shoulder, guiding him back down. She needed time alone. He understood.

She left the main yard. Humidity weighed heavy in the air, remnant of the rainfall the night before. Each breath became a drink of quench-less water. The palms dancing in the breeze were weighed down to a solemn sway.

The sand, moist enough to hold an impression, cast her footprints. When she glanced back, the imprint of her journey lay behind.

She was a distance from the house when a faint ring carried on the breeze. She sprinted for it. Cero's chair sat empty when she entered the house.

Thinking of Kyly, desperate to hear her voice, she answered.

"I'm so glad you called back, honey," she said in airy bursts. An eerie voice on the other end withered all hope.

"So am I," the caller said with slippery satisfaction. "You must be the wife."

"Who is this?"

"*No!*" Cero bellowed from the archway into the family room where Paris stood. He'd been in their wine storage and hadn't heard the phone. His selected bottle was roughly discarded, rattled, leveling out on the coffee table.

"Ah, he's home after all," the voice taunted.

Crossing the distance to her in a stride, Cero tore the phone from her grasp as if it were molten metal scorching her flesh. He ushered her from the room, shielding her from imaginary flames. She required no explanation; she knew the identity of the man on the other end. What she couldn't fathom was why he'd risk calling back.

In the library, out of the line of sight but within earshot, she strained to grasp pieces of her husband's enraged criticism. His voice reverber-ated with fury for the first few moments. She heard him utter at least one threat to the man on the other end. Then his tone changed. It remained laced with restrained contempt. The information shared must've warranted a change in attitude. Curiosity drew her. She walked catlike to the hall where she could decipher whole sentences.

"And you're certain of this?" Cero questioned. "Locke delved into tissue memory research...transplants? I didn't know about the genetic engineering."

After a short pause, he continued, "How many know about it? Is that how he financed buying the island?"

"If they know where it is, why not send in a team to retrieve it?"

She couldn't fully understand Cero's discussion. Half a conversation didn't offer clarity. Silent for several minutes, he startled her when he spoke again.

"Wonderful!" he said cynically. "You're telling me they're afraid of her. What does that mean for my child?"

He paused again for a mere second.

"I know that! Don't be smug about this. And why, in Heaven's name, did you risk getting this information to me?"

Anxious silence.

"Redemption," Cero echoed, then hung up the phone.

The information came down on her husband like a crushing blow, driving him to collapse in the chair beside the desk. He didn't see her watching or know she'd overheard him.

Taking her place beside him on a footstool, she asked, "What happened?"

"You were right," he said, defeated. Head in hands, he refused to greet the worry in her eyes. "Darkness *is* coming for her. Perhaps for us all. And...and I..."

"We can't lose faith." She pulled his hands away to cradle his face. "We won't."

Paris left him briefly to fetch water and a calming naturopath pill— she worried about his heart. He wasn't a young man anymore. Swallowing it down gladly, Cero dispelled the information.

"It sounds as if the young man's uncle got him off the island successfully," he said.

"Well, that's good, isn't it?"

"They made it off the island. Whether they're still alive, I don't know. They were followed by a single combat helicopter and a reconnaissance team sent to track it."

"So the couple from the island are after them, and the military is after the island people?" she questioned.

"Yes. By the sounds of things, this goes a whole lot deeper than we first suspected. The island used to be owned by a Dr. Locke. He specialized in transplant advancement, research on something called tissue memory, and the use of genome editing and CRISPR to alter DNA. His efforts led to profitable and guarded discovery, or power players wouldn't have stepped in, fully funded him, and financed the private island to conduct his work in secrecy."

"I remember watching a documentary on tissue memory in transplant patients. A lady ended up with a young man's heart. After recovery, her personality changed drastically—she craved things she never liked before, listening to her kid's music, things like that," she offered.

"Right. Locke's research stretched far beyond anything revealed to the public, then it derailed. Locke broke his agreement with the government, hid his findings somewhere on the island, and ended up dead."

"Dead. Are you saying a dark government faction had him killed?"

"Worse," he said. "It appears Locke didn't agree with the government's agenda and lost his life because he wouldn't comply. He handed his island and research, they believe, to his protégé. A brain surgeon—"

"Was he?" she interrupted.

"Micael Valeric, the man who stole Christian Cromwell at birth. The one the funeral was held for."

"Did they kill him?" she asked, terrified by the picture-taking form. "I thought he was sick."

"No. Apparently he died from a terminal illness, but that's where the problem lies. With Valeric out of the way, whoever *They* are, decided it's time to strike, retrieve their research, and move forward with whatever plan they set in motion years ago."

It was all so complicated. Paris struggled to pay attention, dreading the moment when its impact on their daughter became clear.

"So what about Ray and this Nick person? Why are they after Chris and his uncle? And why is the military after them?" she asked.

"I don't know exactly. I assume it has to do with the research. All I know is we have to get our daughter out of this and fast. If the government is willing to kill for the information on that island, anyone who knows anything about it is in great danger. And that includes us."

"Why did he tell you?" She was hesitant to ask.

"Redemption."

He shook his head, unwilling to draw conclusions.

Cero stood, jotting down the facts. They searched for an escape route in the labyrinth before them. It helped to be busy. They couldn't stand to be idle.

Idle hands...

They agreed to contact Kyly, despite the risk, after they made sense of things. The more information they shared, the better their chances.

"I wish we'd hear from Mason, be able to give her some good news," Cero said. "The more time that passes...the odds are mounting against them. Why did I let her pursue this cursed story? I sensed the danger. Why did I let her get on the plane?"

Paris shared his inner struggle but refused to submit.

"Stop warring with yourself." She placed a hand on his arm, pulling him from his hovering position over the desk. "She wouldn't have listened. You couldn't have prevented this. For a man of God, you can be very forgetful. She is on loan to us. We were blessed with the role of guide and support for her life, but free will led her to this. It's not for us to judge or condemn. We're here to help, so let's help."

"That's the problem," he said, a cloud of uncertainty obscuring his bright eyes. "I'm afraid what help we give...won't be enough."

30

MASON'S NEPHEW teetered precariously on a tightrope between life and death, while his truck traversed dirty back roads in the dark.

Chris lost consciousness long before they reached the doctor's farm. Mason feared the kid had crossed life's threshold during the trip.

He prayed for divine intervention. He'd been doing a lot of that lately.

Nightfall prevented him from being able to read Chris' color. The old routes he traveled for safety had no streetlights to pass beneath. Hunted, he couldn't risk giving away their location by switching on lights. Odds were good. The kid bore a pasty, anemic shade of death.

They weren't being followed, as far as he could tell. It would've taken Ray time to arrange for ground transportation. Unless she was familiar with the area, she sat at a disadvantage.

Penetrating cold sent a relentless ache through his bones. His damaged shoulder throbbed, dull compared to the gnawing fear. "Dear God, please, I can't lose him."

His eyes diverted from the gravel top to Chris' chest.

Still breathing. Thank God.

Sliding into the doctor's driveway, the truck's tires sent a ten-foot rock spray announcing their arrival. The doctor, though frail in old age, rushed to the passenger side to help remove the patient.

One glance at the blood-soaked fabric concealing Chris' wounds and the doctor's spirits sank.

"Into the house immediately!" he fretted. "He needs a hospital, Stone, not my makeshift lab. What the hell did this?"

"Metal supports on a building's emergency ladder." Mason winced, lifting Chris out of the suburban.

The old man's perplexed expression begged the obvious.

"You don't want to know," Mason assured him.

At the back of the tiny farmhouse, in a small, dimly lit room with no windows, they placed Chris on an old, steel operating table.

After blowing dust off the apparatus, Doc Iberson hooked him up to an IV. He pulled an overhead light directly above Chris' left wrist and unwrapped the wound. Blood squirted through the air as the last of the fabric tourniquet fell away. "Pressure," he commanded. "Here, clench hard." Wiping away excess blood, the doctor irrigated with disinfectant to reveal a gaping hole, a penetrating laceration in the shape of a pentagon.

"He nicked the main artery. Unbelievable. It hasn't burst." Doc leaned inches above the hole, peering through a magnifying eyepiece while he stitched. "When you called, I was half-asleep. I didn't imagine he'd be this bad off. If I had known, I would've sent you to County General."

"It's a good thing you didn't know then, Doc, 'cause General isn't an option."

"Just what kind of mischief have you got yourself into this time?" Doc Iberson's eyes focused on the delicate surgery.

"The kind most people don't survive. You wanna keep asking questions?"

"No, son, I don't. Move that tray closer."

Small enough to induce a claustrophobic state of panic, the room closed in around Mason as the doctor tended to Chris. He *had* time to call his sister, to wake her and tell her he was bringing Chris home. He couldn't manage to find a way to say it might be in a body bag.

The young man's vitals were dropping steadily. Iberson said a blood transfusion would give him a solid chance. Unfortunately, he didn't have any on hand, and without testing blood type, he couldn't risk Mason being a suitable match. Glancing at the archaic equipment, the lack of leftover blood seemed a blessing.

Working quickly, the doctor switched sides, unwrapping the right wrist to reveal the second impalement.

"These wounds are identically shaped. In exactly the same location," he said in disbelief, glancing up through his glasses. "You know what the odds are for two identical injuries, both nicking the main artery, occurring by accident?"

"About the same as this kid being alive," Mason replied. The doctor couldn't possibly understand the depth of his words.

Several minutes later, the last of the stitches sewn, Doc bandaged the wounds while Mason aided in clean up. It wasn't so much a considerate act as a self-serving one. His mind amplified the sight of the kid's blood.

Rivers down the cement wall, puddles on the passenger seat, and here, oceans.

He and the doctor monitored Chris' vitals.

While Chris remained unconscious on a gurney in front of him, Doc assessed the damage to Mason's shoulder, then noticed the injury to his hand.

"Better let me have a look at that too," Doc said. "You can't be falling apart and still be able to protect him."

"It really hasn't bothered me," Mason said, mildly perplexed by this fact but more interested in Chris' prognosis.

"Oh, come on, it's the adrenaline. It had to be a pretty good gash."

Blood caked the outside bandage across the length of the wound. Mason suspected he required at least a few stitches to close the cut. Subsequently, the absence of pain surprised him. None. Not even when he applied pressure.

"Come on, tough guy, let me see," Doc insisted. "Who dressed this?"

Mason pointed to the pale young man on the table, and Doc nodded.

"He must know a thing or two about wounds. This is nicely done."

The old man paying compliments to his unconscious nephew seemed highly out of place.

"Yeah," Mason said dryly.

The doctor removed the fabric one bloody loop at a time. Mason expected seepage. He didn't see any. In fact, with the skin exposed, the deep laceration had resealed itself.

"That's strange." Mason examined his hand.

"Certainly can't be responsible for all this blood loss," Doc agreed, holding the rusty stained fabric up for comparison. "Perhaps this is more his blood than yours. You don't need stitches. I'll glue the worst of it so it doesn't reopen under pressure."

"Sure." Mason stared oddly at his hand, his nephew, and back again.

Turning his attention to Chris' cardiograph, Mason's curiosity intensified.

"Doc," he said, pointing to the cardiac monitor. "That can't be normal."

Figures fluctuated in massive leaps from 195 over 120 to terrifyingly low ratios and back again.

"There must be something wrong with the machine," the doctor said. "I told you, it's a makeshift operating room. It's not the most reliable equipment."

Soon, the numbers stabilized, as if forced by the potency of Mason's glare.

His face cringed and contorted as the doctor reset his displaced shoulder. The final crack-pop riveted such intense pain through his bones and muscle tissue it left him dazed. Doc administered a needle to sedate the pain, then stood with his back to them both, filling a nap sack with food and medical supplies.

After examining Chris' eyes with what he described as his "new ophthalmoscope," the doctor measured his pulse manually. His vitals, though still dangerously weak, were holding.

"With proper care, he should be on the road to recovery," Doc said. "But don't push your luck. When he first got here, I wasn't so sure."

"Me either," Mason admitted, tired and aching badly. "Thank you for everything. I owe you."

"You owe me nothing."

Not wanting to further impose or involve Iberson, Mason reloaded Chris, IV bag and all, with the doctor's help into the bench seat of the suburban. He drove to an out-of-the way motel. With individual suites well separated from each other, no one would witness him carrying in an unconscious man with an IV drip over his shoulder.

Excluding a slight wind and cold drizzle, the parking lot and surrounding streets lay abandoned. The only sound, other than the sizzling hum of outdated light standards, came from his heavy footsteps crossing the gravel driveway.

Scrutinizing the area, Mason considered the ghost town atmosphere appropriate for the small rural community at three in the morning. He unlocked the door to their room, unloaded a few essentials, then returned for Chris.

Ignoring the shooting pains across his shoulder, neck, and back, he carried Chris to one of the beds and gingerly set him down.

Aching and dog-tired, he couldn't have been happier to see a bed. He called the front desk and made a firm request to ensure they wouldn't be disturbed by housecleaning the next morning. A *Do not disturb* sign hung on the outer doorknob.

Two queen-sized beds lay across from each other, allowing him to keep a keen eye on Chris. He claimed the one closest to the door, stripped off his filthy wet clothes and slipped on a clean pair of pajama bottoms from provisions in the truck.

Carefully, he cut the rest of the kid's blood-soaked shirt off him and fought to pry the still damp jeans from his legs. A careful jolt and Chris rolled free from the pants, releasing them before Mason expected. He lost his balance and, while regaining it, tossed the jeans across the room.

Clink, clink, clink.

Bouncing across the floor by Mason's bed, catching the light on impact, a single mysterious key lost its momentum, coming to rest against the baseboard.

Mason laid extra blankets from the closet over Chris, checked his temperature, and then turned out the night light by his bed. Returning to his side of the room, he rummaged around on the floor for a few moments before locating the key. Heavy and worn, he couldn't help wondering what it unlocked. After all, it was the only thing the kid brought with him other than the clothes on his back.

Remembering their conversation in the attic about the package sent to Dr. Valeric, Mason imagined the key might be connected. Believing this, he placed it on the chain around his neck. If it protected Dr. Valeric, it might be the key to their survival as well.

Zavier's last message said he and the journalist were enjoying the great outdoors, gratefully without visitors.

Faxed a recent photo by her father, Mason could certainly understand Zavier's interest. He pictured Kyly walking around the property under a blanket of pine tree shadows and found an odd comfort in her being there. He convinced himself her friendship could prove healthy for Zavier. Hopefully it didn't amount to anything more. Romantic involvement at this stage could become a distraction. This line of reasoning, however logical, failed to explain away his sudden longing for home.

The mystery girl intrigued him. There was something in the sound of her voice. Despite his rationalizing, he wasn't fooling himself. He kept her photo and stared at it too long, wondering if he'd live long enough to see her in the flesh.

Exhausted, he pushed and shoved to close the door on his mental debate. The opposition proved too mighty to budge. The hotel room fell blissfully quiet. His mind did not.

———

"Morning. How are the wrists?" Mason asked, shocked to see Chris looking so normal in the light of day streaming through the hotel room window. He showed no signs of his precarious state the night before, save the white bandages covering both wrists.

"Fine, I'll recover," he said. "Who did the handiwork?"

"An old doctor friend of mine. I drove you to his farmhouse after you passed out," Mason explained. "We weren't so sure you were going to make it. It was touch and go there for a while. Do you want something for the pain?"

"Not now. Sorry I scared you. He does nice work; must know a thing or two about injuries."

Stolen from the doctor's mouth during Chris' unconscious state.

Ignoring the obvious, Mason poured Cream of Wheat into two bowls with brown sugar and milk, swung one in front of Chris, and carried the other to a seat across the room, haloed by sunlight streaming in the window.

"Are you okay...with a spoon?" Mason asked.

"No tendon damage. My fingers work. Missed the vital areas. You don't need to worry. I wouldn't make you spoon feed me."

After a silent breakfast, Mason wrapped Chris' bandages in plastic. Chris showered and Mason networked. Their problems had only begun. In less than twenty-four hours, Chris had stumbled across the threshold of death and back again. Keeping him hidden forever wasn't a realistic option; his life would always be in danger. Alive, he remained a constant threat, and unwillingly placed everyone close to him in jeopardy.

Unlike all the other kidnap and ransom cases in Mason's history, he saw no resolution, no point of hand-off.

A truth he couldn't admit to Brook. She'd be waiting to receive word from him, but precautions had to be taken to ensure a safe meeting.

They had drawn battle lines—declared war.

Survival depended on the return of one prisoner. And they'd never hand Chris over willingly.

Mason showered, cleaned the room of any trace of them, cleaned the truck's interior, and ushered Chris into its back seat after ensuring the parking lot empty.

Their first stop, the neighborhood drugstore. Mason intended to acquire hair dye and other supplies to alter Chris' identity. Confusing him with his younger brother was inherently risky but misdirection seemed their only ally.

Though disguised to impersonate a doctor at the funeral, Mason assumed Ray had acquired Intel on him. And had pinned it up for target practice.

Chris, she knew intrinsically. She lived and breathed him.

She found them the night before with such ease it unnerved him.

With a baseball cap, dark glasses, and oversized clothing, Chris' identity all but vanished. And he used this excuse when refusing to wait in the truck at the store despite Mason's objections.

"Ray won't be shopping for aspirin. No one here is a threat," Chris insisted. "I've been isolated long enough, don't you think?"

"Okay, but don't talk to anyone."

"Can I say thank you at the counter?"

"Don't be smart."

"I'd think that's the one thing you truly hope I am." He brushed by Mason to enter the store.

"Great, a stubborn smartass like the rest of us."

Inside, overstuffed shelves of day-old baked goods and disorganized supplies framed a cramped, badly aging corner store. The condition of the place reflected the condition of its clerk. Behind the counter, on an old metal and orange plastic chair, watching a dingy TV, sat an effete man in his fifties. He looked too old for his years, out of shape, over-weight, balding, and as crusty as the half-price bread loaves on display.

After combing through aisles high and low, Mason located hair dye on the last shelf, closest to the pharmacy, at the back of the store.

"Do you prefer blondes?" he asked Chris, kneeling beside a row of bleaching kits.

"Terrific, first you dress me up, and now you want to play barber," Chris joked.

As Mason stared Chris down, a young woman brushed by them, baby on one hip, toddler tagging sadly alongside the other. Her beautiful thick, auburn hair draped down over her shoulders. Slender, lithe, and perfectly shaped, her figure failed to reflect one having recently given birth. Her face, free of make-up, glowed. She lacked even the slightest pretense. Her children, much to the contrary, were immaculately well kept.

She struggled with too few hands to comfort the unhappy toddler and tend to the baby at the same time.

Clutching her left ear with a tiny hand, the toddler strained with might not to cry. Her tear-stained cheeks betrayed her efforts.

"Don't pull at it, sweetie," the young mother cautioned. "Momma's going to get you medicine and make it all better, okay."

"Okay, Mommy," the little one said wearily.

Mason stared at the woman, knowing if she had the luxury of time, money, and make-up, she'd put most models to shame. A brave exterior, no wedding ring.

Before Mason could stop him, Chris walked up behind the woman.

The pharmacist, a short middle-aged local man ignored her, contin-uing to restock a shelf with anti-nausea medications.

Chris used the distraction. Mason stood stilted, watching the scene play out before him.

Focused on demanding the ill-mannered employee's attention, the woman failed to notice her little girl stop fussing. She didn't face her immediately, but when she did, a surge of instinctive protection shot forth.

"What are you doing?" she demanded. "Take your hands off my child."

Chris had placed his hand over the little one's left ear, and she smiled up at his face in joyous awe despite her mother's reaction.

"No need to worry, Mother. Your child will be fine. It's a mild ear infection. It will pass in a couple of days with antibiotic drops, and they won't hurt," Chris said, looking down to reassure the child.

"Oh, you're a doctor...I'm sorry I didn't—"

"No need to apologize. Everything will be better soon," he professed.

"Yes...I...of course..."

"Nothing you can't handle."

Overhearing the conversation, Mason intervened to get Chris the hell out of the store before he decided to make any more new friends. Pulling Chris from behind, he ushered him in the direction of the old man at the till.

"I don't know what's gotten into you, but I hope it's out of your system," Mason admonished.

"It'll never be out of my system...I'll wait in the truck," Chris offered.

"Good idea."

Mason paid for supplies while keeping one eye on the truck, half expecting Chris to resurface.

When he glanced to the back of the store, he couldn't help but notice the once suffering child bouncing happily around her mother. He entertained the possibility of coincidence to no avail. The child appeared relieved.

Two-year-old children tend to act up purely for attention. Mason knew this. He dismissed the incident and left the store, having far more important issues to address.

Uniting his family without casualties, for one.

Half Moon Bay was a risky location. The Cromwells were certain to be followed leaving the house.

After instructing them to take several diversions to ensure they shook any tail, Mason arranged for them to meet at the Ritz hotel outside town. They were to attend church as usual. Impostors, leaving the chapel in their clothes, would then drive their car to the nursing home where Curt's mother resided so it appeared they weren't varying routine.

Incognito, they'd slip out the back, take an inconspicuous vehicle waiting in the alley, and drive the back roads out of town.

Arriving hours before his sister and brother-in-law, Mason and Chris checked into their room and began his transformation.

Mason regretted his sister wouldn't see the authentic Chris. His dark hair traded for his younger brother's blond locks.

The two had become dangerously identical.

Even Chris' stunning hazel eyes hid behind the blue shields of colored contacts.

Nothing left but unbearable waiting, Mason decided Chris could endure another mild interrogation. Settling into chairs by the window strategically placed to optimize the panoramic view of the sea, he broke the silence.

"They'll be here in less than two hours, you all right?"

"Fine," Chris reported.

"Listen, I don't know what you've lived through, the island, Dr. Valeric, this Ray woman, but I need to know everything if we're to have any chance at surviving this. If what you told me last night is true, our families and others are in terrible danger."

"I'm sorry for that," Chris said, eyes staring out at the distant water crashing on the shore. "It appears there's no other way. The only reassurance I can provide is this: I'm her target. If anyone gets in the way, she will sacrifice their lives to get to me, but it isn't her intention to take your lives."

"The hell it isn't!" Mason shot back. "If luck hadn't been on our side last night, I'd be lying dead on a cold tin roof. She may not require our deaths to fill her twisted mind's quota, but she sure as hell sees us as rabbits along the proverbial highway."

"What I'm saying...she won't keep coming after you if she successfully eliminates me unless you become a threat."

"She won't? Obviously you've lived in isolation too long. We're witnesses. We'll always be a threat. She's damn well going to assume if we've spent any time with you, we know her dirty secrets. You think she'll let us parade around with that ammunition?"

Mason's composure was being eaten away like cotton in a closet of moths.

"And what do you mean 'if she successfully eliminates' you? In case you haven't noticed, all this is to keep you alive. That's not an acceptable outcome!"

"You're forgetting a few important facts," Chris said. "I'm dead. I don't exist here, not really. If she killed any of you, she'd be exposed and face consequences that would eventually lead her right back into the hands she fled from years ago. If she kills me, nothing changes. She knows your priority is to protect your family, and you'll do it at any cost, including letting her go free. Her emotions won't get in the way again."

"Fine, we'll assume you're right. That still leaves you marked and all of us in the middle of a shooting gallery."

"It's not a pleasant journey, but it's the one we're on."

Mason bolted up from his seat and paced the room. Anger seethed from him. Justice became a myth.

After years of believing their son died days after birth, his sister and brother-in-law were supposed to get their child back with a target tattooed on his forehead. Mason couldn't deceive himself. Chris implied he had to die for them to be spared.

"There has to be another way," Mason said as a knock sounded on the door.

31

"NAUSEATING DIVE." Ray scanned the sickly embellished hotel décor, the lame manner of generating a false sense of New England comfort. Blueberries in the wallpaper, ivy patterns on the china. They advertised quaint elegant charm. "Pathetic." An amateur's method of coddling man's insatiable need for homespun comfort. Insipid, insane, and insulting.

And the only bed-and-breakfast available at the late hour of her arrival in Half Moon Bay. Begrudgingly, she tolerated it.

The desk clerk's eyes ravaged her from the ground up. He lacked the intelligence to realize the danger. Words dripped from his tongue like syrup. No pleasure, just the toothache. She grabbed her key card, resenting the warm trace of DNA left by his sweaty palm. She considered extending him the courtesy of removing her sunglasses to stare back but didn't.

She threw open the door to her room and stood in its threshold. Tearing the flower print wallpaper off the walls seemed wise. She would've preferred aged glue stains to daisies. Closing the drapes only revealed more of the same. She turned out the lights, embracing the darkness, and tossed her phone into the desk drawer.

Nick would be stretched thin with outrage by morning. She didn't care. She needed a few hours of uninterrupted rest before resuming her search—the only thing worthy of her attention.

The helicopter was on standby. Surveillance crews stole shadows at every pertinent location. And the computer waited to alert her of any possible sightings. Her escapees couldn't evade detection for long.

Night passed.

By eight o'clock Sunday morning, she'd reviewed the data compiled by her sources, showered, changed, called three of her surveillance men, and e-mailed an update to Nick.

Unappetizing as it was, she abandoned her box of paper flowers for complimentary breakfast in the main dining hall. Even she needed to refuel. She entered the hall to find a mother manhandling a child no more than four. Her grip was setting the girl's arm ablaze, and she was crying with such overwhelming emotion her tiny lungs were gasping.

Ray crossed the distance between them with cat stealth, freed the child, and pinned herself between her and the mother in a breath. Clenching the mother's wrist in her hand with a force that set her back, she spoke before the woman could react.

"If you ever cause this innocent girl harm again, physical or otherwise, I will know, and I'll come for you—"

"Who the hell do you—"

Ray tipped down her sunglasses, leaned in inches from the woman's face, and stared her into a recognition that bubbled quickly to the surface in trembling waves.

"Do we understand each other?"

The woman backed away. Her hand, once released, shook. "I'm so sorry, sweetheart. Mommy was very wrong to treat you that way. It will never happen again."

Ray approached the child, kneeling to her level, and gently brushed her tear-stained cheek. "Your birth mother will never hurt you again, innocent girl. If she does, I'll hurt her."

Downstairs, she ate heartily with the other guests and slipped back to her quarters after nine.

Computer chimes rang out a steely digital warning as she passed through the vestibule. Nick.

Flipping open her satellite phone, his elevated tone could be heard long before the device reached her ear.

"...and I want to know where the hell you are from now on! You've got this damn security system so well rerouted I can't even find you."

"Nick, lower your voice, or the maid down the hall will hear you. I'm a half hour out of San Francisco in Half Moon Bay at a place called Milly's Bed and Breakfast. Calm down. If I could've contacted you sooner, I would've. I spent half the night chasing them and the other half avoiding local police. I'm not in the mood for criticism."

"Were you seen? Did anyone get a good look at you?"

"No, quit panicking. The only thing they saw were bullets, which unfortunately flew by them."

"Bullets? You were shooting at cops?" he bellowed into the line.

"No. Damn it, Nick, if you want to know what happened, quit jumping to conclusions and listen. We don't have time for this big brother routine of yours."

"Fine, explain away." His voice seethed.

Beginning from take-off the night before, she filled in the necessary details, making sure he understood with crystal clarity the precipice they stood at and their directive.

Not in the least bit thrilled with her decisions nor agreeing with her methodology, Nick vented. It didn't sway her conviction. She reveled in her element, organizing, formulating, manipulating, and all out scheming until he abruptly burst her bubble with news of his own.

"They wouldn't take no for an answer. If they wound up on our doorstep and found him missing—which, by the way, they already suspect given the anarchy of our aviation activities—it'd be game over."

"So you handed yourself over like a pawn?" Ray left little doubt in her voice of how catastrophically stupid his agreement to meet on military ground was.

"It was our island or theirs. They don't want me. I can't help them, and they know you too well to assume they could bargain with my life and win. It's a gamble I had to take. I'm not innocent in all this. You think it was a poor choice? It was the only choice! It's done, get over it."

They didn't share the same opinion or the same morality. Actually, they didn't see eye to eye on anything easily. They did share the same gene pool, at least partially. Their blood, however, *was* thicker than water. And, since they were the only two humans in the world sharing their unique blend, it bound them to one another with the strength of iron.

"Damn it! I can't come back until I have him."

"Tell me something I don't know," Nick said. "I have to keep them at bay. This is the way to do that. It may give insight on what they know and what's driving them to come after it so hard. I've a sneaking suspicion it may not have anything to do with Micael's death."

"What do you mean?"

"The last conversation I had with Cage...he had a whip at his back. There's a timeline. I don't know why, but there is one. Cage doesn't sweat under pressure. I could smell it on him. Pressure like that only comes from the top."

"I'd never have asked you to do this...to risk yourself. I know what those bastards are capable of. I don't want you going there."

It was the first time in a long while her voice hit a protective, painful note.

"I know. We don't have another option. We knew there were risks involved, and this was one of them. Look on the bright side. Maybe I'll find enough to get them off our backs for good. I want that, too."

Nick was scheduled to leave the island, fly to a Coast Guard drop point, and rendezvous with the military base security for pick-up on Tuesday morning. Cage wasn't leaving them time to maneuver.

"I can't make it back by then," she said. "I think this overzealous Cromwell kidnap and ransom retriever who snatched MJ is headed for the Canadian border."

"I don't expect you back. Just find him and do it quickly. Oh, and Ray..."

"Yes."

"Try not to get yourself killed or added to any new hit lists in the process."

"Yes, sir," she said with a trace of sarcasm, then hung up.

After an hour reviewing the morning's data, she packed and waited for Intel from her reconnaissance man in the Canadian Rockies. She sent him in for a closer inspection of Mason Stone's mountain cabin with instructions to photograph any activity. Lacking any faith in his abilities, she resigned herself to low expectations and was pleasantly surprised when her computer registered three images. Skipping the screen enlargement, she went directly to print, electing for hard copy clarity.

At first, she considered the insensate nitwit surveyed the wrong place. The young woman in the grainy black-and-white photo had just woken up. The first cup of caffeine in hand. Upon closer inspection, she recognized, if only marginally, the woman in the picture.

"It can't be," she cursed the air. "She left on a flight to Hawaii days ago. What the hell is she doing at his cabin?"

Flipping to the next photo confirmed her suspicions. The shot was closer. The woman, the reporter, wore the colored bands of near-strangulation on her neck and appeared startled. The damn photographer had been spotted.

"Asshole, nothing like warning her. You could've gone up and introduced yourself."

These two images of the reporter alone didn't hold a candle to the reaction inflicted by the single photo of her with MJ.

Ray's gold Cartier sunglasses hit the floor with a scratching impact. The picture shook in her hands, distorting the black-and-white image. And her once smooth brow furrowed and grew thundery as her skin broke into a low-grade sweat.

MJ was with her and had spent the night. He was touching her, protecting her from the intruder with the camera. How was this possible?

Emotion scrambled the mind.

His hands were around her, pulling her close, his flesh on hers. Her face was partially concealed in the frame. She stared up into his eyes. He'd never been that close to Ray, not even when she sat at his bedside during recovery. His posture was protective. Why would he do that? They didn't know each other. He was hers.

Her mind refused to make sense of it. She couldn't accept this.

They were strangers. Why would he be willing to defend her so vehemently? Had she slept with him? Did they share the night in the throes of passion?

Snap...crackle...break.

An eruption came from a place beyond her humanity, an animal place of instinctive right. He belonged to her. She brought him back, gave him life, worshipped him, and risked everything.

"No!!!!" she cried out, forgetting where she was. Forgetting the thinness of the flowered walls. Forgetting the people down the hall.

Dropping to her knees with a bruising thud, she held fast to the picture as if made of heavy steel, her hands welded to it, unable to release.

He wore a housecoat but no shirt, like he had rolled out of bed. Their hair was disheveled by sleep, and there was more. Something about him...wasn't the same.

Something had *changed* him.

She . . . changed him.

Pure when he left her. Tainted by another. No. He wouldn't be shared. Without him, she'd be more alone than any living human. Soiled images rushed forth so powerfully they packed a punch that sent her back on her heels, collapsing in a hunch.

She didn't hear the door forced open or the utter of concern from the owner and her husband as they rushed to where she sat crumpled on the hardwood—deaf as the dead.

Only when they reached out to console her, and made physical contact, did she become aware of them.

"Don't touch me!" she breathed in a low, controlled whisper that halted them.

"We heard you scream." The woman retreated, sensing that comforting this guest wasn't a good idea.

"Get out!" Ray ordered, not looking up, her voice iceberg cold.

Fear overruled any compassion the proprietors felt. They backed out of the room slowly, as if avoiding a rabid dog, shutting the door.

She couldn't tear MJ and the journalist apart by ripping the picture. Their bodies overlapped in the frame. She crushed it into a ball and threw it in her backpack.

Dialing the number, her hands regained stability. Falling into darkness, she found an unnatural stillness.

"Did you get the photos?" a nervous voice answered.

"What, *exactly*, did you see?" she asked.

There was no need to threaten him; the eerie tone in her voice did enough.

"They got up late. There wasn't any movement when I got there. I saw her first. She came from the front of the house into the kitchen. I was right outside the kitchen window. It was the only place without motion sensor lights," he began.

"Was she alone?"

"Yes. He came from a different direction. He didn't pass me."

"Then what?"

"He hugged her. She was at the kitchen table. He came in and hugged her."

"Passionately?" she asked, her voice icy and rigid.

"I don't know. They didn't make-out in the kitchen if that's what you're asking," he complained, instantly regretting it and recovering his tone. "He hugged her, then she sat back down. I had to leave before he spotted me. She was upset and he was comforting her, nothing more."

Ray mulled over the information in silence.

"They caught you taking the photos!"

"In the living room. I setup for the shots undetected, or so I thought, but—"

"Don't waste time on excuses. You probably scared them out of hiding. Now I'll be lucky to track them. And, if I lose them, you'll pay for it with your life."

"Hey, relax. They haven't gone anywhere. They probably think I'm a sicko snapping kinky shots of unsuspecting women," he argued.

"Well, aren't you?" she asked. "What are they doing, and where's Mason?"

"I can't get near the house. They have a dog, and the young guy practically chased me off the property. I haven't laid eyes on anyone else. If Mason's here, he's made himself invisible. I can't go back for a while. I'm stationed at the only road out. They can't get past me without being seen."

"Stay there until I notify you otherwise. Hide in the damn shadows. If anything changes, *anything*, you contact me immediately. Understood?"

"Yeah."

Ray dialed her driver next, gave instructions for him to be waiting outside, and grabbed her belongings. Having prepaid her room, there was no reason to engage hotel staff. Better for them if she didn't. Their intrusion grated on her.

Guarded, they glanced up from their flower-embellished front desk briefly before averting their eyes to meaningless papers. She swung open the front door. It hissed shut behind her.

Jumping into the waiting vehicle, she ordered the driver to rendezvous with her chopper. "Make haste." Her voice dropped to an inaudible whisper. "I have mountains to climb."

I journey into the build window who entered the down on we custom is without chorce." Miley bare. H a turned dropped toun man the Scheper. H premountain to mind

32

"I CAN'T WAIT HERE." Chris broke the unbearable stillness, heading for the hotel room door. "Not like this."

"You can't go waltzing around the building either. You know Ray could still be in the area," Mason warned.

"She's not here, I'd know. I'll be outside, below our window on the coast where you can keep an eye on me."

"Keep an eye on you? It's pea soup out there. You won't be able to see your hand in front of your face."

"Well then, I should remain well hidden," Chris said, undaunted.

"You're meeting your mother and father in less than a half hour."

Mason protested, but they both knew he was worn enough to relent.

"Not like this," Chris repeated. "When she arrives, have her come get me."

"It's dangerous for you two to be—"

"Mason," he interrupted, crossing the threshold. "Have her come get me...alone."

When the door lock engaged behind Chris, Mason circled the room. He thought of taking a shower to relieve the tension tightening the muscles across the back of his neck into a band of rubber ready to snap. No time. Returning to a window seat, lacking the foresight of other options, he searched the haze. Chris appeared below him, entering coastal grounds, then disappeared—a ghost amid white shadows.

"How in God's name is she supposed to see you in this? I'm not sending out a search party to find you've plummeted off the edge of the cliff. In which case, I won't have to worry about your protection anymore!" Mason said out the open window despite the fact that Chris couldn't hear him.

Unable to remain idle, Mason paced the room, glancing down from the window once every lap. Worry was debilitating. Sorrow, worse. Chris' parents felt both.

Chris wasn't free to be with them. An endangered pariah. Chances were, he never would be. And there'd be no opportune moment to explain the gravity of his situation. Brook and Curt didn't know the half of it.

"God help us." Mason's words dispersed in the fog beyond the open pane as the sound of someone struggling with the doorknob snapped his head around.

Crossing the room in quick strides, Mason peered cautiously through the security hole to find Curt and his sister hovering in the hall-way, their faces sullen.

Opening the door, his first words came in the form of an answer, "He isn't here. Come on in, and I'll explain."

He checked to see the hall was clear before closing and engaging the dead bolt, then ushered them into the sitting area.

"He's here, though?" Brook begged. "In the building."

"Yes, your son is here. We have to talk for a minute before you meet him. There are things I have to explain."

"Mason, please," she pleaded.

"I know how desperate you are, but I have to ensure you're prepared for what's coming. Chris can't come home with you. After this meeting, I don't know when or if you'll be able to see him again. Your son is at the center of a conspiracy that could cost a lot of people their lives."

"If, what do you mean if?" Curt demanded. "We will see our son again."

"Curt, that isn't up to you. He is a grown man—"

"Does he hate us? Blame us for leaving him with—" Brook wore her worst fears openly.

"Brook, he doesn't blame you or hate you. He can't be with you because he's a walking target. He's being hunted. We were lucky to arrive merely wounded."

"Wounded?"

Consumed by emotions, she hadn't noticed his condition. He wore the toll of the last couple days wrapped in stiffness and shades of black and blue.

"Are you all right? Where are you hurt?"

"I'm fine, it's Chris. There was an accident. He'll be okay."

"What happened to him?" Tears clouded her eyes.

"His wrists were impaled climbing down a fire escape ladder. He's okay."

"Impaled. Dear God. How did that happen? I need to see him."

"You have to give me your word you'll understand and let him go," he said. "He has to finish this, or none of us will be safe. Tell me."

"I will. I promise. I'll let him go. Please, Mason."

"He's down there." Mason pointed out the window to the coast. "He wanted to wait for you outside."

She didn't require an invitation. Brook flew across the room, then froze three feet from the doorway.

"Does he know...his name?" she turned and asked. "What do I call him?"

"Chris," Mason said. "Call him Chris."

Searching for encouragement and strength from her husband, she admitted her doubts without saying a word. Her blue eyes rivers where regret raged.

"You can do this," he told her. "Go get our son."

Before she turned out of view down the corridor, Mason flashed a go-ahead grin and shut the door. Grabbing bottles from the minibar, he settled in a seat beside Curt.

"You're going to need this," he said, pouring liquid strength into a glass on the table between them. "I'll explain everything I know so far, including what we've learned from Kyly, the writer who escaped with Zavier, and her father, the doctor in Hawaii."

"What writer with Zavier...who?"

"You're going to have to keep an open mind. A *really* open mind. Save your questions until I'm finished. Believe me when I say there will be more questions than answers."

Curt's expression settled into accepted patience.

Squashing expectation right out of the gate, Mason said, "You're not going to like this."

———

A few short steps into a cold cloud, fog engulfed Brook. It hung heavy at her feet where the stone pathway led to the ocean lookout and broke into pockets of clearer, wispy air in front as she walked. Like fabric over a telephone handset, it muffled sound. Birds covered the shoreline in this area. A well-known feeding ground rich with fish, still their cries failed to penetrate. She listened as incoherent sounds fell twisted, and broken through the thickening mist.

According to the hotel pamphlet, one destination lay in this direction, a tiny outcrop with two small benches on the bluff. If Christian was out here, he must be waiting there.

Gazing behind her, ten perhaps fifteen steps in, she couldn't make out even the outline of the grand hotel.

The Ritz Carlton evoked images ripped from an era of kings and castles. Two hundred and sixty-one rooms vanished abandoning her in this surreal place of white silence.

Anxious to see the man who was her son, Brook hadn't contemplated the reality that he was a stranger to her. She didn't allow herself the space to think he'd be anything but loving and kind—until now.

Why had he arranged to see her alone? Why not with his father? And why, of all places, here under the concealment of fog?

Maybe he waited, anticipating this moment, when they were alone, to exact revenge. After all, she'd be a stone's throw from an impossibly steep embankment. It wouldn't take much effort, even for an injured man, to toss her from the high cliff wall to the crashing waves below.

What am I thinking? What's the matter with me?

"Christian," she called. "Son, are you out here?" Her voice echoed hollow, bouncing against a soundless wall, returning unanswered.

"Christian," she tried again. "It's me, Brook, your mother."

Stillness returned so quickly following her words she couldn't be certain she'd spoken them.

Long since halting her approach, stagnant in the drizzle, Brook waited for a force to call her forward. She couldn't move one more step on her own accord. Poised there, she found a strange measure of solace in the smog.

She held herself accountable for a lifetime of lies. Of course, she couldn't have known. She was a young, naive mother back then. No excuse. Alone, surrounded by a sobering conscience and an impenetrable gloom, the full weight of the irrevocable damage of her decision hit. A decision based on the best of intentions.

You know what they say about good intentions, she thought.

"The road to hell is paved with them," she whispered without volition.

Frozen there, her eyes fell from searching the milky distance to the ground. Perhaps she teetered on the ocean's edge. Shattered crystal lay at her feet. Sea salt drawn inland to dry upon the stones. It glistened like glass, shifting beneath her sandals. She heard it crush and crunch, but she hadn't moved.

Ahead on the walkway, the fog parted for him, rolling over his shoulders and out from his sides as he drew near. His skin, as white as the air, was pure and untainted by age as it had been the day he was born. His eyes were the most spectacular eyes she'd ever seen. And this wasn't the opinion of a proud parent. A kaleidoscope of color, they pierced through the filmy mist between them. Lit from within. He stood slightly taller than her younger son and larger in frame. He held out his arms, and her gaze drifted to the white bandages on his wrists. He wore no shoes, no coat, just a white shirt a size too large and loose pants, perhaps linen. The breeze flapped the material against him. A vision.

He exuded a kind acceptance. No hesitation, she ran for his open arms. He embraced her as though *she* was the victim in this dire situation, not him. She clung so that it was miraculous his chest accepted the ebb and flow of breath. He didn't resist.

"Hello, Mother," he said. "It's going to be all right."

They froze, hidden in place in the silence of fog, until several minutes passed. Then, looking down, he said, "We have to go back. They need us. Walk with me."

"I don't want to go," she begged in a broken voice, strained with emotion. "I want to stay here with you."

"I know," he whispered. "You cannot. We have to go back and do what is necessary to protect our family."

He held her in his gaze, eyes of a tenderness she couldn't escape.

"You *will* see me again." He led her back, tears streaming down her face. "Let us go fix this."

Taking her hand in his, his grip felt strong despite his injury. She matched his pace along the path to the hotel, unable to take her eyes from him.

Inside the hotel room, Curt met his eldest for the first time. His meeting was different from hers. Something intensely powerful and silent passed between mother and child. Brook knew she'd never be the same. Life would never be the same. She also knew, though she buried it deep within her heart, Mason spoke the truth—Christian would never come home.

33

PARIS, fine wine, fresh baked bread, French music wafting through the air, and a spirit-devouring desperation demoralizing all of it.

Pensive and preoccupied, Cero didn't notice her slip away and drift down the hall. His attention span withered with worry.

Entering Kyly's room, she closed the door behind her without a creak. Lighting candles on the windowsill and bedside table, she gathered her daughter's energy with her own. She hadn't needed to read their future. Their lives, sheltered in contentment, lent promise for tomorrow until a plane ride changed it all.

Kyly's aura radiated. Paris selected a simple tattered notebook. Placing the pad between her hands, sitting knees folded beneath her, she closed her eyes and centered herself—opening the door to her insight despite a very real fear of what she may find there.

Warm candlelight caressed the walls, casting a golden glow throughout the room. Outside, a gentle breeze brushed palm leaves against the window.

Flames grew beyond her closed eyes. She envisioned Kyly in the sunshine typing away on her laptop, investigating, deep in thought. The computer screen came into view through her daughter's eyes.

Malpractice cases in bits and pieces flashed before her until the Cromwell name appeared. Images of Dr. Valeric. Articles boasting his accomplishments, aligned in succession from past to present, just as they were compiled in Kyly's research.

Water edged out from under her fingertips.

The notebook became damp at first as if dropped in a puddle. Within seconds, the soggy leather cover wept. Water spilled steadily from between the pages, a faucet pouring onto the floor at her feet. Paris stood, watching it fill the room, accelerating to the intensity of a fire hose.

No noise accompanied the deluge. Nor spray, just a constant, ever-widening, freezing flow.

Impossibly cold. Her feet fell numb as the water crept up her legs. She clasped the book between her hands, holding fast while a soundless sea surrounded her in its frigid murk with the strength of a devouring whirlpool.

Hungry, it swelled over her hips.

Unable to move her lower limbs, her body surrendered to the stiffening effects of hypothermia. Air came in short, unsatisfying bursts. Her lungs were helpless to receive as icy liquid rose up her torso and over her shoulders, gaining strength.

Heavy hands strangling out the little air she fought for.

The glacial wave covered her mouth. Her screams froze in her throat, a surge of desperation. Steely water claimed her eyes, solidifying terror. A cylinder of smooth stones surrounded the heartless womb, entombing her.

Freedom from the Arctic cage lay inches above. Paralyzed, she was unable to swim up. As threatening as her freezing chamber was, what lurked beyond its surface was far more lethal.

Shadows burned across the darkness above the churning water, leaving intersecting trails of smoke lingering in the air. Below, thundering bursts echoed through the waves, bouncing off the rock walls in deafening succession.

An irregular, threatening drumbeat resounded in her chest. Not good, signs of her heartbeat slowing, slipping, stopping.

A hand reached below the waterline. No strength to grab it. Two hands clenching her shoulders pulled her from the bottom. Darkness shadowed all but his eyes. Paris recognized him from pictures Cero received. Zavier Cromwell.

Then black. Then only black.

Her hands released the notebook when they found the warmth of open air. Her eyes opened. She was dry, seated on the floor of Kyly's room, gasping for air.

It wasn't her breath that would be taken, but Kyly's.

The premonition ended, offering but a terrifying glimpse.

She had to warn her daughter.

She dried her face of tears, circled the room, blowing out the candles, and rushed for the door. Throwing it open, she swung into the hall and her husband who, recognizing her absence, had come searching for her.

Cero grabbed hold to steady her.

"Your hands?" he said with concern. "They're ice cold."

34

RAINFALL CREATED A STEALTHY HUNTING GROUND, giving Ray an edge of silence on otherwise crunchy terrain.

She reached the property's edge surrounding Mason's cabin, pleased to see a 'no hunting permitted' sign. Wild beauty deserved protection.

Sadly, animals couldn't read.

Hot on the trail of an innocent buck and his mates, two poachers had crawled beyond the perimeter with disregard. Nothing but an easy, albeit illegal, kill on their feeble minds.

Like all of her physical aspects, Ray's eyesight and hearing were impeccable. Despite their preposterous camouflage gear and whispered conspiracy, the two hunters made an easier target than the lone buck in the clearing.

Approaching them from behind, she parted branches with the end of her silencer. Their premature triumphant banter rang with crystal clarity. Every arrogant word uttered from their lips infuriated her more than the last.

Blake said it best. 'Cruelty has a human heart...terror the human form divine.'

A truth she knew and resented. After all, she was one of them. In stark contrast, those on four legs were creatures of divine instinct. Despite the reality of which category she exemplified, her mind drew parallels with the animal.

Slaughtering a magnificent six-point buck with the squeeze of an overzealous trophy hunter's trigger was no less violent than her creator's decision to murder her—a one-of-a-kind, ultimate specimen. Both executioners would brag safe from nemesis. Death had a sick way of granting idiots authority.

Not this time.

This time, evolution fought back. This time, the hunters became the hunted. Arrogant, ignorant, flippant. An easy, albeit illegal, kill.

"Bob's not gonna believe this one, hey Mack?" whispered the scrawnier one of the two. His hat, tilted sideways by an interfering branch at his head, made him appear more pathetic than necessary.

"I've got a mind to drive its bullet-ridden carcass to the son-of-a-bitch's front door after the performance he put on last season." Mack spoke in hushed tones, lining up his shot through the scope of his Savage 270.

"We're never telling that asshole about this place," the skinny guy said.

"Son-of-a-bitch would turn us in for trespassing just to take it over."

"Take 'em down. What are you waiting for, an invitation?" the wiry man prompted.

"What? You're in a hurry to drag this hunk of meat a mile and a half back to the truck?" Mack glared the little man down before refocusing the rifle. "Besides, I want it to relax. Go for a nibble before I knock it off its legs."

"Wanna really surprise the shit out of it, hey."

"You got it, mate."

Ray's Glock slipped out from the brush at head level without so much as a hint of sound. Water from the leaves it touched traced its sides, shimmering down the matte black barrel. She stood at equal height, flanking them inches away. They remained oblivious to her presence while she studied them, one more revolting than the next. Her sleek black outfit revealed nothing but the whites of her eyes. Made whiter still by the colorless pools at their center. Dense brush surrounded her. Silent, she stood, a dark angel in waiting.

"Mack, we don't have ta drag this thing through the creek to get back, do we?"

"No, not like the last one we left on the bank. He was a heavy mother," Mack replied. A smirk slithered across his mouth. "Wasn't even finished dying when we dumped him at the river."

"I don't wanna pull this sucker halfway just to leave 'em."

"Na, truck is on the cut line, remember? We're fine. Besides, I'm taking this one to stuff down Bob's throat. The righteous bastard."

Hearing this, the skinny man shifted his weight, snapping a branch under his boot.

"Don't move!" Mack hissed as heavy antlers rose to investigate the noise in the thicket.

Moments passed, and Ray remained frozen with her silencer's barrel pointed at the gunman's temple.

The buck, satisfied with the returned stillness and unable to smell their excited stench upwind, dropped its head to eat at a low bush.

"Ha ha," said Mack. "The element of surprise."

Whispering smoothly, jamming the gun's muzzle against his flesh, Ray taunted, "Ain't it a bitch."

In an automatic release reflex, Mack's rifle fell hard to the ground through broken branches, sending a shot on impact somewhere low across the terrain. Startled, the buck vanished into the safety of the chaparral behind him. *He* was granted reprieve, at least for today. The same could not be said for his hunters.

Like the crack of unexpected thunder, the shot shattered the mountain's serenity. The large man threw his broad shoulders into a military arch to put to shame any young recruit.

"Holy Mary, Joseph, and Jesus!" the skinny one blurted, staring into the shadowy figure's glaring onyx eyes.

"He's not going to help you. Don't you fellas know...brutality begets brutality?" Ray scolded. "You have a license to be on these premises?"

"License?" replied Mack, terrified but still, by nature, insolent. "For hunting, yeah...I'll show ya if you'll point that thing somewhere else."

Ray removed the cold butt from his temple and aimed it at his nether region with obvious intent.

"You some kind of psycho?" The wiry man, shaken by the blast, shuffled back a foot further from his buddy.

"Shut up, Frank! You trying to get me killed?" Mack protested. "Look, I have a legal huntin' license, and the damn thing got away anyhow."

"I don't give a damn about your hunting license. I asked if you had a license to be on this property," she said, confusing the men, and instilling the deliberate impression she had authority over security for the area.

"Property, you're kiddin' me, right?" Mack asked, shifting his body to divert the target from his privates.

"Don't move. I'll warn you once, which is more than you give the defenseless animals you stalk." She spoke slowly, with an empty tone intended to scare the hell out of the men.

"You're gonna kill us for steppin' across a fence line for a buck?" Frank stuttered in disbelief as inner terror soaked through the front of his blue jeans.

"Not exactly." Ray spoke with an executioner's authority that had the men scrambling to save their lives.

Glancing down to verify the gun's model while Frank spoke, Mack's eyes locked onto the silencer attached to the muzzle of the Glock 18, a military issue. The severity of his situation became dreadfully apparent in his contorted expression.

"Jesus Christ, that's a fuckin' war weapon. Who in God's name are you?" Mack blurted out.

"Your worst nightmare. Name's Ray, *your* god…has nothing on me." She said it as her eyes scorched through him, followed by the burning agony of the bullet tearing into his flesh.

The heavy man fell sideways from the impact to his thigh, and before his slight partner could dislodge his Winchester model 30 off the knapsack behind him, Ray fired again, and he too, hit, the damp grasses. Howls erupted, shattering silence.

"One more sound and I finish the job," she said with venom, retrieving Mack's rifle from its resting place in the brush beside her.

The men wriggled in muffled moans. One outcry was all she needed to provoke their certain demise. Ray fed off the intense pain contorting their bodies. It served to assure them of the validity of their assailant's promise.

Handgun still aimed in their direction, Savage rifle swung over her back by its shoulder strap, Ray hovered over the men, devoid of mercy. She glanced at their attire, then bent down, grabbed a T-shirt hanging from the discarded knapsack, and tore it in half, throwing a piece at each man.

"Wrap it tight around your upper thigh. It'll slow the blood flow. If you don't bleed to death and the animals don't eat you, you should be found by morning. If I ever catch you hunting again, I'll hang your heads above my mantel." She tossed their supplies and Frank's lever action 30/30 within crawling distance but far enough out of reach to prevent bullets from being fired after her.

"Another thing," she said. "I wouldn't waste ammunition shooting into thin air. No one will be out here but me until dawn, and if *I* hear you." She paused for effect. "I may be tempted to come back."

Veiled by her mask, a thin, venomous grin stretched tight across her face as she met eyes with each man. It slithered away as she left the pair thrashing in pain, side by side, in the mud where, in her opinion, they belonged.

Blood poured from the larger man's thigh. Still he raised his head off the wet debris of the forest floor to watch her. She paused, capturing the image to replay later. Mack's empty stare spoke volumes. She'd be the last woman to enter his life, the quickest to leave it, but oh, what an impact she'd made.

Shifting his body, he'd unwittingly lined up the bullet and the main artery in his upper thigh. She gave him minutes, not hours.

The cold, dark night would come early for him. Walking away, Ray's mind drifted back to the fallen buck he'd left to die at the river's edge.

Same injury inflicted, same compassion shown, same cruel fate.

Justice.

The incident was a brief but worthwhile deviation. Broadening the distance between her and the fallen butchers, a profound wave of renewed conviction surged through her.

On determined feet, she continued in the direction of Mason's home.

The night, sensing something sinister, cried icy tears that soaked heavy the thick cloth of fog around her. Ray reveled in the worsening weather, knowing the torrent would conceal her even further and force everyone indoors where she could monitor them.

Every premeditated act had a flaw.

The enclosing night drove forth a haunting.

This was the first time since breaking free from the compound as a child she met such a similar environment. She fought to see reality, aware it had disappeared. What lay in its place was nothing more than a cruel trick of the human mind.

Halted by tormenting flashes, her feet quaked and struggled not to falter.

Draped in weapons, she flailed at invisible demons.

Trees came to life. She flung her arms around her torso in childlike defense of an oncoming attack.

Unable to stop it, she relived the sickening terror she'd experienced so many years before. The passage of time failed to heal her wounds. Instead, they festered, a cancer left unchecked, raw, and running rampant, fed by the dark truth of her existence and her designer's desperate desire to end what they began.

Like an internal homing beacon of the psyche, her thoughts targeted Micael. He'd rescued her. He was why she was here, enduring this cold place of memories. She *would* overcome this lapse of sanity to be with him.

The trees stopped spinning. Her breathing resumed a calm flow. Like the fleeting nausea superseding the countless graphic nightmares that afflicted her since childhood, the moment passed.

She adjusted the rifle, checked her gear, and surveyed her surroundings.

Wiping drizzle from her brow, she focused on the tree line ahead, noting the considerable expanse of mountainside before the crest leading to Mason's valley.

It was an uphill trek through forest moss and mud. Wet-weighted branches slapped at her sides, soaking them through, as she fought her way by. She'd long since re-holstered her weapon to free both hands to ward off the greenery. At one point, she paused to glance back down the mountainside, expecting a broken telltale trail behind her. In spite of her forceful shoving, the branches had snapped back into their original cumbersome positions as if never disturbed.

Circling the cabin from a safe distance, she located a vantage point two hundred yards away. She sought refuge, ducking under a large pine. Thickened with sturdy aged limbs, it sheltered dry ground in a four-foot circumference of its trunk. Crouching under its shadow, she leaned her back against the bark, drying out while reviewing the attack in her mind.

Gory images flashed like Morse code across her thoughts. They overshadowed the serene reality, bouncing back through the Vector's high-powered binocular-like lens she pressed to her face.

Refocusing her attention and her eyes, the cabin materialized. Warm lights glowed from several windows with the invitation of hearth and home, cradled by nature's tranquility. It could've been a damn Norman Rockwell painting. She cursed every peaceful implication.

When a thorough search of each tinted window failed to reveal the slightest hint of movement, she made the call.

"What's your location?"

"I'm still at the access road, as you instructed. Ray, you're coming in awfully clear. Where are you?" Her hired tracker, Nero, asked.

"About two hundred and fifty yards to your left. Don't move your position or come back on the line unless you see someone."

"How the hell did you come in? I didn't see—"

"That's the whole idea, isn't it," she said. "Silence until nightfall. I'll contact you then. Hold your position and stay hidden, understood?"

"Yes."

She killed the connection, pulled a water-resistant sheet from her backpack, and laid it as close to the tree's trunk as possible. Saturation glued her inner layers to her flesh making stripping off the soaked clothing challenging. Her skin, left momentarily exposed, bristled.

Wearing dry clothes, she drank large gulps from her canteen, quenching a deep thirst. Tearing open a freeze-dried pouch of food, she ate lying down in her hidden shelter. Justification and resolution filled her.

Absolution would not.

35

"KYLY'S IN DANGER." Paris yanked her cold hands from his grasp. "I have to warn her."

"Tonight? You know the risks." With all Cero was sorting through, her demand broadsided him.

"Damn the risks, I've seen it."

"A premonition? What did you see?" He needed concrete reasons for contact. "We agreed we wouldn't—"

"I don't give a damn what we agreed." Paris pushed by him. "You're not the one with images of her death haunting you."

"What?" He followed. "You saw her dead?"

"There's no time." She dialed the number using the phone nearest the patio and paced. Three rings sounded before Kyly answered.

"Dad?" Kyly said.

"No, it's me, dear. Are you okay?" Paris asked, relieved to hear her daughter's voice.

"Fine. There has been an interesting development. What's up? Are you and Dad all right?"

"We're fine. What development?"

Paris raised the question. Cero repeated it, wringing his hands in the background. Unable to wait for secondhand information, he left the room, returning with a cordless handset to share the line while Kyly explained.

"A photographer showed up here earlier. We don't know how long he spied on us, but he snapped off a few photos before Zavier scared him off the property. There are motion sensors surrounding the place. He tripped them to get a close-up, then bolted. He hasn't returned. We're certain of that, but we don't know why he came in the first place or who, if anyone, sent him," Kyly said. "I think Zavier and I should leave before dark, but he's dead set against it. We haven't heard from Mason, have you?"

"No, we haven't. Our source confirmed he got off the island with Zavier's brother. We're waiting to hear more. Your father will explain when I've finished," she said.

"Wait a second," Kyly said, then called out. "Zavier, your uncle and brother made it off the island."

The young man's elated reaction colored the background. "I told you, I told you," echoed down the line.

"Zavier just flew around the corner. It's the first good news we've had." Paris lost her daughter's attention as she played on Zavier's excitement. "I suppose you're going to hover around my doorway now? Come in, come in."

Paris inhaled a long, slow breath then began. "I had a vision...about the two of you. It wasn't good. Is there a lake or river around you with rocks?"

Kyly didn't question the validity of her abilities. Instead, she instructed her to wait for a moment while she asked Zavier.

"Is there a river or lake close by?"

"Well, it's not close, but yes. We'd have to cross the river to get out of here if we couldn't use the road we came in on. It's the only other way," Zavier answered.

"Did you hear that?" Kyly questioned.

"Yes. You can't leave. My vision involved you trapped in icy water. I think Zavier's right. You should stay where you are, safe inside until Mason arrives."

"Okay, Mom, I don't think Zavier would've agreed to leave anyway. I'll stay inside, I promise. Zavier won't let me out of his sight. And Mom."

"Yes."

"I'll be all right."

"I'll know you're all right when you're home," Paris replied, unconvinced. "It's not you I don't trust."

———

Sitting next to Kyly on the bed, listening in, Zavier watched her mother's warning sink in and begin to erode.

When Kyly's father got on the line, Zavier seized the opportunity to cut in, asking to speak with him directly.

"I've been piecing this together, and it just keeps getting worse," Cero admitted, knowing his daughter no longer shared the line. "For my daughter's sake, be brave."

Zavier was. His expression remained intense but undaunted. Despite her best efforts, he knew Kyly couldn't read it. Every cold detail was a blow to a stake being driven into the heart of their world. He could almost feel the physical impact. A killer was hunting his brother and uncle, a killer with resources, closing in as he listened.

"I'm certain I'll hear from my uncle soon. If anyone can get us out of this, he can. I won't let anything happen to her, sir. You have my word."

Kyly fidgeted with her hands. Her nerves were showing. Placing his over hers calmed her. Dread darkened her eyes as she waited for him to reveal the ugly truth.

"Yes, we will. I'll tell her," Zavier said into the line, then closed the cell phone. "He said to stay together and stay safe. He's proud of you, of us. If Mason contacts them first, which I doubt he will, they'll tell him about the photographer and insist he comes immediately. I'm sure that's his intention anyway. There is nowhere safer to take my brother than here. At least, he'll think so."

"And what do you think?" she asked.

He didn't answer, but his expression spoke volumes.

"If we're not safe here—"

"The thing is, I don't know where we will be safe." Something dreadful underlied his honesty, and he couldn't hide it.

"What haven't you told me?"

"Take a deep breath." A look of regret washed over her. He squeezed her fingers. "I'm afraid this battle may be coming to our doorstep sooner than we'd like."

36

"SORRY FOR THE INCONVENIENCE, SIR," a voice said from behind Mason. "The pool heater will be up and running in a couple hours if you'd like to come back."

"No inconvenience," Mason said. "I'm a cold water swimmer. I prefer low temperatures, better for the circulation."

"That's rare. Are you from Canada?" the hotel worker asked on his way out.

"No." He lied and walked to the edge.

"Have a good one," the man said, exiting the room.

Alone, Mason threw off his robe at the far end and dove into the pool. Cool waves broke around his shoulders.

Submerged, his mind cleared a little. Like Holy water, the pool cleansed his demons.

The mystery behind his newly acquired nephew wasn't washed away. Their conversations—every word spoken between them—played over in his head.

He reveled in the water's silence. The aquatic chamber provided a certain measure of peace. After ten laps, his injured shoulder screamed with pain, forcing him to quit.

Rolling onto his back, he slid into the water and floated with his ears submerged. Cool air drifted over exposed parts of his body, sending shivers across his skin. He welcomed the frigid sensation. Survival training taught him to be grateful for discomfort and pain. The senses, even reacting to the unpleasant, were reminders you had a fighting chance—you were still alive.

His thoughts drifted to Chris. He hadn't once complained about *his* injuries despite their severity. A man with Mason's background learned to suffer in silence, but Chris? It didn't add up.

Why *did* the young man show no concern for himself? Men his age were all pride and ego. Not him. And, even appreciating his sorted background, the facts remained unnerving.

His diction was even more disconcerting.

"There are things in this world one should not lend the energy of the spoken word to." Chris had warned Mason not to dwell on the evil behind Ray's conception.

Or when they were discussing his coma.

"I haven't really been conscious for the last thirty years or so. Like most people on this planet, I've been alive without consciously living," he'd said.

What the hell was that supposed to mean? And why, when Chris said such things, did he feel compelled to believe him?

He hadn't disclosed the details of the wrist operation with Chris, but the extreme fluctuations in Chris' vital signs haunted him. If there *was* something wrong with the machine, *why* were all the later readings accurate? If the readings proved reliable, Chris shouldn't have survived, let alone recovered as he had.

Then there was the incident at the drug store, his instant recognition of the child's earache. Chris' ease with the mother, a stranger. The strength underlying his vow made before he passed out in the truck.

"I'm not leaving until I'm damn good and ready."

"Leaving," Mason repeated it in a whisper. "Why not dying or going to die...leaving."

Stranger still, Chris' reasoning why Ray could get away with his murder. *"I'm dead already,"* he'd said. *"I don't exist here, not really."*

This revelation loomed like a ghost emerging from murky depths below. Mason slapped the water. From his digging, he knew Chris was accurate. On paper he didn't exist, but what happened to him during all those years? Mason dug into the truth of the medical advancements of those who surrounded him since birth, which equated to a realization that terrified. Chris was his nephew, but he was more. He'd been messed with. CRISPR, gene splicing, and genetic manipulation. What had been done to him couldn't be undone, and whatever it was, Mason couldn't deny, its implications made living on Mars inevitable.

Exiting the deep end, he climbed out of the pool with all the demons he suppressed beneath the broken surface.

As for the unsettling facts, Mason wouldn't share them. Not yet.

Slicking his hair back out of his eyes, he toweled off, grabbed his robe and headed back up to the room.

When he arrived, he paused outside, waiting for the corridor to clear of guests. Alone in the hall, he disengaged the door lock with his security code key and entered, careful not to allow the door to slam shut in case Chris slept.

Beneath a light blanket, Chris moaned and rolled to his side. Mason faced his back, walking to the closet to retrieve clean clothes. Closing the washroom door behind him, he showered and dressed, concealed weapon loaded and holstered at his side.

He intended to leave for Canada when Chris woke. He wanted to land before dark. Animals filtered down from higher elevations at night, making traversing the road in dangerous.

The roar of the fan and running water drowned out the world beyond. But, when they were extinguished, what replaced them was disturbing.

Mason's razor broke on impact into the sink. Chris' voice lost its customary composure as he argued protests. Mason reached for the door handle. The door refused to budge as if vacuum-sealed by steam.

Hearing Chris' pleas intensify, he grabbed the handle with both hands. One solid yank and the door popped free hitting Mason with a jarring thud. Rounding the corner, he called for Chris, slid his gun from its holster, and searched the room, ready to take aim.

No one. The perpetrator had fled.

Rushing to his side, Mason asked, *"Chris, are you hit?"*

He expected to see the hotel door flapping wide open, yet the lock was engaged from the inside. Chris' thrashing suggested he was wounded, but Mason couldn't see any sign of an intruder. Through the French doors, at the balcony's edge, he searched below and above and found the area abandoned.

Blood stained the sheets.

"*Chris, what the hell?*"

Pulling the blanket aside, Mason checked for a pulse. He struggled to keep his hand in one place. The kid's heart rate had to be off the charts. This would explain why his wounds were bleeding through his bandages as if fresh. He couldn't find new injuries.

"*Wake up, please!*" Mason repeated. "*Chris, it's me. Wake up!*"

Chris had spoken coherently before he freed himself from the washroom. Mason had heard words and phrases. Now, only sounds of agony escaped the young man.

"*Christian Cromwell, you wake up, damn it!*" Mason demanded.

Chris ceased thrashing, opened his eyes, and looked up at Mason.

"Jesus." Mason collapsed on the edge of the bed. "Darn near gave me a heart attack."

Taking in the situation, Chris said, "I have that effect on you, don't I?"

"I thought someone attacked you," Mason admitted. "You were having a nightmare. We've got to leave soon. Are you okay?"

"Yes." Chris edged up.

Mason couldn't help but stare at him like he had three heads. His demeanor was calm and unaffected. Mason doubted what he'd witnessed.

"I have to change your dressings first," Mason said. "You...uh...you bled through them in your sleep."

Mason realized that if he found the answers to all his questions, he might wish he hadn't. He believed the old adage '*truth shall set you free*' might not apply to their particular set of circumstances. He remained silent, rewrapping Chris' wrists with clean gauze. And was still mute an hour later when they pulled onto the runway to meet their private airplane.

Trahern met their truck and loaded their packs.

"Is there anything you don't fly?" Chris asked their pilot, hopping from the truck's passenger seat.

Trahern paused, glancing in Chris' direction, then said, "Friendly skies," and drifted out of sight.

———

When the plane reached cruising altitude, Chris and Mason unbuckled their safety belts and shifted in their seats to more comfortable positions. Turbulence was minimal, allowing them to walk about the luxurious cabin. A former client of Mason's owned the plane, a mid-sized Gulfstream G150. The flight had gone by smoothly and they were nearing descent.

"Would you like something else to drink?" Mason headed for the bar.

"Water is fine," Chris said.

"Cheap date," Mason teased, his spirits improved with each mile closer to home.

"I have to return to the island, you know," Chris said.

"That's suicide." Mason's good mood evaporated. He poured bottled water into glasses.

"It's where the documents are. They're the only leverage you have to keep your family safe in the future. If Ray or the military retrieves them before us...there is no other choice."

"There you go again," Mason snapped back, annoyed. "It's not my family, it's ours. Why does everything you say sound so bloody detached?"

"I'm not detached," Chris said. "I'm at the heart of all of this. Whether you're prepared to face facts or not, you know their future safety will depend on you, not me."

Mason knew what he was saying. He wasn't ready to hear it. He couldn't help but love this man. Chris had grown up in the strangest of circumstances. Yet, given his freedom, his first and only priority was to re-enter the lion's den for the benefit of people who were strangers to him.

"Why risk your life for us?"

"I could ask you the same question," Chris replied.

"It's different for me. It's what I'm trained to do. And, as you pointed out, this is my family."

"Yes, but you don't just do this for family, do you?" Chris asked.

"No."

"Why do you help the others?"

"It's my job. It's how I make a living."

"Do you think a human life can be measured in dollars?"

"God, no. I wasn't suggesting—"

"I know you weren't. Your life is put at risk every time you take a job, is it not?"

"Well, not always, but yes, there are risks involved." He raised his glass; the water paused at his lips.

"So do you gauge the value of your life against what you are paid?" Chris said.

Mason swallowed, then set the glass down, spilling water over its edge in waves.

"No, how could I?"

"So, why do you risk your life?" Chris asked again.

"Because I want to help them, because—"

"Because you can."

"It's different," Mason insisted. "You have your whole life ahead of you. You shouldn't be willing to waste it...cut it short so easily."

"You're suggesting my life is more valuable than yours because of age?" Chris asked.

"Yes, I am," Mason protested.

"Why would you assume you can gauge the worth of a life by its duration? There are children who come to this world for a very short time and dramatically alter every life they touch. Do you not agree? Then there are those who live into their golden years, leaving behind a legacy of pain."

"What's your point? I know you have one."

"I'm getting to that. Tell me first, who would you say most positively impacted your life."

"Why should I tell you that?"

"Because I don't think you want me to guess," Chris said, his expression foretelling.

Reluctantly, Mason said, "My mother."

"She died too young, correct?"

"How did you...yes."

"A life should not be measured by the length of time lived, nor should there ever be a value judgment made by one unable to see its full impact. Life is gauged safely by its experiences and choices. The higher the choice, the closer to the heart, the more precious the life becomes. In the end, it's the value we place on our own life, the measure with which we judge ourselves. If I chose not to do this, I'd see no value in the life I've been given."

"You're talking about getting yourself killed. This whole thing started so we could find you, save you. Jesus, are you out of your mind?"

"Calm down. It didn't begin there, and you know it. I don't intend on dying, believe me."

Hearing this, Mason eased up.

"But you have something," Chris continued. "Jesus *was* out of his mind. His choices were made by the heart, not the head. The mind is a place where fear reigns. That is why great accomplishments are called journeys of the heart. Trust me, the mind without the heart is dangerous."

With this, Chris fastened his safety belt, drank out of his glass, and secured it in a cup holder seconds before the fasten seat belt light chimed.

"You see," said Mason. "This is what bothers me."

"I know," Chris replied with a smile.

"We're heading into unstable air heading down." Trahern's voice erupted over the intercom system. "Buckle up."

Regardless of the air pockets throwing the plane around, Mason continued testing for cellular service, anxious to reach Zavier. Chris' definition of self-worth crowded his thoughts.

He picked up a reasonably reliable signal minutes out of their destination.

"It's ringing," he told Chris.

Zavier answered on the second ring, but the connection was weak, and his voice cut in and out through static.

"Zavier, it's me. Are you okay?"

"Thank God. We...to hear from you before..."

"You're breaking up. Is everything all right?"

"We're fine, but someone...and he got a few shots off before...chase him off the property."

"What? Someone was shooting at you?" Mason clamored into the unstable connection.

"Photos," Zavier clarified. "A guy came here taking photos. We're fine...just a...shaken up, but she'll be okay. Where the hell...calling from..."

"The plane. We're on our way down," Mason said. "We should be there inside a half hour."

"I'm glad," Zavier replied. "Kyly wanted to leave...to convince her... father found out some new information...concern."

"Zavier. I'm only hearing bits and pieces. I'll hang up and call when we've landed."

"Mason...we'll...damn glad...see you."

"I'll call you back." Mason was answered by static.

"He said something about a photographer," Mason told Chris.

"Get him back on the line," Chris said, the light draining from his porcelain face.

"I'll try him again when we land. The connection's weak."

"*Get him back on the line!*" Chris demanded. "Your nephew and your w...and the woman are in grave danger."

"He said they were fine."

"They are not."

The gravity of the situation came off Chris in waves. Mason's strong hands weren't as stable when he dialed the number for the second time.

"Zavier, it's me again. I want you to try and explain what happened earlier," Mason asked. This time the line was clear.

"There was a photographer here. He didn't get near the house, except for the few minutes when he set off the back security lights to snap a couple pictures of Kyly," Zavier began.

"Of Kyly?"

"The guy looked like a derelict skulking around, snapping photos of a pretty woman. He wasn't exactly Special Ops material. I scared him off the property with no more than a glance."

Mason relayed the information to Chris, feeling his worries were unwarranted until Zavier called his attention back to the phone.

"Who are you talking to?" Zavier asked.

"Your brother, want to introduce yourself?" Knowing the question was redundant, Mason handed Chris the phone before Zavier answered.

"Chris, are you there?" Zavier asked, his voice echoing inside the fuselage.

"I'm here, Zavier. It's a pleasure to meet you, brother," Chris said.

Those few words touched Mason unexpectedly, and he was

forced to turn away. Zavier would've thrived with another boy in the family, but he'd been robbed of that opportunity. Mason couldn't help but imagine how things would've been between them if life had allowed. These thoughts blocked out Chris' conversation. Mason didn't register a single word until Chris got his attention and covered the phone.

"How fast can we get to them?" Chris asked, his voice insistent.

"We're descending, so less than twenty minutes," Mason said, checking his watch. "She's there. Right now. Waiting."

"Waiting for what?"

"Waiting for a chance to take me back, dead or alive. And she'll kill anyone she deems a threat, including the girl."

"But you're not there yet, damn it! You're here with me," Mason barked. "How did she find them?"

"How she found them doesn't matter." Chris continued with conviction. "What matters is she thinks he is me."

"How do you know?" Mason questioned.

"The pictures."

"Are you sure about this?" Mason's luxury airplane had transformed into an iron cage leaving him helplessly suspended.

"Don't waste time with questions you don't want answers to," Chris said, handing the phone back. "Keep him on the line."

Somewhere along the way, they swapped roles. Mason was taking direction from a man half his age. Nothing about it made sense. Yet, an inner urgency beseeched him to trust Chris.

"Zavier, are you and Kyly together?" Mason asked.

"No, Kyly is lying down in the guest bedroom. Why?"

"Go there and take the gun with you," Mason instructed. "The photographer could've been sent in for reconnaissance. When did you see him last?"

"Three hours or so, I guess." Zavier's voice strained.

"That's plenty of time for backup to arrive."

"Okay, you're scaring the hell out of me. Why would they come after *us*? I thought they wanted Chris," Zavier asked.

"You saw the photo in the paper," Mason reminded him. "They think you're him."

"Oh shit! How the hell did she find us? We were so careful."

"Doesn't matter. Do the checklist with me." Mason said anything to maintain a connection.

"Security measures are all in place," Zavier said. "Perimeter alarms are active. I reset the motion sensors. All the locks are engaged. The gun is in my side holster, and extras are loaded. How long until you get here?"

"Less than fifteen minutes," Mason reassured him. "Try to—"

The first alarm sounded, piercing into the line, cutting their conversation to send a signal.

"Zavier! Zavier!" Mason shouted. The phone dropped to the floor. "Get this plane on the ground, now!" He hollered into the cockpit, knowing his demands were pointless. His safe house, with his nephew and Kyly inside, was under attack by someone he'd barely survived.

37

"DOWN AND DIRTY BOYS." Cage roared above the chopper blades and driving rain as his team jumped into action. "This was their LZ. Find me something!"

When the military touched down in Half Moon Bay's industrial holding site, Ray and those she chased had long since vanished from the landing zone. Intense training and motivation paid off. It didn't take long before the trackers located spent ammunition from her handgun. Prints weren't viable on outdoor surfaces. Poor weather swept any chance of such evidence from the rooftops. Likely Ray had worn gloves anyway. Two specific dent patterns showed men landing in a leap, presumably from a chopper.

"Scan out in a radius from the point of impact," Cage commanded. "Hunt 'em down." Like a pack of wolves, the men followed the scent.

Identifying two areas of refuge, they discovered evidence that one or both men were injured during the ordeal.

Minutes passed while the men scoured outlying sectors. A sodden soldier returned with an update. "Major, a SKO was raided in that abandoned warehouse." He pointed to a decrepit building a few rooftops away. "Minor repair gear missing."

"Any chance they left their DNA behind?" Cage asked.

"Nothing yet, sir. We'll keep at it. Boys are checking the goat trail."

The soldier added, referring to the dirt road used for escape, then he disappeared back into the night.

Another burly man unearthed a few clues in a nearby attic. Ray's prey had fled into the hideaway. Inside, once wet footprints defined by dust led the tracker to a resting place but offered little else.

"Security for the area confirmed reported gunfire," Cage's lead man said. "Their search yielded nothing. They didn't get out of the damn car, grunts."

As inept as local enforcement was against this particular opponent, their fledgling effort didn't come as a surprise to Cage or his men. What they found trailing the escape route, however, did.

Rain blew in off the ocean. Protected by walls in its direction, bloodstains under a broken ladder remained reasonably untouched. Samples were collected for DNA testing, evidence photographs were taken, and the dislodged section of a ladder hauled away. Whomever the blood belonged to, they lost enough of it to place their life in serious jeopardy.

"Dispatch a team to canvas district hospitals and medical centers," Cage ordered. "Track anyone with a medical degree."

"Yes, sir."

He didn't expect to find them hovering nearby, but all options had to be exhausted for the potential of a new lead.

They located a small privately owned practice that served as an evening emergency center. After gentle prying, a secretary informed a handsome and persuasive officer that one of the head doctors on staff had a facility at his home. To her knowledge, it hadn't been used in years.

Cage recognized a suspicious scent and followed it.

Old and wise, the small-town physician—a Dr. Iberson—refused to confide in an outsider. His defensive behavior was indication enough.

"He provided medical attention to someone at the ranch in the last twenty-four," Cage's man said. "We found bloody bandages in the garbage. He wouldn't let us near them. And, a vehicle entered his property at high speed, left a trench in the loose gravel and fresh tracks on a connecting back road heading out of town. My wag, he knows him."

"Snap the tracks, run the photos, and get me a make," Cage said.

Surveillance had locations the injured men could've held up in narrowed to a select few. All of them dead ends.

Cage reviewed flight patterns for every bird within fifty miles, hoping to find a red flag. Two small commuter planes failed to follow their registered flight plans. Bad weather forced one to alter course. The other had no excuse, nor did it lodge a passenger manifest. Its owner and pilot couldn't be located—bingo.

The new information posed a serious problem because the airplane in question landed across the Canadian border. RCMP officers wouldn't be inclined to share information with him unless they were given significant reason to do so. Reasons Cage couldn't provide.

Knowing this, he instructed his team to go after the medical link. If further care were administered once the injured men safely reached Canadian soil, he'd find out. It didn't turn up the lead they were hoping for. Instead, it proved more lucrative.

Cage landed outside a small Alberta town in the Canadian Rockies, twenty minutes southeast of Banff National Park at dark o'clock. Two maimed hunters had been discovered a couple hours prior to his arrival. In the woods for thirteen hours, their attack had come late morning. The larger of the two was slain, the smaller man lay in recovery, having undergone surgery for a bullet wound to the left femur. Despite being terrified, doctors said he was healthy enough for questioning.

"We're optimistic this was our guy," Cage explained to the chief of staff. "He put a bullet in a kid last night. We tracked him here. It's our intention to apprehend him and take him back home before he inflicts any more damage."

"I see. When I was called in, I expected victims of a bear attack, not this. We don't need that sort destroying the sanctity of this area. I'd rather it be a grizzly," the surgeon said, leading Cage into the wounded man's room. "I'll leave you to talk. I'll be down the hall if you need anything. I'm sure local authorities will arrive soon to aid in your search."

"Thanks, Doc." Cage hoped the doctor was wrong. He needed time alone to clean up what he assumed was Ray's mess. The last thing he wanted was Canadian police embarking on his investigation. Yet, he feared the kind of attention Ray drew would result in nothing less.

"How you feeling, son?" Cage said. His words were kind, but his voice projected an icy authority. "I have a few questions. I know you're still smarting from the burn, so I'll keep this quick and to the point."

The uniform, metals, and all made the position transparent. Even Frank Scallynn appreciated complaining to a man of his stature would be pointless.

"Yes, sir." Frank sat up straighter in his bed.

"We need details, son," Cage explained. "The who, what, where. Start at the beginning of the attack."

Frank relived the events of the morning in graphic detail.

Leaving out, of course, the fact he and Mack were poaching and illegally trespassing at the time of the encounter. A detail Cage surmised but saw no benefit in divulging.

Frank pointed to the exact location on the map and gave the precise time of the attack. He was unable to offer an accurate description of his assailant.

"She wore camouflage gear, nothing but the eyes exposed...strange eyes," he said nervously. "And it was dark. Rain clouds moved in. Hard to see. I was afraid to look too close, you know."

"You said, she?" Cage questioned. Ray might have been responsible for the attack, but he'd bury that fact and anyone who held to it. "Are you certain this was a female? Doesn't sound like a woman's work."

"Well, the voice was muffled through the hood. I guess it could've been a guy...I...I don't know."

"The guy we're after is about your height, skinny fella, and a hell of a good aim," Cage said.

"Yeah, that's him," Frank agreed. "He's a damn good aim, eh. I have the scars to prove it. He meant to kill Mack. He was pissed we were hunting. Hates hunters, I guess."

"Sounds like our man." Cage made eye contact with his men flanking the door for effect. They nodded back. "We'll find him, son. You've been a tremendous help. Rest up, and don't let anyone give you any shit about this. You must've done something right. Everyone else he came in contact with ended up in a morgue. You're a brave man."

With Frank's ego sufficiently padded, Cage exited the room satisfied.

Local police rolled into the parking lot as Cage and his crew pulled away. Fortunately for them, the ER had a busy night. The hunter's death was one of a few in the area. The others were the result of a multi-vehicle accident on the Trans-Canada Highway. In a peaceful town, this kind of activity was uncommon. Local authorities would be scrambling, giving Cage a solid lead.

Using the economic development department, he identified all the residential sites within five miles of the shooting. The team needed time to weed through them to ascertain Ray's target.

Preliminary blood analysis confirmed there were two men involved in the industrial site pursuit. What he couldn't piece together was who they were or why she'd gone after them with such vengeance. He had his suspicions.

He'd confront Nick with it, though he presumed Nick wasn't being kept abreast of his so-called sister's movements. Her arrogance worked in his favor.

He established base camp at a local alpine hotel, spread the gore photos of the half-eaten hunter across his bed, and made the call.

———

"I'm afraid we're going to have to change the location of our meeting," Cage said. Nick stared out his island estate's window to the ocean, the phone loose in his hand; he expected nothing less.

"We've decided to have you on hand when we bring Ray in."

"Bring her in?" Nick asked, no longer enjoying the view.

"Better us than the Canadian authorities."

Nick believed Cage relished in toying with their lives. He prayed for a day when he could return the favor. "Canadian authorities?"

"I guess you've been kept out of the loop. Ray guards her secrets—"

"Tell me what the hell you're implying, or I'm hanging up you, smug son-of-a-bitch."

"I wouldn't do that if I were you."

"Well, you're not me," Nick said. Scenarios of how Ray managed to engage the Canadian authorities swarmed his mind.

"She killed one civilian and wounded another. Not to mention the two men she chased here from California. It's time you and I had a frank discussion before she ends up in a heap of trouble even *we* can't save her from."

Nick fell silent. If Cage was telling the truth, and chances were likely, Ray had lost sight of logic and reason. The inevitable had arrived.

The only way to avert disaster and halt Ray's spreading shadow of destruction was through resignation.

After a full explanation from Cage, he consented to an immediate pick-up at a predetermined Coast Guard launch pad. He would then be flown into Canada to rendezvous with Cage early the next morning. He hoped Ray wouldn't inflict more damage before he arrived.

No one would get between Ray and MJ without consequence. Nick expected her to kill the man who had abducted him from the island, but Cage said the two other men she attacked were simply rogue hunters in the area. Her actions had been calculated and savage. What was worse, Cage's bloodhounds weren't far behind her.

Cage reiterated the unlimited resources at his disposal before the two hung up. At first, Nick assumed it was nothing more than an intimidation tactic. It soon became obvious he wasn't lying. The authority necessary to command the situation the way Cage explained it could only come from the top.

Alone again in quiet, Nick's mind replayed the conversation. Cage had mentioned bringing Ray in safely a total of six times. If they didn't intend to kill her, as was their prior prerogative, they sure as hell intended to use her.

The question remained, for what? Whatever it was, it couldn't be in Ray's best interest. Her saving grace was that they needed her alive. For now.

"Keeping a savage assassin alive," he whispered to the empty shell of the home they once shared. "Risking her coming back for revenge.

"Be wary, gentlemen. An angel of death knows no mercy."

38

ZAVIER SLID INTO the kitchen doorway, gun in one hand, phone in the other. He dropped the cellular to his pocket and cemented his grip on the pistol, leaving his left hand free to grab Kyly. He had only to follow the resounding crash echoing from the kitchen.

She was mid-lather on a dish when shock from the alarm caused her to lose her grip, sending it colliding into the granite countertop. The stoneware broke in a powdery explosion. White dust lingered as he took hold of her arm.

Hauling her from the mess and the window into a crouch below counter level, they crawled, backing out of the kitchen into the hallway. Avoiding visual access from outside, they stood together.

Frantic and yelling to be heard above the alarm, she asked, "This is it, isn't it?"

"Yeah, it's them," he said. "Mason's less than twenty minutes away. He'll get here."

"That's twenty minutes too long," she said. "I'm not prepared to die, are you?"

"No."

"Where's the safest vantage point in this place?" she asked.

"The loft, Mason's bedroom."

"Then that's where we're headed. Our supplies?"

Zavier pointed to a duffel bag a couple feet farther down the hallway.

"I'll grab the bag. Where's Riggs? Riggs, hey boy."

The dog emerged, hindquarters first, from the kitchen, glancing back at them while defending the space ahead.

Misinterpreting the dog's reaction, Kyly asked, "Could they already be inside?"

"No. These sirens are outer perimeter alarms. They engaged when they crossed onto the landscaped property. I can tell where and how many when we reach the loft. The monitoring system is activated from there. It may be our photographer back for round two." Zavier's voice trailed him as he ran.

"But it isn't," she hollered from behind.

Crossing the great room and its wall of windows to access the winding log staircase to Mason's loft, the three stayed tightly knit, moving as one.

"Remember, it's all security glass, bulletproof," Zavier reassured.

They spiraled upward, scanning the room below. Riggs's perpetual low growl underlined their every movement.

"If they come within ten meters, the second alarm will sound. Brace yourself," Zavier warned.

Kyly glanced at him, both catching their reflection in a mirror. Disbelief painted her pale. Her feet, like his, pounded solid ground, but Kyly appeared adrift. She hadn't seen a ghost. What he read in her eyes was worse. She feared becoming one.

The cabin was the sole structure within two miles. Shrouded by dense forest surrounded it on all sides. They fled *here* for *protection*?

"Jack," Kyly said in a flash of hope. "What about Jack and the alarm? Police will be dispatched."

"Yeah, you're right. Jack's linked to the system. He'd know the second it sounded. But it takes police fifteen minutes to respond," Zavier yelled. "And that's wishful thinking. I doubt they've ever had a call up here before."

Kyly skirted the corner from the wide hallway overlooking the great room and headed into the loft. "I hope they're set on making a solid first impression."

Three sides of the master bedroom were adorned with windows.

Zavier shifted the heavy chocolate drapes aside, searching the property for movement. "The back's clear. Right side too." When he peered out the front, a security light shone back at him.

"They're closing in from dead ahead."

He pointed to a nearby desk set into beautifully crafted built-in bookshelves. "Push the panel. The computer's hidden."

She pushed the wooden panel behind the desk, releasing a mechanism that revealed a flat-screen monitor and keyboard.

"James Bond," she said.

It didn't take her long to access the security system. "It's asking for a password."

"Riggs one, in numeric form," Zavier answered.

"He really trusts you," she yelled, punching in the code. "Your uncle."

A flash of movement caught Zavier's eye. "I can't see shit," he cursed. "I think he's moving into our blind spot."

Their field of view was hampered by thick brush to the west. If Zavier was right, the attacker approached from the one side lacking unimpeded camera surveillance.

"We need that system." He abandoned the window to join her.

"If these red dots are movement indicators, there are two of them," she said. "One almost out of range and one approaching from the west."

"Yeah." Zavier backed away to grab the duffel bag. "You're going to need a crash course in firing a weapon by the looks of things."

"You're serious?"

"As a heart attack."

In combat mode, he pulled an old .38 Special from under the wooden bed frame and loaded it.

Placing it in her hands, he said, "You have to lead your target. It's like driving. Look ahead and steer for what's coming. Your hands are the wheel. When your target's in sight, you lead and squeeze. Don't jerk; squeeze steady."

"How the hell do you do that when your hands are shaking?" she asked.

"You don't," he said. "You don't shake."

Their eyes met. He'd risk his life defending her. He hoped she knew it.

"I won't shake," she promised. "And I won't miss."

Her words were barely airborne when the second alarm sounded. The computer screen confirmed Zavier's suspicions; the intruder approached from their blind side. Coming in alone. The second indicator light hadn't moved. It remained by the access road leading onto the property.

"He's surveying the house, looking for weaknesses," Zavier said.

"You mean looking for a way in."

"Yes."

"Well, that's comforting."

"Not really. They're using combat tactics. One attacks hoping we'll flee—"

"Hounds to the hunters," she said.

"Yes. I hope your mother's dire predictions are wrong more often than they're right. The only other way out of here is the river she warned us about. It's damn cold, even at this time of year. And it's moving fast enough to—"

"To drown. We can't leave this house, Zavier. She's not wrong. It's us or them."

He grinned. "Mason has a theory about positions like this."

"And that is?"

"Don't aim for the kneecaps."

Typing into the computer, Zavier silenced the alarms, sending a loud and clear message to their intruders. They weren't coming in without a fight.

They watched as the red dot encircled the house, ending up back out front. Zavier ran to the window, opening a crack in the drapes to peer through. Security motion sensor lights illuminated the ground below, exposing their adversary.

"It's a woman," he said.

"A woman?" Kyly echoed, her ears ringing. "It's her, oh god. It's Ray."

Zavier hesitated. "She thinks I'm him. The pictures were surveillance to locate Chris and now...she thinks I'm him. If she gets in here, you have to stay the hell away from me."

"I will not! I will not let her take you!"

"If she thinks I'm him, she won't kill me."

"Like hell she won't. What happens when she realizes you're not? That ought to take her about thirty seconds. You told me Mason's warnings. She's a lunatic, not your run-of-the-mill type, more the born and bred. I appreciate your brotherly protection, but I'm years your senior, and I'm pulling rank. You'll remain glued to my hip until your uncle gets here. You hear me? And don't think for one minute you're going out that door without me. I'll shoot you in the leg if I have to," she threatened.

Zavier smiled. "Guess we should've had this conversation *before* I handed you a loaded weapon."

The first of Ray's bullets impacted a side access door to the garage. Logical. The door had a small half-window and an unassuming lock. It appeared weak, but it wasn't. Its glass, like all the outer windows, was bulletproof. The door was dead bolted top and bottom, only visible from the inside, with steel pegs mounted long into lower foundation cement and upper reinforced steel framework. It wasn't budging. Still, the shock of the attempt made them wish the exterior walls were constructed of solid concrete.

"What's next?" Kyly asked. "Is there an attic door, a hidden cellar hatch, anything?"

"No attic door, no cellar hatch to crawl through, and the chimney's a metal pipe too small for raccoons. We should be okay," he replied.

"Then why don't I *feel* safe?"

On guard at Kyly's side, Riggs's canine ears reacted to something they couldn't hear. Darting away from them, he headed to the staircase.

"*Riggs, no!*" Kyly commanded.

The dog barked insistently at the edge of the stairs.

"She's still outside according to this." Kyly reviewed the computer's indicators. "This couldn't be malfunctioning, could it?"

"No, he's sensing our fear."

"No, he's not. He's trying to tell us something," she insisted. "Riggs, what boy, what is it?"

Ignoring orders to stay put, Riggs started down. Kyly ran after him, leaving Zavier no choice but to follow. They had extinguished all the inside lights on their way up to remain hidden. With the aid of a small flashlight taken from the desk, Kyly kept one hand on the dog's back letting him lead her down to the garage side of the house. As they drew near, the scent of gunpowder tainted the air.

At last glance, their intruder had circled to the front of the cabin.

"This is a bad idea," Zavier whispered at her from behind.

Riggs stopped in the doorway to a mudroom between the lower and main floors. Below waist level, the narrow beam revealed why.

Following behind them, Zavier plowed into them.

"Sorry," he apologized. "What are we doing here?"

Kyly stepped aside, her flashlight illuminating a dog entrance dead ahead. "Is there a way to block it off?"

Though too small for any man to fit through without considerable difficulty, a woman Kyly's size could access the tiny opening.

"There's a metal shield that slides shut on the inside. Mason locks it up when he goes away," Zavier whispered. "Jack must have taken the cover off. Search the walls, but watch your light. If it seeps outside, she'll see it."

Pulling a pen light off a key chain on a nearby hook, Zavier scanned the walls with her. Both were careful not to allow their beams to reflect off nearby windows. Respecting the intellect that brought them to this point, Kyly solicited the dog for help.

"Where's your door, boy?"

Riggs quietly stepped back. He couldn't be more obvious; he was standing on the shield. Jack had discarded it onto the floor.

"It's here," Kyly whispered. "Riggs has it."

Zavier slid the metal piece off the ground with a slow scraping sound. On either side of the miniature entrance metal, locking clips secured the door. Both had to be forced out of the way before the door could enter the metal tracks and slide down to seal the exterior hole. Kyly propped up her flashlight on a small wooden doorstop and aimed it at the doorway, hoping its rubber flap would prevent any light from escaping.

Zavier couldn't unlatch the clip on the left. It refused to budge. Its size and shape made for an awkward grip. After struggling for a few seconds, he pried it loose. It popped free with a loud snap.

"She would've heard that," he warned. "Stand back from the door."

Shifting her stance to a spot against the wall to its right, Kyly tried the remaining clip. To her surprise, it unhooked without much effort. Zavier steadied the door above as they lined it up with the metal tracks and guided it into place. The rails were a snug fit, preventing the door from dropping easily. They were forced to shimmy it back and forth, clanking metal to metal every inch.

At Zavier's side, Riggs snarled, freezing their movements. They listened for noise from outside. A twig broke.

"Did you hear that?" Kyly's whispered breath caught in her throat. "Get the door down. Now!"

Riggs's low growl said he too equated silence with survival.

Two inches from the bottom, the door jammed. Wrestling it back and forth ceased to be effective. Panicked, Kyly leaned over, placing her hand at the center point of the panel's bottom edge. Pulling evenly, it slid lower, but before it sealed, something reached through from the other side.

Cold, wet leather, like a withered corpse's hand, brushed against her skin. Tripping over shoes and dog toys, Kyly fell to the ground, knocking the air she held out of her lungs. Riggs lunged at the remaining opening, snagging enough material to tear a piece of the glove free. Zavier hammered the top of the panel. It slammed down with a reverberating blow seconds before the intrusive hand disappeared beyond its sharp edge.

"Come on!" he urged, lifting Kyly from the floor. "Let's get the hell out of here."

As he dragged her from the room, she stared past him, eyes glued to the torn leather by the door.

In mid-stride, Zavier slammed and locked the mudroom door behind them.

Kyly fought to regain her footing. He clenched her hand, retracing their steps back to the loft, and bounded up the stairs two at a time.

"Zavier, wait," Kyly pleaded.

When they reached the main level landing, he rounded the corner and broached the first step of the second flight before she hit solid ground. Sliding like a puppy on a waxed floor, she collided with the railing post. Struggling to remain upright and prevent him from dislodging her arm from its socket, her feet scrambled to keep pace. Riggs followed, twisting left then right, defending their exit.

Zavier maintained a death grip until they were back at the loft computer.

"She's still the only one near the house," he said, winded.

"Are there any other doors or windows Jack could've left open?" She rubbed her sore shoulder.

"I'll check." Changing the screen, he ran a search of points of access. "There's no other easy way in."

"So what, we wait it out? I doubt she's going to make it that simple. She has to assume the police are en route. She doesn't have the luxury of time for a standoff."

Picking up the desk phone confirmed Kyly's fear. "The landline is dead. How could she do that so quickly? She wasn't close enough to trip the second alarm until minutes ago."

"She cut the main," he said.

"And where is that?"

"On a telephone pole, half mile away."

He watched panic brighten Kyly's eyes. Pulling out her cell phone, she tried dialing out. No signal. Desperation swelled.

"We can call out online, separate uplink, but I can't monitor outside at the same time. We'll lose our eyes for a few minutes," he said.

"Do it."

The indicator light traced Ray's movements at the back of the cabin, then the screen disappeared, replaced by a police link. Typing in, Zavier informed the RCMP they were under attack by unknown intruders, shots had been fired at the house, and the perpetrators were breaking inside. He gave his name and failed to offer Kyly's.

"Tell them they're heavily armed and wearing combat gear," she said. "Maybe it'll light a match under them."

Confirmation flashed across the screen, and he switched modes back to monitoring the perimeter.

It hadn't taken more than seconds to send the message, but they'd lost Ray's location. A tiny red light still flashed at the property's entrance. The second beacon had vanished. Kyly assumed control, focusing and extending the search to the back of the house, behind the rock wall on the east side. A faint light flashed.

What was she doing there?

"She's almost out of range," Zavier said. "Why has she backed off?"

"I don't know, but chances are it's not a good thing for us. How long till Mason arrives?"

According to the timer on Zavier's watch, eleven minutes had passed. "You're kidding, right?" Kyly fretted.

What their adversary wanted was them. She couldn't be bought off. The levy placed on their lives loomed ever closer. And the collector was an iconoclast, bleeding away all hope of a hero's rescue.

Despite what Zavier said earlier, he knew if he walked out the front door, Ray would kill him the second he reached her.

They kept watch over the blinking red dot on the screen—a sentinel of doom. Tension streamed up Zavier's back, settling at his neck with the weight of a cement block.

"What's she waiting for?"

He didn't expect Ray to come in quietly. He gathered she'd prefer a direct approach. He just never knew how direct.

Set off a bomb and blow them to hell.

———

The explosion rocked the cabin at its foundation, throwing Kyly and Zavier to the floor, buried by fallout debris. Destroying inward from the lowest point in back of the house, but the explosive device hadn't completely shattered the structure. It blew out a large enough section to send everything not nailed down airborne. Interior alarms blared. This time, Zavier couldn't silence their screams as the computer, like much else, was in a heap.

Riggs found Kyly first, licking at her face. Zavier moaned from a pile nearby. Kyly rushed to free him from the wreckage. Adrenaline pumping, she tossed aside heavy wooden furniture.

Ray was inside. Every second counted. If she lived to be one hundred, Kyly would never know a time when mere minutes stretched across eternity as they did now.

The explosion must've been heard if not seen, she told herself, freeing Zavier. His lips moved. She couldn't hear his words.

He led her to the balcony. If Ray was inside, they were going out.

Security lights knocked out by the blast left them scouring the ground below with a flashlight Kyly snatched from the pack she'd reached for before impact. If the bomb was intended to disorient and lure them into a trap, it was a chance they had to take.

Though neither of them could hear, their communication was clear. Zavier would lower Kyly, then jump. Riggs had to stay on the balcony. His eyes pleaded to go with them, but he moved aside.

Climbing over the railing, Kyly clenched Zavier's hands. He lowered her down to the extent of his reach before releasing her. The forest floor was soft where she landed. Springing to her feet, she dashed out of the way. Her eyes fought the dry burn of explosives as she surveyed the area for movement.

The extra distance Zavier's aid provided made a difference. Without it, he hit hard. His ankle twisted beneath him. He struggled to stand. It was obvious he couldn't walk without assistance, much less run for his life.

Kyly propped herself under his shoulder, and together they limped to the back of the rock waterfall located on the yard's east side where indicators showed Ray had hidden while waiting for the blast. And, hopefully, the last place she'd search for them. Setting Zavier down, she pulled his pant leg up, exposing his injured ankle.

"We can't escape like this. We have to stay hidden until help arrives."

Zavier's boyish good looks contorted with pain as he mouthed, "You can...escape. Go! They'll find me."

"Remember what I told you," she said, peeking around the side of the rock formation.

"What are you doing?" he hissed through grinding teeth. Her hearing was returning.

"You dropped the duffel bag. Our ammunition is in there. I have to grab it before she realizes we're not in the house."

"Don't."

"Stay here and be quiet." She disappeared around the corner.

Making her way back to their drop point, Kyly thought she detected sirens in the distance, but the house alarm and the ringing in her ears from the blast made it impossible to be sure. The duffel bag and its contents lay strewn across the ground. She gathered the scattered items back into the bag. Tossing it over her shoulder, a noise above marked defeat.

Her heart waited to hear the click of a trigger.

Only panting. Riggs had struggled through a broken section of railing and perched on the edge.

"Then come on, boy, jump." She motioned with relief.

The dog sprang from the deck into a mossy bank, shook free of the mire, and hurried to her side. They made their way back through the darkness to where Zavier waited.

"I think I hear sirens." She set the bag down, scouring the darkness ahead.

"God, I hope so. I only hear ringing."

Guns loaded, and backs to the rock wall, they waited. A storm had sent buckets of rain into the area earlier in the day. Yet, now, the night shone crystal clear. Stars hung like rhinestones on black velvet above them and the moon, though not half full, set aglow the remaining scarf of a cloud as it blew by. The night dripped of surrealism.

Beautiful. Deadly.

A gunshot cracked through the trees in the distance. She couldn't be certain, but it seemed to originate from the upper west side of the property.

"The man at the entrance?" Kyly kept her voice to a shallow whisper, mouthing the words more than speaking them. "You don't think Jack would come unarmed?"

"If that had anything to do with Jack, it's the other guy you should worry about." Zavier rubbed his swelling ankle and searched the darkness.

"He must be here. We're going to be okay."

Kyly wanted to call out to Jack and let him know where they were. Logic kept her silent. Riggs twitched his head to the left. Kyly raised her gun.

"Hold up." Zavier threw up a hand, halting her. "His ears are probably as shot as mine from the explosion. If someone *is* there, it could be Jack."

"Quiet." Kyly moved slowly around the left of the rock wall, then back. "There's only one way to be sure. I'm not going to stay here waiting to be cornered."

Her eyes darted left, movement at the back of the cabin. Darkness prevented clear identification. The shadow appeared to be a man's, perhaps Jack.

It made sense; if Ray heard gunshots out front, she'd investigate them, fearing it was Chris fleeing the area. Jack could use the opportunity to get close.

She strained her eyes to track the shadow's origin. It bent, turning on a low beam flashlight to inspect the ground at the opposite corner of the cabin below the loft deck they had jumped from.

It wasn't Jack.

The illuminated slender figure traced their footsteps. There was no time. The tracks would lead Ray right to Zavier.

Slinking behind the rocks, she turned her attention to the dog. "You stay here." Smiling at Zavier, she placed her finger to her mouth instructing him to remain quiet, and slipped away.

She gave him neither time to protest nor the benefit of knowing what threat waited beyond the safety of the wall.

She crept past the blown-out portion of the house. Witnessing the wreckage firsthand, it was amazing they'd survived. If she could get inside, she could create a diversion. Police were drawing near. Their sirens floated up the mountainside. She needed to buy a few more minutes.

Too late.

Her foot scraped against a piece of fallout from the blast zone. Ray heard it and spun to the sound. Kyly dropped to the ground, avoiding the first bullet. Ray's flashlight beam sliced the night, brushing Kyly's right leg. Another bullet ricocheted, sending plumes of debris into the air near her foot. Scrambling to her feet as Ray approached, Kyly fired one shot in her direction and sent Ray diving for cover.

Coated from head to toe in soot and debris, Kyly flailed like a fish out of water. Ray, on the other hand, came up nicked, bleeding, and primed to kill. She transformed in a glance from woman to weapon.

An old fallen tree stopped the next bullet as Kyly ran for shelter.

"*Kyly!*" Zavier called out from the waterfall, his weapon's report adding punctuation.

Ray was thrown back as a bullet ripped into her shoulder, forcing her to lose a firm grip on her weapon. She glanced down at her torn flesh but never stopped moving. Crouching low, She flung the gun into her other hand and fired in his direction. The bullet shaved through the air above Zavier's head, sending him rolling off balance.

"Keep your head down!" Kyly screamed, deliberately drawing Ray's fire, buying Zavier a chance.

Sorry, Dad.

———

Before Zavier reached a vantage point atop the rock wall, another bullet cut through the night. An unearthly scream followed in its wake.

Sliding off the stone face, he limped around the corner with complete disregard for safety.

"Kyly!" he screamed, making his way into clear view of the cabin.

Sirens wailed in competing octaves from all directions.

His flashlight caught a blood trail in the opposite direction, Ray's. He wished his shot had been fatal. Kyly was nowhere in sight. Hobbling the distance to the house, he called her name. His lungs drank in fresh gunpowder lingering in the air. He prayed Ray hadn't taken Kyly with her.

"Kyly!" he bellowed again, searching through the rubble inside the house.

"Zavier?"

His name filtered down from inside the upper floors of the house. Jack.

"Jack, I'm down here. I can't find Kyly. I think she's hit."

Out of the corner of his eye, blood and an unmoving pile of copper fur.

"Riggs, oh Christ no!"

Hobbling to the dog's side, Zavier's heart sank. The pup was alive but bleeding. Hit in the back right side. Riggs whimpered as Zavier approached the waterfall. Kneeling, he ripped off his shirt holding it tight over the open wound.

"Jack, get over here!" he said, anger laced his tone. "Kyly...Kyly!"

Climbing through what was left of the exterior basement wall, Jack crossed the distance with gun still in hand.

"I can't find her!" Zavier panicked. Slime shifted across the water next to him as words fell from his lips. Hair floated below the waterline of the cold plunge pool.

Located at the base of the waterfall, it appeared to be no more than a decorative pond when, in fact, it was ten feet deep.

Riggs had been shot protecting Kyly. Lunging his torso into the water, Zavier grabbed her by the shoulders and lifted her from the depths. The water was freezing. She didn't respond to his touch.

Pulling her over the side next to Riggs, Zavier began CPR. She wasn't breathing and had sustained a serious head injury falling in. Jack threw off his heavy coat, and Zavier used it to cover her upper body.

"*Come on, damn it*!" Zavier begged her lifeless form. "I haven't even graduated. You are *not* dying on me! *Breathe*! One, two, three, four, five, six."

Kyly's beautiful face became pallid porcelain, her features forever frozen.

"Breathe, Lee. Please, baby. Breathe. One, two, three, four, five, six."

Zavier refused to give up even if Jack's expression told him it was too late. He shrugged off the strengthening grasp of defeat.

"Damn it, you breathe right now! One. two, three, four, five, six," Tears spilled freely from his eyes. "Don't leave us, Lee...breathe."

His sodden appearance could've been the consequence of dampening emotion, not immersion into icy water. Focused only on Kyly, he didn't see Mason and Chris round the side of the cabin. He didn't sense them hovering over him. It wasn't until Chris kneeled beside him, placing his warm hands over Zavier's numb ones on Kyly's still chest, that he noticed them at all.

39

EYES ARE windows to the soul. Ray's were black.

Empty voids retreating further into darkness.

From the first moment she knew about the journalist pursuing MJ's case, she disliked her. Every moment since, her dislike intensified. Kyly's meddling caused it to mutate into incomprehensible hatred.

Valiantly, the dog had been caught in the crossfire during the siege at the cabin—a disturbing repercussion. Alive when she fled the scene, its chances of survival were bleak. This loyal creature's suffering fed her animosity.

The nosy word jockey had been dealt a deadly hand.

Ray lavished the thought, clutching her wounded shoulder with her functioning hand.

She paused to tie a tourniquet to minimize blood loss, tightening the noose with one hand and her teeth. The pain drove her as she cleared the wooded area in a sprint.

Heading to the river, she maneuvered at breakneck speed through thickets of wild brush, fallen trees, and uneven ground. The flashlight in her belt dimly lit her way through the night. She'd prefer it unnecessary, but the canopy above laid a blanket of black between her and the moonlight. Still, if choppers neared the area, she'd kill the light and run blind. She'd done it before.

Engorged by recent storms, the river ran like a herd of unleashed

Mustangs. It rushed forth, rising, diving, and slamming against itself and the mountain rock embankment containing it. Swimming it with two functioning arms would be challenging enough. Injured, Ray didn't stand a chance.

She'd never seen anything quite like the fury of steely Canadian rapids slicing through rugged mountain caverns. A lifetime of isolation had robbed her. From here on, she vowed the future would be one of atonement.

Sirens soiled the silence as she stopped to inject herself with a numbing agent. Zavier shot her—with well-honed police accuracy—near, but not in, the brachial nerve, forcing her to drop her weapon. His uncle taught him well. Beyond this, MJ's look-alike had talent.

Tantalizing. Tactical. Zavier.

He was to be envied. Many wanted to be behind the bullet that would end her life. His would always be the first to come close. She had to admit, he *was* courageous, a rare, admirable if not annoying, family trait.

The resemblance to MJ was uncanny. It explained why the Cromwells reacted with such vengeance. He was definitely theirs.

Despite sporting a significant laceration, Nero fleeing, and MJ's whereabouts unknown, she considered the evening a success. She'd hit hard, killing one of their co-conspirators, leaving awkward explanations for authorities. Tongue-tied and terrified.

It would've been rewarding. Watching them wither over their fallen friend with grief-stricken with regret. No rest for the wicked.

She'd loved that expression. She equated rest with death. In her version, it simply suggested the wicked lived forever. A truth she intended to prove. What mankind wasn't able to comprehend was the inevitable overlap between spirituality and science. There came a point where the two merged. The ability to control life and death made her a God.

The bullet had torn clean through her shoulder, leaving a worm way from back to front. Fortunate. No digging for shrapnel.

The positive aspects of the evening would elude Nick. He'd been adamant about not drawing police attention. She'd deviated.

Despite blood loss, her current conquest invigorated her. She fed off the strength in her heartbeat, the solidity of her muscles, the rise and fall of her lungs.

Approaching the raging river's edge, hounds yelped behind her, their response quick and determined. Lowering herself down the four-foot embankment with the aid of an exposed tree root, she half-traversed and half-slid down, taking with her a trail of falling dirt and rock. They'd know she came this direction.

Checking her tourniquet for seepage, she wrapped the wound again and pulled a poncho from her pack over her head.

Her feet struggled to cling to the wet rocks without losing balance. She wanted to rip the boots off. She'd be far more effective with nothing between her and the earth, but she'd leave a potent scent trail.

After two hundred yards, the river narrowed, pushing up the bank, making it impossible to pass without being swallowed. Though an easy climb sat in front of her, she backtracked to a more difficult and less obvious rock wall. She scaled it, careful not to disturb its natural state. Back on semi-even ground, she picked up pace, ducking and weaving until the dog's barks were a whispered reminder.

Stopping to survey the distance behind her, she drew in great bursts of mountain air, letting them erupt from her lungs. Her breathing steadied.

Hunched below an overhang of heavy pine branches, she checked her GPS and activated a signal for pick-up at the next cut line road. Police wouldn't imagine her capable of crossing such a vast distance so quickly. Average foot speed over uneven ground, barring injury, was four miles an hour. Ray's superior physique managed twice that speed. And, given at least a fifteen-minute lead, she'd exit outside their search perimeter undetected.

Bleep, bleep, bleep.

The readout confirmed her ride waited half a mile west. Panning her light into the night, she ran for it.

Fragile red blooms, crushed by her boots, bled in her wake.

She anticipated the fallout of the attack. MJ would see his choice to abandon her came at the cost of at least one innocent woman's life—his perspective, not hers. He'd be persuaded to rethink this decision.

"Wisdom is always the first trait to be auctioned off by emotion,"

Ray whispered. Either by choice or by force, the circumstance of his return mattered little, only its inevitability.

Dissecting the situation, she discovered a vital clue hidden beneath surface clutter—the human mind held secrets. There was only one, other than hers, that she revered, and she'd tried so valiantly to save it intact.

Mason was with MJ. They had fled the Half Moon Bay area. If they hadn't, her Intel would've alerted her to a sighting. Money could and did buy eyes everywhere. It wasn't logical for Mason to stay in the area. They had to be heading her way when she ambushed the cabin, thinking Zavier was MJ.

Why was the younger Cromwell son there with the journalist? The two collaborated their information and efforts. They were in hiding to escape the repercussions of their probing.

Mason was circling the wagons, managing the situation. Fruitless labor. MJ would be there soon. And, when he arrived, he'd witness the death and destruction firsthand.

She may not need to come after him a second time. He'd trade himself for his...family.

Her train of thought screeched, skidded, and derailed.

They weren't his family. They were strangers he should've cared nothing for. Why had he drawn an alliance with them?

Unless.

Tell your mind not to go any further. Stop before...

"He remembers."

The words fell from her lips, and her feet lost all momentum. She stood frozen three feet from the cut line. With her shoulder torn, her body covered in mud and debris, her eyes, cold shadows in the darkness, lost sight. A wave of sickness shook her.

Meek and low, the driver's voice startled her back into motion.

"Ray, is that you?" he mumbled. The flash of the truck's headlights coming at her drew her eyes. It slowed to a stop, and she tossed her pack into the back through the open window, flung open the passenger door, and slid in.

"What the hell happened to you?" the driver said, taken aback by her disheveled appearance. "Forget I asked."

"Drive." She threw off her tattered layers for new clothes. "If I see your eyes shift in this direction, death by explosion will seem merciful."

Folding down the ear covers on his hunting hat, blocking out his peripheral vision, the driver maneuvered down the rough mountainside terrain. He bounced along, destined for the main highway like a puppet on a string.

Once bandaged and changed, Ray discarded her soiled clothes into an incineration bag on the truck's floor by her feet, lit a match, and watched the evidence go up in flames. Designed to contain the fire within and burn to ash without threat to flammables outside it, its flames extinguished harmlessly. She pulled down the vanity mirror; reflection of the flash burn licked her black eyes setting them ablaze, then abandoned them to smoldering darkness.

40

THE DAY AFTER KYLY DIED, shadows cast by an eagle's vast wingspan caressed her face, leaving in its wake the soft embrace of early morning sunlight. His high call overhead whistled on the wind, dancing upward through the mountain chasm into billowing white clouds suspended at its peaks. Cascading illumination airbrushed her delicate features, setting her skin aglow. Like the light through the window, Mason's eyes clung to her.

A Madonna. A living Madonna.

Heavy drapes dampened the day's intensity, but skylights overhead couldn't be dimmed. She didn't stir beneath his watchful gaze, immersed in a deep slumber. Tranquility reserved for the most innocent among us. He'd remained at her side throughout the night.

Shshshsh...hummm...shshshsh...hummm

Sound breath. Slender shoulders sheltered under soft blankets and whispered words of comfort. "You're safe now," Mason said. "You're not alone."

Kyly moaned against memories. Her face contorted, then relaxed again.

The others slept. Worn and wounded, rest became the sole salvation in an evening of chaos. Police stood guard, vowing to maintain a perimeter until they could convince Mason to relent and accept more desirable lodging or apprehend the suspect. Mason's instincts assured him, that, despite his own stubborn will, the latter of the two appeared far less likely.

Plywood sheets replaced the once picturesque family room window, his panoramic alpine view gone. Though neither attractive nor in the least bit formidable, it gave the illusion of security, sealing the hole left by the bomb.

Police photographed, categorized, and removed debris inside the house for lab analysis. Ravaged, the lower level resembled a demolition sight.

Outside, bloodstains—splattered, scattered, and pooled—painted a grim story. Upstairs, the main level of the cabin appeared almost normal. Jack and Zavier, despite his ankle injury, spent hours exhausting their anxiety on restoration while Mason collaborated with local authorities.

He issued a statement pertaining to the attack, giving all the necessary details, withholding a healthy portion of the truth. "My nephew and the others will volunteer their complete statements at the station tomorrow," he told police. "You can ask them anything you want then. Tonight, they're off limits."

Police resigned.

Mason refused to allow Kyly to be taken to the hospital. He told them she was his girlfriend. And, since she appeared physically out of danger, they allowed him to care for her at home. With cops visible at every turn, the cabin was more secure than a hospital.

Zavier and Jack collapsed under a blanket of fatigue before the clock hit midnight. For Mason, sleep didn't come. Even his skilled psyche became powerless to control the deliberation plaguing him.

In an oversized wingback, he tried and failed to make sense of things. Riggs, bandaged and tired, panted at his feet. Leaning down, he stroked the soft matted fur. The dog stretched out under the security of his master's heavy hand. Riggs had been spared. Logic no longer reigned in Mason's world. He doubted it existed in any of their lives.

Did Chris save them both? Somehow, in darkness, had his touch changed fate, or was it simply not their time? Was there an order to life we could not see?

Riggs should've died on the cold rock pad as certainly as Kyly had.

Death was denied, not once, but twice by his count.

He remembered the chill in the night air. How it seeped past his skin, settling in the marrow of his bones. The thought shook him, and he drew his blanket over his chest.

His eyes lingered on the two spared souls sleeping peacefully before him. What had he witnessed, miracles or the stumbling path of life?

Grasping the truth was like clutching water. Chris wasn't just a perplexing medical anomaly. Convinced by the ebb and flow of breathing around him, Mason knew his nephew's existence dawned a new age.

He wondered, who else shared this secret?

———

Mason Stone's face was beautifully etched by time. Compelling with character, yet smooth in unexpected places, disguising many of his years. Kyly studied it. His eyelashes were thick and lengthy, like a child's. His hair was long enough to be sexy. Blond waves, highlighted in an array of tones like ocean reflecting sunlight, distinguished by the few places drawn shimmering silver. She dreamed of his eyes up close. In pictures, they appeared aqua-hazel and kind, full of laughter and life. She didn't dwell on his perfect physique, unlike most women who she imagined made spectacles of themselves to impress him.

Kyly trusted no one, save her parents. History made her reserved and watchful even with those she counted among friends. She was private and guarded. These natural protective responses abandoned her in his presence. She wasn't sure why.

His handsome face was rugged and radiant.

Her eyes drank him in. His hands, folded loosely across his chest as he slept, were strong and large, mysteriously scared in places. Thick skin, not stretched or weathered, but infused with a golden hue.

From his bed, the haven he'd given up for her, she watched him.

His was the first face that came into focus out of last night's darkness as her lungs fought to fill with air. He carried her inside the cabin through gathering police, search dogs, and sirens. Memories of concerned faces were scattered along the way. He was the constant. And, as she lay recovering her strength, he remained her guardian.

According to the wall clock, it was after ten in the morning.

A noise at his feet alerted her they were not alone. Wrestling her covers, she leaned down, peering over the bed's edge to come face to face with a weary but jovial pup.

"Hey, boy," she whispered, reaching to pet his soft head, saddened by his bandages. "I'm really glad to see you. I thought we were both goners."

Riggs curled his lips up in a sheepish grin, stating he, too, had his doubts.

A foot or two from Mason's chair, she absorbed every detail. Why did she find him so intriguing? The world slipped away, and she was lost in this intimate gaze. Until he woke to meet it.

"How are you feeling?" he asked, groggy. She retreated into her covers.

"I'm okay. I'm glad Riggs is too," she said hoarsely, averting her eyes to smile down at the dog.

"You should go back to sleep," he encouraged, stretching.

Sitting up in the center of the bed, she asked, "Where will you be?"

"Not far." He stood bedside.

"Is everyone else all right?"

"Yes, they're okay. They'll be better knowing you're awake and talking. You gave us quite a scare."

"Sorry."

"This wasn't your doing." A protective force shadowed his tone. "Close your eyes. I'll be back up to check on you after I make my rounds."

"Mason," her raspy voice called after him as he headed for the doorway. "I'm glad you're here."

"Me too," he said with a smile, then rounded the corner out of sight, leaving her and Riggs nestled in the safety of his lair.

———

Mason found Chris standing with his back to the great room, facing the cracked windowpane overlooking the blast area in the backyard. He stood encased by a sunbeam streaming through pine tree branches.

"Morning, Mason," Chris said without turning. "It's a shame, all this destruction. How is she?"

"Coming around. I told her to rest. Hopefully she'll go back to sleep. Have the guys got up yet?"

"Zavier's in the shower, and Jack's out there." Chris gestured to the back of the property.

"Can you keep an ear out for Kyly? I need to check out the area."

"Go ahead. She'll be fine."

Throwing on a sweater, concealing the gun tucked into his belt at the small of his back, Mason slipped on his hiking boots and headed outside. He met with the officer stationed at the front of the cabin, discussed the state of things, then excused himself to join Jack around back.

"Find anything useful?" Mason asked, kicking through debris.

"Nothing you don't already know about. I wanted to wait for you to follow the blood trail, her escape route. The hounds have made quite a mess of it," Jack warned.

"Lead the way, old friend."

A symphony of scents engulfed them as they delved deeper into the forest maze, disappearing from Chris' fractured view. Rocky mountain terrain challenged many stereotypical beliefs. Here, beneath an emerald canopy, the perfume of leaves choked out the flowers adorning the forest floor. Pine tingled the nostrils.

Pausing periodically to examine telltale signs of passage, they made their way to the river. "She slid down the wet embankment over there." Jack pointed to an area with upturned soil. "Where she headed from there is hard to say."

Covering her tracks between water and stealth, she left little to go on. "The search dogs crossed and re-crossed this bank," Mason complained. "Looks like a cattle herd passed through here."

Turning his attention to broken branches Mason traced her exit path.

"Square depressions," Jack said. "She stood right here. See the feet, close together?"

"I think I know her escape route." Mason pointed ahead. "The cut line road." Albeit faint and subtle, the meager clues were enough. After an hour or more of chasing her ghost, they found the confirmation Mason sought.

Trampled in the direction of the road, a smear of crushed crimson petals gave her rendezvous point away. The flower's dye left them with a clear shoe impression. "She planned her escape." Mason kneeled to inspect the ground. "She's good."

"The kids never had a chance," Jack said.

Having what they needed, they returned to the cabin leaving local authorities to make their own discoveries.

When they entered the house, the aroma of bacon wafted through the air. Mason proceeded upstairs to wash up while the others chatted and poured coffee. Heading into the closet to change, his clothes damp and sodden from his hike through the brush, he didn't notice the empty bed. He grabbed a clean T-shirt, tucking it into his back pocket. Pulling off his sweater one handed, he re-emerged with his head stuck and walked full force into Kyly.

Damp from her shower, shaking droplets from her hair, they collided. The impact left her clutching the shirt she wore with its buttons opened. Embarrassed and stunned, they apologized at the same time. Making an awkward situation even more tongue-tied.

"My fault," he said, retreating but never taking his eyes from her.

"I didn't know anyone was out here. I would've asked—"

"No, no. You go ahead and finish getting ready. I should've knocked. Sorry. I'm not accustomed to having guests here...sharing my room. Anyway, they're itching to eat downstairs, so whenever you're ready." He backed out of the room bare-chested with his shirt still dangling from his pants pocket.

"You don't have to go—" He heard her say.

He smiled all the way to the kitchen.

Everyone was happily surprised Kyly appeared not to suffer severe consequences from her time beneath the water. Mason was particularly grateful.

By mid-afternoon, a detective offered to take remaining statements at the house rather than request they make the trip to town headquarters. Prepped and memorized, one by one they fed their version to local authorities. Giving them enough to keep a keen eye on the area without interfering.

After the police car vacated the driveway, Mason revealed their next tactical maneuver.

"Chris and I discussed this. The documents hidden on the island are the only insurance we have against these warmongers," he said. "Be it underground government officials, their genetic scientists, or Ray herself. Keeping them at arm's length is going to require diversions. If they're not onto us, they will be soon. Chris will make contact, throwing Ray off our trail by offering to meet her in a few days. If she agrees, it'll buy us time and keep her close—away from our target destination.

"Zavier, if you pose as both yourself and Chris, it'll leave Chris free to return to the island discreetly," Mason said. "Chris, you need my protection."

"It won't work," Chris said. "She'll be looking for us."

Chris insisted Mason stay behind. The idea sat in the pit of Mason's stomach like a cup of lard.

"How's your ankle?" Mason asked Zavier. "If you're limping—"

"I'll be fine. I'll favor it when I'm me," Zavier said.

If Ray couldn't survey them, she'd have someone watching their every move—Mason's absence would immediately alert her to deception. Chris was right. It was too risky. What he and the others failed to anticipate was who would take his place by Chris' side.

"I'll go with you," Kyly offered.

"Are you nuts? You barely survived your last encounter with Ray and the one before that with her hired assassin. You want to put your life in jeopardy again so soon? You've barely recovered." Mason struggled not to sound military.

"That's the point. She thinks I'm dead. Chris will be far less suspicious traveling with a wife than alone. My family is in terrible danger. I have to do this."

Chris agreed with Kyly. "It's the one advantage we have."

"I'll have to make the necessary calls to create the illusion of Kyly's demise with local authorities," Mason said begrudgingly. "Alert the news media of a suspicious death. Kyly was never admitted to the hospital. Careful maneuvers might ensure a believable deception."

"Ray's arrogance will prevent her from questioning the report," Chris added. "She'll be too focused on me to care."

Chris and Kyly planned to sneak away the next morning, traveling under an alias as a married couple.

The plan made sense. Aiding Chris was paramount. Still, Mason found no comfort in it.

"I don't like this," he said, encircling the living room and coming back to stand by Chris. "We're going to have to contact Cero. If they catch that news piece...you don't want them thinking Kyly's dead. And I'll have to call Brook."

"Do that when we're in the air," Chris said. "Have them announce the death on the evening news. Leave her identity unknown. I have to contact Ray tonight."

Mason searched the other's eyes. Their expressions mirrored his disbelief.

Mason said little throughout the rest of the day. And, as the hours passed, Kyly grew edgy. He wondered if she questioned her sudden determination to share the next dangerous steps. Perhaps it hit her; she was headed straight for the lion's den. What the hell was she thinking? If she had reservations, she admitted them to no one.

Recent events left them all mute. Their true fears silenced. What was the point of pessimism; it wouldn't improve their odds of survival.

Zavier and Jack were outside instructing the clean-up crew. Chris was nowhere to be seen. He'd retired to the guest room to prepare for his call to Ray. Kyly cornered Mason in the kitchen.

"I don't have a death wish," she said quietly.

"I know. I wish we all didn't have to be placed at risk. I didn't mean to sound so harsh earlier."

"Sure you did. It's fine. It's not smart, but I feel it's necessary. You're going to have your hands full with keeping the illusion going here. Besides, he'll take good care of me."

"You're in good hands." He wanted to tell her those hands were responsible for saving her life, but he didn't.

"So, why aren't you married?" she asked, throwing him off track.

"Nothing ambiguous there," he replied, buying time to form an intelligent answer. In all his years as a bachelor and the countless times he was confronted by this obvious question, this was the first time he searched his repertoire for a meaningful response and came up empty.

"Journalist," Kyly reasoned, her eyes fixed upon him, beseeching an answer. He couldn't escape.

"I was never compelled."

"Hmm. Compelled, eh."

She searched his eyes, not acknowledging that he was staring back.

Eventually, his all-knowing gaze caused her to shift visual directions. Too late, he read her thoughts.

"I hate what happened here." She shifted topics abruptly.

His expression caused her to rephrase.

"I mean...I don't regret meeting you or Zavier at all. Just this mess. I—"

"You didn't bring this to my doorstep," he assured her. "Don't apologize, Kyly. It's not necessary. It's me who should be apologizing. Your life has been in danger ever since you first laid eyes on my family. I'm sure you'll be glad to be rid of us when this is over."

"Don't bank on that happening anytime soon. You may have to get comfortable with me being around."

Zavier walked in just in time to hear Kyly's last words. The mischievous grin he was known for was back on his face.

"You have to be convincing. There can't be any doubt in Ray's mind that Kyly is dead," Mason said. Chris listened to his guidance, knowing none of it would apply.

"Be outraged. It'll lend credence to your time demands, but don't provoke her," Mason continued. "It won't do us any good if she decides you're not worth the effort."

Pausing to breathe, Mason asked, "Are you sure you're up for this?"

Admiring his loyal group of supporters, Chris replied. "A man could have no greater incentive. However, you may not want to be present for this. It won't be a pleasant conversation. It may not go exactly as planned."

"We can handle it," Mason answered for them all.

Dialing the direct line to the island estate, knowing Ray would redirect incoming calls to her satellite phone, Chris was certain they couldn't.

She answered on the first ring.

"I expected to hear from you," she said, her voice laced with poison. "Just not quite so soon. How are things?"

"The answer to your question is beyond your comprehension. You possess but a superficial understanding of the grievous loss caused by your reprehensible intention. You've made an inescapable error." He started.

"Error? What error? My only error is trusting you."

"Your error is thinking you know me, anything about me. Who or what I am." His voice gained an indignant strength. It rang back at him. "You think you're my creator, saved my life, worse still, made my life. You're a fool. There's only one of those, and it's not you."

"What are you saying? Do you know whom you are speaking to? Who made me, what I am—" Her voice was showing cracks.

"I know better than you." He paused for punctuation. "The how doesn't matter. The why all comes from the same place. I'm on borrowed time, but not because of you. You're a genesis of ineffable bereavement. Resisting the depth of human character, you hold an obscure but undeniable arrogance for an action inciting tremendous remorse and consequences you can't yet imagine. Some day you will, and it will crush you, break you open, but I won't be there to see it. I feel the remorse now."

Chris spoke to Ray with words that matched her advanced IQ. All his listeners, save one, were silenced.

"Remorse!" Ray shot back. "Why the hell should you feel any remorse? For an insignificant, meddling, second-rate journalist? I didn't kill her. She hit her head diving for cover and drowned. Call that ordained! Why question it or allocate blame? How could she have become so damn important to you?"

"You wouldn't understand," Chris stated. "Not yet."

Realizing the conversation turned to her, Kyly's eyes met his with an all-knowing certainty.

Ray was far from finished. "How can you possibly profess to know where her head was at? She was breaking a case to get her name in the paper. On the other hand, I broke all the laws to save your life. And the thanks I get for my efforts is condemnation?"

"I did not require saving."

Each word carried depth. Chris caught Mason and Kyly exchanging a curious glance.

"Your exploits serve only as a reflection of your inner pain and, therefore will never achieve the results you so desperately yearn for," Chris continued.

Chris fell silent in the wake of a full-out verbal attack. Mason had warned him not to provoke her. He knew there was no way around it. Seconds passed with them bending their ears to pick up selectively accentuated words, none of them the least bit palatable. Then Chris countered.

"From you, I've witnessed a conspiracy so Machiavellian in nature it has served humanity with a vast injustice that, regardless of brevity, dispels a dark force with sufficient magnitude to span the distance between this life and the next. All medical miracles require respect equal to their impact. It doesn't matter what happens to me, Ray, you will pay, and then you will break—"

"I doubt it," she countered.

"You *will*, vowing an allegiance to war, kicking and screaming, see your dark desire fade to white. First, do no harm. The Hippocratic oath protects both sides of the table. *You are no different!*"

"It may serve to remind you I was manmade. Engineered. Designed to kill!" Ray said with steely contempt. "Do you believe they followed any damn oath?"

"You're not *only* that, wait. Every medical scientific advance of the human race has the same source. You think you're so special. You and I are evolution. It's not new. I know what you're capable of. What will you do with it? Muddy the line between this life and the next and the consequences will be...evil."

These last words, unlike the others, struck deep. "You can't know that," she said, her voice lost its rage and quivered. "He...he whispered it on his deathbed."

"Who have you become?" she asked.

"Let's find out."

"Two days," she said faintly. "Call me, same time. I'll arrange your transportation."

"Fine. And Ray, no more killing."

Chris placed the phone back in its cradle and faced a room full of bewilderment.

"What the hell was that?" Mason asked.

"A dialogue she needed to hear."

———

Through the kitchen window, the night appeared peaceful and calm. Kyly captured a mental snapshot to carry with her. Finishing her milk and placing the glass in the sink, she wondered how the cabin could still feel homey. Everything from the reason she came to the night of the attack, told her to flee and never return. Her heart said something else.

Tiptoeing up the winding staircase to the loft, she was careful not to make a sound. It was one in the morning; she wanted to avoid waking Mason, who was sleeping on the sofa in the sitting area. But he was already awake, headed in her direction, bound for the kitchen himself. As the gap between them diminished, she realized, too late, his eyes hadn't adapted to the dark. He couldn't see her. Before she spoke, he walked into her.

"Mason, it's me, Kyly," she whispered.

The sudden impact scared the hell out of him.

"Good Lord, next time, warn me," he stammered.

"You were staring right at me. I thought you saw me," she explained, brimming with laughter.

Pressed against him with his hands clenching her shoulders, neither of them pulled away. His vision improved, captured by her eyes.

A silence passed between them, then, "I'm sorry."

"I'm not," he said. The warmth of his body against her was welcomed.

"We have to quit running into each other." She made no effort to free herself from his strong embrace.

"Why is that?" he asked.

"It's dangerous."

41

BLINDING fluorescent lights screamed into Nick's retinas, inducing a sharp, piercing pain with a throbbing ache chaser. In vain, he fought to shelter his eyes, slamming his wrists hard against the chains linking his cuffed hands to a waist belt.

Night had passed in a windowless cell, where darkness folded in on itself with the incessant nature of a black hole. He believed it was brighter when he closed his eyes than when he lay wide awake with them open.

Far beneath the earth's surface, the room was designed to provide a safe harbor for high-ranking government officials. In emergency scenarios, where ground-level destruction was imminent, a select few were welcome. It wasn't intended for adversaries.

Light came with an intensity he was certain would burst the bulbs containing it.

The walls smelled freshly painted. A cream color. Constructed of solid cement-like material, and the bed had been built into the wall, with a firm mattress pad fastened by friction belts to the platform. A flat-screen sat inset high on the adjacent wall, though not activated, and a sub-wall sectioned off a shower, sink, and toilet.

When the guard left the area, the lights were extinguished.

During his stay, for the many hours that passed, he remained in dark seclusion.

Cage gave him time to shower, provided a change of clothes and a dull razor, then sent guards back in. They shackled him like a condemned murderer for the long humiliating, walk down the underground hallway. The hairs on Nick's arms bristled as a waft of cold air blew down the corridor. It brought with it a stale stench of cigar smoke not yet swallowed by the filtration ducts. Nick coughed out the offensive air. Putrid. The breath of an enemy.

Cage hadn't the decency to speak with him the evening before. Intent on adding insult to injury, he left Nick in the dark, both figuratively and literally, to ponder his fate and the fate of his sister. Nick expected nothing less.

Breaching the threshold of a small conference room, Nick's eyes adjusted to the harsh drill of the lights, recognizing Cage's sanctimonious grin as he stood, a looming shadow, in the far corner of the room.

"Take the cuffs off, boys," Cage ordered. "Leave us gentlemen to talk."

Gentlemen. Cage's reference dripped of low-grade irony. Nick stood while two soldiers began the complex procedure of unleashing him.

"You sure you want to risk it, Major?" Nick said. "I can be a real asshole before my first cup of coffee."

Cage waved the men out of the room, then kicked a rolling chair across the floor at Nick.

"Have a seat, smartass. This slide show you're about to see could prove rather interesting."

Cage revealed data acquired by filtering through Ray's computer firewall. He clearly enjoyed toying with their lives. Nick was emboldened by their ineptitude. As Nick drew in the first measure of relief, Cage used shock treatment to gag him. It worked.

Rain-soaked, bloated, and corroded by the feasting of beasts. It was difficult to determine the cause of death or even if the corpse was, in fact, human. The photo showed flesh torn from numerous places. One leg was detached from the body, discernible by the boot at its end. No recognizable features remained, only what appeared to be remnants of camouflage gear worn by hunters.

"What the hell is this?" Nick demanded, outraged by Cage's morbid indulgence. "Your idea of intimidation? A drill sergeant's version of a subtle threat?"

"No, no. Apparently it's yours. Or more to the point, your sister's." Cage drew out each sarcastic word. "His buddy got off lucky. He's out of surgery, but he'll spend significant time recovering. In good spirits though, I spoke with him yesterday. Simple fella. I managed to convince him his attacker was male. The rest are going to be far more difficult."

"The rest?" Nick asked, dumbfounded. He could only imagine.

"Oh yes, the RCMP, for instance. A random kill like this one." Cage tapped the macabre image that remained enlarged on the overhead screen. "Could've left them baffled, but blowing out the side of a local hero's house...a direct attack demands equally aggressive action. Killing his girlfriend? Well, it's an insult Canadian cops won't tolerate. If they reach Ray before we do, they'll shoot to kill. After all, to them, she's a deranged foreign terrorist."

"What house? What girlfriend?" Nick demanded, spinning the chair to face Cage.

"Oh, while you've been busy playing diplomat, your sister—the assassin—engaged an unsuspecting society. You thought she'd be controllable? You can't control her any more than we can. She was designed to do exactly this." Cage stabbed at the screen. "*And you set her free!* If we can bring her back alive, we will. It's our prerogative, but chances are she'll meet her death first."

He closed the distance to loom over Nick's chair; reflected bloody images from the projector lit his face.

"*Know what you've done?*" Cage whispered. "*You've unleashed hell.*"

———

Nick prepared Ray before she uttered a word over the speaker. "Don't say anything you don't want Cage to hear."

"What could I possibly have to hide from him?" Ray's seductive voice amplified into the room. Cage grinned. Nick wanted to punch him. Granting him the use of his hands might prove a grave mistake.

"How did you sleep?" Cage asked her. "Nightmares keeping you awake?"

"Not hardly," Ray said. "I slept like a baby—"

"How would you know?" Cage taunted.

Nick hit the mute button, then said, "Any more of that crap, and I end this!"

"Fine. Put her back on."

"Nick?" she said.

"Yeah, I'm here. They've narrowed down your location."

"Don't worry. He doesn't have the capacity to outsmart me."

"That must inflate the ego," Cage replied.

"No. Knowledge is pain. I've become comfortable with both. I'm lying back on my pillows reviewing rendezvous maps, agent profiles, safe house locations, photos of potential targets, and methods of infiltration. You haven't a hope in hell."

Nick knew she would hole up a safe distance away, across the Montana border. He pictured her surrounded by documents of deception. Blueprints for MJ's domination formed her security blanket. "We have to talk."

"I'm sorry you're in such poor company," she said.

"You have no idea. Without graphic details, your escapades during the last forty-eight hours annihilated our squeaky-clean image. You've raised some high-profile eyebrows. The only way this situation can resolve itself amicably is with a certain measure of cooperation."

"Cooperation, is that what he's calling it?" she asked. Contempt steeled her voice.

"Ray, cut the shit. This thing will bury us if you're not careful. They want you to come in willingly. They can't harm you, they need you."

"Is that so? How long do I have?"

"Not long. They expect you to surrender tonight."

"Not possible. Cage, are you still eavesdropping?"

"Of course, darlin'. It has been a long time since I heard your pretty voice. I wouldn't miss it for the world."

"How sweet. Two days and I'll come peacefully. We'll sit down for a real one—on—one chat about old times over tea, and crumpets. You can scold me for reckless behavior and I'll help you earn a few more stars. 'Til then, you so much as snap a hair on Nick's head and people you favor will start disappearing in the most unpleasant way. We understand each other, sir?"

"As a matter of curiosity, why did you feel it was necessary to kill an innocent hunter along your travels?"

Nick knew the question was intended for his benefit.

"*Assassin.*"

Ray's one word explanation proved Cage's earlier point. Extraordinary. Flawless. Cold-blooded killer. Cage's arrogant grin almost dislodged the cigar hanging off his lip. Nick hoped he choked on it.

"Ask one who's known me if I'm really so bad...I am." Ray quoted Gowan's song, *Criminal Mind*. Touché. It could've been written solely for her.

Refusing to bask in airwave silence, Ray demanded to speak with Nick off conference. It wouldn't guarantee privacy, but it would annoy Cage. They had reverted back to adolescence. Nick clicked off the speakerphone and listened in.

"I have the situation well in hand," she said.

"Are you okay? Cage said you were hit," he asked.

"Shoulder wound, repaired by a very well-paid, discrete, local physician. Throbs relentlessly. A trade off."

"Better be the last," Nick warned. He ended the call. Resting his head in his hands, he contemplated their impending doom. 'Assassin.' The word echoed between his ears.

"It's not as bad as it seems, son." Cage's tone became strangely supportive. "We do need her, and if we need her, we need you."

Nick longed for the isolation of his windowless cell. Instead, Cage escorted him to a more luxurious room two floors above the impact safe zone level. It resembled a penthouse suite with all the expected luxuries. For Nick, it was still a cage.

A soldier delivered a breakfast cart minutes after he arrived and freed him of his cuffs. Nick poured coffee and stared at a changing computer-generated image built into a windowpane. It mimicked a lakeside view.

Here he sat, hundreds of feet below the surface, hidden from the world and it from him. God, how he wished he was back in his Saleen S7 with the purr of the engine to soothe him. No roads, only walls.

They knew everything. Almost everything.

Ray lost control of MJ. He was fleeing the island when they began monitoring. They knew about the family helping MJ in Canada—the family who called him Chris. They hadn't put all the pieces together. It was a matter of time. Chris had a strong hold over Ray. Why else would she have gone after him with such vengeance? They saw it and when the timing was right, they'd use it against her.

Ray didn't realize Chris had been injured during the roof chase. She wasn't aware that Cage's men followed her there with the intent of tracking and capturing her. She'd led them straight to him.

Typing and analyzing his blood and DNA from the warehouse wall, they stumbled onto something of far greater value. They confirmed Chris wasn't Micael Valeric's biological son. The fact he'd been kept in hiding for over thirty years spoke volumes. His DNA revealed him to be exceptionally unique.

The average human DNA contains forty memo groups. Their analysis revealed his had over 100,000. Compositional elements of his DNA chain were the same. They were simply compounded. He, in essence, was somehow tightly packed with infinite genetic knowledge. They couldn't be sure yet, but it appeared he shared DNA with every human on the planet. The Eve Theory had found its Adam thousands of years in the making. Cage admitted they couldn't fathom how or why. He also said Chris shared extensive genetic markers with the man who helped him flee the island.

"Transplanting every organ in the human body can't alter the recipient's DNA. That kid was born that way." Cage paused, letting the information hover in the air.

"*Before* Doctor Valeric or any of us got our hands on him."

What Ray didn't know, what Nick couldn't tell her, was they didn't just want her. They wanted Chris. She may get her wish of being reunited with her lost love, but it'd be hard to celebrate from behind bars.

They'd engineered her. Years had been spent perfecting the art. An art Valeric improved upon, deceiving them. Secretly developing a weapon far superior to theirs.

Nick couldn't comprehend all the data Cage showered on him. Information overload seemed to be Cage's intent. All he knew for sure was Chris wasn't who they thought he was. Valeric had kept his greatest achievement hidden, even from his family. As hard as Nick fought to make sense of it, he came up with nothing but a full-blown migraine.

He remembered the night of the operation, telling Ray it was a mistake.

She'd refused to listen to reason.

He wanted her to accept limitations, the existence of things out of her control. He waited for her to collapse and admit defeat so he could help her mend. That moment never came.

That night, in the lime green glow of the monitors, the fire of her fear ignited, incinerating her grief. In its wake came pure rage.

He knew then, as he did now, it'd be a slow burn.

Staring at the distorted image of a bluebird, he tapped the screen, warping its dimensions to the echo of Cage's warning. "You ever wonder why her eyes are black? There's a growing school of thought that we're the genetic product of beings. Half human, half animal, that colonized this planet with weaker DNA. Ray's pure predator. They're shark eyes. And like them, when she stops hunting, she'll die."

42

TYPING a message in the dark can be a dangerous practice when the information has the potential to boomerang and take your head off. Concealed in the closet, Brook's fingers worked the tiny keyboard nonetheless. She pushed the send button, watched an icon confirm receipt at her father's end, and was about to dump the blackberry into her pocket when the house phone startled her into losing her grip. The cellular collided with shoes, purses, and bottles of leather protector at her feet.

No time to rummage.

Fear of her father being brazen enough to contact her on the main line fueled her exit. If Curt, or worse, Mason, found out she'd involved her father, there'd be hell to pay. Both men had sworn never to speak to the man again. She had no choice. He knew people that could be called out of the shadows. Mason needed that kind of backup, whether he'd admit it or not.

"It's Mason. Where were you?" Curt asked, holding the receiver to his ear.

"Needed a sweater," she said. "Closet."

"Then, where is it?"

She shrugged the question off as he handed over the phone. His expression said neither he nor Mason knew anything. She kept secrets before. It didn't end well. Listening to Mason, she knew he had his own brand of silence. Their family of transparency had clouded over. And the storm brewing was sure to drown them all.

———

"I hope I didn't wake you." Mason sat upright, leaning against the back of the couch when Kyly entered the sitting area.

"No, I've been up for a while," she admitted. Her voice softened when they were alone. She wasn't sure why. "I heard you on the phone with Brook. You love her very much."

He smiled in response, blinded by sunlight, unaware her gaze left his eyes to drift down to his exposed chest. She couldn't help noticing his masculine beauty; white sheet crumpled around his waist, barefoot hanging out one side, tanned skin in a backdrop of sunlight. In a threatening world, he brought a reassurance something good remained.

A comforting silence passed between them, and, for a moment, she forgot the burden they carried. Despite her usual defensive nature, she stood back lit before him in nothing but the shirt he'd loaned her to sleep in. The worn cotton held a subtle aroma of musk.

"I guess I'll be leaving today," she said, rescinding the moment's serenity.

"I still think your leaving is a bad idea."

"It's a day or two, then we'll be back. You'll be there? When I, when we get back."

"I'll be there," he said with a telltale grin.

In the most nonchalant way, the essence of his ability to light up a room resonated in his smile. It was too easy to be entranced by his gaze. Dark, thick eyelashes like Egyptian paint highlighted his sparkling eyes, enhancing a flawless profile. No matter what happened, she'd hold this image.

It might be the last or the first of many. She prayed for the latter.

———

Mason wrestled with his thoughts after Kyly left the room. He'd caught a glimpse of something. Paradise.

Throwing off his blankets, he grabbed his jeans from the floor and headed downstairs, desperate for fresh, cold mountain air.

Riggs waited happily in the foyer. After a few extra pats, they headed out onto the front porch barefoot. Cool, crisp waves of pine scent washed over his bare skin. He drank it in, admiring the pristine mountain morning while Kyly lingered on his mind.

She was too young for him. He was too old for this. She'd return to her life a thousand miles away once this was over and forget. He would not.

The sound of the door interrupted his introspection. Jack arrived with a fresh mug of coffee.

"Thought you might need this," Jack said. "Kinda crisp out here, isn't it?"

"Thanks," Mason replied, taking the warm mug. "I needed a little fresh air."

"She has that effect on most, I suspect. Poor Zavier spent the last week accepting sisterly affection."

"Zavier? He and Kyly—" Mason asked, awkwardly alarmed.

"Whoa there, cowboy. In her eyes, Zavier's a kid. She's older than she looks, like someone else I know. So you gonna tell her or let her leave here wondering."

"Tell her?"

"Yes," Jack said firmly. "Tell her."

The native wisdom in Jack's expression said it all. Mason didn't argue. Instead, he dropped his head for a moment. Leaning against the railing he stared at his feet, then looked back at Jack's waiting eyes.

"She knows."

"You sure?" Jack questioned, heading back inside. "If I were you, I'd want to be sure."

Alone again, Mason wondered if he may have attributed more significance to the subtly seductive moments that had passed between Kyly and him than deserved.

"Man, I'm in some kind of trouble here," he said to the dog.

Riggs groaned, shaking fur free from head to toe in agreement.

"Don't get smart," he said. "You're the one who put your life on the line for her."

Riggs whined in protest, then abruptly fell quiet, taking on a pointers pose, staring into the forest.

Flying low, three white birds, too far away to discern breed, broke free from the entwined maze of tree branches and soared upward, seeking the freedom of open sky. Distracted by their flight, Mason didn't see Chris emerge from a pathway beneath them. He walked alone.

Mason's gut reaction said to chastise his nephew for risking himself a day after the attack. He swallowed hard against it, knowing it wasn't his place. Not with this man.

Riggs padded down the curved staircase and across the driveway to greet him. The fact that the dog was living and breathing still astounded Mason. Watching him play as if he never sustained injury was, in a word, disturbing. As he wrestled with this, Chris looked up. Mason sensed him reading these thoughts.

He found it odd how hastily he ascribed preternatural qualities to this man and, odder still, how he always managed to comply with this assessment. Others would label Chris eccentric, distant by a life of confinement, exceptional at the very least. In truth, mere words couldn't accurately describe him.

Neither spoke, but Mason could tell, as Chris drew nearer, his disposition wasn't that of a joyful man.

"You worried about going back?" Mason asked when Chris came close enough to speak discretely.

"No," Chris said dryly.

"Worried about how this is going to turn out?" Mason persisted.

"I know how this will turn out." Chris stared back into the woods.

"What then? You seem...well, you seem angry."

"I am angry," Chris said firmly. "In fact, I'm furious."

"About what, exactly?" Intrigued, knowing every bit of information drawn from Chris provided another window into his true identity, Mason pushed.

"Life." Chris bowed his head and offered nothing more.

"Life. You're young. There'll be time. I realize you can never get back the years taken from you. We can't erase the past, but don't lose the time you have focusing on it."

"It's sound advice but inaccurate. You don't understand. My life isn't served by acquisition." His tone had become somber.

"I know your circumstances are unique, and you have a very real sense of obligation to protect your family—"

"Obligation?" He raised his head. "I have no obligation."

"Okay, you've committed to protecting them, to making things right, but you still deserve a life of your own."

"Yes. I deserve to experience my family and, perhaps, one day, a wife and children of my own. I deserve to grow old watching those I love flourish, but I will not." Anger deepened his voice.

"Why are you being so negative? We can find a way—"

"There is only one way."

Mason wanted to grab Chris, shake sense into him, and force him to believe in the possibility of a happy ending, but one glance into his kaleidoscope eyes and he fell speechless—a wisdom existed behind their reflection that defied provocation.

Chris walked to Mason, placed a hand on his shoulder, smiled graciously, and turned to leave. He paused at the threshold, staring back at him.

"Kyly feels the same, by the way, but you still need to tell her," Chris cautioned. "She'll need your support and your love."

If Mason's speech hadn't been frozen by shock, he would've erupted into a line of questioning indicative of the Spanish Inquisition. Once again, he was blindsided by Chris' uncanny gift for hearing words unspoken.

The door sealed shut behind Chris, and Mason collapsed onto a lounger at a loss for words.

———

Placing her bags in the foyer, Kyly memorized the cabin. It wasn't how it appeared when she arrived, peaceful and still. Equipment and luggage now lay strewn across the floors, abandoned in hallways and doorways to trip over. Paperwork and files littered every flat surface. Loaded guns were left in open sight.

The once perfect glass framing the picturesque property mirrored her shell against the darkness, fractured, weakened, and unstable. The view became a cruelly etched metaphor of her faith—tainted by destruction.

Changing perspectives, she turned to the window flanking the front door and a clear view of Mason in the lounger, bare feet crossed on top of the railing, wearing nothing but wrinkled blue jeans, top button undone.

God, he was easy to love.

He held a coffee cup on the chair's arm. His eyes were closed, though not with the tranquility of a sunbather but a deep thinker's secession from the world.

She wished she had more time, but time was an elusive treasure. Her hope lied in living for the day when she could return, her debt paid, her conscience clear.

Zavier startled her. She'd been so focused on the man outside that she was deaf to his approach.

"I'll be sorry to see you go," Zavier said, not blind to what held her attention. "So will he."

"I thought you'd be glad to be rid of me," she replied. "I know he will."

"Yeah, right."

Like other men in the family, a lot could be conveyed in one of Zavier's many sly expressions.

"You need anything?" He scanned her luggage.

"Yeah, a foolproof plan and an invisibility cloak."

Zavier hugged her, and they stayed there for a quiet moment until he pulled away to face her.

"Take care of yourself. I expect to see you back here in one lively piece in a couple days. No excuses," he instructed.

"Yes, sir." Kyly saluted. "Zavier?"

"Yeah."

"You're an amazing doctor and a wonderful man." With that, she leaned in and kissed his cheek. He graciously accepted.

"You're not so bad yourself. I'll miss you, and I won't be the only one. You better go say goodbye."

He left her there, and for a moment, she thought about waiting inside until Chris came to tell her it was time, but she didn't. Shyly, she opened the door, rousing Riggs from where he'd been sitting under Mason's free hand.

"Didn't mean to disturb you," she fibbed.

"You're not." He slid into an upright-seated position. "Have a seat."

He patted the chair next to him and Kyly walked around back to reach it.

"Actually," he said. "I was going to come find you."

"You were? I know you're very concerned about your nephew's safety. I give you my word I'll do everything I can to help—"

He placed his left hand over her right as she settled into a seat.

"I know you will. That's not why I wanted to talk to you."

"It's not?"

Nothing in life prepared her for the sensations she experienced in his presence. The simple touch of his hand flowed through to her soul with its promise.

"Life isn't bent on providing ideal circumstances. A person could waste away waiting for that. I won't."

His voice commanded her full attention. She gave it, anxious to hear his every word.

"I'm a lot older than you. I've been witness to such a vast array of tragedy and triumph that little surprises me. I've been down enough roads to be keenly aware of one I've never before traveled."

She wasn't sure where he was heading with their conversation, whether he would drill home the seriousness of their situation or reveal something far more personal. Her heart hoped.

"I don't think anyone has ever been down the road we've all been forced down," she contributed.

"I'm not talking about Chris. I'm talking about us."

"Us?"

"I can't breathe when you walk into the room. I swore I'd never commit myself to all the demands and heartbreaks of a long-term relationship, but I find myself suddenly longing for them. I don't know how you've done it, but you're under my skin. I've spent my life defending a wall I built to turn and find you on the inside. I don't want you to go. Not because I think you're incapable or don't trust your decision, but because I don't want to lose you, which makes no sense since I hardly know you."

"Okay," he whispered. "This is the part where you get up, tell me I'm delusional, and walk out."

She said nothing, shaking her head while keeping her hand beneath his.

"No?" he said.

"No, I don't want to go with Chris. And it's not the danger holding me back. I don't want to go because I don't want to leave here." Tears welled in her eyes. "I don't want to leave you. And that wall you mentioned...you were on the inside of mine before we met."

43

CERO GRABBED the phone in the bedroom in a state of forced semi-consciousness, battling exhaustion. The voice on the line came filtered as if drifting down a long corridor. "Cero, it's Mason. I know it's late. I imagined you'd be up."

"You were right. Why isn't Kyly calling?" Cero asked, fear his constant companion.

"She's fine, Father, but we discovered unwelcome visitors here, so I had to relocate her. For her own safety, she's going to be out of contact for a couple of days. Please try not to worry."

"It's been rather difficult. She's...she's all we've got."

"No need to explain, Cero, I know. She's..."

Seconds passed without a word, and Cero waited.

Clearing his throat, Mason continued, "We've had to use the media to throw them off our trail. Do me a favor, and don't believe everything you hear or read in the paper. If I could prevent it, she wouldn't be exposed to..."

The strength in Mason's tone shattered, exposing more than a professional interest in protecting Kyly.

"Are you all right, son?" Cero asked. His genuine concern was met by silence at the end of the line. Cero admired Mason's chosen profession, but the man was more than a hardened ex-cop driven to serve and protect. Not jaded by the evils of humanity, Mason Stone's heart beat strong. His emotion championed Cero's respect.

"Son, I'm here if you need to talk. I know this can't be easy for you. You're carrying a burden for us all."

"It's not the burden I mind, Father," Mason admitted, his voice falling to a whisper. "It's the fear of failure. I love these people. I can't let them down. I'm supposed to keep everyone positive and lead with confidence, but today...seeing her go. It's more than I can take."

Before all else, Cero was a minister. He wouldn't betray this by allowing his own fears to render him useless at this moment.

"Mason, you've kept everyone safe up to this point. You have to keep your faith. You're not walking this path alone. You're being guided, son. I believe this. And you must know it as well. I've entrusted my most precious treasure to you with confidence. You mustn't let fear cloud your judgment. Stay focused. Save your tears for another time. I'll do the same. And, when this is over, we'll shed them triumphantly."

This constituted a consideration of hope.

"Thank you, Father, for your trust. I'll do my best. I don't know what to say."

"There is nothing to say. Protect my daughter, take care of yourself, and keep in touch whenever possible."

"Yes."

Cero hung up feeling less isolated.

Wrapping his arm around Paris, he whispered to his waiting wife. "She's fine, honey. In fact, I think she's in very good hands. Sleep."

This night, their thoughts would not be quite so troubled. This night, friendship reigned over fear. This night, they found peace inside the eye of the storm.

But it watched, weighed, and waited.

44

MASON INHALED PLUMES of evergreen-laced dust as tractors, cranes, and heavy machinery growled, screeched, and tore into the once serene woodlands behind his cabin. All traces of the bomb's debris had been cleared away. Landscapers worked overtime to finish restorations to the yard by nightfall, while construction inside was scheduled to continue into the wee hours, if necessary.

Waiting for the cop's interest to subside, waiting for a plan to hatch, waiting for a bolt of lightning to zap his mind into some kind of clarity, Mason surrendered.

New security system. New walls. New level of frustration.

Busy hands distracted the mind, lessening the constant intrusion of worry and debate. It was a toss-up who was under greater demand. Mason with ceaseless questions from all directions or Zavier, who for several hours had changed continually between two outfits, effectively maintaining a split persona.

Sporting a cap, jeans, and T-shirt, he directed workers outside the cabin, talked with Mason, limped openly and drank coffee. Wearing khakis, sunglasses, and a long-sleeved shirt, slightly exposing the mock bandages on his wrists, he impersonated Chris. Mason insisted on replicating this medical detail, unsure of whether Ray had knowledge of Chris' injuries.

Zavier altered his demeanor as well. Ankle compromised, he still moved light-footed and youthful as himself, then adapted to a more conservative stance with slower deliberate movements as Chris. After the first three hours, Mason became convinced if medical school proved too tedious a venture for Zavier, acting was a viable alternative.

Shaking the insanity of the situation off with the dirt on his gloves, Mason pulled his hands free from the worn calf leather, smacked the fabric together in a cloud of dust, and collided with Zavier dressed as Chris.

"Whoa, just about trampled ya," Mason apologized.

"It's okay," Zavier said, noticing they were alone. "I've got to tell you, this feels too weird."

"For us both, kid," Mason agreed. "Do a double take. I'll tell them we're going in to eat and have them break for lunch."

"Good idea. Being both of us has increased my appetite," Zavier joked.

Mason ran interference while his nephew performed quick changes, scattering himself as two one last time around the cabin. Though, he doubted the validity of their efforts.

Like cockroaches in a flashlight beam, workers fled the area in search of the nearest diner. In moments, Mason, Zavier, and his alter ego were abandoned.

A delivery from one of Mason's favorite taverns waited for them in the kitchen. Stealing the bag from where it sat on the counter and three cold beers from the refrigerator, Mason called for the young Dr. Jekyll to join him upstairs.

"Okay, kid, you have an hour to amalgamate your split personality and chow down."

"Very funny," Zavier replied. Clearing the staircase, he noticed the three beers beside Mason. "Thirsty, or do I get a beer for both of me?"

"Pretense," Mason explained. "We'll leave them in the sink in case a crew member is being paid to be nosy."

"I like the new digs, a little cozier," Zavier said, unwrapping his lunch. "Your idea or the designer's?"

Mason didn't answer, electing instead to bite into his roast beef sandwich. Zavier's comment was intended as a precursor to the underlying topic he was itching to discuss, and Mason knew it.

"Come on, you're not a throw cushion type of guy. You're metal and stone. Admit it, you're decorating for her."

Mason maintained his silence, refusing to be drawn out by his nephew's banter.

"I think she's worth it, that's all," Zavier relented.

After a moment of chewing, Mason conceded, "Yeah, kid, she's worth it."

"She'd be a great addition to the family, but I'm never going to call her aunt Kyly. She's too much like a sister for that."

"Wait just a minute." Mason choked on his second bite. "I hardly know this woman. I haven't even taken her out on a date, and you have us married?"

"No, that's true. I mean, she has lived in your house, slept in your bed—alone mind you—escaped certain death under your protection, and had her parents firmly place her life in your hands. I can see how important a first date would be at this juncture." Zavier smiled.

"Shut up and eat," Mason grumbled, trying hard to squash a grin. Clearly, they both saw the connection. He wasn't fooling anyone, especially his nephew.

Mason ate, content in the silence, happy to be free of the noise and intrusion. New glass panels were scheduled for installation in the upstairs living room in two hours, making Zavier's quick changes more difficult. Both men were becoming anxious for privacy to discuss the voice of concern growing louder with every passing hour.

"So, what did you think of your older brother?" Mason asked, cracking the cap off the third beer.

"He's, I don't know. There's something...uncanny about him. He's the spitting image of me, but he's nothing like me."

"You mean you're the spitting image of him," Mason corrected from his relaxed perch on the window seat. "He has dark hair. It's too bad you didn't see him before the dye job."

"Dye job wasn't so great. You've spent the most time with him. What do you think?"

"I think your assessment is more accurate than you know. He's unearthly and strangely soulful." Mason stared out the loft window. "I think it'd take a lifetime to understand him."

"Because of what he's lived through?" Zavier shifted his position on the floor, leaning his back squarely against the lower portion of the sofa.

"Yeah, and how it has...changed him." His voice had grown solemn. "We better finish up and get ready for visitors."

Zavier didn't pry. He didn't have to. Mason knew a part of him wasn't ready to acknowledge what happened to Kyly and Riggs. He was there. He had experienced it. Kyly responded to Chris' efforts not his own. Though grief-stricken and refusing to accept the situation, Zavier conceded her death before Chris appeared. Medical training led him to this truth. More than that, he'd admitted to Mason he sensed Kyly returning to life that night. He claimed to feel the energy flow through his own flesh into her and back again beneath Chris's hand.

Mason witnessed Kyly's rebirth. Zavier experienced it firsthand.

Riggs spent the day with Jack and his son. Mason wanted to keep the dog out of danger and out of sight. So, Jack's truck coming up the road mid-afternoon surprised him. Walking out to the driveway to meet it, he noticed it wasn't Riggs smirking in the passenger seat. A very serious, square-jawed cop nodded curtly in Mason's direction. The Royal Canadian Mounted Police officer wore dark sunglasses, concealing his eyes and intentions. He posed no threat to Mason.

Alastair Beron was a veteran officer with three years to early retirement. They'd become pals seven years earlier when Mason moved to town. Aside from their mutual loyalty to their chosen career, both were bachelors, avid sportsmen, and comics after a second scotch at the Bearspaw pub. They shared intimidating dispositions that sent criminals cowering, but in the right setting, they were the best kind of fun.

Bear, as friends called him, smiled away his stern expression and rolled down the window, resting a beefy arm on the doorframe.

Tipping his glasses to peek over the top rim, he said, "Hell of a way to redecorate. Looks like a bomb exploded."

"Very funny. I don't remember you making house calls," Mason said. "Either you're disgracefully late, or you're breaking policy."

"Thought we should chat," Bear said, lifting his burly two hundred and thirty pound frame from the truck's front seat. Shorter than Mason and packing a few extra, Bear remained the picture of authority, well-suited to his nickname, with a trigger finger and aim capable of threading a needle at fifty yards.

Mason leaned in the window to talk to Jack. "You comin' in?"

"Nah, I'll check around, say hi to the boys, and meet you back here in ten," Jack said.

"See ya in ten."

Bear smacked Mason on the back with a hardy paw and followed him into the house with a solid stride. Mason laughed at Bear's overconfidence. Criminals did not. His appearance announced zero tolerance, leaving those who crossed him praying for divine intervention. The only saving grace when it came to Bear. He wasn't a big proponent of second chances.

"So you've managed to once again attract the very worst of 'em," Bear said, sliding onto a bar stood in the kitchen, concealing it in such a way he appeared to hover mid-air.

"What do you have for me?" Mason pulled a chair up on the opposite side of the café bar.

"Seems we have a hunter in recovery who has been questioned by an American covert crew. Can't find any trace of them through standard channels. They convinced the guy his attacker was a man. A renegade they traced here."

"And your assessment?"

"It's bullshit. A woman in combat gear sportin' a weapon amateurs couldn't get their hands on shot the guy. Who did you pick to dog fight this time, 'cause the damage report would suggest she's rabid?"

Mason smiled, locked eyes with his fellow public defender, and then shifted his gaze to the granite countertop.

"Okay. How bad is it?" Bear asked.

"Bad."

"Anything we can do?"

"Yeah." Mason made eye contact again. "Stay outta this one. Drop the trail and give me a couple weeks."

"I'll hold off inquiries for the time being, but sooner or later, I'm going to need answers."

"Later," Mason suggested.

"You've been bombed, buddy. You sure you don't want me in on this?"

"I'm sure. I may need you in time. I need a handle on this first."

Bear agreed, shifting their conversation from what he didn't know to what he did.

"They're hunting this one like a fugitive. One of their own gone rogue. She's holding the cards, or they wouldn't be pouring manpower into this."

"Doesn't make sense," said Mason. "They knew where to find her before. Why hunt her now?"

"She's off the reservation, man. In more than one way." Bear glanced down at photos of the bomb's damage lying on the counter.

After he disclosed the information they had, Mason thanked him for his discretion, patted him on the back, and walked him out to Jack waiting in his truck.

"The guys are planning the annual escape for October." Bear jumped into the cab. "You in?"

"Hey, if I'm breathing, I'm in." Mason shut the cab door behind Bear. "Call me in a couple weeks. We'll catch up."

"I'll do that."

Jack tipped his hat. Mason watched the truck clear the driveway and disappear beyond the tree line, then he headed inside.

Grinding, screeching, and snarling discontent, the new living room windows were being set in place. Be it ill-fitting glass or mental anguish to blame, his brain ached.

Ray's pursuers were hot on her trail—professionals with powerful contacts backing their movements. Bear hit nothing but dead ends unearthing who *they* were and what they were up to.

They couldn't know about Chris, or at least not everything. If they did, they would focus more on him. At present, Ray appeared their primary target.

If Ray became their captive, she'd barter with Chris' life for freedom. It wouldn't be long before the mystery unraveled. There would be no refuge for his nephew.

"Damn it," Mason cursed out loud, not caring who overheard him.

Crushing a paper coffee cup, he let the dark liquid spill over his hand before tossing the contorted cardboard into an open trashcan. Lingering droplets slipped through his fingers.

"Something wrong with the fit?" an installer fretted, glaring down from the top of a ladder where he hovered, applying sealant to the frame.

"No, no. It's...nothing. The window looks great," he said. His tone was anything but convincing.

New glass didn't comfort. It only made Mason's urge to smash something harder to resist. He fled downstairs and out the hole where a new lower level door waited to be installed. The noise of landscape machinery and workmen yelling orders didn't soothe his agitation. Deciding to put his aggressive energy to constructive use, he jumped in behind two workers struggling to insert a large bolder into the rock garden by the waterfall.

Hard labor was good medicine for attitude readjustment. His father swore this time and again. Today, Mason decided he had a point and wondered what had driven him to emotional fracture. What did he hide from his family when they were still his?

By nightfall, Mason and Zavier were exhausted, one from being two men and one from doing the work of two. Covered in dirt, transformed to mud by the onset of salty sweat, Mason earned a long cold shower. The interior reconstruction was finished by midnight. Once again, Mason shut out the world behind the cabin's new doors and sought solace under a high-powered faucet.

Crisp, clear mountain water washed away the grime of the day. It did nothing to clear his conscience. His muscular frame emerged, refreshed. His thoughts remained muddied. Worsening with the weight of worry.

He swept a towel over his wet skin. The shirt Kyly slept in the night before lay draped over the corner chair. The memory seemed a thousand years ago. He pictured her body beneath it in the sunlight. Cold shower or not, he ached for her. He threw his towel across the room, dissolving the memory, and stood naked with tense hands clasped to his temples.

How could I let her leave?

Driven, he threw on running shorts and a T-shirt and headed downstairs. Slipping by Zavier's room, he set the house alarm and embarked on a moonlit trail.

Heavy feet pounded against solid ground, heavy heart against fate.

45

"CHRIS, WAKE UP." Panic muddled Kyly's voice. "Wake up, you're bleeding."

Crimson seeped through the white gauze wrapping his wrists, soiling it. Droplets beaded at his scalp until their weight became sufficient to journey down his face. She wiped them with her sleeve, protecting his closed eyes. The airplane climbed altitude, avoiding rough air. Perhaps this fed his condition.

"Wake up!" Kyly clasped his face in her hands. She knew about his wrist injuries. At the cabin, Mason had explained the gruesome accident that happened during their rooftop descent, escaping Ray. She wasn't aware of any related head trauma.

"Chris, wake up! Please, for the love of Christ, wake up," she begged, holding him close.

He resumed control of his body and pulled against her hands.

"Chris?"

With no sign of the typical dreary transition from slumber to alertness, his kaleidoscope eyes popped open, and stared back at her.

"You look worried?" He adjusted his position. "I'm fine."

"You're not," she shot back, gesturing to his injuries. "You're bleeding from your forehead too."

"I'm okay." He slid his legs over the edge of the sofa. "Nightmares, that's all. Thanks for waking me. How close are we to the drop?"

"I don't have a clue. I was busy worrying you'd bleed to death."

Smiling, he grabbed his duffel bag from the floor and headed to the washroom, leaving her pacing the cabin. For the first time in her life, she became airsick. When he emerged from the washroom refreshed with clean bandages, she fled past him, slammed the door shut, and threw up.

His resemblance to his younger brother was striking, yet the two were as different as night and day. Where Zavier announced who he was, what he wanted, and what he thought, Chris stayed a well-guarded mystery. Kyly couldn't anticipate what demons lay ahead, and she wasn't comfortable confronting them with this odd stranger.

It made her head spin.

Her body seconded the rejection. She leaned over the porcelain rim again.

When she finally crept out of the washroom, Chris met her a couple feet from the door and, ironically, helped her to a seat. Handing her a glass of watered-down ginger ale, he placed his hand over her free one and instructed her to relax. She sensed color returning to her face.

"I'm sorry...I got mad. It's just—"

"You have nothing to apologize for," he said. "Drink. It will help settle your stomach. We have a long swim ahead of us, but we're going to be fine, Kyly."

The calm in his voice or honesty of his eyes, somehow she believed him.

"The scars on your head, are they from the accident when you injured your wrists?" she asked.

"No, they happened first, but I'm fine, and so are you," he reassured.

The pilot came over the intercom system, announcing they were a half hour outside their destination.

"We better get suited up," Chris suggested. "You're feeling better?"

"Yes, thank you."

"I'll go out first," he said with a sympathetic pause. "Then, you'll follow."

She wasn't nervous anymore. Parachuting didn't bother her, she grew up cliff diving, but something underlying his words turned what was a soft chill into a leaden weight.

Kyly rose from the water. Its film drained off her wetsuit as she glanced back across the distance to where their boat lay in wait. If clouds blew in or they were forced to wait until dark to swim back out, relocating it would be like finding the shadowed hump of a whale in the bleakness of midnight waves. Peeling free from the rubber mold, she said nothing of her fears.

Creeping along the wharf's edge, every sound was an alarming intrusion. The sailboat, yacht, and high-tech custom motorboat moored at Valeric's private dock swooped and clanked as incoming waves broke around them. Metal fittings on the masts chimed in the breeze while the vessels moaned out warnings in their berths. Kyly jerked and flinched against their every sound.

Above them, the hillside sat beneath a blanket of tall grasses, not lengthy enough to walk through undetected but a moderate concealer if one maintained a crouched position. In a gorilla's hunch, Chris led the way up, pausing first to check on Kyly. She nodded the go-ahead, and he trudged up the steep incline.

Currently uninhabited, the island's hidden surveillance cameras became the occupants they evaded. Ray's watchful eyes lurked everywhere via satellite. Chris mapped a path through the blind.

Warehouses and a shed lay to the right of the estate, and an expansive home to the left. Below, the marina was centered between them. Making their way to the top of the embankment, Chris angled their ascent for the storage buildings.

He reached back for her as she met the lip of the hill and eased her to level ground. She caught her breath, surveying the surroundings in awe of the island's beauty. Eerily familiar to her tropical home.

The estate sat not far to her left. The grounds were impeccable, the home itself majestic. She paused, realizing what an enormous feat of character it'd take to abandon all of this.

Chris had shown Kyly a picture of Ray on the plane, along with photos of others involved. Smiling seductively on a boat deck, she was breathtaking.

Kyly hadn't gotten a clear view of her during the attack and preferred to avoid running blindly into their enemy. Ray's appearance wouldn't have triggered any suspicion. She didn't *look* threatening—a supermodel selling expensive toys. A movie star on vacation, or a

Caribbean princess, perhaps. Not, by any stretch, the poster child for cold-blooded killers with explosive finesse.

Chris remained unmoved by the view, tapping Kyly back into motion when she lagged behind.

Approaching from the ocean side, the first building they reached appeared to be an impenetrable fortress of thick metal walls and high mounted security cameras. Behind it lay a much older, subdued storage shed surrounded by overgrown foliage. As they rounded the corner, Kyly thanked God out loud when Chris pointed to the less formidable structure.

"You had me worried for a moment there," she said.

"The window is at the back," he urged.

Nearing the shack, she maneuvered between carnations, red roses, bellflowers, lilies, jasmines, and strawberry beds. Chris stood admiring the flowers and then whispered, "Sonnet 64."

Sun reflected off Chris' arms as he yanked the window open with a thud. Trailing plumes of dust and cobwebs declared the structure officially abandoned.

Interlocking his fingers, he made a step to boost Kyly through ahead of him. Hoisting herself up, she met a large yellow and black spider. It crawled by her hand from its' disturbed resting place making her less enthusiastic about going in headfirst.

"Something wrong?" Chris whispered.

"I'm introducing myself." She glanced back with a quirky glare. "You wouldn't have antiserum in one of those pockets, would you?" Her voice faded as she dropped through to the inside with a clumsy crash.

"You okay?" He peeked his head in before leaping through to his hips.

"Fabulous, just give me a minute to do something with my hair," she complained from a disheveled position on the floor, brushing webs from her clothes and checking her long locks for six-legged visitors.

"Well, you were right about one thing," she said, dusting off. "No one has been in here for a long time."

She stood upright and stretched out her long legs as he pulled free from the windowsill and jumped to the ground gracefully—adding indignity to her awkward entry.

"It's in one of the brown file boxes in the pile behind you." He made his way past her.

"What are we looking for, exactly?" She pried open her first box.

"A very old package with a tan folder attached. It will have a title in the right bottom corner in black ink," his description became muffled by hollow echoes of cardboard friction from prying a box top apart. "It will say **'Recon Project A, Subject Y.'**"

"Doesn't have much of a ring to it for an earth-shattering experiment."

Moments passed between the soft sliding of box tops, the fanning of paper, and the solid thud of uneventful documents sent back into their resting places, shoved aside for a more hopeful discovery.

Soon logic and perseverance lost momentum to frustration and fatigue as Kyly stood wedged between rows of the next line of cartons, panting hot, dusty air.

"Ray's afraid," he said. The last thing she expected him to blurt out.

"*I'm* afraid. She didn't exactly give off the 'damsel in distress' thing at the cabin. Then again, I couldn't see past the bullets."

Kyly spoke, eyes fixed on the ground, dislodging her foot from an entanglement of rope and wooden debris between boxes. "Everyone has an area of vulnerability. Hers will only surface if you regain your memory and leak damaging information to the wrong people. But afraid?"

She continued, tugging her ensnared limb free. "She's a murderer. What could she possibly be afraid of?"

"Me." He bent over and shuffled through his sixth box of documents.

"Aside from her makers." Her foot popped free, sending up a new plume of dust.

"It's me she's afraid of," he clarified without looking up.

"They pose a real threat," she said, frantically waving her hand in a futile attempt to clear the air. "What evidence do *you* have on her? She diagnosed you with retrograde amnesia. You can't remember anything before the funeral. No threat there." Doubt shadowed her conviction.

"You think?" The question a deliberate challenge.

"What haven't you told us?" She clutched his arm, forcing him to face her. "Have you remembered something?"

Angelic, his face was captured in a halo of light filtering through the tiny storeroom window behind him.

"The nightmares I told you about on the plane. What if they weren't nightmares? What if they were memories?" He opened the flap to yet another box.

"Memories? You weren't even born when they engineered their genetic weapon. You couldn't have anything to do with it," she reasoned.

"No, I couldn't."

At least on this they were in agreement.

"Strange dreams or not, you're not responsible for Ray's life in captivity. What evidence does she think you're holding over her head? What crimes has she committed?"

"I'm the evidence." He paused to meet her gaze. "I'm the crime she committed."

"What do you mean?" Kyly's patience eroded.

"Have you ever heard of cellular memory?"

"Yes, in relation to organ recipients claiming to experience behavioral or character changes linked to their donors," she replied matter-of-factly, slipping into her journalistic role and turning her attention back to the boxes.

"It's actually a far more complex theory, traveling not only into the memory of human tissue cells but beyond, before their formation."

"Tell me you're not a believer in past lives and regression therapy?" Skepticism drove her piercing glare. "Next, we'll be discussing the probability of Astro travel."

Isolated, a world away, and still facing the same debates she'd painstakingly avoided with her father her whole life.

"You can't get away from this stuff."

Her thoughts became transparent.

"How do you do that?"

"Are you sure you want to know?"

His face was heavenly beautiful, his honesty obvious, and his voice strangely soulful and tender.

"Yes." Her assertive tone rang back tentative as some files she'd been rifling through piqued new interest.

"It's going to change everything," he vowed. "Knowledge can be both a burden and gift."

"So I've realized as of late." She opened the document, recognizing the content. "I saw this on a docuseries." Her attention split between him and the information in her hands.

"This life yet another," he said cryptically.

Her career taught her to wait for clarity to be revealed and gave her time to skim through content.

"I've lived this life as two men, one following the other, but I know of many."

"I'm confused," she admitted. "You're Chris. Do you mean as Doctor Valeric's son and then as Chris?" She continued reading until, "Why was Michael Valeric funding cave excavations in the Middle East?"

"I was born Micael Larenzo Valeric," he said.

Her eyes stayed on the research in her hands. "You mean you were born Christopher Cromwell and became him after being taken," she corrected, distracted.

"I was born Micael Larenzo Valeric forty-eight years ago."

"What?" The curious documents had a competitor. "What did you say?"

"I was reborn as Chris days before my first funeral. I'm both men and neither."

"But how can? What about? You're my age and..." Her voice caught in her throat and faded into wordless bubbling sounds. The research in her grip became secondary.

"Chris Cromwell had a perfect body but lacked a sufficiently functioning brain. Micael Valeric's body failed as his mind grew stronger. Ray's surgical prowess is the equivalent of a medical fountain of youth. Designed to kill, to acquire her target, and use her genius to aid in her own survival and mine," he explained.

He really *had* been dropped on his head after birth. She didn't believe any of it. Staring blankly at the expression on his face, he aged before her eyes—not by way of wrinkles and fallen flesh, but in the wisdom of experience hidden behind youthful eyes. For a second, she could've sworn their color changed from hazel to blue to green and back again.

"It's going to take a lengthy explanation, and this isn't the place." He shook the illusive package, having found valuable documents of his own.

"Got it. Let's go before one of them returns. It's not something I'm prepared to discuss with Ray, Nick, or any of their enemies."

Kyly put her hand to her mouth as if afraid of what might spill out. She took one last glance at the box beside her, and the file labeled 'CI Evidence' and then dropped it back inside. Her ethics professor's voice echoed in mind. 'A story is never one story,' he'd say. She was inclined to believe him.

Taking her arm, Chris prompted her out of the storage room. She let him guide her to the shoreline. Her eyes never left him, not even to ascertain her footing down the embankment. Taking a nose dive down the hill seemed inconsequential when holding the hand of the only man on earth claiming to have resurrected other than Jesus.

One thing was clear: he wasn't leaving her sight until she had the whole story. As the pledge drifted through her mind he locked eyes as if hearing every word and smiled with assurance.

She fought and failed to wipe the rapt expression from her face.

No words were spoken as the pair slid back into their rubber sheaths on the sand and escaped into the calm of the water. Clouds overtook the sky, pushed in by the power of the rain behind them. Within a few reviving strokes, darkness swallowed them as they crossed the length to their raft.

Chris directed their efforts. Synchronizing their movements, they came upon it at the same time. Kyly almost swam into its side, unable to discern it from the ocean waves. Her eyes remained fixed on Chris while he removed the cover, threw the precious contents of a watertight bag inside, and climbed aboard. When he offered to pull her over its edge, she searched his eyes for a glimpse of wisdom, a shadow from beyond the grave. She hesitated, then accepted his hand.

They paddled silently for an unbearable duration. It wasn't fatigue but suspense dragging out time. When they reached what Chris described as the 'safe zone' to activate the motor, Kyly could no longer hold her tongue.

"Couldn't these memories stem from overhearing conversations while you were unconscious?" She had to ask, as it plagued her since they left the shack on the island. "Intimate conversations, reliving of the past, emotional details, discussed in your presence during such a traumatic time."

"It's more than that, Kyly." He quit rowing and prepared to start the engine. "I remember being him because I still am him."

With this, Kyly froze as cold reality reduced the marrow of her bones to frail icicles. A part of her desperately longed to leap over the edge of the raft and swim for the shores of sanity, but there were none to be found.

"Would you like to know what area of the brain you're using at this precise instance of panic? Or perhaps the chemicals it's releasing into your system? Maybe how to avoid damage or where its' weakest flaws lie, because I can tell you."

His tone frightened her in a way only a confirmation of your worst nightmare could.

"Don't be afraid, Kyly, this was foreordained. I'm not Satan or any variation of. And, although you don't believe it, all of this is a gift."

Kyly held her head in her hands as if to prevent the painful splitting of her brain caused by cognitive dissonance. Having learned the term in college, she'd chuckled at the prospect of ever having a need for such linguistic acrobats. She faced the disturbing reality that it held the only accurate description of her emotional state.

On one hand, she held fast to her relentless belief in facts and logic. On the other, she fought the innate and undeniable knowledge that truth had found oxygen. Freed, it burned like a wildfire, leaving nothing but ambers where solid conclusions once stood and her world ashen.

Relinquishing the oar, Chris placed his right hand on top of her head as if in blessing. "It's going to be okay, Lee. You're stronger than you imagine. You'll get through this."

"What about you?" She lifted her head, questioning him. "Will you get through this?"

He smiled while reaching for the pull cord, preparing to break the silence between them. "You're not asking me, of all people, if I'm afraid of dying, are you?"

46

SEETHING with fury in the confines of her hotel room, Ray cursed the air, "*Damn you!*"

Tuesday afternoon, late morning on the island, and one day after MJ had negotiated a window to get his *affairs* in order. He bided time to acquire information he could use against them all and blindsided her. Underhanded. Offending her in such a way was detrimental to one's health. This time, it could prove fatal.

Pulling out all the stops, throwing caution to the wind, Ray bypassed her computer's safety measures and honed in on circling sharks in the waters off the island coast. The island held their secrets. The tagged sharks were her early warning system. They trained on live prey, seals, or humans.

Certain biker gangs took pride in utilizing the Florida Everglades' reptilian population to dispose of those who crossed them.

No bodies. No witnesses. No convictions.

On one hand, she hoped her deadly friends of the deep would eliminate the intruder or intruders the same way. On the other, she waited for the chance to handle it personally. She was certain what had the sharks' interest was worthy of hers as well.

Throwing a wide ban net over air traffic in the area, it'd be a matter of time before her trespassers led her to MJ.

Fighting claustrophobia, a remnant of her early years trapped in a one-room cell, Ray paced from balcony to doorway and back again, circling the room in anticipation. Every lap acted like the turn of a guitar string key, winding her to the brink of rupture. The breeze filtering through the open balcony doors was alive with scents. Bread from a bakery below, car exhaust fumes, and deli meats. Ray couldn't brave stale air, nightmares from a childhood housed behind glass breathing only what the vents allowed. Lost in unsavory memories, the bellboy's heavy-handed knocking brought back visions of doctors pounding on her cell's glass walls. Bad timing.

"Do you suffer from cataracts?" she said two inches from his face.

"Excuse me?"

"A clouding of the lens of the eye," she continued.

"No, no...I—"

"Then I assume you recognized the 'Do not disturb' sign."

"I have the package you were waiting for. I thought—"

"Insistent flea. Next time, I suggest you wait in the hall—that is what you are paid to do—instead of rapping intrusively on my door."

She ripped the parcel from his hands and slammed the door. Unleashing her loathsome mood on the young man proved invigorating.

After, a disturbing calm washed over her. She stretched her long legs across the sofa, keyed into the travel link, and began arranging transportation. Her destination remained vague. It would narrow soon.

Her body stiffened with expectancy.

With a tap on the keyboard, she zoomed in on the sharks' movements and traced their curls through the water with her finger across the screen.

"We're much alike, you and I," she whispered. "Impertinent creatures, immune to the pitfalls of virtue. Taking liberty without license. And so we should. We're practically immortal. We're Olympians, deadly and unforgiving."

On cue, as the words fell from her lips, the cluster of sharks abandoned their aimless circling and formed an attack line, cutting through the ocean a mile and a half off the dock. Minutes later, reaching their intended target, the most aggressive of the group confronted an area too small for any hard bottom boat.

"Don't tell me you were fool enough to leave swimmers waiting for pick-up in open water," she spoke to the screen. "Remains won't require retrieval, but the chopper will lead me to your next location, with or without live cargo. Rookie move."

Setting the alarm volume on her laptop to alert her of a breech in nearby airspace, she pulled herself from the image of circling sonic signatures to pack her remaining gear. Retrieving a medical kit from a duffel bag, she produced a ready needle and injected her damaged shoulder. She couldn't afford distraction, even to flinch in pain.

Earlier, she'd downed a handful of supplements. Now, her stomach grumbled for something substantial. She ordered foods high in protein and low in fat and wondered if they were drawing straws in the kitchen for the sorry soul that had to deliver it. The image made her laugh. The girl handling her order became overly accommodating.

"I'll put a rush on the order and make certain it arrives in less than twenty minutes, as requested," she said. She failed to offer her name. Smart girl.

The pain in her shoulder faded with the release of the numbing agent, restoring her mobility. Cloaked in a bathrobe, concealing her combat attire from another witless delivery boy, she moved her equipment out of sight.

Transferring the computer from table to bed, the screen flashed a notification beacon in the bottom left corner. Nick.

Unable to open the message without allowing a crack in her defenses for Cage's technicians to crawl through, she was forced to shut down all other sensitive programs.

Whoever floated in the water outside the island couldn't be left adrift much longer. She hated cutting the signal. She did it anyway. Nick wouldn't be contacting her unless it was crucial. She had no choice.

The message was encrypted, unreadable to anyone but her and Nick. Why Cage would allow him to use it was obvious. His arrogance made him believe he could break the code, decipher their secrets, and use it against them.

Quickly, she downloaded the document, filtered it through a battery of virus scans, and shut down Cage's possible link to her world. She decoded the encryption and reviewed the information. The first part came as no surprise.

The government hounds were advancing hard on any potential

medical breakthrough Dr. V had uncovered. The message lost its predictability when it mentioned Chris. She hated their insistence on calling him by that name.

The military retrieved and analyzed his blood left at the scene. They knew he wasn't Micael Valeric's biological son. Apparently, he wasn't any one man's son.

Nick's tone sharpened as he described what they concluded about Chris Cromwell's genetic make-up. Ray's posture lost its rigidity as evidence of a second, far more devastating betrayal trickled across the screen. Chris wasn't *just* a donor, a viable human specimen. If Nick's assessment was accurate, Chris' DNA was far more advanced than hers —*engineered* to be more advanced. If true, this begged her to question whether Dr. V. had willingly participated in her own creation.

Had she devoted herself to one of the vile men responsible for her years in captivity? Had they left her alone all this time because she was living under the watchful eye of one of their own? No. She knew Micael Valeric, knew his heart. He wasn't capable of this level of deception. Or was he?

When she'd questioned Micael about what he was doing the day he rescued her off the coast of the compound, he swore he was mourning the loss of a friend. Was it a lie from the start?

She refused to believe it. He'd treated her with such kindness and compassion. But what other explanation existed?

Their time together flew by in her mind like a movie on fast forward, pausing at relevant intervals as she reread each scene from this haunting perspective. She had time to ask all the questions while he weakened but never did. Why? Why do we sit beside the dying in silence? Was it because she knew he couldn't face his own end, or was it because she couldn't? If MJ, damn, Chris, had stayed put, if he trusted her and not these bloody strangers he'd aligned himself with, none of this would've happened. Her memories of Micael would stay pristine, how she needed them.

Her introspection ignited a fury from deep in her. The closer she reviewed her life with Micael, the more distorted the picture became.

The film reel snapped as the unlucky soul who drew the short straw in the kitchen rapped on her door.

47

THE OUTBOARD MOTOR died four miles outside Kyly and Chris' pick-up zone, forcing Chris to re-enter the water. A decaying net snagged the propeller. Every detail of their mission depended on precision. The failed motor placed them out of range and almost out of time.

"If I jump in and pull from the other side—" Kyly offered.

"No," Chris warned. "You have to stay in the boat. If it drifted, we can't both be in the water."

Chris pulled from below the water, loosening small sections at a time. Leaning over the backside of the raft, Kyly yanked the entangled mass upward with strength born out of terror at the notion of missing their rendezvous. Expecting to manually restart the engine, neither was prepared for the blades to regain momentum without prompting.

The raft pitched, throwing Kyly to its floor. When she jumped to her feet, Chris had turned his back into the slashing steel arms, catching a barrage of lacerations before escaping the churning blades. Kyly witnessed the atrocity as metal met flesh.

Chris closed his eyes *before* he was hit. In that fraction of a second, he appeared prepared for impact. His expression did not contort in terror. Kyly must've misread it.

Wrestling him into the raft, stripping her wet suit down to her waist, she tore her shirt off and wrapped it as a tourniquet around the worst of the gashes. Lying face down, blood trickled along Chris' arms, over the raft's edge, and into the water.

He didn't utter a sound. No scream of torment. No cry of anguish. Nothing.

Ripping her undershirt into strips, shivering in nothing from the waist up save wet lace, she wrapped his lacerations.

Though it would exasperate his tortured condition, in a barely audible voice, Chris asked her to "pour salt water over the wounds."

In a hush, he spoke words in a language she couldn't decipher.

She did as he asked, not knowing why.

Reaching to scoop up the liquid in her cupped hands, fear consumed her. Focusing on her task, she saw nothing but the water in her hands and his injuries. A close jarring splash broke her trance.

An angry ocean wasn't to blame. She stared into a black abyss, the unforgiving eye of a shark. Shock had her hurl the eroding fluid over Chris' ravaged flesh. She scanned the circumference of the raft in sheer terror. They were surrounded. And the propeller, free of debris, sat silent. In shock, Kyly had cut power to Chris' assailant.

They were sitting ducks.

Rubber ducks, to be precise.

The sky blackened above, becoming a pall, blanketing their deathbed.

"Sharks." Her voice shuddered up through a palpitating chest. "We're surrounded by sharks. The blood. Oh, god."

Growing up an island girl, she heard the stories, saw the pictures in the local paper. They smelled the blood.

Below the surface of serene seas, savages slept who couldn't decipher us from the prey in their natural habitat. Blood was blood.

Chris sank his hands into the water before she could stop him, flushing fresh blood into the sea. She assumed he'd gone into shock, and his delirium was bound to cost them their lives. Then, something unexplainable happened. The powerful creatures defied expectation, and retreated from the edge. The water encircling the raft smoothed like soft ripples surrounding a dropped rock.

Kyly's blood turned to ice as the warmth of common sense left her.

Liquid glass encompassed them. Stillness radiated out from where Chris lay with hands in the water, and, as it did, the sharks drifted further and further away. Disbelief caught in her throat like a wet rag, rendering her speechless. Kyly tripped the motor and steered the boat for the flashing beacon indicating the helicopter on the onboard computer screen. Anxious to wake from her nightmare, she welcomed the roar of the outboard, the crash of the waves, and the slapping rhythm of the boat's underside smacking the water's hard surface.

When they reached the waiting chopper, though weak, Chris climbed the ladder above her. He didn't lose consciousness until they were both safely inside. Fitful, while the chopper cut a line inland, he spoke in his sleep words of an unfamiliar language.

Cleaning his wounds with supplies from the onboard medical kit, the depth of the lacerations surprised Kyly. When she first tied her shirt around him, they appeared deep, severing all layers of skin. No, surface wounds serious enough to present a very real risk of infection but not life threatening. Patching the last one with ointment, gauze, and sterile bandages, she paused over him. Anticipating another astonishing event, she waited for him to vanish before her eyes. He slept.

She asked nothing of him when he woke.

She said nothing to him other than 'you're welcome' when he thanked her for tending to his injuries.

She spoke not another word until they arrived at the safe house Mason had arranged for them. And even then, she hesitated. Avoiding the inevitable, she sought refuge in a long hot shower—it proved futile. Memories of blades tearing through Chris' flesh wouldn't be easily washed away.

"Making sense of it?" Chris startled her, entering the old stone house's reading room, where she padded across the plank floor.

"Quite frankly, none of this makes any sense." Tension weighted her brow and fueled a headache. "There are too many unknowns here, and..."

Having hit a brick wall in understanding, she halted, crumpling in defeat into a heap amid pillows and blankets piled on the floor.

He pulled her to a seat beside him on the worn sofa. "We must elevate your perspective."

The journalistic background that urged her to search for the truth, to hold fast to logic and fact offered no help either.

"It's pretty muddied, trust me—"

"Experience tells you not to, trust, I mean," he said.

"Yeah." She looked hard at him, then the room. "So, honesty. I don't know what the hell I'm doing here. Why I wouldn't let go of the story. Why I almost died for it, and I still don't know the half of what's going on. And, here's the kicker. Every cell in me is screaming that knowing is a really bad idea."

Chris left her to stare out the window. He spoke without facing her. "Honesty...yes." Walking closer to the crackling wood in the fireplace he appeared deep in thought, guarding a trove of wisdom.

"Great," Kyly said under her breath, then rose to retreat to her own space.

"You better stay seated for this." His tone held a certainty.

Cloaked in an old bedspread the color of sand, firelight casting a glow behind him,and windswept hair and two-day shadow, he was raw and compelling. Despite herself, she sat back down.

"Genetically, we contain infinite wisdom. That's an accepted fact," he began.

She propped her hand under her chin, crouched on folded legs, and leaned in.

He left the warmth of the fire and knelt before her. When he spoke again, his voice was but a whisper.

"What we lacked was an avenue to directly access it. The problem is like all things; we want to view it through separation and not inclusion. Science and spirituality merge at a point. The earth looks peaceful from a distance. Cells appear still when, in reality, under closer inspection, they are rapidly moving."

"Okay, I'll bite, but what does that have to do with your kidnapping or Ray?"

"I wasn't anything until I was...kidnapped." He stood again, walking the room.

"Explain that."

"Do you have any thoughts on adoption?" he asked.

"What does? Yeah. I do. I believe children find their parents by many paths, no one more valid than the other. You weren't adopted. He stole you."

"Christopher Cromwell would not have survived without intervention, and he was meant to be born in a hospital where a doctor who knew how to preserve his life worked. Everything that happened did so because it is time. It's evolution."

Seconds passed before it sank in, then she asked, "You're telling me there was a grand design at work, and it's somehow worth the trail of destruction?"

"I'm trying to let you see the importance of—"

"I wouldn't have chosen to experience this for anything!" she protested. "For all of us to be immersed in this dangerous web of treachery with no way out."

"No, you wouldn't. We wouldn't choose most of the pathways leading us to the greatest experiences if we were made aware of all the pitfalls and consequences, would we?"

"I think I would've avoided a few," Kyly said, feeling her heart sink, weighed by bad memories.

"Life is given. How you choose to be determines what you take with you."

On waves coming off the thriving fire, his warm words melted into her. Her eyes burned. She fought not to close them.

"If you focus only on the tragedy of a circumstance, you miss the point. There's an awakening in how far mankind has come, where some of us are now. What's next…"

Silently attentive, fire flickering in the backdrop, Kyly sat still as a china doll.

"It changes everything about being alive. What we do with our lives."

She pondered this for a moment. "I wanted to warn the world about blind trust in doctors. I wanted to tell others what could happen, share stories of suffering, bring awareness—"

"You wanted to be a messenger."

She thought for a moment. "Yes. I suppose I did."

"Believe me, you are. The message is just a whole lot bigger than you anticipated."

After a brief silence, he continued, "It may not be easy to deliver or accept, but it's time."

Her eyes bore into him as if seeing for the first time. "Who are you?"

"That's a matter of perspective," he said.

"You're not Chris Cromwell or Micael Junior," she said, a deep fatigue filtering out from her core.

"None of us are only that which lies in the confines of a name."

With a thousand things to say but no strength to say them, Kyly mustered one final sentence. "I feel like there should've been signs, fire, and brimstone, you know."

"Everyone, so intent on what was, never seeing what is," he said.

Teetering precariously at the threshold of understanding, key pieces of the puzzle came into focus only to disperse on an upward draft. Blown from her mind without warning. Confused and exhausted, she wondered whether her eyes were open or closed. His voice seeped in as if squeezed down a long tunnel in the distance.

"You must rest," she heard him whisper. "I will watch over you."

———

Candles flickered on the bedside windowsill and from a small table in the corner of the room, giving off a discrete glow that didn't betray their presence in the old house. The nearest neighbor lived twenty acres away, but from their vantage point on the hillside, anything brighter than candlelight put them at risk of discovery.

On top of the covers, wrapped in a blanket, Kyly searched the room for familiarity. She couldn't recall entering it. Was she that exhausted, or had Chris carried her?

Clutching the blanket tighter around her, she rose and followed his voice down the narrow hallway and into the reading room.

It, she remembered.

She stepped through the doorway. He leaned on a large wooden table by the window. He was clean-shaven, in blue jeans and a sweater that concealed his wounds. He so resembled Zavier she almost forgot his true identity, whatever that was.

"Oh, you're awake. Perfect timing." He handed her the satellite phone. "Someone is anxious to say hello."

As she reached for the phone, she couldn't help wondering if she dreamed of their conversation. The man in front of her failed to reflect the vision in memory. He smiled and gestured to take the call.

"Hello."

"Kyly, thank God. I've been so worried about you."

The mere sound of Mason's voice put her at ease. "Everything's fine. You both okay?"

"All according to plan. I'm anxious to have everyone back in one place."

"Me too," she exhaled.

"We have to keep this call short. Chris has all the details regarding your return tomorrow. See you soon."

"Yes, soon," she said, her heart sunk.

"And Lee. I'll be thinking of you."

"Take care, Mason."

Moonlight swept the room, and Kyly was drawn to the viewing window where Chris was sitting.

"Wow, that's impressive." She surveyed the panoramic skyscape beyond the windowpane.

Built to harbor the owner's passion for stargazing, the tiny house sat tucked away from civilization and its metropolis of light pollution. On an outcrop of rock overlooking the vast ocean, it offered the perfect spot to appreciate all the night sky had to offer.

"Hungry?" Chris pointed to a basket of warm bread and a bottle of unopened wine on a long handcrafted wooden table behind them.

"Yes."

"Eat. I'll explain the next leg of our journey in the morning."

She agreed, not wanting the lingering warmth left by Mason's call to dissipate. They sat together, staring out at the endless skyline. He poured the wine into stoneware cups and handed her one.

"They look so different from here," she said. "I can't recognize any of the constellations I see back home."

"They haven't changed. You're just viewing them from an altered perspective." He broke the bread in his hands and passed her half.

"The Heavens are beautiful, amazing." She sunk her teeth into the warm loaf.

"No matter where you see them from," he added as a flash shot across the sky.

"A shooting star," she said.

From the sparkling skyline, his kaleidoscope eyes shifted to rest upon her. "Fierce, inescapable inferno," he whispered. "They burn out before impact. Usually. Other times, they transform in darkness."

48

FORTY FLOORS below the earth and feeling every inch of it, Nick shuffled into Cage's conference room accompanied by stone-faced soldiers. The afternoon was about to be wasted on yet another slide show with Ray cast in the role of villain. Florescent bulbs intended to simulate natural sunlight did a poor job. They flickered, sizzled, and hummed before capturing enough electricity to burst on full blast, blinding anyone fool enough to have diverted their attention to the annoyance.

Back on the island, in the freedom of open air, isolation had eroded Nick's spirit. Here, encased by a mile of rock with Cage as a cellmate, he labored moment to moment to maintain his composure.

No longer shackled by chains, he was constantly reminded of his prisoner status. Guards clung to him everywhere. The cafeteria, lounge, even the men's room. He couldn't escape.

Years spent in virtual seclusion and now, never alone.

Fighting to appear undaunted by this drastic change of environment, Nick strolled into the room and flopped into the nearest comfortable chair. His body language hummed a melody of contentment. His brain gyrated to the thrash rock of imprisonment.

"You know what I think?" Cage entered the room behind Nick with a coffee mug in one hand and an unlit cigar hanging from his lower lip.

"What you think is paltry," Nick interrupted.

"I think your little sister needs to find a healthier outlet for unresolved childhood issues."

Cage nodded to a guard straddling the doorway. He flicked off the unstable overhead lights and sealed the glass door shut behind him. Starting up the projector, Cage revealed the first of his horror show pictures.

Nick was glad he'd skipped breakfast.

Blood splatter covered a hallway, defiling the pleasant wallpaper's attempt at cheery, warm tones. The man's body was contorted, laid half in, half out of a luggage trolley. No hand smears down the wall or on the carpet. No signs of a struggle. Only a brutal end.

Cage, gauging Nick's mortified expression, skipped to the next slide—a close-up of the young man's lifeless eyes, a timeless face of death. He couldn't have been much older than twenty. Nick had seen enough.

"You are one twisted son-of-a-bitch!" Nick protested.

"Don't think I *enjoy* this?" Cage rifled back, shutting down the overhead, leaving them both in the dark. "I told you to tell her no more deaths! You said she'd listen. Obviously your opinion doesn't mean a damn thing to her. She fled the scene late last night."

"Ray isn't capable of *that*. She wouldn't kill a kid," Nick argued. Cage hit the switch, awakening the sizzling overhead.

Tossing a file across the table at him, Cage said, "Think again."

Inside, tracking documents confirmed Ray at the location of the hotel. Eyewitness reports described her as the occupant of the room where the attack occurred.

"Sweet Mother of God," Nick said. "I'm not going to believe any of this! It could all be fabricated lies."

"Fair enough." Cage turned the conference phone sitting on the table between them toward Nick. "Call her. Ask her yourself."

Nick wouldn't.

The gray walls of the briefing room became bleaker. Nick felt dirty, though he'd showered before the guards came to get him. Intended for the sensitive nostrils of the commander-in-chief, the compound possessed an unsurpassed air purification system. Still, Nick sensed a pungent aroma seeping in around him. A vile truth.

Cage exuded too much confidence for it to be a lie. Ray had

executed at random, with complete disregard for human life. She elimi-
nated anyone in her way.

Cage tossed the pictures onto the table. The dead man's blank stare
beseeched Nick. His image forever begged for his life. Nick couldn't
allow the killing to continue.

Head bent in defeat, he whispered, "What do you want?"

Gathering the file and gore photos, Cage waved the guard back into
the room to retrieve them. Alone again, he pulled a chair close to Nick.

Speaking in a quiet raspy, tone, Cage outlined their plan.

"We have to bring her in before she kills again. We're having trouble
anticipating her direction. We need a way to track her current movements so we can head her off. If there's any way to bring her in
unharmed, we'll do it. I have my orders. They don't want her dead, but
they want her, and they're losing patience. Where is she going?"

"Wherever he is, she'll be there," Nick said in a shallow voice, his
head still swimming with morbid images of Ray's victims.

"The Cromwell kid?" Cage asked, shocking Nick back to attention.
"Yeah, we know about him. Haven't quite sorted out the medical
connection, but we're working on it."

Slow to reply, Nick said, "Yeah. You find him, you'll find her. I'd
recommend getting to him first, or he might end up like your bellboy."

"We haven't made contact with the family yet, but I intend to when
we're through here. In fact, it might be wise for you to sit in on the call."

"What happens to her when you bring her in?" Nick asked, uncon-
cerned with Cage's agenda.

"Can't tell you that, son, but I will guarantee she won't be harmed in
any way while I'm involved."

"You put her in a cage, and you're harming her. Your assurances
mean nothing," Nick stood from his chair. "Make the call."

"The Cromwell residences are under surveillance. After we were
alerted Mason Stone, Brook Cromwell's brother, had initiated a few
suspicious phone calls, our ears were perked. Evidently he pulled in
favors. Researched doctors associated with Micael Valeric prior to the
funeral in order to get on the guest list."

"The guest list?" Nick said without volition.

"Requests concerning any known associates were red flagged for
obvious reasons. Mason's intrusion, though curious, was deemed trivial

until Micael Junior disappeared from the island. When blood typing from the industrial area evidence confirmed Mason extracted him out from under Ray's watchful eye, he became a whole lot more interesting. I've become quite familiar with Stone. Definitely enough to have his number, quite literally."

———

"Stone." Mason stared at the scrambled signal off his call tracing system.

"Mason Stone?" Cage questioned.

"Yeah, who am I speaking to?"

"Name's Cage. Seems you and I have common interests. It's about time we discussed them."

"Who are you?"

"We don't have an official title. Then again, we don't officially exist," Cage replied. "We're interested in a certain individual, the one responsible for remodeling your Rocky Mountain retreat. She's our property, and we mean to retrieve her. You, on the other hand, wish to keep your family members as far from her as possible. Your cooperation could prove favorable for both of us."

Of all the possible scenarios tossed over in Mason's mind, he never anticipated a faction of the government stepping in to eliminate their problems. *Nothing* was *that* simple.

"Why ask me for help?" Mason questioned. "If she's your *property*, why isn't she in your custody? You're capable of re-acquiring her without me."

"You, of all people, should understand the complications of military missions. For instance, the governor's daughter, what a pretty mess that was, and yet you were able to handle it with such discretion. Discretion we're counting on you to exhibit now."

Cage came off threatening and was too informed to dismiss. And he'd done his homework. Only three men knew of Mason's involvement in the retrieval of the governor's daughter. One lived at 1600 Pennsylvania Avenue.

"I won't do a damn thing for you until I have ironclad assurances my family will remain unharmed," Mason replied.

"What I *can* assure you of, if you don't cooperate, is that one or more of you will end up in a body bag."

"Is that a threat?"

"Call it a warning. She's coming for your nephew. We can't stop her without your help. Are you with us or not?"

"I'm not *with* anyone. My priority is my family...period."

"Can we count on their silence?"

"My family and I want nothing more than to return to an ordinary existence. I guarantee we haven't shared what little information we know, nor will we. You forget us. We'll do likewise."

Cage, of course, wouldn't believe him, and he didn't need to. He held enough power to wipe the entire family off the face of the earth, if necessary. Of that, Mason was sure.

"We have a vested interest in Ray's continued existence and no interest whatsoever in any of the Cromwells," Cage promised.

Crafty. Chris was neither a Cromwell nor a Valeric in the eyes of the elitist group that hunted him. He was an enigmatic anomaly, a medical miracle.

Him, they'd want. Mason kept his opinion to himself.

"We can't keep cleaning up after her. It's drawing too much unwanted attention," Cage said. "We can't afford any more deaths. We'll do everything we can to ensure the safety of your family."

Despite his delivery, Cage held a degree of truth. Chris couldn't be studied, analyzed, or used if he were dead.

A latent motive clung like cellophane to every reassuring word Cage uttered. His mission to capture Ray could provide an added distraction Mason could use to his advantage. He didn't have a choice. Working against Cage only narrowed the odds of survival.

Mason disclosed the time and place he was to rejoin Kyly and Chris, giving himself a lead time. He said nothing about where they were now or where they had been. They were in hiding, was all he'd admit. He also failed to mention the evidence Kyly and Chris retrieved from the island nor would he, until such time as it became absolutely necessary. The documents they held provided the ace up his sleeve. He preferred to leave Cage and anyone else involved, believing Micael Senior had taken the trump card to his grave.

———

Rubbing his hands together, Cage smiled across the room at Nick. Nick answered him with a scowl. Regardless of Cage's thick frame, Nick wished him puny and pathetic. A part of him figured if Ray was going into custody the least she could do was expose his interest in her first. Nick didn't know why but Cage's attachment was feeling less duty and more personal.

Once details of the meeting were outlined, a high-pitched static shrieked across the airwaves. Mason hung up on Cage. No window for further questioning. Cage shrugged it off.

"I've got him in a corner. The guy knows it, can't expect him to be friendly."

"He didn't *sound* scared," Nick taunted.

Actually Nick admired the way the man had handled himself. Most people wouldn't have remained so composed. Stone sounded completely calm. Cage may have underestimated this civilian.

"As I understand it, Stone told you nothing but where to pick up your renegade weapon. You're taking a risk trusting him. It could be a trap. He doesn't have the benefit of all your so-called top-secret information, yet he has managed to lure Ray to him, keeping his family safe in the process. You have no clue as to the depth of his involvement or what he's potentially holding over your head. He just manipulated you into giving him exactly what he wants and you think *you* have *him* in a corner." Nick laughed and stood up, happy for the two-inch rise he had over Cage.

"Get him outta here," Cage called to the stiff figure guarding the outer doorway.

Nick smiled, shuffling across the floor in mocking disregard. Slowing his exit out of the room, he said, "Personally, I kinda like the guy."

49

AT HARBOR MIST Ship Yard ghostly, wind swept between the abandoned loading docks. For years, even local kids, desperate for a hideaway to accommodate notorious backseat indulgences, steered clear of the yard.

The article Ray found when researching the site suggested it was haunted. The story flooded back as she walked its forsaken streets.

A string of accidents claimed the lives of seven workers over its last summer of operation. Deemed unsafe, the yard was shut down by county officials. Many of the teenagers in the area believed it carried a curse.

The tragedies were of such a disturbingly bizarre nature; they lent credibility to the myth its closure had less to do with relocating to a more efficient plant and more to do with avoiding a lethal poltergeist.

The story explained that all ship loaders gained worthy nicknames during their first year on the job. Heavy lifters like Popeye, Hammer, and Tank fit their new identities. Each herald embellished recollections of the events that earned them their handles. Other titles were acquired by default. Lucky, Dozer, and Kid. Then there were those that came brandishing hard-won warnings. Quickfire, Hot-wire, and Ripper. None came into the world with such labels, none except Anchor Archer.

Anchor, it said, was a third-generation port town laborer, and everybody knew it. His grandfather arrived by ship and died, never straying more than a couple hours inland from the dock. Raised on the dark side of Half Moon by his paternal grandparents, Anchor grew up honorable but tough inside and out. He was kind if you were brave enough to get to know him. At six foot four and two hundred and sixty pounds of raw muscle, his sheer mass and chiseled face left most too intimidated to approach.

Labeled at birth by a father who saw him as nothing more than a burden pinning him to a town he longed to break free from, the Anchor weighing him down. The article said Daddy Dearest abandoned Anchor at the age of four. They never spoke again.

Like his grandfather, Anchor found pride in his work. Dedication and appreciation for gainful employment, meager as it was, skipped a generation and landed squarely on his beefy shoulders. Known to be steady and reliable, he never caused trouble but became a force to be reckoned with in turbulent situations between other workers. He married a local sweetheart who was as delicate and soft-spoken as he was strong and commanding. Their union endeared him to the town's folk. Illianna was a constant reminder of his gentler side. Their son was three months old when Anchor was killed in a freak crane accident. His death was a grievous event on many levels, but it struck a nerve with all the young men in town who worked under his watchful eye. To them, Anchor was invincible.

His sinking made them fear Harbor Mist and the bad karma it carried.

Perhaps this explained its instant appeal for Ray. She scanned the dreary area, smiling before entering the abandoned warehouse.

Wedged into a space large enough to plant her size eight feet tightly together alongside her weapon, she relied on the gap accommodating the window frame for breathing room. Tilted forward, the sill taking the place of a table, she lined up pieces of the rifle and snapped them together. Despite the cramped quarters, she moved with the unhampered accuracy of a seasoned assembly line worker.

The impulse to wipe a hazy yellow film from the glass in front of her to allow a clear view of Christian's arrival tempted her. She let it pass. The clinging chemical tar impeded anything more than a blurred perception of the world beyond. It gave her a strategic advantage.

Regardless of visual confirmation, Ray knew the window looked down the center of the main dock out to sea.

Through a hallucinogen-like smear, Zavier approached the water's edge. The rhythm of his youthful gait, though attractive, lacked the sexy weight of maturity that underscored his older brother's. Chris had spent so little time on his own two feet after surgery, but, oh, how she knew that walk.

To think she could be deceived into believing Zavier was him? She expected more. As always, she found her adversary's inferiority typical and disappointing.

The suffocating wreckage of dispelled fumes painted on the glass surface confirmed her general view of humanity as weak, pathetic, self-destructive, and arrogantly asinine.

The force of her grip on the weapon intensified. "There it is," she hissed. "Beauty choked out, potential extinguished by a lumper's insatiable thirst for the empowerment of nicotine, the self-deprecating sucking of smoldering cyanide."

She spoke to the limiting air, cursing invisible ghosts.

"Human beings, a lazy, evolutionary inept group. One suitable form of mankind derived from a species teetering between disappointment and detestability. Well...perhaps two."

She stared at soldiers storming the area. Through the film, they transformed into cockroaches scattering from the light.

Cage's men swept the building in combat gear worthy of a war zone infiltration. Ray swallowed her laughter to prevent jeopardizing her position. One nervous soldier hovered mere feet from her but couldn't detect a reflection in the polluted window.

The man with the gun held a solid tactical stance, but the bead of sweat forming on his brow belied his self-assurance.

If the external temperature reflected the ice in Ray's heart, her exhaled breath would transform into fog. She blew. Wicked wind drifted around the corner of the crate and brushed the soldier with a ghostly tickle. He flinched, sweeping around in a reactive circle, scanning the area with the flashlight held beneath his gun, seeing nothing. She remained deathly still, telling him telepathically he should leave. He didn't linger long before proclaiming the area 'Clear' and moving on.

"Coward," she whispered.

The team moved out of the warehouse to take their marks around the shipping yard, leaving her plenty of time to do what she came for. There'd be no escape—it didn't matter. Vengeance had a price.

Ray nestled in the crack between stacked crates and the steel wall. Dust coated everything in the place with a veil of abandonment. Cage's men missed her footprints and muddied the path in. She wore their same boots.

Folded boxes lay over the top edge of the crate above her, sheltering the area below where she waited. Her long trench coat remained dust-free and as black as her raven hair and her intentions.

Free of intruders, she locked the scope into place, completing the weapon's assembly. The McMillan Tac-50 rifle stood to her left, almost the same height as her. Inching her arm free, she checked the adjacent door to ensure it hadn't been locked from the outside preventing her access to the dock. As anticipated, it inched open.

Confident, she shut it, putting a shallow barrier between herself and Cage's men.

The bitter secondhand stench and acute confinement would've driven most into a state of sudden claustrophobia. Ray's hand rested near the window's latch. Its glass wouldn't contain her. She pictured the airduct that granted her escape from the compound as a child. The memory anesthetized. It sweetened the moment when crisp, clean air would fill her lungs as she expelled sorrow for the satisfaction of revenge.

Certain she'd allowed enough time to lapse to escape detection, she squeezed out of the cramped quarters, stealthily opened the window, and lined up her shot. She loaded the weapon, full metal jackets, bullets capable of piercing through almost anything, even from a mile and a half away.

She'd need only one.

The wharf comprised an endless walkway along the shore, an inverted T jutting four hundred yards out to sea in the center. It's distance necessary for nothing other than accommodating romantic strolls. The old shipyard was in the process of being revamped into a converted warehouse district, a calculated effort to rid the area of its lingering bad karma.

Two buildings sat parallel to each other, flanking the parking lot.

The central building Ray decided to hole up in ran horizontally across the back of both. Together the structures formed a U-shape, with the sides pushing closer to the ocean. At her right, an abandoned warehouse awaited reconstruction. On her left, a revived version is in the final remodeling stage. Scheduled to open at the end of summer, its promotional sign promised shop fronts adjacent to the boardwalk and an open market.

Using Vectors, Ray's eyes sliced through the loading area, roadway, parking area, beachfront, and dock. Combined, they put her over 2600 meters from the dock's furthest point in the water. The binocular-like device confirmed the range to target. Impossible.

She loved defying odds.

She needed no reassurance of a perfect kill shot, save the weapon in her hands and an assassin's motivation. She had both. Her bullet would pierce the distance long before the military could undermine her attempt. It was almost sad how easy they made it for her. Almost.

Using the Nightforce NXS scope, she verified her adversaries' positions flanking her in the nearby warehouses. Drawing in another slow, deep breath of stale air, she waited. After today, the old shipyard's cursed fate would be sealed, and it wouldn't be alone.

50

THE HILLTOP HIDEAWAY marked the last stop on the road to hell, and Kyly wasn't anxious to leave it, regardless of Chris' reassurances.

He'd explained Mason's plan in detail without so much as a hint of emotion. He showed no fear, no worry, no opposition. For the life of her, she couldn't understand how.

Mason negotiated a deal with the men who were responsible for Ray's existence. They'd arrive in time to capture Ray before she descended on Chris or anyone else. So they promised. In return, they expected Mason to set the trap and lure Ray in. Kyly wasn't happy hearing Zavier was the bait.

"It's you, not Zavier, I fear for." Chris' voice was tempered with regret.

They slid into the truck's cab. Before pulling away, she questioned, "It's Mason's plan. He wouldn't let anything happen to me."

"The outcome is out of his hands," he said. "Mason is orchestrating the impossible. Too much room for error. Life doesn't exist in the confines of our control."

"What are you saying? This may all go to hell in a handbag?"

"I'm saying we, you and I, are Ray's prime targets, and she's willing to give anything, including her own life, to seek revenge on you for interfering and me for leaving. The other side of hatred is a dangerous place to be."

"I don't understand. Why us? Why such vengeance?"

"You have a hallow soul," he answered, first smiling with approval, then hardening with conviction. "Ray's is hollow."

"How do you mean?"

"You're full of virtues hard earned. The death of your mother and sister weighed heavy on you, but you used it to form your character with a keen dedication to moral integrity."

She hadn't told him about her mother. Zavier could've, but why would he? And how, in the midst of their situation, did he find the time?

"Ray used the injustice served upon her to fuel her contempt for the world—the exact opposite of what you chose to do with your hardship," he explained.

"You can't really compare the two. I never knew my mother. I was too young to sense the grief. Ray was born into a cruel life of captivity."

"You suffered the loss. Every day your father grieved," he said.

His comment stirred painful memories.

"Ray knew nothing else," he said. "Many children endure abuse worse than hers and choose to be heroic, an example of strength and faith for others."

"I fail to see why she's so driven for bloodlust," Kyly admitted. "Why risk recapture?"

"Immediate gratification." His voice surged with conviction. "A large portion of the world's population sacrifices peace for it. It's the source of all addiction and perpetuated pain."

She stared at him as they rolled down the gravel road. "I'd have to agree there."

"You cannot heal a wound by slicing it open further," he warned.

"Then how do you deal with people like her? I don't believe she's capable of change at this point."

"Most aren't, by choice," he said. "The goal is to strive to find understanding in the face of frustration. Acceptance in pain, of pain. None of us know what's coming on this journey or how long we get to be on the path, so live in every moment and hold nothing back."

Kyly let silence pass and then said, "It's asking a lot. To trust without a safety net."

"It has always been there."

"No one believes that," she admitted.

"I know of at least one who does, but I've had a glimpse."

Kyly never answered this.

"Life isn't a game for the weak of heart. It's an unconditional choice to *be* blind to reason, understanding, or outcome. It's leaping off the cliff, never looking down."

As they came onto the stability of the main road, he placed his hand over hers. It was tender and kind. He bestowed grace, though his skin became strangely cold. She studied his face as he spoke. There existed a radiant wisdom in him.

"A new world is but an answer away—"

She hadn't dreamed of the deep conversation with him the night before.

"—I'm offering a perspective—"

He guided the old pickup blindly while locking his mysterious eyes with hers.

"—an insight you'll need from here forward—"

An unknown weight fell heavy on her heart, and with it came a resurgence of faith.

"—I'm offering you the words most sought after, written, interpreted, and desired."

Everything transformed in the wake of his sermon. Yes, as a minister's daughter, she recognized the rite. This wasn't merely rhetoric.

"—I'm offering you truth."

Inside the old beat-up pickup, as it clanked and moaned down the road, an unseen passage opened to Kyly's soul. Her hands became dewy. Her heart accelerated with exhilaration. She would find the justice she sought.

She'd been called. Humbled. He'd brought her back from death's abyss. No one was willing to speak of it. She didn't need to be reminded. She knew more than anyone.

Approaching a row of parking stalls designed to accommodate the beach bound, Chris withdrew his hand from hers to maneuver the rickety pickup into place. He left behind a folded paper.

Recognizing the aged parchment as the same paper she'd seen him writing on late the evening before, her eyes questioned him before her lips formed the words.

"Not now," he answered. "Read it later."

Sliding the odd folded paper into the small front pocket of her blue jeans, she was uplifted by the mere indication there might be a later in which to read it.

The mission weighed heavily on her conscience. What would be asked of her? Her stomach turned as she questioned her resolve. Back at Mason's cabin, she'd been saved. For what? That was every person's question and path.

The truck stopped at a spot along the boardwalk closest to the dock. She kept her silence though there was much her inquisitive nature desired to know. The deeper halls of her being understood what was revealed and left hidden was precisely intended.

Taking her first steps away from the security of the vehicle, across the boardwalk, and onto the sand, she held fast to her faith. The faithful accepted wisdom without question, even when it appeared they'd been led into hell.

Kyly glanced down at her feet. Instead of sand, she envisioned the ash of fire and brimstone.

51

DEMONS POSSESS MANY FORMS. The shipyard was said to have at least one. Mason prayed the one he fought hadn't arrived yet.

In his line of work as a Kidnap and Ransom consultant, he'd witnessed a haunting array of depressed, deranged, destitute, and enraged souls. Normally, the motive was terror, politics, or money. Not this time.

Even through the static ridden line, Ray's darkness penetrated.

"Don't be recalcitrant," she hissed. "You're no rival adversary. No sustainable alliance can be formulated to safeguard your Cromwell clan. He is not who you want him to be. He is mine."

"He's not who you want him to be," Mason corrected. "And he's not yours."

"He will be," she whispered.

"You're wrong," he warned.

"Never," Ray replied. "I've spent years with him, not days. And you think you know him?"

He didn't attempt in-roads; they'd all lead to the same dead end. In Mason's opinion, she was higher than a kite in a tornado and just as twisted.

An expert in negotiating, Mason knew the drill—contact, demands, negotiation. A game forced on unwilling opponents. A game they were given no choice but to play—here, a game without leverage. Negotiating with Ray constituted a pointless waste of time, and time was precious.

"Let me be clear," she said. "Hand him over, or I'll kill your family."

Backward and upside-down, Mason fought to maintain his footing as the world slipped off its axis.

"While we're being frank, you touch my family, and I won't stop coming until you're dead," he promised. "And that includes Chris."

Accustomed to retrieval, he found nothing comforting about offering up his nephew to grant his remaining family asylum. It violated every moral fiber in him.

The trap set to catch Ray was enough to ensnare them all. They were playing with the most lethal inferno—one lit from within. It didn't matter what you threw at it, gasoline or holy water. Greek fire, Ray's hatred only burned hotter.

"Don't waste your time hunting ghosts," Ray said. "I don't die easily. You, on the other hand..."

The banter fed her insanity. A drug fabricated in her DNA. Hearing the venom in her voice, he decided direct was best.

"Is it your intention to kill my nephew?" he asked.

"Which one?"

"Don't toy with me."

"If I wanted him dead, I wouldn't have brought him to life, now, would I?" she said. "He will be yours no more, but no, I will not kill him. He's one-of-a-kind, like me."

In all his years of successful missions, he dreaded the day when good luck and training failed him. Hunched over, hiding, awaiting a nightmare, he begged, 'Let it not be that day.'

"I saw your picture," he said. "You could have any man. Why him?"

Silence. Then static.

Mason swallowed the profanity screaming from his mind until he physically choked. "Did you get all that?" he asked Cage through his headset. "The signal emitted locally, within a twenty-five-mile radius." Cage said. "She's close."

Cage remained in flight, monitoring air traffic, picking up nothing out of the ordinary inbound, which meant she'd anticipated their location long before the phone call. How? God only knew.

Mason speculated her brother, Nick, held in Cage's custody, leaked the information to Ray. Cage was sloppy, or Ray too clever. Either way, the shadows around the construction site became newly menacing. Ray's infiltration options were limited to the shipyard behind where Mason stood.

"None of this feels right," Mason said.

"We swept the entire area. Every building. She's not here, so she's coming from outside."

The situation, wrought with defects, had gained too much momentum. Mason and those he cherished most on earth had become astronauts strapped to a shuttle of faulty workmanship. He sat waiting for their world to blow apart and rip them into a thousand indiscernible pieces. In a word, they were 'FUBAR.'

His mind washed over areas of vulnerability, dragging him along for the ride. It left him psychologically battered and bruised. "She's smarter than you, right?" Cage didn't answer.

Instead, his sister's face, anguish deepened by guilt, Curt's regret and liability etched in memory lingered. Pain he couldn't erase. Pain still hungry and feeding. Restrained, he stewed, crouched in a fenced-off storage area left of the main warehouse. Cage's team members were assigned positions further out. Mason insisted on being as close as possible to the dock's midpoint.

Through his rifle's scope, he saw Zavier waiting- bait hung out at the ocean end. Kicking out two fence boards, he established a clear access route. A garbage bin covered him from the parking lot, a fence and rusty equipment concealed him from the front. Stench from rotting waste filled his nostrils.

Confronting maniacs ceased to unnerve him, yet his hands shook. The thought of Zavier, or any of his family, in the crosshairs of anything but a camera made his stomach turn.

He'd convinced Brook and Curt to stay as far away as possible, though they refused to wait at home. Understanding didn't diminish danger. Cage held them at a safe distance out of visual range, waiting with commandos. It wasn't reassuring. If Ray could get to him, blow a hole out of his cabin, and walk away unscathed, she was certainly capable of taking out a few armed troops.

Without confirmation of Ray's precise location, they were all targets.

The second hand on his watch echoed in his ears like a time bomb.

Frustration and anxiety mounted inside him until it couldn't be contained.

He waited until a beat-up garbage truck bounced over a pothole, then erupted, slamming his heavy left fist into the side of the metal garbage bin with sufficient force to inflict a dint. The sound of bent metal ricocheted through the air, followed by Cage's voice over the radio.

"Stone, do you have a visual? Confirm."

"I'm rearranging my line of sight," Mason said. "Nothing but a junker."

"Junker my ass. Put a lid on it," Cage chastised. "The woman has ears."

Mason tossed the radio to the ground and rubbed his sore knuckles. The pain was superseded by the ache in his chest, the place where his heart raged.

Kyly had interfered with Ray's plans and would be viewed as a rival who refused to die. When Ray saw *her*, she'd finish what she started.

This was the source of his deepest fear—the thought of losing Kyly. He couldn't bear it and hated himself for not focusing more on his nephew.

Chris was Ray's primary target. He'd lived through hell, estranged from his family, isolated by a lunatic. No one was more deserving of a normal life, and odds were he'd never have one. Even if Ray were apprehended without incident, the military would be all over him. He embodied the ultimate specimen, and they knew it.

Mason, trained to absorb and analyze detail knew Chris was filled with insight and experience no one his age could possess. He drew conclusions beyond his years and far beyond any isolated patient in a coma. Who came out of a coma stronger and wiser than when they went in? The way he dealt with pain, how fast he healed, his fearless nature, he was not normal. How far from normal, Mason didn't know, but those behind the genetics that created Ray would certainly want to find out.

Still, Mason's heart stayed with Kyly. Images of her filled his head. Standing in his bedroom in his shirt, sleeping with the face of an angel. He wanted her with him. He couldn't do this, stand back and give Ray a window of retribution. What the hell was he thinking?

Drawing his attention to the soiled, broken pavement, the radio came to life.

"We have incoming," a voice said. "Two civilians in a pickup. One male, one female, both late twenties."

"Kyly...Chris," Mason said to the air.

Cage's commands followed. "Hold your positions, boys. I don't want anyone screwing this up by being overzealous. We get one shot at her."

Holding his rifle with one hand, Mason withdrew his Beretta from its resting place in the middle of his back. He snapped open the chamber, confirmed it was fully loaded, and slammed it closed again. Slipping the back-up weapon under his belt, he inhaled sour air through his nose, a long, slow, tainted breath.

52

"*DAMN YOU!*" Ray threw the laser, binocular-like, device to the dirty warehouse floor. "*You're supposed to be dead!*"

Behind the haze of the warehouse windows, she waited until Chris approached. Through her Nightforce scope and the Vectors, she confirmed her range to target and locked on the journalist.

The fact Chris wasn't alone complicated things. She came for him. She didn't want him dying in Kyly's arms. A choice had to be made.

If she had time, she would've reloaded. The full metal jacket was selected for Chris. One shot clean through. For Kyly, she'd prefer more tissue damage—enough to rip her in half. No mercy, but the clock counted down, sparing no second chances.

They'd expect her to arrive from the parking lot or roadway soon after they did. Allowing the necessary time for the military to apprehend her before she breached the safe distance to where Chris waited at the water's edge. Again, they were wrong.

"Hate to be late," she breathed.

On an art-film angle, through a stained lens, Ray monitored the scene.

Other than Cage's chopper, there was no sign of the military.

No sign of Mason.

Concealed in a holding pattern necessary for the element of surprise, they waited on her. She would not disappoint.

———

Chris' hand came alive with urgency as he steadied Kyly's final step to level ground. No longer chilled, as it had been on the truck ride over, she drew strength from his tightening grip. They ascended the wooden stairs at the sand's end, midpoint down the pier. Clearing the last few corroded steps, Zavier came into view ocean-side.

Apprehensively, he waited for the chopper in the distance. Blown by sea winds sweeping off the waterfront, in a loose cotton shirt and jeans, he mirrored the man beside her. If they stood together, it'd be difficult to tell them apart.

Chris' pace quickened when he saw Zavier. His determination came off him in waves, sweeping over her, leaving her breathless. Like running in the wake of exhaust fumes, the air failed to quench the need of her lungs.

Racing against sinister forces, each footfall became accentuated by the pounding of Kyly's heart. With the rhythm of a ritualistic African drumbeat, it sounded a haunting, advancing dread.

Recognizing she and Chris weren't in the chopper, Zavier's expression became terror stricken. Swiveling between his older brother and the chopper, she read his confusion. He welcomed the incoming helicopter, thinking they were its cargo. And now, he suspected it harbored the enemy.

Chris directed her attention to the plank walkway, wanting her to keep eyes on the far end of the pier opposite their approach—Ray could surface at any second.

She remembered his words. Zavier wasn't Ray's intended victim.

Squinting to see more than a fluctuating blur between steps, Kyly caught a reflection from deep in the distance, an onyx shine.

Thump, thump. Her heart slammed against the walls of her chest.

Kyly's feet impacted the dock in a racer's stride, legs stretching beyond comfort to keep pace with Chris. Where was Ray? Where was Mason? Where was their damn backup?

Thump, thump. Acid inched into her throat. She swallowed it down.

His words came slow, drowned by the reverberation of panic rapping against her ribcage.

"We're in her sights." Chris released Kyly's hand and ran ahead.

"*No!*"

The absence of physical contact with Chris left a gaping hole where security once reigned. She needed to touch him as if her life depended on it. Branded, she wore a bull's eye on her back.

Thump, thump. The angry beat would not subside.

Thrown off balance without Chris' momentum to steady her, Kyly's feet dispelled a conflicting rhythm with her heart, overlapping the pounding in her head. She couldn't move fast enough. She wanted to stop time, to catch it, and hold it until Mason found Ray and they were safe, but it slipped away.

Thump, thump. The air she gasped was thin and empty.

Zavier turned as the chopper closed in, dropping to collect him.

It was a military chopper, not Ray's. How could they've known? Mason must've called them in.

A ladder dropped out the side door as an officer leaned out, yelling over a loudspeaker. "Jump!"

Out of range, Zavier spun back to see how close Kyly and his older brother were and whether he should trust the instruction of the man.

"*Go!*" Chris hollered. "*Get outta here!*"

Looking beyond his brother, and past her to the dock entrance, something froze Zavier in place.

Time failed to compete with the amplified throbbing beneath Kyly's ribs.

Reading the terror in Zavier's eyes as he leaped for the rope handles dangling above him, Kyly twisted mid-stride, her stare drawn by a distant sound burst. Time pulled taut while she imagined Ray's soulless eyes glimmering through heat waves rising off a gun barrel. It burned.

The echo inside her head overlapped.

Men in combat gear dispelled like ants from warehouse buildings across the roadway and flooded the sidewalk leading to the pier. They heard it too. For them, it was an all too familiar sound. They'd reach Ray, but too late.

Out of the corner of her eye, Zavier hovered above the wooden planks on the rope ladder. From the right entrance to the dock, Mason sprinted for the blast.

The fabric of time ripped. Kyly's mind tore with it, splintered by devastation and doom. Mason closed in, moments away from a close-range bullet if Ray saw him approaching. Zavier hung, an open target. And she and Chris were placed in the line of fire, one after the other. Death would visit one of them.

The trigger was pulled.

Thump, thump, a single heartbeat, and time stopped.

Sweeping motion spun Kyly in a complete circle. Her eyes fought to find focus. Out of nowhere, Chris clenched her by the arms, twisting her with combined velocity. He grabbed her, then slipped away, leaving her rocked on her heels. A force expelled her breath in an explosive exhalation. Her lungs deflated without the ability to draw replenishing air. Her legs buckled beneath her, driving her knees a crushing blow as they impacted the unforgiving weathered planks. Her head flung back, a contorted glimpse of Mason, then the sky.

———

Closing the gap between himself and Ray, Beretta drawn, Mason chased her. Ray exploded from deep in the old shipyard's central warehouse and flew across the loading dock in a vampire's charge. Having served its purpose, she traded the rifle for her Glock and ran, gun arm stiff in front of her.

He collided with her at the dock's T-section, slamming his hands under hers. The weapon catapulted into the air before she engaged its auto-fire feature.

Crumpled in a heap with Chris, Kyly's body was still at the far end of the dock, Chris beside her. Mason's heart broke with their fall.

Statue stiff, deaf, and heartless, he fell into a robotic state, immobilizing Ray until Cage's boys tore her loose. She grinned as they grabbed her, her face so close to his. Those eyes, dead, and yet glistening with hatred.

He'd never forget.

He'd never seen a demon up close.

A scream broke his hardening cast. His heart slammed hard back inside his chest—Kyly.

———

Bees swarmed between her ears, jumbled thoughts confused. At first, Kyly couldn't understand why she was on the ground. Shifting from one side to the next, she couldn't feel her legs, her arms, anything but the pain in her chest.

Breath returned to her. Not wholly, but in the form of broken bursts, fragmented by the firm grip of terror choking out life-sustaining air. Gasps. Warm liquid flowed across her hands. It wasn't welcomed.

"*No!*" The core of her being railing against a reality too harsh to bear.

It wasn't supposed to end this way. They knew the dangers, but not like this.

"*God, no!*" She pleaded for mercy, but mercy didn't come.

Looking around them, frantic for optimism, she searched for even the slightest shadow of promise, but paramedics were nowhere in sight. Abandoning Ray, as Cage's men swarmed in, Mason raced to her.

A pounding sensation coursed through Kyly's body. Mason's heavy steps, her own heartbeat, a drumbeat of doom? She couldn't be sure.

When Mason crouched behind her, she read his expression—it offered not a shred of hope.

Kyly's world broke free from those around her. Every sensation deadened. What could reach her came through a surreal strain that sifted Chris' pain with the contrition in her soul. Staring back down to the man she cradled, she watched his luminous glow fade into a shroud of eternal darkness.

"*Oh Chris, no! Don't go.*" Her voice bounced back at her from a distant tunnel. Their bodies lay together on the damp dock, but Kyly felt its solidity give way. "*It should've been me.*"

He said nothing but brushed his index finger over the back of her hand.

"*No!!!!!!*" From the far end of the dock, Brook's scream echoed her pain and desperation. Defeat driven from the hollows of a broken heart. "*No!!!!*"

Dashing past the executioner being cuffed and manhandled by military officers, across the remaining distance down the dock, she ran, arms reaching to protect a child already fallen.

Kyly absorbed the impact of Brook's racing footsteps—dread gaining velocity. The worst fear answered. Meeting an expression riddled with tragedy, her tear-stained face said it all.

Dropping to her knees, Brook gathered her firstborn in her arms. Forcing her sobs back down, she silenced herself to hear him. Kyly witnessed their exchange, drinking in the anguish as her own.

"I love you." Brook's words were hardly coherent through convulsing sorrow.

"Do not...mourn me..." His words came slowly, his speech broken by the blood seeping into his lungs. His tone delivered not a request but an instruction. Somehow managing to recapture a weak but steady voice, he continued.

"My death...could change everything."

The wisdom in his dying eyes wasn't betrayed by the certain anguish of his body. Kyly's hands, drenched in blood, couldn't cover the gaping wound, yet she held them, determined to replace his missing flesh. The bullet had torn through him at an upward angle from his right side into the heart of him—he should not be breathing.

"No victim..."

Brook did not interrupt.

Gurgling impeded his pronunciation. "I...will never love you less."

Kyly struggled to feel his life force pulsing beneath her buried hands but couldn't. She strained to hear his breath, but it had grown too shallow or no longer existed at all. She bowed her head to his chest and stared into his eyes as Brook's filled and spilled above her.

"I'm parting of the clouds," he whispered on feathered breath.

"Without you..." Kyly's doubt, fear, and heartbreak transformed into simple words.

His hand slipped from Brook's. Kyly pulled back believing he was reaching for his wound, where her hands still were. He was not. Stretching beyond the bloody mess that once was his perfection, he rested his hand on her lower abdomen. Strength waning, he didn't possess the ability to reach above to her heart.

"Not...without, within," he whispered through the fluid so faintly only she could hear his words.

His last words.

Kyly collapsed over his body. Her head rested upon his chest. Her tears fell over a lifeless heart—the emptiest sound in the world.

No matter how many days she lived, she knew she'd never hear anything as silent, lonely, or painful as this. It consumed her, for she alone knew who the world had forsaken. She couldn't hear the helicopter blades chopping the air above them, the ambulance sirens wailing toward the dock, or Brook's heart-wrenching sobs beside her. She did not feel Mason's strong hands clasp her shoulders from behind, his chest press against her back, or the wind sweeping everything around them. She saw only Chris' lifeless eyes, blackening as the light fell from them, drawn away from the inside—then white, then only white.

53

GONE, the radiant youthful glow. Gone, the sparkling soulful wisdom. Gone, the alluring vibrancy. Kyly's fiery auburn eyes burned out. When Mason peered in, no one stared back. Instead, glass replicas emotionless as a wax museum reproduction.

The windows to Kyly's soul—once mesmerizing and alive—became cold and impenetrable. No words escaped her lips. Not a sound. In silence, tears pooled and spilled down pallid cheeks.

Under his secure grasp, she moved with a zombie's stiff gait. Her feet skimmed the dock's planks as he led her to the parking lot. Once there, he lifted her into the waiting truck's bench seat. Numb, she flopped inside like a wet rag doll. Bloody.

Dying, Chris had laid across her folded legs, head pressed into her chest. All of her, save her porcelain face and silken hair, wore evidence of his demise.

Mason remembered the strength necessary to tear her from Chris's lifeless body. She fought him, then went limp in his embrace.

Elite military units stormed the dock seconds after he knocked the gun from Ray's hands, leaving mourners precious moments at Chris' side before flooding the scene to remove his body.

"You let him die! You made this happen. He's my son...my son." Brook's shattered pleas had been futile. Soldiers seized Chris while Curt gathered his inconsolable wife under one arm and his younger son under the other.

Coldly and systematically, Chris' body was placed on a gurney, covered with a thick white sheet, and ushered into Cage's waiting chopper.

Ray wasn't airlifted in the same unit, which was a small comfort. Even in death, it would've been an abhorrent injustice to allow her anywhere near Chris.

Brandishing a government-issued Colt .45, Cage's authoritative mannerisms were as easily recognizable as his combat boots. Mason spotted him immediately. The man standing beside him remained a mystery. Wearing casual clothes, he didn't appear to be active military, though his stance said he'd served.

Ray had recognized him. Actually, if Mason's eyes hadn't played tricks on him, she'd smiled at the stranger while being escorted away. They knew each other.

Watching his surviving family walk away, dependent on each other in a clutch of support, Mason knew they'd all been transformed and weakened.

A shroud had fallen. An unmistakable illusion that once provided a destructive but oddly comforting understanding had disintegrated, unveiling a pure, raw, transforming truth.

Hours later, standing in the master bedroom of his beach house, Mason wished Kyly's eyes would reflect something other than the chandelier's candlelight glittering overhead.

Frozen before him, a scarlet mannequin, she stood in the threshold of the washroom. He knew of the delicate place where her sanity teetered between shock and acceptance.

Like a priest baptizing away sin, he prayed he could bathe her back to life. He had to coax her away from the edge of hopelessness, but with what lure?

She knew, intimately, the power of dark forces. They were real and, at times, inescapable. Simply brandishing a crucifix or clasping hands in prayer wouldn't ward off evil. Even the best among us couldn't be saved, not always.

He pleaded with everything holy in him she could be.

Walking to the washroom, he kept her close. Inside, he reached beyond the white linen shower curtain for the faucet, adjusting the water's temperature and force. A soft spray of water washed over his hand.

"Lee, honey, I have to get you out of these clothes," he whispered. "It's going to be all right."

Removing his hand off the small of her back, he reached for clean towels on an overhead shelf. Tremors quaked through Kyly's body.

"It's okay," he reassured, stroking her arms. "I'm not leaving your side. Let's get you cleaned up."

Unfastening tiny smeared buttons, he removed her blouse, peeling it off one arm at a time. The saturated fabric made a sick suction sound as it broke free from her undershirt. It dropped in a heavy lump, a blemish on the pristine tile floor.

Unbuttoning her blue jeans, he leaned in to balance her weight against his. Mechanically, she lifted her legs. Reaching down with one hand, he folded the denim back on itself until the jeans lay inside out in a heap beside her shirt on the floor. Barefoot, in lace panties and a wet undershirt, she trembled.

"I've got you, Lee. The water's nice and warm." He coaxed her to proceed on her own accord. She would not. His words broke against a stone exterior, never reaching the inner core. Mason tore off his shirt and stood facing her.

"Honey, I've got to take off your T-shirt," he said. "It's all right, you're safe with me."

Focusing his concerned gaze on her beautiful face, he removed her blood-soaked undershirt. Her arms raised automatically above her head, accommodating its removal like a sleepy child before bed. Her face was barren of emotion.

Backing into the warm spray, jeans and all, he led her, keeping her close. Minutes passed while the clear water turned pink between them, vanishing bad memories beneath the drain. His eyes, trained on hers, avoided the crimson reminder of devastation. Chris couldn't be saved. His hope stayed with Kyly.

Eventually, the rigidity of her body loosened. He did not rush her. Lathering his hands behind her back, he let suds flow over her shoulders. She remained still in his arms. He glided soapy hands over her. Dried blood lost its tacky grip and slipped free. Awaiting a flicker of life behind her haunted eyes, he never saw the efforts of his hands.

Warm water sprayed his face. He blinked it away. He guided her around to the showerhead. With her back to him, he poured shampoo into his palm and massaged it through her long mane.

Pain and passion were overwhelming. They hit with a combined force.

Pulling away, he stepped backward onto the bathmat, drenched denim restricting his movements. As the curtain closed in front of him, a gasp pierced the silence. Kyly had come back to life.

Deep sobs erupted from her, compelling him to jump back into the shower and take her in his arms. He wanted to forget as badly as anyone, to bury himself in her tenderness, but he dared not compromise her, or take advantage of her sorrow. The pain of passion sent a crippling ache through him.

"Don't leave." A heartbroken plea shuddered out from beneath the waterfall, stopping him.

"Please, Mason, don't leave me alone."

He opened the curtain and stepped back inside to see her head bent, propped against the tiled wall ahead of her, her anguish unleashed.

"I'm not leaving you, Lee...I'll be right outside."

Reaching back, she clung to his arm, drawing him in, wrapping it around her. Placing his right hand over her left breast, she reached for his other arm, crossing it over her. Pulling him too close.

"Kyly, I can't do this," he said. "You need time, space to grieve. I'm a man. I can't—"

Her lips drowned his words as she spun, pressing her chest against him, kissing him with a deep, soulful passion. In one breath, his gallant protest was swallowed whole. He held her with all the strength in him. She wanted him, needed him. And he was powerless to deny her. Stepping as a unit onto the wet floor, she pulled away to reach for the buttons on his jeans.

"Lee, are you sure?"

She popped the buttons free.

As the sun fell, their passion rose until the night surrounded them in serene darkness. For one night, love replaced pain.

Nestled in, pressed against him, Kyly rested her head on his shoulder. Her hand clasped in a delicate fist beneath his. He transformed. He lived now for what he could give and be to her. A life of resistance ended. His heart fell prey to an all-consuming devotion.

Pledged in utter silence.

———

Strewn in a littered pathway to the shower, the bloodstained clothes were a gory reminder of the death Mason couldn't prevent.

In all his years of protecting and serving, he never lost a civilian life on his watch—until now. And Chris was family. Guilt weighed heavy. How could Brook ever forgive him?

He knew she would, already had, and never blamed him for any of this—she was too busy blaming herself. It didn't matter. He harbored enough penitence for both of them.

He should've checked the main warehouse. He'd trusted...

Cage's men should've done their damn job.

Chris should've survived.

His training instilled reflex reactions. Why hadn't he shot Ray from the stairs instead of disarming her? She deserved to die.

While emptying Kyly's blue jeans pockets, he tortured himself. He piled retrieved items beside him on the floor, forgot he'd gone through her front pockets, searched them again.

A mysterious crumpled piece of aged, brown, paper-like material caught his eye, preventing him from rummaging through the jeans for a third unnecessary time. Crinkled Kleenex and a tube of lip-gloss were not quite so curious. He wanted to inspect the strange paper, but first, he had to properly discard the bloody clothes. He set the items on a shelf and tossed the Kleenex into the toilet.

Opening a wooden garbage container, he pulled the unused liner bag free and placed everything except Kyly's undershirt inside the plastic. Removing a box of Baggies from the cabinet and a pair of scissors, he cut two one-inch squares out of an area where the material was most saturated. He stored them in zip-locks, then added the damaged shirt to the contents of the garbage bag.

Taking a clean washcloth from the shelf, he turned the sink tap to hot and submerged the cloth while pouring hand soap over it, moving it under the water until covered in suds. On hands and knees, he scrubbed the white tile free of bloodstains left behind from the piled clothing. Satisfied, he placed the stained cloth in a separate baggy, sealed it, and tossed it in with her clothes.

After tying the garbage bag, he crept down the hall to the back entrance, across the moonlit yard, and to the detached garage. He punched in the code and waited for the door to disarm. In modest light, he placed the white trash bag safely in a locking cupboard and headed back inside.

Sealing doors along the way behind him, he reentered the bedroom. Kyly lay in the full moon's silhouette. He longed to lie beside her but passed by, his work unfinished.

Inside the washroom, he returned to the shelf where he stored the strange paper.

A shudder ran through him. He shook off bad memories.

Peeking around the corner, he checked the rise and fall of Kyly's chest.

Using tweezers and a Q-tip, he unfolded the blood-soaked paper. Fragments of writing, unlike any he'd ever seen, were concealed inside. Prying the upper right corner free, his breath caught in his throat.

Do not burden your heart with blame... A familiar voice echoed the words in his head. Chris.

A cold film slithered between the middle of his spine and the shadow hairs at the nape of his neck. He wasn't alone. Turning on his heels with a catlike reflex, he expected Kyly to be standing in the doorway. Empty.

He stared out the window at the night's lidless eye. The passage of time had become the enemy. The moon glared back, cold and heartless.

———

Dawn brought a scorching brand of injustice. Mason resented the irony of these baneful emotions in the wake of indescribable passion.

His world had flipped upside-down.

Walking outside to meet the courier, he checked the skyline, expecting to see waves hovering above and clouds below his bare feet. The courier snatched the manila envelope from him, placed it in a thicker waterproof jacket, and then requested Mason's signature for delivery to the San Francisco DNA lab. An old friend worked there. He needed answers he'd never pry from Cage. It was far too risky to even ask the questions.

Following the paved drive, he spotted Kyly beyond a window. He couldn't help but smile. She was wearing one of his shirts again.

He headed back inside. Focusing on her quieted the inner turmoil.

Making her way down the hall, Kyly complimented, "This place is amazing. Did you design it yourself?"

"I had help." In the sunlit kitchen, he sat at a built-out nook.

"This room's like a yacht's eating galley." She sauntered beyond its threshold to peer into the next room.

"Yeah. All the promise of sea, none of the escape." He picked up his coffee cup, having forgotten it was empty, and put it down again.

The house had been remodeled using subtle elements of maritime style, making it homey and uniquely seaworthy. Paneled passageways led from room to room, carved corbels, wooden ceiling beams, and white wainscoting topped in pencil thin trim added to its architectural allure. Window seats and hideaways, conducive to captain's lookouts, nautical windows, and roof hatches, washed the comfort from the sea ashore.

The kettle began whistling as Kyly rounded the corner.

She slipped onto his lap and wrapped her arms around him, smothering his guilt and self-doubt in her love.

Bracing her elbows on the table behind her, she faced him. "We can blame ourselves until it destroys us. That will only make us useless. I won't be made useless. We didn't put Chris in the position that led to his death. The criminal that killed him did."

She brushed his cheek with her fingertips. Her touch soothed, but her eyes were afire.

"He wouldn't want you to blame yourself. Please, for him, don't."

He didn't say a word but absorbed her wisdom. He *would* make peace with himself, but not today. Perhaps not until Chris' killer was dead and all the payback was paid.

54

"THAT BASTARD STOLE MY SON!" Brook's hatred simmered behind bloodshot eyes. "I want him back, Curt. You hear me? I want him back."

"I can't make that happen—" Curt reasoned.

"They can. Why did we let them take him off the dock? Why—"

"Why? Cage had two choppers full of armed men. Let them? We never had a choice."

Their raised voices flooded the house, seeping out cracks in the windows soiling the otherwise peaceful neighborhood. This is what true anguish did; it bled out, scaring everyone into fearing they could be next.

"Not good enough." Brook stared past her husband to the mantle above the crackling fire, her eyes stealing its amber glow.

"Try to be reasonable—" Curt said, his voice worn by the emotional grind.

In one violent thrust, Brook's arm became a sword, sweeping the once pristine collection of Cromwell family photos to the floor. Expensive crystal frames shattered with her tolerance into a heap of regret across the marble.

"My son!" she said, her words a rite of passage. Then, the fury that sustained her released its grip. She sunk to the floor, a centerpiece within the wreckage.

"He wasn't *just* your son," Curt said. "He was mine too."

"I'm sorry. I didn't..." Her voice faded as Curt left the room.

A photo showered in fragmented glass caught her eye. In it, Chris stood alone, isolated by the drift of fog across Half Moon Bay. Fitting. This was where she'd reclaimed him. Where he'd always been and forever would remain, embraced by everything unseen. Never close enough to touch or taint. Set apart and more present than any other human on earth.

A morose veil hung over Brook, casting a murky shadow that reached back into her past, clinging to the moment of Chris' birth and stretching across her future, corrupting the void beyond death. No memory abided that it did not alter, no thoughts it didn't plague. All their skeletons were unleashed. It wasn't liberating.

She licked her lips but couldn't swallow. The walls of her throat sifted like sandpaper.

By the time she approached Chris at the dock, all that once was him had fallen away. A beautiful, ruined, empty shell remained. Not how she wanted to remember him.

Nightfall darkened the room. Brook fingered through broken memories, not ready to move beyond them. She plucked the photo of Chris out of the debris and pushed back across the floor, the scraping sound of crushed glass shadowing her movement.

If she was cut, she couldn't feel it. The emotional scars ran deeper.

———

Morning brought muted sunlight and a dull ache across the top of Brook's shoulders from sleeping upright in a chair.

Stepping out of the car, she scanned the cemetery. It had never appeared bleaker. Not even the day she buried her mother. Like a funeral shroud, a bank of gray clouds gathered above, casting the grounds into shadow.

She rubbed her neck, glancing down at the photo of Chris in the fog that she'd brought from home. Summoning her strength, she made her way to the headstone.

Curt exited the car and stayed a few paces behind. The distance between them couldn't be measured in feet. She arrived at the plot alone.

"It has your name, son, but not your body." Her finger traced the engraved letters. *Christian Cromwell, taken too soon.* "I want to know whose ashes lie here."

Curt's brow furrowed at the mention of the tiny casket beneath the surface. "You're not suggesting—"

"He was somebody's son. Not ours, but somebody's."

"It's too late for that." Curt approached the opposite side of the headstone, careful not to step on the area directly in front. "The baby's parents don't need to suffer for us."

"Our son must be properly laid to rest." She propped Chris' picture against the cold stone. It was a copy. The original was at home where he belonged.

"It's our right. I want him back."

"So do I, damn it, but we can't hold our breath waiting for that to happen. The odds of them releasing him aren't good, and you know it." He kneeled and placed a photo of him, Mason, and Chris beside the other picture.

A sad silence fell with the first drops of rain.

"You have two other children who need you," Curt said.

Brook's eyes stung with a fresh swell of tears. She thought of her father, and his efforts to help his son without question for the first time. It was too late for all of them. They'd all failed each other and themselves.

"Let's go home." Curt reached out to take her arm and lead her away from the grave, his hair matting into wet waves. She pulled away before he touched her. There'd be no consoling her, not today. Not anytime soon.

55

"THEN FIRE ME!" Dr. Gordon dared Locke. "*That* I can live with, but I'm not touching a scalpel to him!"

Their raised voices carried down the corridor leading to the medical research wing of the underground facility. Bouncing along the bleached cement tunnel, folding in on themselves, they arrived at Cage's ears an offensive reverberation.

"You'll do what you're told, or unemployment will be the least of your worries!"

Locke's sanctimonious tirade made Cage's skin crawl. There were countless men in recruitment Cage knew weren't worthy of a life of honor. It was never personal; they simply weren't cut from the cloth. He'd seen every type of poor excuse for a man, James Lawrence Locke the II, held a category all his own.

"You have your precious blood analysis, your DNA sample. I ran the whole gamut; it's all in the report. You know how he died. I'm not laying another hand on him." Gordon's protests escalated as Cage closed the distance.

"And why the hell not?" Locke said. "I'm sure he won't be offended. If you haven't noticed, the guy is dead!"

"Keep your bloody voice down!" Cage ordered from behind them. "What the hell is going on here?"

Dr. Lance Gordon was a brilliant medical examiner and a damn fine human being, even by Cage's high standards. Dedicated, hard-working, extraordinarily intelligent, and the least squeamish man Cage had ever known. What earned him Cage's admiration was a tour of duty that cost him his left leg.

"This excuse for a forensic pathologist is refusing to do his job," Locke said. His words slid together a screeching train wreck. "That's what's going on. And if he doesn't have an immediate change of heart, his new career is going to be remarkably short-lived."

"His career isn't your concern, Locke," Cage admonished. "How about you do *your* job and let me worry about things down here with the doc."

"Fine! You deal with him, but I need those results...yesterday," Locke whined.

Cage stared Locke down. Weak men crumbled easily. Intimidated, Locke and his scowl stormed down the hall out of sight.

"Nice fella," Gordon said, wiping his brow.

"He's a piece of trash that refuses to be thrown out," Cage said. "What's the problem?"

With a sullen expression, Gordon shook his head, walking in a circle before coming back to meet Cage's inquiring stare.

"Out with it, man!"

Gordon remained silent, staring past him into the white walkway.

"I've never known you to be silent or stumped," Cage said. "What the hell is it?"

"I *can't* do an autopsy on his body," Gordon replied.

"And why is that?"

Gordon struggled with his explanation. "He isn't like the others."

"We know that. That's why he's here, hidden forty floors below the surface."

"No! You don't understand. I believe there'll be dire consequences if I take a scalpel to him."

"An infection, something deadly? We have precautions for that."

"Not those kinds of consequences."

"LG, the investigation has been ordered from the top down. No one's coming after you—"

Incensed, Gordon cut Cage off and grabbed his arm, pulling him toward his operatory. "I'm not worried about those assholes in the White

House. I've worked under them long enough to know how to protect myself. My concern is for repercussions from someone much more powerful than them."

"Okay, LG, I've been patient, but you're starting to get on my nerves."

"Come with me." Gordon slammed a hand on the security pad while forcing Cage into the operating room ahead of him.

"No one but you is supposed to have contact with the body," Cage protested but couldn't stop the momentum of Gordon's iron leg shoving him across the threshold.

"I could be cutting into..." Gordon spoke as the door air sealed shut behind them, leaving them hovering four feet away from the corpse.

"Jesus Christ!" Cage said, astonished as his eyes drank in the room.

"Exactly," Gordon echoed from behind him.

Cage knew the root of the word *Autopsy*. It derived from a Greek word meaning, 'to see for oneself.' In this particular case, seeing was *not* necessarily believing.

To prevent contamination and protect their covert operation, Gordon was ordered to deny all access to the body. No one but him had been this close to it since its rush delivery. Though Cage rode back with the corpse, it remained covered in sheets applied on the dock where Christian Cromwell died. No one thought to have a peek, absorbed by the euphoria of capturing Ray.

"Fools." Her voice floated across the gray matter between his ears, tainting it.

The examiner's operating room was a wash of static white and stainless steel. Its walls consisted of the same bland cement that made up the entire facility. Encircling them on three sides at chest level were x-ray surfaces, designed to accommodate large eleven by fourteen-inch photos or x-rays for analysis on backlit boards. Their size and strong fluorescence allowed Gordon to reference certain interesting aspects of the subject's anatomy from a distance during autopsy. All the spaces were occupied like a macabre art exhibition for a deranged Robert Berdella wannabe.

Cage stood surrounded by enlarged photos of Chris' injuries, enough to make the toughest marine nervous, not through gory detail but by implication.

Every facet of the room screamed of cutting-edge advancement, each piece of furniture, the surgical tools, and the inventory of equipment—most appearing strangely futuristic.

They did nothing to prevent Cage from feeling he'd been sucked back through time two thousand years by some cosmic vacuum.

The body lay swathed at the lower torso by thin white sheets, bathed in a soft glow, which he assumed was the result of overhead lights. Reluctantly, he moved closer. The strong bulbs above the operating table were not lit. Just the same, the glow remained. An odd castoff from the x-ray backboards or inexplicable like everything surrounding him.

Without warning, the cosmic vacuum switched into reverse, and Cage found himself spit out between the afterlife and the Twilight Zone.

Chris had died as a result of Ray's first and only shot. The images before him disputed the facts. Minutes passed before Gordon reminded him he wasn't alone.

"Now you see why I refuse to cut him open?" Gordon broke the silence.

"Jesus Christ," Cage whispered again.

"Yes, duly noted."

"Who have you—"

"No one but you," Gordon replied. "Locke did everything but put a gun to my head to get in here. I didn't budge an inch. You tell me, am I wrong?"

"Don't lift a scalpel," Cage ordered. "Go over all your findings with me. I'll hand deliver the information straight to the top. I don't want you leaving this room. I don't care if you have to move in a cot and sleep alongside him. You understand?"

"Yeah, I understand," Gordon replied, noticeably miffed.

"Been a while. You still know how to use one of these?" Cage handed Gordon a concealed .38 Special he removed from an ankle holster beneath his right pant leg.

"Yeah, I remember."

"If anyone but me tries getting through that door, you stop them *before* they see this. If you can't, make sure they end up on a gurney next to him."

"I'm not authorized to kill anyone!" Gordon protested.

"You are now." Cage turned his attention back to the pictures on the walls. "Explain this."

"I'll try to ignore the implications." Gordon set the gun aside to retrieve his file on Chris. "I'll tell you what I can, but I don't think anyone alive could explain this. There's conflicting data in every detail."

Encircling the room, drifting as if on air from one image to the next, Cage questioned Gordon every step of the way. Unlike the tender luminescence cradling the body, the backlights of the x-ray panels were harsh and unforgiving up close. Standing inches away, Cage became captivated, drawn mercilessly close to the brutal images.

"These wounds through the wrists, he suffered those injuries eluding Ray at the industrial area off the coast," Cage said. "Are they consistent with that incident?"

"The holes are the result of direct trauma caused by identical iron stakes six inches in length, thrust at an extreme velocity with excessive force," Gordon said, slipping into clinical detail. "Your report says he was impaled by broken ladder rungs?"

"Correct. The ladder broke during his descent. Pinned him to the wall," Cage confirmed. "Why six inches?"

"Long enough to pass through the thickness of the wrist, leaving sufficient excess on either side to suspend him without making it easy to pull free."

"Well that's a pleasant mental image," Cage whispered, entranced by the portrait before him.

"The wounds are the exact size and in the same location," Gordon said.

"Makes sense, two sides of the same ladder," Cage replied.

"You're not listening!" Gordon carried the file over and slapped it against Cage's thick chest. "I never said *approximately* the same. I said *identical, absolutely identical.* Do you have any idea the odds or accuracy required to create those injuries? If we strapped someone unconscious to a table, measured precisely, and applied exact force, we couldn't replicate his wounds."

Cage didn't respond. He leafed through the file, skimming the measurements and other pertinent data confirming Gordon's assessment. Investigation photographs magnified the lesions. The holes, larger than a quarter in diameter, revealed entrance wounds of exact shape, size, and placement—perfectly formed pentagrams.

Cage's grip on the file tightened, creasing the photo paper, warping the images.

"Careful," Gordon warned.

"This doesn't make sense," Cage murmured beneath his breath.

"Tell me something I don't know."

"I was there." Cage stared at the photo of Chris' wrists. "I saw the ladder brackets. These wounds should be an L shape, not a star?"

"If you're looking for logical conclusions," Gordon whispered, "you're in the wrong place."

Flipping to pictures of the kill shot didn't bring Cage any relief. They only served to make matters worse.

Gordon held an aged leather-bound book open to a page depicting the death of Jesus. In it, a biblical reference to the wounds Christ suffered, the final injury responsible for his death. The illustration, hand painted in faded colors, could've been drawn from the photo Cage held.

The men made eye contact.

Referring to the body, requiring confirmation of the photo's authenticity, Cage loomed over Chris' side where the bullet entered, inspecting. He reached out his left hand and touched the flesh. On contact, his arm retracted as if he received an electrical shock.

"His skin's warm! You have him lying on a heating pad?"

"Yeah, right. It's standard protocol," Gordon said sarcastically.

"This isn't possible," Cage murmured. Backing away, he tripped over a rolling stool and cursed under his breath.

"And you expect me to lock myself inside this room with *Him* and sleep on a cot," Gordon protested. "It's not going to get any easier, I warn you. I'm a man of science. I rely on facts. And, every step forward I take in this investigation, the more logic fails me. Read the blood work-up with a bottle of scotch."

"That bad, huh?" Cage closed the file, his composure returning.

"That good," Gordon replied hauntingly. "By the way, the bullet's missing."

"Do you need this?" Cage waved the file at him.

"It's your copy. I have all I can handle, thank you very much. And I'm not coping well as it is. The file I gave Locke is incomplete."

"I'll keep him off your back and buy us time to review your findings. We'll figure out where to go from here. Until then—"

"I know," Gordon offered dryly. "I sleep with the dead."

"Did you determine TOD?"

"Fifteen hundred," Gordon replied.

After outlining certain precautions, Cage headed for the exit. Before activating the lock release, he insisted Gordon view the exterior hallway on his computer to ensure no one lurked beyond the doorway.

Gordon gave him a look he read instantly. "What aren't you saying?"

"It's not that...you know he researched this extensively, even called me about it once or twice." Gordon's face registered a deepening fear.

"Who? Researched what?" Cage demanded.

"Micael Valeric. He delved into a belief that scientific advancement would tip the scales of faith. He spent his later years reviewing every credible document he could get his hands on that supported his theory." Gordon stood frozen between the exit and the body, glancing at both.

"What theory is that?" Something about this line of conversation disturbed Cage more than the evidence within reach.

"If we went too far..." Gordon turned and fixated on the body as his voice trailed him. "If we screwed it up, crossed too many lines...someone watching it all might step in."

"You're not buying into that?" Something about being away from the room pulled at Cage in uncomfortable ways.

"Whatever you're going to do, please do it quickly," Gordon pleaded.

"When do you have dinner?" Cage snapped back into delegation mode.

"When do I have dinner?" Gordon wasn't following.

"We can't afford suspicion. Locke's watching every move you make."

"I normally leave in a half hour for the dining floor."

"Not tonight. I'll make your excuses and bring you something to eat. There'll be no more access through ordinary channels. I'll get back as soon as I can."

"Don't bother with the food. I lost my appetite some time ago," Gordon admitted.

"Remember what we discussed, LG," Cage emphasized. "No one but me gets through that door alive."

Gordon stepped back, retreating further into the room as Cage crossed the threshold. The cold, thick, metal door that once offered isolated security slammed shut with an unforgiving slide and thunk. Heavy bolts, present every three inches, engaged with calculated precision. The burst of suction sounded like the slam of a judge's gavel sealing his fate, condemning him. The problem was, he didn't know what crime he'd committed to deserve such a sentence.

Facing away from the gray steel, Gordon's attention returned to the body.

"Now what?" he asked the lifeless flesh.

No answer, and none expected. Curiosity lured him to the table. Tentatively, he placed one hand on Chris' still chest.

Cage was right. It *was* warm.

Cage walked the expanse of the long hallway back to the elevator with Chris' file clenched under his left arm. Inside the dark metal shaft, he pressed the button for his office floor. The doors shut, and ascending floor numbers flashed by overhead, bringing the reality of his situation ever nearer. He knew what he must do.

Ding, ding.

Before leaving the shelter of the iron cell, he reached for his sidearm and popped open the stiff latch of his gun holster, exposing the top of his government issue Colt .45.

He never left the safety on his weapon. Such precautions demanded time. Time had just run out.

56

CAT STEALTHY, Nick maneuvered beneath lazy eyes. He'd memorized Mason's number from the one time Cage dialed it in his presence. He lifted a cell phone off an unsuspecting soldier. And, though it demanded craft, convinced Cage to authorize a trip to the surface for a half hour to breathe unprocessed air.

Maintaining a stable connection forty floors below land level was more than a slight bit tricky. Nick needed to be topside for the call.

"I'd prefer to be alone," he told his burly escort.

"I have orders. We go back at 1500 hours," the guard said.

"At ease, solider." Nick ran a hand through his wavy hair and squinted, adjusting to the harsh climate. "We're surrounded by miles of desert. Where could I go?"

"No more than fifty feet, sir."

Nick sauntered across the tarmac, knowing in a few strides, his conversation would be drowned out by the jet engines of nearby planes.

"Just checking out your hardware." Nick gestured to a nearby Stealth.

The guard nodded. Despite military obedience, he didn't make an effort to track Nick in the scorching sunlight. He hadn't seen the phone but scanned the barren earth, then shrugged his shoulders as if to say, "Easy target."

Once far enough away for his collar to conceal the small cell phone, Nick auto-dialed the number. Stone picked up on the third ring.

"Stone."

"Mason Stone?" Nick asked.

"Yep, who's this?"

"The only friend you have this side of the military and the last person you'd imagine. There's no time. You'll want to listen if you value your life and the lives of your family."

"Who are you?" Mason asked.

"Ray's in custody. It's not a matter of justice. They don't need to study her, and they sure as hell don't give a damn about the people she offed. They simply require her services. I don't know how much of the puzzle you've put together. And I don't know how much your nephew, Chris, explained to you. Whatever you know, it's only the first card dealt in this hand."

Nick's words had wings. There was no guarantee of when, or even if, he'd be able to make another call. He didn't leave enough air space for Mason to interrupt.

"Your nephew's body is being held under the strictest security measures. I don't think Cage is even allowed access, which means they've unlocked the mystery, or at least part of it. They know what Ray is capable of. She has become indispensable."

"She may be a valuable weapon, but—" Mason interjected.

"They've never had any intention of using her as an assassin. You're way off base. The reason they panicked over her private war wasn't due to a rising body count. They didn't want her getting her hands dirty...or damaged. Those hands are designed to hold life or death. They're sacred. Her purpose doesn't lie in being a programmed killer."

"What the hell are you saying?" Mason's voice disclosed mounting frustration. "And who the hell are you?"

"She's a doctor, Stone. Not just any doctor. *The* doctor. He's sick. She's the only one capable of saving him. The men around him invested too much to allow him to fail because of something as pathetic as death. I'm telling you, it's not over. It's just begun. She knows what they need her for. She'll use it as leverage, and she'll escape. It's a matter of time. You are not safe. Your family isn't safe. Kyly isn't safe. When she negotiates her freedom..."

Nick paused while empty air fell heavy across the line.

"She'll come straight at you."

"They won't let her out," Mason argued. "They can't."

"They won't have any choice. She's holding all the cards. Everyone who crosses her path falls prey to her will," Nick promised. "Stone?"

"I'm listening."

"This is your warning. She doesn't believe in mercy, I'd know."

"How's that?" Mason asked.

"I'm the closest thing to family she has. I'm her brother Nick."

The line went dead. No more battery. No more time.

———

In a wingback leather chair, Mason sat staring out the window with the phone in his hand. Its dial tone hummed like a high-tension wire. It didn't register. What did Nick mean by *The* doctor? Who was sick? And how exactly was Ray holding all the cards?

Mason remembered the man who got out of the chopper when Ray was apprehended—six-three, coffee-colored hair like Ray's, and over-confident. It made sense. Military training, official but dressed down, and the one man Ray smiled at.

Her brother.

Adding this new piece of information to an already complex puzzle didn't bring clarity. It painted a scarier picture. Unwillingly, his family had been cast into a Greek tragedy. He replaced the receiver and cradled his head in his hands.

"Let who out?" Kyly asked from behind him.

Rubbing the back of his neck, he came up smiling. "You're so beautiful," he said.

"No charming your way out of this one. Let who out?" she repeated.

"Ray. One of my buddies in the service says he thinks they may transfer her out of maximum security. I told him, there's no way." He twisted the truth.

"There isn't, is there?" she worried. "I mean, there isn't a chance..."

He stood towering over her, held her tight in his arms, and kissed her. He couldn't tell her. Not yet. Not until he'd confirmed.

"I don't think we should worry until we have good reason," he said.

"If there is a reason, tell me." Kyly's slender frame stiffened beneath his hands. "Don't keep me in the dark."

"If anything solid materializes, you'll be the first to know."

———

Mason brushed by a drift of indoor trees inside the library's atrium and spotted his mark buried behind a stack of historical text. Closing the distance, Ash caught him in his peripheral and waved him over without taking his eyes off the open book of interest.

Seated at the far back table, with a lovely view of the landscaping central to the building's new appeal, he'd filled two seats with his wreckage of backpack and hoodies to ensure privacy.

"Good to see ya. I have the results. Thought you'd want them right away," Ash said.

"Quick turnaround," Mason complimented.

"You're one customer I hate to keep waiting," Ash admitted.

Having a forensic scientist on speed dial had its advantages. The fact he had been a child protégé, one of the best in the business, reinforced the value of their alliance. Mason helped him find anonymity, so Ash kept his secrets in kind.

"So give me the lowdown, brainchild," Mason said, plucking a nearby chair off the floor and placing it within whisper zone.

"What I can say, unequivocally, is I'd like to get my hands on the full page before the Vatican sanctifies it."

"Who said anything about the Vatican being involved?"

"Oh, come on, I thought you trusted me. I know you have your code of secrecy and all—"

"This has nothing to do with any code or any church," Mason replied, confused.

"Not yet. Give it time," Ash said, making a tunnel between them with his collection of books.

Mason leaned in. "What are you talking about? I've had my share of cryptic conversations today. Are you going to tell me the results or not?"

"You really don't know anything about this?" Ash's tone became serious, and he glanced around his stacks, confirming the safety of their isolated corner.

"It kind of fell into my possession." Mason shifted his weight. "The results, Ash?"

"The substance is a form of parchment developed and used over two thousand years ago," Ash began.

"Could it be manufactured today?"

"I'd assume there are labs capable of it." Ash pushed his heavy glasses back up the bridge of his nose.

"Where? How do I find out who made it?"

"That's complicated."

"It can't be that difficult. I'm sure it's not a particularly common practice, but—"

"You could find a manufacturer to replicate it, but that's not going to help you find out who made this."

"What do you mean?"

"The piece of parchment you sent me isn't a replica. It's over two thousand years old," Ash explained. "It's the real deal. And it doesn't take my IQ to realize the implications. I ran it three times, solid results. I also carbon dated the ink. Same era."

"That's not possible," Mason whispered under his breath as a thin line of sweat formed across his back. He looked out the window. The serene view wasn't helping. "I'd buy the parchment being original. I can see that as possible, but not the ink. Someone is toying with this."

"I threw everything I have at the sample, and I happen to know a little bit about this. It *is* possible. My results are indisputable. The only ink on record that's a close match is on the Dead Sea Scrolls. I don't need to tell you the awkwardness of confirming *that* without giving anything away. I flat out lied my ass off." Ash deked out from behind his books to scan for intruders and then settled back into his tunnel. "I *can* say with absolute certainty what you have in your possession is a valid piece of history. Only the smudged name at the bottom is from this era. If this is a forgery, whoever is responsible has better contacts and a higher IQ than mine. And that's saying something. I'm worried for you."

The kid was more jittery than normal. "Ash, you haven't shown—"

"Never, big guy. It's our secret."

"I owe you," Mason said. "We'll meet again soon. In the meantime, keep it safe."

"I've just the place. Watch your back, Stone." Ash slid the book tunnel closed as Mason stood. Disappearing back into the comfort of facts. Mason wished he could do the same but there was no comfort to the facts mounting against him.

There had to be a logical explanation. To find it, he had to pry open the rest of the blood-soaked paper and expose the writing inside.

Walking heavy-footed back to his truck, he swallowed hard on Ash's results.

———

The warm scent of aged paper. The smell associated with books left too long on the shelves lingered in Mason's nostrils. An aroma unleashed at the first crack of interest.

Like opening an ancient Bible, the zip lock baggy released a musty scent. Strange. Peculiar a paper received only a day prior, blood stained and locked away from air would emit the perfume of a sage's text. Yet, it did.

It lacked the pungent, sour smell that, under any other circumstances, accompanied blood. Or, perhaps, that was all in his head.

Under the dim light of a tiny desk lamp angled over the contents, he extracted the crumpled parchment out of the bag with the aid of tweezers.

Rich paper, smoldering brownish gold. There were areas burned crimson by his nephew's last fleeting moments. He tried not to think of that. He unraveled the crinkled mass with the aid of Q-tips. The blood remained tacky. Not dry, sticky, and resistant.

The sun had fallen from the sky, leaving the room illuminated by mild moonbeams, casting a Herculean shadow of Mason's form hunched over the tiny paper.

He struggled to unfold each wrinkled section one at a time. Labored minutes passed before the slightest hint of text became visible. He couldn't read it. Symbols more than letters, Egyptian to the untrained eye. All his attention became wrapped within the creased paper between his hands.

He didn't hear Kyly enter the room. It wasn't until a large piece of the bottom right section laid flat, revealing the signature of its intended owner, that his eyes searched the ceiling in astonishment to glimpse he wasn't alone. Kyly loomed over him.

Blood had washed away three letters of his nephew's name, leaving six legible, which would've appeared unimportant if not for the pattern the stain left behind. The ink was not new but not by any means ancient and differed in language and handwriting from the rest. The last three letters were missing. Damage left the letter signed not by Christian but by **Christ**.

Without a word, Kyly reached across the desk in front of him, grasped the paper in her hand, and turned it in her direction. Untrusting of her own eyes, she sought a closer inspection. It remained, clear in heavy ink, the letters C H R I S T.

Staring up at Kyly, her confounded expression mirrored his own.

"I see it, too," he said. "The remaining letters have been smudged away and..."

Before he could finish, she bent over, gagging. With quick hands, Mason rushed the wastepaper bucket to her. "Still nauseous, hey?" Her concussion worried him.

"Christ." She fought for voice. "It fits in so many ways though, doesn't it?"

He stared at the paper and her.

Locking hands onto the desk's edge for support, Kyly threw up repeatedly before he could pull her from the office and usher her down the hall and into the washroom.

Cradled in the soft glow of a 20-watt bulb, an ancient message lay crumpled and abandoned in the silence of the empty room.

Even as he held her, rubbed her back, and pressed a cold cloth to her forehead, he knew her reaction was warranted. They had experienced only a taste of what they were yet to endure. Kyly's body shook and quivered beneath his hands. Tremors they shared. An earthquake erupted in Mason's chest cavity. She was right. It fit.

"He said he only had the days he was meant to fulfill like he wouldn't be granted more time," she whispered. "Do you think he knew he'd be killed?"

"I don't know. Every time I think I have a handle on this, a new piece throws me. I know there's more to it."

The parchment dated back two thousand years. The ink that flowed from pen to paper originated from Galilee. It was draped in mystery, and the same could be said about the man who had handed it to Kyly.

An untold discovery resonated from the depths of their situation. It wouldn't be silenced. It was simply a matter of time before the rest of the world heard its echo.

57

RIGID. Cold. And lifeless as ice.

This constituted a fitting description of the tainted politician and the hands he stared at.

His once agile fingers were now frozen, feeble digits. The buoyancy of youth long since receded. Wrinkles and weathered skin that lay in its stead were hard earned. He would've celebrated it, rejoiced at the tell-tale signs of experience, if the disease hadn't also eaten away his life force along with his zest for living.

The entourage left him alone in the room, save for his right-hand man Alerio—he knew everything.

"You should brace yourself, sir. They say it's graphic."

Alerio stood by him through all of it, dating back to the first campaign trail. Sometimes, he wondered why his trusted confidant was content to remain in the shadows. His capabilities were extensive. Other times, it became blatantly apparent his was the wiser path of the two.

Carefully, Alerio handed him hot coffee, his eyes revealing sympathy despite valiant efforts to conceal it.

"I'm okay, Al. Start the film," he instructed.

"Yes, sir."

Hours of painstaking work had edited hundreds of minutes of tape down to this three-hour film. It contained the most pertinent information, with an added narration from the head of his surgical team. Nowadays, thanks to the Discovery Channel, even children had hardened to watching graphic operations seemingly anesthetized.

It was one thing to watch a random dissection. Quite another to foresee the invasion soon to be inflicted upon your own flesh.

If illness shadowed him publicly, he masked it with a beaming persona gifted in the art of deception. For over six months, he'd performed as the perfect picture of health, a living testament to strength and self-assurance. It was expected, and the world believed.

Acting was a requirement for anyone in politics. Blood, sweat, or tears? Yes. Visible? Never. He wasn't alone. Kennedy and Addison's disease, Reagan and Alzheimer's. Lincoln's brush with malaria, small-pox, and depression to name a few of the great pretenders. Lately, his symptoms ravaged him in an arpeggio of pain—one affliction after the other. Too difficult a lead.

He didn't want to play anymore.

Just to close his eyes, he fantasized, to feel no more pain, no more weakness.

With effort, he swallowed the thoughts down with steaming coffee as images flooded the screen.

Ray was quite beautiful. Depicted in operating room scrubs amid the unpleasantness of surgery, she glimmered across the screen's surface.

Strange, given what he knew of her. She appeared compassionate in the care of her patient. He reviewed the crime scene photos of her other handy work, unthinkable—the pretty doctor, a brutal killer with no conscience.

"Masterful," he said, quietly enamored.

"I'm sorry, sir?"

"Nothing, Al."

Like the finest conductor's hands, each precise, fluid movement sang a note in the symphony of salvation. On the screen, death turned to life beneath her fingertips.

It never struck him, the injustice of it.

His eyes saw only the miracle of her delicate hands tearing life from death's grip.

Shakily, he lifted the hot coffee cup again.

His hands were so cold.

In his interpretation, Ray had saved not one but both lives. Replacing what lacked in one through a gesture of goodwill to another. Though, the burden handed to the Cromwell family did not go unnoticed. His situation wouldn't be quite so amicable. No way around that. It's a consequence of his position. No point in dwelling on the unavoidable.

When they reached the transplant portion of the film, the human brain had the consistency of uncooked liver. Alerio hated liver—a fact he'd reiterated over the years. Still, he stomached the graphic images in silence. His disgust emanated from him nonetheless.

"You can leave for this part, Al," he offered.

"No, sir. I'll stay with you," Alerio said. "She's an abomination."

"Al?" he disagreed but understood.

"You see what she's willing to do," Al warned. "No one knows how far. After you, no further."

"We have contingencies in place, but we can't undo her. She exists. No way to backpedal out of this." He stated dryly. The screen captivated his attention. "Everything we truly are." He resented the frailty of his voice.

"Sir?"

"She's holding the summation of human existence in her hands. The intellect is all that sets us apart."

"No, sir," Al corrected. "There's no heart involved in this procedure."

———

Sea salt clung to the air.

One lick of her lips and Ray could taste it.

It stuck to the ground.

With every step, its gritty residue transferred onto her bare feet. Washing in, overshadowing every scent it perfumed. A dusty white film covered, indiscriminately, everything inland. A haunting mist crept in, silently polluting.

She'd visited this place so many times before to contemplate life, and destiny. Never, until now, had she been there in her dreams. Recognizing the walkway to the ocean's edge, the stone path, and the lookouts, she became aware her subconscious had drawn her back to that one moment of consideration.

Why now? Micael was dead, this time without reprieve.

The dream mirrored that first night he died. The ominous storm, its gale force winds pushing in off the water, turning the waves into lashing mountains of black crude.

The frigid breeze matched the chill in her heart, icy reminders of a cold, unforgiving world.

One after the other, her footsteps led her to the dock's end. Further and further out to sea until the storm all but swallowed her into its bleak void. Anger swirled around her, whipping her for her sins.

Before, she was brazen and brash. Adding her fury back into the night, howling and screaming defiant protests. Here, in her dream, she stood silent beneath Mother Nature's vengeance.

"Do with me what you will." became her motto. This time, she wasn't so impervious.

Answering without warning, a wave of intense magnitude was back-built until it stood fifty feet high. It crashed down with the force worthy of the wrath of God.

She woke in her cell, coughing imaginary water from her lungs, gasping for air.

"Ah, you're awake. Perfect." Locke's sniveling voice filtered through the air ducts in the outer glass wall. Three inches in diameter, ten feet from the ground, thirteen holes were placed a foot apart. They spanned the length of the cell front, allowing for crystal clear conversation between prisoner and patron. Ray wished the glass would solidify.

"Missed watching me sleep?" she asked.

"Never again," Locke said triumphantly.

"Never say never. You can't see in the dark." She paused for effect. "But I can."

Stretching, she slid out of the cot located at the far end fifteen feet from him. Hers was the voice of darkness. With the security light dimmed at its entrance, the room's layout concealed her.

Locke, wobbled on an interrogation chair beneath a hallway light, depicted an illuminated portrait of failure, sloppy and sleazy.

"I expected visitors." She rested against the wall behind her bed. "Just not quite so soon. Aching for me, huh?"

"Oh, I wouldn't go that far."

"Really. What else would force you to sneak out in the middle of the night and bribe guards to have a moment alone with me?"

"You know why I'm here," Locke shot back in a heated whisper.

"Yes, I do," she said, her tone sinister.

"I'm not prepared to have everyone in this place angle for control over this situation! I—"

"Own me. Isn't that what you were going to say? You have too much invested in me to lose what's coming to you. I understand, believe me."

Fool, he almost *did* believe her. His pause made her break out in laughter.

"There is nothing remotely funny about this," he snapped.

"You ought to see it from this side of the glass."

He shifted in his seat, crossed his legs, and then uncrossed them, swiveling the other direction. It was so easy to unnerve him.

He *was* visiting her without approval, which was against protocol. The moment he stepped into the maximum-security hallway, his ass was on the line. And she was right; he *had* bribed a guard for clearance. There was no other way in.

"I think you're sweating," she said. "I can smell salt in the air."

He hated her. She hated him more.

Like a wolf, her fine-tuned senses fed off his fear. It wasn't the consequences of breaching security scaring him. It was her. She'd always had that effect on him. Her memory served up an image of him, a high school senior, avoiding her coal eyes when he passed her chamber in his father's lab. He knew her blackened core, its potential. And she held close all he'd suffered upon her. She *would* kill him. She'd hunt down everyone who crossed her and exact revenge.

"It's a simple dilemma." She rose from her perch in the darkness. "You need me to secure your fame and fortune—topple dear old Daddy's record once and for all—I need to get the hell out of this place. Perhaps a trade's in order."

"I can't trust you to follow through. Besides, breaking you outta here would take no small measure."

"Tsk, tsk, the mire of pessimism. You'll find a way. For your effort, you'll have my loyalty. After all, you're my salvation from a life of probing. You know, been there, done that. Wasn't much fun. This is your one chance to redeem yourself."

"What assurances do I have you'll perform?" He stood near the glass, eyes darting neurotically, desperate to pierce the darkness.

"Don't let me go until after the surgery. You get what you need, I get what I need, but don't consider failing me," she hissed, a viper ready to strike.

"If you do..."

She waited until his face pressed hard against the four-inch-thick glass wall, searching in vain to see her outline lurking at the back of the cell. Her voice bounced off the transparent walls, making it impossible to determine its origin.

Slam!

Her fist hit the glass wall hard enough for impact waves to reverberate into his chest cavity. The smack landed where his shriveled heart lay, thrusting it into overdrive by shock.

"I'll destroy you like a Category 5."

There, then gone, swallowed by shadows.

"Run along, Lanky Locke, before they suspect something's amiss."

Leaving his pride and the lingering scent of perspiration behind, Locke fled the maximum-security corridor.

————

Locke's heart rate was racing when he returned to his living quarters. Shaking, he pulled up the computer and accessed the program monitoring Ray. Every aspect of her existence was under the proverbial microscope. The device taped to her chest confirmed *her* heart rate remained steady, an optimal rhythm, unaffected by his initial intrusion or their heated negotiation.

She *was* a masterpiece.

He couldn't help but admire the biological perfection.

After erasing the fifteen minutes of tape that spanned their meeting, he rummaged through the medicine cabinet, desperate for Xanax. Thirty minutes later, the drug kicked in.

He dreamed of making the cover of Fortune magazine. It wasn't good. Half his face was missing in the photo, and the caption read,

'*Genius in Genetics, Victim of His Own Design.*' He sat bolt upright, cold sweat adhering the silk nightshirt to his pasty skin.

Changing into jersey PJ's, he brought up Ray's cell on his monitor. Several floors below, in a concrete cage in the darkness, she stretched under the sheets. The camera's night vision feature allowed him a closer look at her. She shifted positions, staring into the lens. He wondered if she suspected he'd be watching.

Her voice echoed in stereo, "Sweet dreams, Simpleton."

She hated him.

She'd stolen his father's attention for over a decade, the most formative years. And rejected him countless times.

He hated her more.

———

In another area of the compound, unbeknownst to either Locke or Ray, Cage echoed Ray's sentiment as he stared down at Locke's employee dossier.

In a T-shirt and boxers, smoke wafting around him, Cage poured over classified files on those involved. He prioritized people and events initially from his own perspective, then as interpreted by other key players. By 0500 hours, he'd devised a plan. One hour later, he executed it.

Freshly shaven after an ice-cold shower, he dressed in his meticulously pressed uniform. It stood at attention without starch. He glanced for a split second at the image in the mirror. His intimidating demeanor left the room before him, overshadowing all his finer elements. A necessary persona he accepted.

He had to speak to Ray alone. Her contempt targeted everyone except Nick. What wasn't so obvious was how much she knew about Christian Cromwell. He'd watched the operation tapes, confiscated from Ray's office when he stormed the island property, long before anyone else got their hands on them. He absorbed the highlights and had seen enough. He'd also located the hidden equipment used to preserve Christian's body until it was needed. Ray's improvements on Dr. Valeric's design enhanced the body's perfection in ways never deemed possible.

Chris hadn't given anything away. There was no indication of who he really was or what he *remembered* if you could call it that. But Cage needed to be sure.

He found the elevator abandoned.

Wearing an interference device to cause static sufficient to disable the recording system, Cage approached the holding area.

"At ease, soldier. I have to talk to our prisoner," Cage said.

"Yes, sir."

The armed guard stepped aside while Cage swiped a security card through a detector, placed his palm on a scanner for confirmation, and gave his name and rank to a voice identifier. A series of bolt-action locks disengaged. Passing a row of empty cells, Cage's footsteps echoed back at him.

"Good morning, Cage," Ray said long before he was within view.

"Hello, Wild Thing. How're they treating you?"

"Like a prisoner. Can you believe that?"

"You did kill a handful of innocent people."

She stepped close to the glass, leaving breath marks. "No one is *that* innocent."

"Here to talk business." He flipped the provided chair around and sat facing its backrest. She retreated. "Locke's not going to spring you, honey. His days of—how did you put it—*toppling dear old Daddy* are over." She spun to meet his gaze. He gave her no time to process. "Couldn't sleep," he continued. "You'd be amazed what's playing on night monitors these days."

Ray stood immobile, black eyes fixed on the adjacent wall.

"The chief needs your services, and you know it. What I want to know is if your war is over or if I'm going to have to hunt you down again."

"He's dead, isn't he?" Ray's voice could've cast a chill in a meat locker.

"Cold as the steel slab he's lying on," Cage confirmed. "What about the others? You able to square with that?"

"They wanted their kid back. The family's safe."

"All of them? What about Stone? He stole him off the island. I figured you'd take that personally."

"He made the chase more interesting," Ray said. "If I wanted to, I could've killed him a long time ago."

"Fine. And the reporter?" Ray paced at the mention of Kyly. Cage twisted his head, following her movements, reading her hatred. A pirate's grin turned up the left side of his mouth. "Struck a nerve, huh?"

"*She* isn't family," Ray said with contempt, spinning back around.

"*She* is off limits. You want your freedom. You work for me and with me. You cross me, and I'll shred you in the time it takes to blink."

Ray approached the glass wall. "I don't think your superiors would approve of you threatening me."

"It's not them you have to worry about." Cage stood eye to eye. "He breached her black barriers with raw intention. Make no mistake, little girl, *I* am your gatekeeper. I can free you or condemn you to hell. What's it going to be?"

Ray said nothing; she lowered her black eyes from his.

"Eighteen hundred," he said, not pulling back. "And Ray...be polite."

A grin crept across her face as he moved away from the cell.

"Get the prisoner fed, showered, and shiny," he told the guard at the far end of the hall. "Open the gate."

58

MASON PULLED onto Oscar's family estate, spitting gravel behind him. Oscar was a trusted friend and an expert interpreter of ancient languages. Hidden amid a productive vineyard, Oscar occupied a historical barn turned eclectic, ancient archive, laboratory, and wine-tasting cellar. Having deviated from the family business, he told Mason he considered himself fortunate not to be evicted from the property altogether.

Though not tailored, traditional, or in the least bit well kept, Mason found Oscar's residence the most inviting of the six estate homes. Isolated far off from the other clustered houses, it bordered the back west edge of the land.

Dust swirled and encircled the truck as Mason came to a stop, engulfing the vehicle in a cough-inducing cloud. When the air cleared, it gave way to a vineyard vision out of time. Original barn doors, modified with glasswork, denoted a common entrance, welcoming visitors into the aged structure. A stone pathway preceded it, then snaked up its walls, accenting arches and window boxes. Its appearance and aroma were vintage and the perfect place for Oscar's prized wine collection.

"Stone, how the hell are ya?" Oscar leaned out the doorway with an opened, half-emptied bottle of wine. "Started without ya. Better come in and catch up!"

In a tattered sweater, homegrown distressed jeans, disheveled hair, and three days of uneven growth over his lip and chin, he seemed an ill fit for the crisp, pristine white lab coat draped over top. It was standard attire for Oscar. He was a sight for sore eyes.

"I need you sober for this one." Mason climbed out of the cab. "When you're done, I have a sneaking suspicion we'll both need a bottle or two."

"Sounds like a plan. Come on in."

Casual and unpretentious, Oscar was entirely serious about his work. So much so he lived surrounded and consumed by it. This explained his fifty years of bachelorhood and the organized chaos decorating every aspect of his life.

"You need to hire a maid," Mason joked.

"We bachelors have no need." Oscar handed Mason a glass he wiped off with the bottom edge of his shirt.

"Sure it's safe? I wouldn't want to catch whatever you're suffering from."

"With what I'm pouring into it, any bacteria that survives has a god given right to its existence," Oscar proudly proclaimed.

Mason laughed and held out the dirty chalice to be filled.

"So let's have a look." Oscar walked through the kitchen into an open laboratory that doubled as his living room. Strange, but fitting.

Stepping strategically through the mire of strewn papers, lab texts, and empty bottles, Mason cleared an area and placed the parchment on top of the examining table. Oscar set his wine aside, freeing his hands to adjust a soft overhead light and gather the meager equipment necessary for a thorough inspection. A matter of seconds passed before Oscar lost his lighthearted demeanor, froze over the image, and stared up at Mason through the top rim of his glasses.

"Where did you get this?" he asked, his voice void of all humor.

"I can't say."

"Who else has seen it?" He leaned in closer to the specimen.

"No one."

"Keep it that way. I don't think I even want to know how you came to have this in your possession, but I strongly suggest you safeguard it," Oscar warned.

"Because of what it says?"

"Because of how it says it. The language interwoven within the English text is a specific form of Aramaic."

"Aramaic?"

"It's the language spoken over two thousand years ago in Galilee, around the time of Jesus. And you said it was dated back to that era?"

"Yes," Mason confirmed.

"This message is an improbability and unnerving and unbelievable." Oscar loomed over the paper for several minutes before coming up for air.

"I don't know what to tell you, Stone. I can't explain this. I wouldn't believe it myself if I wasn't seeing it through my own eyes. And I'll wake up tomorrow with a hangover and convince myself it was a dream."

"Can you tell me what it says?"

"I can interpret the words."

"Do that. At least I'll know that much." Mason ran a hand through his hair and walked in a circle, coming back to the table no less anxious.

Oscar stared up. Distress loomed behind blue eyes. "Are you sure you want to?"

"I don't have a choice."

"Aramaic comes from a different basis of thinking, so its translation isn't black and white. For example, the first word, Hokhmah, refers to Holy Wisdom. It's a crucial feminine archetype, one largely neglected throughout the history of Christianity."

"It's the name of a woman?" Mason hated sounding ignorant but valued clarity more than pride.

"The Greek called her Sophia, but no. It's more a descriptive process of acquiring Holy Wisdom. There's a sea of background to understanding this dialect," Oscar explained.

Mason leaned his large frame closer, resting his elbows on the table. "I suppose you'll have to give me the crash course."

"Here, when He says, 'Child of God, Haimanuta.' He's asking the child of God, whomever that may be, to have faith. Peshitta is easier to interpret. It means simple, true, straight," Oscar continued.

"Well, which is it?" Mason asked.

"That's my point." Oscar looked up from a magnification loupe he held over his right eye to further inspect the handwriting. "Its meaning encompasses all of them."

He glanced down again, then stood, blinking repeatedly and refocusing his eyes.

"At the end, the sign-off 'Ethphatah' is both an instruction and a practice Christ used when performing miraculous cures. Eth-phatah means to 'be open.' Jesus said this in preparation for divine healing. Ptah, a portion of the word, is rooted deep in Egyptian history, where it named a god they considered the open mouth from which all creation flowed. The full Aramaic expression's translation could mean to 'be open to the healing wisdom of God,' 'to expand,' 'clear the way for' and such. In this context, I'd read its general meaning as an instruction and advancement that changes and expands the knowledge and capabilities of the human race.. There's a warning."

"Warning for what?" Mason asked, mystified.

"There's much more here than missing words you can't decipher. Aside from the fact that it's attributed to Christ, the manipulation of the language reveals a powerful, multifaceted purpose underlying the message on the surface."

"You're the expert, Oscar. I'm afraid there's little I can offer. What I can guarantee you is it wasn't signed by Jesus."

"I never said it was signed by Jesus. This has little or nothing to do with Him. You're going to have to pay closer attention if you want to understand what I'm telling you," Oscar scolded.

"Sorry."

"I said it's attributed to Christ. There wasn't one, but several messiahs, anointed ones, who used that title at the time of Jesus—either self-acquired or issued upon them by followers. In general, it was reserved for a messenger, but in this context, it refers specifically to one who holds medical wisdom of our intended nature. It's promising a path to eternal life, but not in theory as an afterlife but here. Physical renewal. It is far less spiritual and far more practical. 'For those who stumble on this discovery.'"

"This discovery?"

"Yes, one worth guarding and intentionally hidden until now." Stepping back to reclaim the wine bottle and top up Mason's glass, Oscar became solemn, "You drink, I'll interpret." He poured wine into the goblet, wiped the edge with a clean white cloth, and offered it back.

"To the blood of Christ," he toasted with grave sincerity.

"Man," Mason replied. The wine lost its flavor.

Oscar hauled out a dozen books on the language and the historical significance of each word. After three painstaking hours, he covered as much territory as Mason could comprehend and more than he wanted to know.

When Mason's truck pulled out of the dirt driveway, both men were weary. Oscar collapsed in his favorite chair with a copy of the precious letter and a new bottle of red wine. Mason drove away with a heavy heart and a full case of Oscar's family's latest batch. Despite protests, Oscar insisted he not leave without it.

Hours later, back at his house, under frail candlelight in the living room, one of the bottles sat unopened on the coffee table beside him. Holding the parchment, absorbing its contents, he couldn't help being impacted by what he read between the lines.

Kyly remained unaware; he delayed telling her. He'd have to soon. He wanted to give her one night of peace. One night to sleep in the blissful illusion that the nightmare had ended.

One night to breathe a sigh of—

Dunnunununa, dunnunununa.

His business line sounded out a high-pitched ring that flew through the air across the roofline and rebounded off the outer walls.

Dunnunununa, dunnunununa.

He couldn't reach the desk before it repeated, severing the silence. Nerves plastered to the soft white ceiling, Mason fumbled into the receiver, "Stone."

From the adjacent bedroom, Kyly shuffled in half-awake. Choosing an uncomfortable perch on the edge of his desk, she listened to his curt responses.

"How the hell did that happen?" Mason barked into the line. "Why would you even consider that...you couldn't come up with anything better? Where is she now?"

The implications of Mason's response weighed heavy. When he didn't offer clarity, Kyly left for the washroom down the hall. Walking back a short time later, she paused by the parchment and a mound of wax that was once a full-length candle. Taking the paper with her, she returned to him with it outstretched in her hand. The phone rested back in its cradle.

"It's not over, is it?" she asked.

"No, Lee, it's not over," he admitted, rising from behind his desk to hold her.

"Tell me." She pulled back to face him.

He couldn't soften the blow, and he couldn't keep it from her. "Ray's been released from her cell."

"What? Why?" Her brow dipped into a mass of anger.

"She's confined to the compound, and she's not allowed surface clearance—"

"Surface clearance? The woman should be thrown in front of a firing squad." Her heated words, barely absorbed, were followed by a contemplative whisper. "You can't heal a wound by cutting it open further."

"She should meet her maker," Mason said, lost in regret. "I should've made sure...cutting what?"

She didn't respond.

"Lee...Lee?" he repeated before getting her attention.

"What?" she asked, confused.

"Are you okay?"

"No! I'm not okay!" she snapped back. "None of us are okay! We'll never be okay if that woman escapes custody, and it sounds like she's halfway there."

Ray's release was imminent. Nick warned Mason of the coming turn of events. What once seemed implausible had gained ground.

"We need to stay calm, think this through," he cautioned. "She's a thousand miles from here, under armed guard. They won't let her out. They need her."

"Need her for what?"

"I'm not sure." He escorted her down the hall. "We don't have all the pieces yet. Come with me."

"Who are you getting this information from?" she argued. "And where are you taking me?"

"To the kitchen, tea. This could take a while."

"I don't want tea. What I need is a drink and answers."

Being ushered ahead of him, Kyly grabbed the wine bottle off the table as they passed en route to the kitchen. Picking up pace, he lost contact as she stomped to the utensil drawer and pulled out a corkscrew.

"Put it down," he said. "Lee."

"Why?" she asked, her tone softening. It wasn't him she was angry with.

"I'm making us tea," he replied. "That's not a good idea."

Disquiet laced his words.

"Why not? You saving it for a special occasion?"

He confiscated the corkscrew. "You're healing from a concussion." He pushed the wine bottle to the back of the counter and led her to a chair.

Without answering, he removed the plastic bag she had forgotten lay clasped in her left hand. He set it in front of her with such precaution it could've been constructed of thin glass and not have sustained adequate impact to fracture.

"I need you to stay calm." His eyes said what he couldn't.

Staring at the parchment in the dark of the room, Kyly whispered, "I can't make out the writing." Her attention was fixed on the unusual, frail paper. "What does it say? Mason...what does it say?"

"It says unraveling our genetic code is a certainty, and it will lead to a new race and a new way of life and disaster."

59

RAY DIDN'T MIND that Alerio insisted on keeping her shackled. His high-profile boss disagreed but indulged him. He'd been persistent in his justification. Seated in an oversized chair that accentuated her small frame, she appeared timid and harmless. With her injured arm wrapped in white gauze and her long raven hair and dark lashes, she evoked the image of a fallen black bird with a broken wing exactly as she intended.

"It's a pleasure, sir," she said. "I watched your election with much anticipation."

"Yeah, right," Al murmured. Her indifference to him was eroding.

"Thank you," her distinguished captor said. "What do you prefer to be called?"

"Ray is fine. I'm an Anthropogenic Mortal." She glanced to Alerio, suggesting it was he who required clarification. "A manmade human being." Then back to the man in charge, "My official name has thirty-seven syllables, which I find rather daunting. Doctor Locke's idea, I suppose."

"Ray, I brought you here to speak with me in private because, as I'm sure you've gathered, we have a great deal to discuss."

"The surgery is for you," she said, wanting to gauge his reaction.

"Yes."

"How long?"

"They've given me six weeks before the symptoms heighten and become unmanageable. I don't know that to be an accurate estimate," he stated dryly.

"The pain, it has intensified." Her voice was deliberately quiet, weighing conclusions.

She admired the man. He'd become so accustomed to displaying perfect health that it was difficult for him to attach emotion to the grim reality of his prognosis. Of course, he knew he teetered on the edge of a crumbling cliff. He'd simply become numb to it. Kindred spirit.

"You can't be too careful," she warned. "You've crossed the threshold."

"Yes, it would seem so," he agreed.

"When would you propose I perform the operation?"

"Soon. I'm afraid I have a summit meeting to attend at the beginning of next week. After that, we've blocked out my schedule," he answered matter-of-factly like she was proposing a business luncheon.

"Have you begun preparations?" She stared Alerio down as he pondered a reply.

"Yes. They had me following your medical protocol after receiving that information."

"And the host?"

"Taken care of," Alerio jumped in.

Interesting.

"I'm sorry I wasn't made aware of this sooner. I would've accommodated you," she said.

Al huffed in disbelief and glared down his nose at her. Despite his urging, she wouldn't be provoked into eroding the veil of ivory silk coating her evil blackness.

"I've no reason to break the alliance," she said. "I never wanted to be in this position."

"Then you shouldn't have killed innocent civilians," Al blurted out coldly.

"Alerio," his superior admonished. Al fell silent again.

"I'm sorry you see it that way." Ray never made eye contact with Alerio, priming her attention on the powerful man in the wheelchair ahead of her.

"I've relocated you to a private suite," he said. "You'll still be under lock and key with escorts, but you'll be given privacy while in your quarters. I'm certain you'll feel quite at home. And your medical texts have been transferred from the island, so you'll have access to any relevant information. If there's anything you need, please notify your doorman—he answers to me alone."

"I appreciate this more than you know, sir." Ray spoke carefully. This man's dependency guaranteed her survival.

"We'll have to form a measure of trust, you and I, won't we?" His eyes carried more power than his words.

"Of course," she agreed.

Al scoured the ceiling, mumbling under his breath.

"Al," he ordered. "Kindly escort our guest to her living quarters."

"Gladly, sir," Al replied.

"Sir, one last thing," Ray asked. "Could I see the body?"

"Of Christian Cromwell?" he clarified, surprised by her request.

"Yes."

"I think that would be unwise."

"It's not for the reasons you might suspect. It's research. This procedure has only been successfully executed once. Several integral questions remain. His body may provide answers," she reasoned.

"I'll consider it," he said. "What unanswered questions?"

"You're aware he was removed from my care during recovery? This denied the opportunity to verify the surgery's level of success. It made it impossible to gauge how much of the original memory survived the transplant."

"The Cromwell boy's memory?" he asked.

"No, sir, Dr. Micael Valeric's. Christian Cromwell was a host. Micael's brain lived inside him. And, due to the family's intent to reclaim what they ignorantly assumed was their son, I was never able to confirm to what degree Micael existed. Without that, I can't guarantee your *mental* survival."

"How can staring at a dead man verify his memory?" Al said.

"I can view the brain. Assess the synapses and connective tissue to determine what areas exhibited healthy growth and which, if any, indicated rejection. You'd be amazed at what you can learn from death."

"I'll make arrangements for a viewing tomorrow morning," her new patient agreed. "In truth, I hold very little faith in the surgery's success. In the end, it matters little—at least to me. I'm a dead man either way."

"Sir," Alerio erupted. A glance silenced his protest.

Those around the proud politician, those who depended on his knowledge and popularity to lead them into the future, clung to a positive outcome tooth and nail. He wore the strain of their death grip tearing through his flesh, deep into his very spine, grappling and scraping at the core of him. Ray recognized the look. She'd seen it before. He wanted them to let go. He didn't know there was another way. *Her way.*

"Until tomorrow, then," she said. "Good night, sir, and thank you again."

Summoning Al to his side, he whispered a clandestine order into his ear. Al nodded, then instructed Ray to remain seated while he pushed the wheelchair into an adjacent room equipped with a wall of screens monitoring activity in the compound. From there, even a feeble man could wield tremendous control.

"You are a pathetic actress," Al whispered seconds later as he ushered her outside the corridor and into the hallway.

She didn't respond. He'd bend to her will soon enough. No more indifference.

————

Floors above the safe zone, Cage disabled the security monitoring system in his office as he'd done in his quarters an hour earlier. He couldn't risk Locke checking up on him by hacking into the computer mainframe. And he knew the weasel was capable and motivated to do so.

Radioing one of his men topside, he ordered the custom Hummer fueled, loaded, and waiting. Then, he double-checked the system, keying in coordinates to the parking garage to observe the execution of his request.

As he gathered up the last of the sensitive documents, his phone rang.

Gordon.

In all their years together, through witnessing everything from the bizarre to the blatantly sick, twisted, and ungodly, Gordon had remained reasonably unaffected until now. Quivering over the line, his voice sounded shocked and shaken.

"I don't think I can handle this for much longer," he pleaded. "Locke phones every half hour. He won't stop calling here."

"Don't answer the phone," Cage said.

"It's not that simple, and you know it. If I don't fend him off, he'll insist on coming down here! He's about ready to do that. We can't let that happen."

"Calm down," Cage ordered. "I'll be less than twenty minutes. I have one more stop to make."

"Hurry!"

Cage ended the connection, glanced around his office, and headed for the door. Without his presence, the room was a stark, cold reminder that rewards for service and loyalty were fleeting. A shrine of metals and photos of him shaking hands with the most powerful men in the world adorned the walls. No one would be there to tell the stories, no one who cared. Without his explanation, precedence would be lost.

Checking his watch, he headed for the elevator. A key control locked it off from use by others. When he arrived on Ray's floor, he used this feature. A cryptic catalog of Ray's worst nightmares lay concealed within a locked leather case he'd confiscated from the island. It and other boxes were left safely behind the elevator's thick metal doors.

He couldn't help feeling a certain triumph strolling down the wide passage. He anticipated Ray's astonished expression, and a grin escaped his hardened face. He knew what none of them would ever understand. What she really was and what she desired most. The acceptance she believed could never exist, one only he could give her. The doorman outside her room thanked him for the fifteen-minute break. Cage waited until the man's footsteps receded to a faint echo down the stairwell.

Pounding with adequate intensity to wake a dead man, Cage rapped mercilessly on Ray's door. Conveying, despite the leniency of his superior, her stay would not be a pleasant one. His fist landed the first solid reminder.

A welcoming voice resounded from the opposite side. She expected someone else. Cage loved the element of surprise. Using his security key, he released the lock. As the door drifted inward, he anticipated from which direction she'd strike.

Cornering a cobra was risky business to everyone but a deadlier cobra.

60

LOCKE, on a conference call from hell, snubbed the authority of the devil on the other end with reckless rebellion.

The caller's inability to see him wringing, twisting, and tearing at the once pristine tablecloth in front of him remained his saving grace. Terse, his voice squeaked and ground forth an arthritic compliance. Discontent softened into arrogance awkwardly restrained.

"I've issued Ray a private residence. I expect you to recognize her essential role and accommodate," said the government voice on the other end.

Locke wanted to vomit, but that *would* be obvious over the speakerphone.

Deluded, they failed to realize what they were doing. The language in Locke's head turned the air drifting between his ears a smoky blue. She played them all. They let her, hell, encouraged her to do just that.

He wasn't willing to be one of her pawns.

Outrage clogged his throat, suffocating. And to think, once, not so long ago, she was his caged pet. Now, she had the rich and powerful eating out of her hands.

He couldn't stand for this. He wouldn't.

His teeth clenched around his hatred. In moments, his jaw ached. His words compressed between locked incisors. "I need her local...for clinical reasons. I understand. I wouldn't have chosen this particular avenue, but to alleviate consequences..."

He negotiated his way out of the conversation, careful not to jeopardize himself.

"Your delivery is as transparent and clumsy as your walk, Locke. Your words, like your frame, are far too large for your small-footed intellectual foundation. Just so we avoid confusion...do as you're told and stay out of the way!"

When Locke hung up, red smears soiled the button. He'd dug his eccentric long nails right through the torn cloth and into his palms, lacerating the flesh.

"You'll pay for this," he said.

He paced the room, waiting for the smoke ignited by his foul thoughts to clear. Think. He wasn't dealing with an idiot. The situation was precarious.

"The enemy of my enemy is my friend." His intention, from the day Ray escaped, was to manipulate the circumstance to benefit himself. She would come for him. His only reprieve was to become a necessary asset. The question remained: what would he be forced to endure in the process?

———

Longing for the island's isolation and the luxury of ignoring incoming calls, Ray begrudgingly lifted the phone in her suite. In thirty seconds, she'd stomached her fill of Locke's empty, sugarcoated wisdom.

"Assumed you had the upper hand again. You must be so distraught with disappointment." Ray drew immense pleasure from whipping Locke with his apparent loss of status. "You know what they say about assumption. Our distinguished transplant candidate didn't even regard you as a member of his team. He *did* express a desire to form a mutually beneficial relationship with me."

"Don't flatter yourself, Ray," Locke whined. "You're his surgeon. What's he supposed to do, piss you off before you cut into him?"

"Point is, *you* are of no use to him, or me for that matter. I'm not even sure why I've wasted time entertaining this conversation. I must be bored."

"Don't get too cocky," Locke threatened. "You might need me. Think about what I said."

Locke hung up. A thunderous slamming diverted Ray's attention. The door to her suite shuddered as if ready to implode. Untangling herself from the phone cord, she feared a medical emergency threatened her new patient.

It filled her with genuine concern—for herself, of course, not the patient.

If he expired before the surgery could be performed, the military's immediate use for her would die with him. It would threaten her position of limited freedom. They may even view her as a liability. She rushed to the door.

Her patient's status had not worsened. Her own had.

"Expecting someone else?"

Ray shrank backward as Cage pushed past her.

"What the hell are *you* doing here?" she demanded.

"Don't get worked up over me, darlin'," Cage said. "Just a friendly visit. Thought I'd check out the new digs."

"Great. You've seen them. Now, get out!"

"Is that any way to treat an old friend?"

"*You* may be old, but *we* are definitely not friends. What do you want?"

"You're right. We're more than friends. Jack on the rocks."

"You'll excuse me if I'm a little short on hospitality. I'm not accustomed to entertaining tyrants. What the hell are you here for, and don't tell me it's a drink?"

Her mounting frustration colored Cage's face with satisfaction.

"What are you grinning about? Wipe that smirk off your face."

"*You* declaring *me* a tyrant, now that's the pot calling the kettle black." Cage laughed, continuing to toy with her. He pushed further into her space. "Make it a single, I'm driving."

"They haven't stocked my bar yet. I just got here." Ray backed into the living room where a wall screen simulated a tranquil view of a wilderness landscape.

"Yes, but you'll be staying for quite a long time, I'd imagine," he mocked.

"Don't bet your life on it," Ray snapped back, her eyes drilling hard at his core.

"Oh, I won't, but there are some—"

"Is this what you came here for, a verbal game of cat and mouse?"

"No." In a word, Cage's tone lost all its playful buoyancy. "I came to tell you that you lost, in case you haven't figured that out."

"Oh, but it's early in the game," she countered. "Too early to call."

"You think so? Tell me, did the nightmares end in the good doctor's bed?"

"What?" Ray held a poker face with a hand to hide.

"You suffer from the same human weakness. Heard you made plans to visit your boyfriend tomorrow. Not sure why. From what I hear, he's a cold fish, non-conversationalist. In fact, one might say he's a regular deadbeat."

"You have a seriously sick sense of humor. Did anyone ever tell you that?"

"They were all too afraid to."

"And they call me arrogant," Ray replied.

"Oh, you are," Cage agreed. There was something disturbing underlying his tone. "But *you* are not the only one."

Walking close enough for her to inhale his stale cigar breath, he towered over her steely frame. His demeanor transformed as he spoke. His voice lost its raspy character and became something steady, far more dangerous. Ray knew dangerous.

"Your hateful eyes will never again be given the grace to lay upon him. You'll never be granted a reprieve from the living hell you have created. There will be no mercy for you. You take false comfort in your abilities."

The sudden and striking change in Cage's demeanor left her speechless, though his fierce prediction hadn't yet burned through the icy mantel. Retreating from the room, never breaking eye contact, he backed into the threshold before administering a final blow.

"*You are a bad seed,*" he said with chilling finality.

Her trance broke with the slamming of the door.

No wineglass was pitched to shatter and smash against his exit. Ray internalized anger. It nourished and cleansed, a high-octane fuel in a racecar. Inhaling it, she drew it in, anxiously awaiting its rush like a cocaine high.

It fed her.

Burning with ammunition, her black eyes found new depth.

Still behind the door, she listened to his footsteps recede down the corridor.

How dare he demean her? How dare he dismiss her brilliance? No one alive compared, and he knew it. He was there at the beginning, all the way through, from conception to capture.

Each of his heavy footsteps landed an insulting sting of non-acceptance on her ego. She never stopped to ponder why he possessed the ability to rattle her in ways others were incapable of.

The guard outside her suite had not returned. She walked to the bedroom, turning out the lights en route. Prepared to make at least a modest effort of concealing her intentions.

Slipping pillows under the covers with her, she faked fitful slumber, tossing and turning until she could slip down the side unnoticed, leaving a well-positioned mound of fluff in her stead. Crawling back to the foyer on her belly with the silky ease of a snake waltzing through sand dunes, she escaped the cameras. Sliding one arm up the edge of the doorjamb, she disengaged the lock using a key card she stole earlier from her doorman.

Pressed against the floor, she slithered down the hall and into the emergency staircase.

This act of defiance would cost her freedom. She *would* be caught. Yet, at this moment it meant nothing. Cage was wrong. She would prove it. She would see her creation again and soon.

Red emergency lights inflamed the vacant staircase's gloom. A tunnel to hell, spiraling deep into Satan's caverns, it drew her lower. She uncoiled, glissading upright in one deadly fluid movement. With her back pressed hard against the curved cement wall, she shifted from step to step, watching for shadows of resistance approaching from below.

Glancing overhead at each landing, she confirmed her progress by the amber-lit floor levels. Her heartbeat increased in unison with the diminishing numbers.

The odds of making it to the morgue undetected were dismal at best. Knowing this, she pressed forth ever more determined. The ninth-floor access door came into view. Red caution signs overhead announced required clearance to access this sensitive area. They filled further the crimson glow of the stairwell into a bloody pool of light.

Grasping the doorknob, she almost expected it to resonate with heat. Contradicting its flaming luminescence, it was cold to the touch.

The temperature on this somber level maintained a crisp 65 degrees F, unpleasant for the living. Accommodating for the dead. Work performed within these haunted halls didn't exude a comfortable atmosphere, nor did the morbidity of its occupants. Ray imagined the many available rooms filled with numerous faceless, nameless, decomposing guests. Her interest remained on one.

Uncertain of the layout or security measures, she didn't know how she'd locate the body before they detected her absence.

Focus. Find him.

As softly as smoothing hair from a baby's brow, Ray guided the knob to disengage the bolt action without causing the typical click and pop that could alert a guard cruising the outer hallway. The pin withdrew into the door, revealing an unimpeded hairline view between it and the doorjamb. Suction held it firmly in place. Formidable and constructed of solid steel, it provided a soundproof, windowless panel strong enough to withstand repercussions from a nuclear blast.

Scanning the framework, she searched for signs of secondary security measures. There were none. Her hand stayed in play with the knob twisted open. She drew the door inward against her weight. Her effort met with resistance.

Designed by engineers expecting to be protected by this labyrinth tomb, safety measures abound to the point of overkill. Three-inch thick pins formed from impenetrable classified metal were set to engage in emergencies for added security. They were not in use.

Evidence gave way to logic.

Perhaps it was not what but who obstructed her passage.

Cage trapped her.

A rat in a maze, he wound her up and unleashed her. No coincidence the guard at her suite hadn't returned at his leaving. Cage accommodated the opportunity for escape. He'd allowed her access to the key card she lifted. She stood bathed in an amber glow equal to the inner rage ignited by gullibility.

She stumbled. Unacceptable.

Bracing herself for impact, she held the knob with both hands. Then, with blunt, jarring force tore it inward and watched as it was yanked back to its original place. A game of tug-a-war played out with someone on the opposing side.

An impending ambush left no room for games.

Glancing first below, then above, Ray waited, anticipating leagues of Cage's troops to flood the staircase. Surely, they were en route to apprehend her.

"Damn you."

Turning back wasn't an option. She'd rather confront the enemy beyond the door and protect even the slightest possibility of reaching Chris than retreat back the way she came and sever all hope. Ray stood her ground.

Her grip remained strong, vehement.

Exhaling in quick, short breaths, she delivered a sudden, violent thrust. And crumpled Locke's six-foot-five frame to his knees. Shocked, she stared down at the scattered mass of flailing arms and legs at her feet.

"What the hell are you doing?" Locke hissed, clambering to regain a less humiliating position. "Are you *trying* to get us caught?"

"No. Where did you come from?" Ray scoured the hall with censure as Locke brushed the wrinkles of embarrassment from his smock.

"The same place you did. I didn't think I could trust you to go it alone. Evidently, I was right! It's miraculous you're not already back in handcuffs. If you pulled that little stunt of yours ten seconds earlier, the guard would've seen you, and we'd both have a lot of explaining to do."

Locke moved in close enough to whisper. "I saw your little encounter with Cage. The sound feed scrambled to the point of being incoherent, but the confrontation appeared less than amicable."

"You just can't get enough of me, can you?" Ray asked.

"Are you going to tell me what he said to spur you into mindless action, or shall we stand here staring at each other until the guard detail shows up?" Locke fanned out his frame peacock-style. Foolishly thinking height alone served to impress after she'd sent him flying to his knees.

"He said I'd never lay eyes on Chris again," Ray replied, her voice lacking any inflection of emotion.

"I knew it!" Locke erupted.

"Knew what? Keep your voice down."

"I've been demanding to view his body since it arrived. Cage has a lockdown on the morgue. He's been shutting me out!"

"Well, you're not alone." Unmoved by Locke's outrage, she leaned past him to survey the corridor beyond the doorway. Carrion tainted air. Decaying flesh.

"If that cretinous jarhead has convinced himself he's calling all the shots, I'll—"

"Why?" Ray interrupted.

"Why? 'Cause he's a sanctimonious moron."

"No. Why do you need access to Chris?"

"This project is my birthright—"

"My birthright," she coldly corrected. "Save the rhetoric."

"Yes, yes. Yours as well, certainly," he stammered. "I've never seen information so protected. Ever since his body arrived, it has been like pulling teeth to—"

"They're keeping secrets from *you*?"

"Yes! It seems classified has become top secret, and unattainable for some godforsaken reason. And I'm damned determined to find out why."

"I think I already know," Ray said under her breath. "Which way?"

"Well...I...I'm not sure," Locke stuttered. "That's why we need to work together."

Ignoring his last, Ray clarified her question. "Which direction to Chris?"

"Left."

Her foot hit the hard marble, transforming it into a thousand-square-foot pressure activation switch. Alarms blared, and sirens screamed. The murky depths of the manmade catacomb flooded with their intrusion.

"What did you do?" Locke erupted. "What triggered the alarm?"

Ray swung back to meet his terror-stricken expression with a glare that silenced. A thin veil of fresh resin coated her deadly black eyes.

"Cage." His name oozed over her nerves like burning tar.

Under a wailing entourage of warnings, she spelled it out, "A rat and a Cage."

61

GRABBING LOCKE BY THE SHOULDER, forcing him ahead of her down the corridor, Ray issued demands. Her voice sliced through the relentless racket of sirens wailing around them.

"Which way? Move! Now!"

"We don't stand a hope in hell of—"

"Shut up and move!"

Scampering nervously forward, Locke's hunched frame shrunk relative to his diminished confidence.

Amateur.

He shuffled down the halls with Ray prodding him from behind.

"We can use this to our advantage if we can get to the lab before the guards do," Ray said, her voice fought to hit a clear octave.

"How?" Locke bellowed, pausing long enough to be jarred ahead by another tenacious jab to the ribs.

"I said move!"

The hall was a mass of confusion despite the fact they were, thus far, its only occupants. Circling lights spun overhead. Doors slammed bolts into place with punctuation. Signs flashed warnings.

Rounding the final turn leading to Chris' body, Locke received the last in a series of insulting blows to his backside.

"How much farther?" Ray demanded with a shove of insistence.

"We're here, damn it, stop pushing me." Locke jumped and shifted in a ridged full circle, scanning for armed assailants. "You're going to get me killed."

Ray grinned. Pressing him to the side of the entrance, she swiped the key card she used to break out of her suite.

"That'll never work," Locke said, his voice a dull roar. "Cage and Gordon are the only ones with clearance. And, besides—"

Locke fell mute when the indication light flashed a welcoming green and the security measures disengaged.

It didn't make sense.

"Even with card clearance, Cage and Gordon are required to use secondary protocol measures. Eye scans, voice recognition...I've seen them."

"It's never this easy," Locke warned. "This doesn't feel right."

"Because it isn't." Ray glanced back at him one last time before crossing the threshold. "We'll be fine once we're inside."

"No offense, Sherlock, but you'll forgive me if I fail to trust *your* instincts."

Locke grimaced as Ray disappeared inside the morgue's foyer.

Autopsies were performed in the pristine confinement of oversized, frigid operating rooms adorned with cold, polished, stainless steel or whitewashed with carbolic disinfectant and bleach. Most of them smelled of peroxide sterilization and the toxic aroma of death.

This particular room exuded but one scent—metallic.

Bodily fluids were the first to be removed. Stored in labeled beakers, the system of their analysis and eventual disposal was mathematical and clinically precise. The gore diluted to the point of nonexistence. This held true in all cases.

Except here.

Ray hadn't come but four steps into the room. Paralyzed, she stood along the break between its entrance and a much broader inner chamber, slippery surface under her feet. Shoeless as always, the liquid beneath them formed an undependable layer between the flesh of her soles and the marble flooring.

From behind her, someone screamed. It didn't register that the high-pitched panic belonged to Locke.

The persistent blare of the alarms vanished. Silence reigned, an invisible bubble swallowing her whole and leaving her suspended inside the aftermath of a bloodbath.

The floor and the walls, even as high up as the x-ray screens were doused in thick red splatter. Tools left out, primed for surgery, were stained where they lay in perfect placement. Extra smocks, hanging in convenient reach, were splashed in patterns that gave way to visions of off-spray from a killer's proud pirouette. Ribbons of blood cast off in circles, trailing each hand.

Locke vomited behind her.

It wasn't the gore impacting Ray. The lone empty table centerpiece amid the macabre surroundings froze her in place.

After an unearthly calm, she erupted.

"Where?"

Her voice filled with unbridled rage. Rage capable of crossing eons of time to emerge, drifting back on the thrashing winds of a doomsday storm, having never lost a fraction of its girth.

"Where...is he?" A plea and a demand from her darkest depths. And as terrorizing as her tone was, Locke's reaction said he preferred this to the immobile zombie she'd been.

"I don't know, damn it." His words were accented by guttural urges to vomit again. "This is...I've never been allowed inside. I...I'm not responsible!"

"No! He can't do this to me!" Ray shrieked.

"Raw emotion? I don't recall ever seeing you quite so—" His fascination with her reaction was interrupted by a warning flashing across the computer screen monitoring the outer hallway.

"They're here." Panic punctuated his pronunciation. "And this doesn't look good for us."

"Really, you think?" Spilling forth at an increasing rhythm, her tone equal to the brutality she wished to inflict, she threatened, "You tell them we discovered the room in this condition! You say you suspected Cage couldn't be trusted. You brought me along to inspect the body for tampering. You tell them the alarms sounded when we were on our way here. And you convince them of our good intentions as if your life depends on it!"

It did.

———

Locke had seconds to pull himself together before armed troops arrived.

"Holy Mother of God!"

The first man to round the bend crossed himself at the sight before him with his free hand while pointing his gun at Locke—the nearest target.

"Get that thing out of my face, you imbecile!" Locke screamed. "It's about bloody time you showed up! We could've both been sliced and diced into tiny pieces by now."

"Show me your hands," a senior officer demanded.

"Show me a towel, asshole. They're covered in puke! And while you're at it, get CSU down here before you contaminate the scene!"

While Locke ranted and raved, Ray stood protected from clear view behind him. The soldiers couldn't see the expression on her face, but glancing back, Locke read mild approval in her eyes.

He might pull this off after all.

"Sir, we have to ask you to remain where you are until they arrive," the officer stated.

"I didn't plan on leaving for a nightcap," Locke shot back. "Hurry up!"

An officer transmitted over the radio, struggling to hear over the noise.

"And turn off those damn sirens before we all go deaf!"

To Locke's surprise, the soldiers followed his direction without resistance. Perhaps the vicious nature of the scene acted in his defense. They didn't question his innocence, at least, not yet.

At the back end of the entourage, unable to see beyond his many brothers-in-arms, a soldier yelled newly acquired information ahead.

"We have a prisoner escape as well, sir," he said. "Her suite has been searched."

"Oh, for the love of God!" Locke countered. "Ray's in here with me. She hasn't escaped. I brought her here because I suspected the body was being tampered with, and she's the only one with knowledge of its condition prior to arrival."

The man in charge stood beside Locke, careful not to place his feet near the blood pool. He leaned around him to find Ray. Standing pale and silently frozen. Her face wore an expression of such convincing shock the soldier became compelled to reassure her.

"Miss, we'll have you outta there soon. You're going to be all right. We won't let anything happen to you," the man said.

Locke stood in amazement. Ray locked eyes with the officer. Terror and sadness emanated from her. Locke shook his head disapprovingly at the officer. The idiot had no clue who he was consoling.

"Don't make promises, do your job, and get us the hell out of here!" Locke demanded.

Radio static announced an incoming transmission and the officer cupped his hand around the microphone by his ear.

"Yes, sir. We found them halted in the doorway. No. They weren't in the room when the event occurred. Yes. He says he was suspicious and came to check on the body. Yes, sir, she is. No, I haven't...in a deep state of shock..."

Masked beneath wailing sirens, Locke inhaled a cleansing breath. Once again, he'd slip through the fingers of justice...and right into the talons of turpitude. Evil had a wicked grip.

———

After a half hour of immobility, Ray's feet were numb and bloodstained. She stared down at them without seeing. They'd yet to determine whose blood she wore. That remained the question of the hour, among others. Like, where the hell was Cage? He and Gordon couldn't be located. Back-up tapes of activities within the compound proved useless. Any potentially beneficial footage turned to static at relevant intervals. They knew the unlawful opening of an outer ground-level door triggered the alarm.

It didn't dispel the mystery, but it served to support Locke's suspicions.

In a conference room several floors above the crime scene, Ray refused to speak.

Playing the role of shocked and shaken victim, she never uttered a word until her prestigious patient entered the room. Guards wanted to get her cleaned up, but her unresponsive condition stopped them. They left her in her disheveled state.

She sat at the edge of a table as if someone had propped her there. Her feet dangled cold and exposed, tacky and bearing the dye of blood and ink from CSI imprints. Her upper torso was hidden, cocooned in a blanket.

Rolling into the holding room, her future patient asked Alerio to fetch another blanket, and then requested they not be disturbed.

Alerio handed the throw over and left the room, sealing the door behind him.

"I'm sorry," he said once they were alone. "Is there anything I can do?"

Ray hung her head lower. He wheeled himself over and laid the blanket on her legs and feet.

"I'll get to the bottom of this if it's the last thing I do."

His words fell heavy, given the precarious state of his health.

To this, Ray lifted her head.

"I can't help you," she whispered. Shame and defeat masquerading true emotion. "Without examining—"

"We'll manage," he said. "Did you see anyone? Pass anyone in the halls on the way there? Anything you remember may be crucial."

"Cage came to see me before Locke brought me down." She set the stage. "He told me I'd never see Chris' body again."

"He never approved of you having access," he said.

She'd coax him to follow the dark, accusatory path she laid.

"He believed punishment for your crimes far exceeded all other priorities. He didn't agree with any of the concessions I've allowed."

"He sounded as if he planned to make certain I couldn't see Chris." She pushed the possibility of Cage's betrayal gently. "And now...they're both gone."

"Yes, in more than one way, I'm afraid," he said, sparking her full attention.

"What are you saying?"

"The blood. Close to a gallon spilled down there. Save for a few pools, which were identified as Gordon's, it was Cage's blood type. There's simply no way for him to sustain injuries generating that level of blood loss and survive. I'm afraid he died defending Chris' body. By the looks of it, he put up one hell of a fight."

Against her will, her body shook. He was still speaking but it wasn't his voice she heard. It was a voice from childhood, at a time of terror. He had broken into her cell, held her in his arms, and told her the truth. What had he said? She saw Cage's face, much younger than it had grown. "It's going to be so hard," he had said. "I can't protect you from that, but I will get you out of here someday. I will never let them kill you." A deep chill overtook her. Rapidly, it increased to a state of convulsion. Falling from onyx eyes, crystal tears streamed in growing numbers down her face. Why had he done that? He had told her. Her mind couldn't recall the words, but her heart felt them.

"Alerio," the man in the chair summoned. "Get some help in here!

"Yes, sir." Voices withdrew. Became distant. Someone entered the room, then empty words again, "Medic! Get in here!"

Nurses. Cold hands grabbed at her. No sensation of touch, their fingers like putty. A doctor's face appeared, swimming in tides of distortion. His expression was one of unbridled fear.

"Jesus...if we lose—"

"Shut up! Get the crash cart..."

Needles. How she detested them. Intrusive but she didn't fear the diminishing light.

She was designed for the dark.

The staff doctor had administered a fast-acting tranquilizer. She knew the feeling. Nurses supported her until the drug did its work.

"Al, please escort them back to her room." She heard her esteemed patient order.

"Sir. What happened?" Al asked, whispering as Ray was lifted onto a gurney across the room.

"I told her about Cage," he replied. "I don't understand it."

"Odd," Al agreed. "I'll post a medical detail to monitor her around the clock."

"Al," he whispered. "Get her cleaned up. I don't want her waking up with any visual reminders. And Al."

"Sir."

"Stay with her."

"Suicide watch, sir?" Alerio questioned. "My place is with you."

"If you protect her, you protect me. My fate lies in her hands. For both our sakes, don't argue this."

That was the one good thing she heard.

———

Locke's interrogation was unpleasant—particularly for the interrogators.

The soldiers said his reputation for being a whining, sniveling, spoiled rotten to the core, arrogant, pretentious, neurotic, know-it-all preceded him. He exhibited every undesirable personality trait and breathed new life into previously held claims during the two hours he wrestled under the strain of relentless questioning.

Those involved maintained loyalties to Cage or his superior. Locke realized quickly, following the first initial inquiries, the closest thing he had to a friend in the complex was Ray. And she'd be the first one chanting "off with his head."

His father's hard-earned acclaim had paved a smooth, affluent way for him. He never needed to form beneficial relationships to manipulate compliance or push forth his own agenda. Those benefits came with the name. After his father's death, money and controlling stock of his legacy provided a subsequent free ride.

He hadn't anticipated ever needing anything more.

Now he wished he had the forethought to unearth a few skeletons. They could've proved useful.

Without them, he seethed, fumed, and proclaimed his innocence with a level of annoyance that grated down the nerves of his accusers. Eventually, the need for justice paled, withered, and shriveled to dust. Relentless irritation managed to break the will of any decent human being.

The soldiers before him, however, were not so decent.

A call came from above. Locke was expecting a visitor. They had a half hour to make him presentable. Smart enough not to injure his face or hands, they relied on his pride to protect their dirty secrets—administering injuries to places quick to heal and delicate to expose.

For Locke, it proved his acumen. Trust no one. Value no one. Betray everyone.

New recruits suffered far worse without complaint, but Locke's pampered background inflated the humiliation and degradation. Showered and thrown into clean clothes against his will, his face still displayed the flush of anger when his boss entered the room. A fresh, steaming cup of coffee in front of him and a blanket around his bony shoulders gave the distorted illusion he'd been treated with kid gloves.

He'd been treated with gloves all right, just not the welcome kind.

"My men say you've been quite helpful in detailing tonight's events. It's impressive after what you've been through." The man rolled his metal chariot into the room.

"Yes," Locke echoed, accusation on his breath. "After what I've been through."

"You need your rest. We have a great many issues to deal with tomorrow. You should return to your room. I'm surprised to find you here at this hour."

The cat was out of the bag. Locke eyed the men around him but said nothing.

"Did Ray have anything of interest to add?" Locke asked, worried she'd thrown him to the wolves.

"No. She had a breakdown and was sedated."

"Sedated, what did they use? Her mind is a well-oiled machine...I hope they didn't—"

"She is being given the absolute best care. And you know why."

"Yes...yes, of course," Locke retreated. "Sorry, I'm a little edgy."

"Well, that's understandable. I'll have my guards escort you to your quarters."

"No!" Locke protested, his tone overzealous. "I...I've seen my fill of guards tonight. I'll find my own way."

His boss signaled for the door to be closed behind him and Locke, who slowly and stiffly rose from his chair.

"Gordon's notes are gone," he said, hushed but still audible. "Do you have copies?"

"Yes, sir. The initial autopsy report and some of the test findings I demanded. It's pretty sotty."

"Where are they?"

"In my quarters."

"You haven't been back there since you left with Ray," he reminded. "I didn't send in troops because I didn't think you'd want them rifling through your personal property and other sensitive documentation."

"I appreciate that," Locke said. Visions of hedonistic creeps defiling his prized possessions muddied his thoughts. He was certain his face showed the internal struggle. "I'll check on things and call you when I get in."

"Fine. I don't need to tell you how important those documents have become."

"No, sir."

Locke was only too happy to leave the conference level on the same elevator as his superior. The elevator arrived on his floor, leaving no opportunity for thirsty soldiers, who hadn't had their fill of brutality, to sneak off and make the few night hours left a living hell.

Ducking out of the lift, he turned with a prudent nod of respect, though he had none.

"Call me."

"Yes, sir, right away."

The hallway was empty. Locke's feet flew ahead of him off the lift, and he stumbled. Overcompensating, he tripped on the carpet and failed to recover gracefully. The aches and pains of odium sapped his energy. Slamming the door to his suite, he engaged his security system, collapsed in a chair in front of his desk, and searched the unopened mail. Scattering the others to the floor, he clutched the contents of a simple manila envelope to his chest. Gordon's report had been expressly thorough. A fact he'd safeguard. He'd hid all he'd discovered about the Cromwell man. He'd read everything about Ray. Years of information he'd poured over every graphic detail in the dark hours of isolation on the island and kept those secrets all these years. He sat armed with the fruits of his obsession.

62

OUT OF CHURNING BLACKNESS, with the rabid eye of an animal stalking the night. A broken moon glowed jaundiced yellow above Kyly. Tilted on a leery angle, it hung in the metallic sky with a twisted glare. Ribbons of clouds cowered beneath it. Their edges scorched as they drifted by. Below, the sea raced back and forth, unable to escape it. A fate she shared.

The tiny mound beneath her hand confirmed what Mason suspected. She had more to protect than just herself. She safeguarded this new life and the secret Christian bestowed on her with unwavering dedication.

No one else knew what he'd confided, no witnesses, no one to collaborate the truth. She understood the ancient note without interpretation because he had explained it to her in detail that one night in the cabin. Christian's fate had been sealed from birth. Micael Valeric did not randomly choose him. He'd been searching for him, his bloodline, for decades. A bloodline she carried in her womb, created by his uncle, with a stronger genetic link than his mother's. A bloodline rooted in every living human. Scholars knew well of the Eve Theory. They knew nothing of Adam. Micael Valeric found a link to him. One with the potential to map out the story of mankind and drastically alter its future.

Chris left no validation. No way to substantiate, with unequivocal proof that what he told her was the truth, and he did it to protect her. There may come a time when the world needs to know. Not now.

She told Mason their child would be in grave danger if the men who held Chris' body decided he was not an anomaly. Mason hadn't doubted her, even without evidence. He didn't question her or judge. He kept his blessings and curses separate. He didn't speak of it, but the late-night phone calls and the deepening worry behind his eyes told her peace wouldn't be sustained.

Standing on the upper deck of their house, peering into the night, she imagined it swallowed by the sea, like her adrift. The wind whipped her silk nightgown and robe into waves of white.

Coming up behind her, Mason wrapped her in his arms, letting the breeze swirl silk between them. "A vision to behold against the dark night," he whispered. He slid his right hand over her abdomen, warm and protective. Kyly let her head drop back into his shoulder. "Our future," he said.

Her fingers found comfort flipping the antique key on the chain around her neck. The second keepsake Chris left behind. She wouldn't part with it.

"I don't know what fate has in store for us." She searched the unsettled night.

"No one does." His grip tightened. "Know I love you, and whatever it is, we'll face it together. Speaking of, I could use your help with the crib."

A glance wouldn't reveal it. Her height and build carried their secret well. There, at the center of her, a legacy waited, hidden discretely, protected beneath her flesh.

Mason announced her pregnancy to the family proudly but warned given their circumstances it be kept private for as long as possible.

A storm cloud had threatened their wedding ceremony, but as the opening prayer fell from the lips of her father, the sun broke free. "God's blessing," he told them. He let her go, and she'd come back to stay, he said.

Kyly knew the break in their storm was but a temporary reprieve.

The faces of their families, Cromwells and Zuriels, united during the service, burned in her memory, Brooke's speech welcoming her to the family. She'd lost a son but gained a sister-in-law who grieved his loss with her. A formidable union tested. She held to sacred moments, but the wind carried change. And it blew fiercely.

They had been forewarned.

Chris left her words to cling to in hours of darkness. He told her not to fear, to live in the light. He asked her to have faith in difficult times and give all her love. This was salvation. She held her doubts.

Looking down under the moonlight, she recited the Aramaic translation aloud.

"Do not fear Pure of Heart, live within Unity and you shall see there is no opposition and you have no need of protection. The Giver of Life has given you life unending through the source of lifeblood. Without qualification or limit the answers you seek are in his code passed to all in his line. When the time has come, seek within. When the ONE is discovered, the gift of knowledge will reside within him. All expansion meets its other but cannot be withheld. The time you dread will come. The time you seek will follow."

Christ...

Kyly fought to push out lingering fear—dreaded fear—to hold fast to Christian's strength. But it clung like the fabric brushing her skin. Distant enough. Diminished by faith, quieted by love, but whispering.

She knew from thousands of years foretold, there was no stopping the next steps no, matter how terrifying the cost.

63

GHOSTLY SHADOWS POLLUTED Nick's vision.

He couldn't trust his eyes or much of what they saw. Light resonated so intensely across the marble floor he worried it wore a florescent jelly and feared for the safety of his footing.

The fog in his mind became self-aware, growing legs to spring from its trapped cavern, rolling into this new outer realm.

He winced, blinked, rubbed his eyes, and blinked again. He shook his head to dispel the cobwebs, massaged the back of his neck, and fought to focus past the ethereal mist. Still, it wouldn't disperse.

Cascading across every surface, the apparitions clung.

Too many hours under unforgiving manufactured strobes gave birth to these luminescent monsters. Now, he couldn't rid himself of them even when a source for them to draw upon no longer existed.

To anyone else, the room was cast in the dull shadow of a dying day.

Closing his eyes garnered no relief. It served only to shut out the tangible, leaving him watching them slither and shift against the black backdrop of his eyelids.

He was a disturbed man. He would fix that.

He waited for the phantoms to fade from his sight and his thoughts. When the Pacific Ocean came into view beyond the glass, he pulled a hidden phone from his pocket. There wasn't much time. Tiny green numerals meld together into one glowing lump on the faceplate. By memory, he dialed the number and waited for the deep and distant voice on the other end.

"Stone, it's done," he said without inflection. "I'll call again in a few days. I told you he was on our side...like all of us, he has his reasons."

Stone gave everything for his family. He wouldn't save them all, but he'd die trying. He liked the guy.

Sliding the phone off, he lifted his heavy frame from its seated position and sauntered, half-dazed, back down the hallway to his suite.

The passage remained empty, thankfully.

For a fleeting moment, he moved back to a time when the island was theirs alone and intrusion an ocean away—it was not so. A home once so familiar had become alien, forever tainted by the invaders that now shared it. Bringing with them firepower and the unpolished truth of Ray's sordid existence. They saturated it with an open evil, making no attempt to conceal their intentions.

It was strange and unnerving how this sorcery hung so heavy in the tropical air. Choking humidity called forth a brewing storm none of them would survive.

Locking doors behind him, he stripped, threw on Ralph Lauren pajama bottoms, and fell into bed.

Underlying complete fatigue, a fire flickered behind his eyes. It gave him strength.

Pale from weeks basking under track lights, thin from loss of appetite, and disheveled from long hours of operating, Nick was anything but the picture of health.

It was impossible to sleep. Strangers lurking about the house upset him. A fact, with time, he'd have no choice but to accept.

The island was their hidden oasis no more.

Security clung to every exit. They were, however, far more interested in Ray's activities than his own. The medical wing had been instantaneously revamped into a full-fledged military surgical unit more capable of handling a level four biohazard than the CDC. Two extra helicopters sat in a constant state of readiness on the helipad. And Ray's computer had been taken over by a military operations specialist. Thus far, she was the model of accommodation—another in a long list of charades.

"He's only a kid, a computer geek," she said. And she was right.

Barely eighteen. Ray didn't seem the least bit threatened until Nick told her the "Kid's" IQ. Still, she was resolute. No one existed whom she'd fear matching wits with.

She'd forgotten who her creators were, a foolish mistake. Suspicious, Ray did nothing to hide her contempt. Despite his explanation, she didn't trust that he'd remained under lock and key, unaware, during Cage's murder and the body snatching at the compound.

She wasn't designed to trust. Life taught her not to. Testaments to this hovered all around her. They included him.

He'd crossed the line to the other side. No one suspected how far across he'd gone.

———

Those with a vested interest and top-level clearance lined the viewing window. In decorated uniforms, they became a prestigious audience. Their eyes moved over Ray, analyzing and scrutinizing her body, mind, and synthetic soul.

Nothing new.

She'd managed to avoid the intrusive microscope for well over a decade. It didn't unnerve her. She'd hardened to the prying eyes of bloodthirsty onlookers. Present circumstances differed greatly from those of the past.

This time, they held their breath while she performed miracles. With scalpel and suture, she decided the fate of her patient, the hope of her spectators, and the key to her freedom. Here, on *her* island, with *her* entourage, she rose to the height of power. A champagne bottle uncorked inside her chest cavity with sinister effervescence.

Her black pupils pierced the operating room's glass wall. *It* existed to keep them out, not to keep her in.

In a white hospital smock and moss green booties, with a surgical facemask covering all but her charcoal eyes, she began the journey.

After painstaking hours, the surgery ended. The patient was critical. An expected condition. Assisting staff vacated the room even before Nick had slipped out, leaving her and the man on the table alone in the steady rhythm of the machines—the automated breath that sustained her patient's life and hers by association.

Prior to surgery, the powers that be wanted to pry every ounce of pertinent information from her—as if they'd recognize it from the useless garbage she fed them. They sent Locke to do their bidding. Their choice couldn't have been more asinine. Her patient's cardiac arrest prevented much time for probing.

Surgery expedited Ray's power play.

Now she stayed, peering down at the handsome face of her latest creation long after her presence was required.

Locke rapped against the transparent barrier like an annoying seven-year-old at a pet store window, choosing to ignore the signs pleading for silence.

Time to let him in.

One of the remaining three superior officers admonished Locke for his persistent interference before filing out of the observation room.

Ray signaled to the airlock, inviting Locke inside.

Passing through a "clean room" preparation corridor, he was washed down with a harsh antiseptic, followed by a burst of intense air before an airtight door opened to a second holding vestibule. Not a speck of contaminants could survive it. After the door behind him sealed shut, a green light indicated the door ahead would disengage, allowing him passage to the surgical unit.

Booties kicked aside, Ray waited barefoot.

"Have a full report in my hands by 0800 tomorrow," a stern voice echoed through the intercom system. Ray nodded to the last of the dignitaries shuffling out. The men didn't make eye contact. Her colorless pools were unnatural, disturbing reminders of her unique DNA. Staring into the eyes in which your image reflected back was disconcerting.

Even for war heroes.

"Yes, sir," Ray said.

"Let the doctor rest, Locke. She's had one hell of a day."

Locke's eyes gleamed with resentment. He never spoke.

Perfect.

Ray consulted the monitor. The men exited the hall.

Locke leaned over her shoulder. "You put on quite a performance. They're all sold."

"That's what I'm here for." She stretched on new gloves and

removed the last surgical tools from the sterilizer. "Why are you here? Risky business."

"We need to talk. I assumed you'd selectively control this room's surveillance. Safe from intrusion."

"Yep. No sound. Limited exposure. I'll kill the feed. What's troubling you?" Ray keyed a code into the computer and rested against the counter behind her. Relaxed in the afterglow of achievement.

"You have the leverage you need. You're where you want to be." He surveyed the room in mocking admiration of the state-of-the-art equipment. "And Valeric said it couldn't be done."

"He said it shouldn't be done. Where I want to be...and you're not?" She slid closer and stood up to him. "Worried you've exceeded your usefulness?"

Locke stepped back, tripping slightly. "I wouldn't say that."

"No. You wouldn't." Ray sunk her hands into her lab coat pockets and drifted close, brushing against him. Locke's eyes fell from her onyx pools to her chest.

"See something you want?"

"No. I was thinking—"

"Nothing you haven't seen before." Ray's smile teased. "Remember?"

"It's been a while. What were we—"

"Your usefulness." She held his right hand, caressing it seductively.

"I'm invaluable to you," he said as she flipped it over, inspecting his palm. "What are you staring at?"

"Your lifeline." A chuckle escaped her.

The tension in Locke's shoulders abated. "A medical genius and a fortune teller?"

"Yours is very short." Ray spoke with her head down, still focused on his large hand.

"My what is short?"

"Your life." Ray clenched his upturned hand, pulled a scalpel from her pocket, and cut deep across his wrist, severing the main artery in one fluid movement. She stepped back, avoiding the spray. "Don't look so shocked. It's been a long time coming."

Blood spewed from the gash. Arching in front of him, it splashed lower cupboard doors and splattered across the high-grade Italian marble.

"You're ruining my clean floor." Ray laughed.

"You crazy bitch!" Locke flailed, rummaging through every available door in search of something to tie off the wound. He found a roll of gauze and shook it free of its outer box but couldn't unfurl it.

"Mending glue," she offered. "Works on anything."

"What the fuck do you hope this will accomplish? They'll—"

"I'm killing you. They won't do a thing to me. You said it. I have all the leverage I need."

Locke cleared four cupboards and the counter. Blood trailed his futile efforts. Smeared. Spattered. Spoiled.

He slipped and stumbled on his own wreckage. Ray laughed louder.

"Dizzy?" she asked. "You're losing volume fast."

Locke found a towel. Shivering with panic, he wrapped his wound, pulling the fabric tight with his teeth and good hand. His face came away, muddied by blood. His eyelids fluttered, searching for a clear line of sight to the code button on the wall. He didn't see the second attack coming.

She cut deeper on his left wrist. Bored, he wasn't ending as quickly as she'd like. This time, the blade ran lengthwise, opening the artery in a two-inch span.

Locke screamed. The realization he was dying took hold. He staggered to the wall phone, knocked it off, and pushed at the buttons. A second or two passed before he saw the unplugged cord. He picked it off the floor. The warm liquid made it slippery. She watched as his fingers lost the dexterity needed to reinsert it. He fumbled twice.

Ray's laugh was almost lyrical. Pretty. Airy.

Unable to maintain his balance, Lock stumbled and slid across the counter to the code button. Ray made no effort to stop him. He locked eyes before he hit it. Victory, or so he assumed.

"It's too late to save you," she said. "I know the doctor on call. She's not particularly fond of you. Besides—"

Locke slammed an elbow into the button and collapsed on the floor. The alarm sounded, echoing overhead. He crumpled his wounds together, a final effort to slow blood loss.

"There's a problem with the prep room door. When they find you, six minutes from now, I'll be locked inside with the shower going. Ready to start a new life."

She tiptoed around the blood trail and bent down so he could see the blacks of her eyes. "Sad, really. All the years you—ached for me to want you. I want you. I want you dead."

"Who do you think you are?" Locke's voice shuddered, a mixture of terror and rage. "You're—"

"Reconnaissance Assassin Y, the killer you bastards created. Proud? If Daddy could only see you now."

———

Tonight, she'd released that which plagued her. She drifted on a cloud of contentment.

Nothing resembles the sleep of the just more closely than the slumbers of an assassin. The poets were right.

She'd checked on her patient. He slept.

He would wake.

When he did, it'd be her face he saw.

No one would take *him* from her. *He* would never leave.

His chest rose and fell. With every inhalation, they were one step closer. Every surge of blood through his veins brought forth her purpose. Every day from this forward, they'd become stronger until they were invincible. They were so much alike, she mused, both created for greatness.

The machine to her left announced a change in his brainwaves.

Like her...he was dreaming.

Locke's mess was gone. Still, he'd tainted the air inside.

Outside, living statues of metal armor, instead of marble or stone, flanked every entrance. They held space two feet from the outer edge of the dock at opposing ends, straddling where Ray strolled to admire the ocean, breathing in the fresh night.

These watchful war hounds scanned the sky and marina with robot reflexes, smothering her union with nature.

Eyeing the men and the sea, Ray hadn't noticed the unusual sky. The men had. In fact, when she glanced at them, their eyes remained solid upon it.

Bizarre.

Black and smooth as far as one could see. Like a satin sheet, it feathered out without the blemish of a cloud. At first glance, it was not a rare or unnatural event until one noticed the lack of stars that typically scattered this dark canopy. Not one solitary twinkle.

A shadow light sent a dull glimmer across the sky. It came from the only luminescent source, a half-moon, as white as an Arctic snowdrift, shone above. A perimeter, a deeper blackness, held this abnormally bright lunar surface, and beyond it, above and below, laid an unbroken formation of gray clouds. Separated, they meant nothing. United they sent a chilling message. Together, they formed an unforgiving eye.

Ray's sinister eyes perfectly reversed.

The guards glanced at each other, at Ray, and back again. She knew what they were thinking.

The Eye of God.

A short time before, NASA captured the rare spectacular space photo with the Hubble telescope, a phenomenon believed to occur every three thousand years. Upon seeing this universal reproduction of a human eye, encased in bright golden hues, blazing in a fiery ring encircling a white perimeter and a bright blue core, most agreed it couldn't be more aptly labeled.

Here, on the border between water and land, on the edge of reason and at the end of sanity, Ray was being watched and not by God.

God should be proud. From death, she created life.

Perfect life.

This time? Flawless. Even *He* didn't get it right the first time out.

The lidless eye, hovering overhead, wasn't pleased with humanity. If the kaleidoscope of color the Hubble had captured was the Eye of God, this demonic glare was that of a dark angel. So bleak, the soldiers retreated back indoors, abandoning Ray on the dock.

Letting out a long, slow sigh, she inhaled the essence of the night.

Micael's words played in her head. "Tread with care in matters of life and death. A time will arrive when we are able to choose." His warning was issued by way of the Hippocratic oath. "Above all...do no harm."

Her thoughts shifted to the man recovering inside her fortress, what she'd given him, and how much he'd love her for saving his life.

"...you're not ready to choose wisely. None of us are. You'll take it too far."

Ray walked back inside and brushed a hand over her patient's sleeping face.

"Welcome to your rebirth, Mr. President," she whispered. "It's amazing the length some are willing to go to hold on to life and power. Let's see what you're made of."

IF YOU LIKED THIS, YOU MIGHT LIKE:
DEATH SECRETS: AN ANNA HALE, PI THRILLER

A gripping thriller that explores the lengths one will go to for family, and the resilience needed to stand against the darkness.

In the shadow of Alaska's towering peaks, Anna Hale is haunted by a past painted in flames and betrayal. Marked by the tragic death of her mother and the scars of a childhood marred by violence, Anna has fought tirelessly to build a semblance of normalcy, only to have it shattered again and again. The latest blow comes when her sister, Tia Pace, vanishes without a trace, reigniting old wounds and casting Anna into a nightmare where she's the prime suspect.

As she grapples with her stepfather's execution and the weight of suspicion, another crisis looms: Zoe Pace, her other sister, has disappeared in an eerily similar manner. The only clue a sinister black rose and a chilling letter. When her brother Josh, now a dedicated cop in the Anchor Police Department, begs for her assistance, Anna is pulled back into the fray. Despite the agony of reopening old wounds, she embarks on a desperate quest to unravel the mystery of her sisters' disappearances.

Faced with the unforgiving Alaskan frontier, Anna must confront a tangled web of corruption and deceit, with a copycat killer moving in the shadows. With every tick of the clock, Anna's hope for a normal life slips further away, but her resolve to find her sisters and bring them home burns fiercer than ever. Will Anna's journey through the cold, dark paths of Alaska lead her to her sisters, or will she find herself lost in the depths of a conspiracy that threatens to consume everything she holds dear?

AVAILABLE NOW

ABOUT THE AUTHOR

As a thriller author, owner of a successful developmental editing company for authors, a ghostwriter, and journalist, J.L. Hughes is grateful to be immersed in her respected field working with other accomplished writers. On the inside cover of dozens of novels, she contributes as editor or ghostwriter to both fiction and nonfiction in every genre from true crime to fantasy, sci-fi to horror—all for the love of story.

Her DARK JUSTICE Broken Jade trilogy will release in the summer of 2025. J.L. and her family enjoy city life against the adventurous backdrop of the Rocky Mountains.